Cartel King

The Cartel Brotherhood

Sabine Barclay

OLIVERHEBERBOOKS

The end of the world is coming... At least, the end of The Syndicate Wars world is. Welcome to the final family's story.

Find me writing Historical Romance as Celeste Barclay.

Happy reading,
Sabine

Subscribe to Sabine's Newsletter

Subscribe to Sabine's bimonthly newsletter to receive exclusive insider perks.

Have you read *The Syndicate Wars*? This FREE origin story novella is available to all new subscribers to Sabine's monthly newsletter. Subscribe on her website.
www.sabinebarclay.com

Sabine also writes Historical Romance as
Celeste Barclay.
Discover her Highlander, Regency, Viking, and Pirate Romances.
www.celestebarclay.com

The Cartel Brotherhood

Chapter One

Enrique

She's going to fall off that fucking ladder.

I slow my pace to a jog as I approach a house with a woman far too high on her ladder, leaning far too much to the right as she tries to fish something out of her gutters. She's got to be about five-five to my six-three.

I could reach whatever she's fishing around for. She's more likely to fall off and break something. I should mind my own business and keep going with my run, but there's no way I'm doing that. I wouldn't if it were a woman of any age, and I wouldn't if it were an elderly person, either.

If it were a guy my age, maybe I'd let him deal with it, but for her—there's something in how she's reaching. Some frustration I can feel even from here. I approach slowly as I walk up the driveway. I'm only halfway to her when a humongous dog comes bounding toward me.

No wonder there's a baby gate across the entrance to her open garage. The massive beast doesn't bark, but he growls. It's a Mastiff, much like the one Laura Kutsenko has, except this one is a different color and easily weighs about fifty pounds more than her giant companion. I wonder if this one is as much of a love bug as Laura's. At least, that's what she's always claimed.

The woman on the ladder speaks to her dog, giving him a command.

"Hush, Constantine. Lie down."

The dog immediately obeys, but he inches closer to the baby gate, still growling at me. It's only then that the woman notices me. She grips the ladder as she jerks away. I hurry over and grab the ladder, tempted to demand she come down from there.

"Who are you?"

If anybody's going to do the demanding, apparently it's her. Not that I can blame the woman, since I'm a complete stranger.

"I'm Enrique. I saw you as I was running. You looked a little wobbly up there."

"Well, I was okay until I was startled—but thank you."

Dismissive is the only way to describe her now. I don't blame her for that either. She's a woman in a precarious position with a strange man looking up at her. Now that I'm certain the ladder won't fall over, I step away. I don't need to look like a perv staring up her shorts.

"Would you like some help? I can easily reach whatever you're going for."

She glances at the gutter before she looks at me, clearly debating whether she should trust me. Never has there been a more misguided decision than when she backs down the ladder. I'm probably the least trustworthy person she could ever meet. At least to anybody who's outside my family. Within my family, I'm absolutely trustworthy. I'm more loyal than anybody you could ever meet. Family is everything in my line of work.

She steps aside once she's back down on the ground. She walks closer to the open garage door, and her dog stands. She pats him between the ears, and his tail waggles so much that his entire body shimmies. I don't wait around.

I don't ask her name, even though I'm dying to find out. Instead, I scale the ladder and quickly see the problem.

There's a branch packed in leaves lodged in the gutter. It's a miracle the weight of the leaves and this practical log hasn't pulled the gutter from the roof. I know this house has been on the market for some time, so she's a recent buyer.

I'm able to reach, just like I said, so I scoop out all the leaves, then wiggle the branch free.

"Here, I'll take that."

She reaches up, and it gives me a fine view of the loveliest tits I've ever seen. She's wearing a sports bra and tank top with workout shorts. The tank top's cut just as low as the sports bra. I tried not to stare at her ass as I walked up the driveway and failed miserably, but at least her back was to me.

If I keep looking at her, she'll realize what I'm staring at are not the most piercing blue eyes I've seen in a long time. She's going to know I'm looking at what must easily be double, if not triple D tits, and there's no way they aren't real.

She's waiting for me, but I'm tongue-tied like I'm fourteen years old, seeing my first pair of boobies. I shake my head as I lift the branch out and fling it away from her. As I climb down, she frowns and looks over to where the branch landed.

I know she's thinking she'll just have to pick that up later, along with all the leaves I pulled out. I'll take care of it. When I'm on the ground, she steps forward, but instead of backing away, I move the ladder down a few more feet and climb back up.

"You really don't have to do that."

"It's fine. This'll go faster if I do it. I can reach more than you can. It'll only take me a moment."

Well, I take more than a few moments. It's closer to ten minutes to do the entire front of her house. It wouldn't surprise me if the other three sides have just as much clogging them as this one does. I want to suggest there are services that do this, but I don't know her well enough. And if she's just bought a house, perhaps she can't hire people to do things for her.

"You really can stop now. I've already done the rest of the house. It was just up here that got a little more difficult. The company I hired flaked on me, and with the weather that's

3

supposed to be coming soon, I wanted to make sure I had the gutters clear."

"April showers bring May flowers."

What the hell? That is the most asinine thing I've said in ages, but it's true.

I noticed when I approached she was wearing gloves to do this work, but I'm not. Since those leaves had been up there all fall and through the winter, they were a mushy pile of mold. I don't even want to think whatever else there is besides just the leaves. My hands are disgusting, but it doesn't stop me from grabbing the open composting bag I see and going over to scoop up what I dropped on the ground. When I finish that, I break up the stick I fished out and put it in the bag as well.

I left her little choice but to accept my help. She watches me as I move around like this is my front yard rather than as a trespasser. I watch from the corner of my eye as she steps over the baby gate and grabs something from the garage. Her dog could've easily cleared the gate in one leap. He's that well-trained he just growled instead of ignoring the obvious barricade.

Just as I put the last of the leaves into a bag, she comes out with a bottle of water, a bottle of hand sanitizer, and some paper towels. She uncaps the water but doesn't hand it to me. It takes me a moment, but I realize she grabbed it so she could rinse my hands for me.

I stick them out, and she pours the water until everything is off of my hands. I accept the paper towels and dry them off before taking a pump of the hand sanitizer.

"You said your name is Enrique, but I was remiss in telling you mine. It's Elodie."

Neither of us offers a last name, and I don't blame her. I didn't offer mine because a quick google to make sure I'm not a psychopath is enough to prove I am. My name will come up as the *jefe* of the Colombian Cartel here in New York. No police or federal agency has caught and prosecuted me to prove it. It's just known. I'm certain she didn't give her last name because she doesn't need some strange man looking up her life history, even though I now have her address.

Constantine's staring up at me while Elodie and I chat. I feel as though the dog is taking stock and deciding whether I pass muster. His head tilts to the side. If he were an old man, he would sit with his thumb and index finger cupping his chin with his finger tapping his jaw.

I don't know why that came to me. It's one of the most ridiculous thoughts I've had in a long time. It's like that old-fashioned picture with the dogs playing poker. But he once again wags his tail and wiggles. Maybe he's not judging me, or I've passed.

I'm tentative, but I offer the back of my hand to the animal, and he sniffs. His tongue sticks out for a moment as though he'll lick me, but then he looks up at Elodie as though she would give him permission. She does nothing, so the dog sits and offers his paw to me instead.

"You have a very well-behaved dog."

"I do. It took some training, but he's a sweet animal to begin with."

"How old is he?"

"He's two. My sons got him for me."

"Your sons?"

With gloves on, I couldn't see a wedding ring. I glance toward the house, and she smiles.

"They won't come out and grill you over who's talking to their mom."

I don't want to tell her that's not even what I was thinking about, but that's good to know. Since she didn't mention a husband coming out either, I assume there's no angry man who'll want to know who's been picking leaves out of his gutters. Even better to know.

We stare at each other, and for once I'm at a loss for words, so I smile instead. I've been told I can be charming when I smile, but it seems not to affect her as much as the way she affects me.

"Well, I'm glad I could help you. I've got to finish my run."

She looks toward the street and then at me and nods. "I really appreciate it. I have to admit my heart was beating a little hard as I stretched up there. I knew I should've moved the ladder down, but it still wouldn't have mattered that much. I'm not exactly tall."

"Just being a friendly neighbor."

Her gaze passes over me before she looks at the house next door. This is a great neighborhood with homes that cost more than most people can afford. However, I'm certain she can tell I have more money than the average family here. It's not that I have a ton of jewelry on or have ridiculous high-end clothing to work out in. I've just been told I reek of money.

"It was nice meeting you."

She pulls her right glove off and sticks out her hand. Her skin is smooth, but I can feel calluses at the bottom of her fingers pressed against the palm of my hand. I noticed the workout equipment in her garage.

It's a three-car, and the main two-car part has a bunch of fitness gear. She parked her car in the single. I walk to the end of the driveway. I'm nowhere near done, so I turn away from the direction I came and continue my run. I'd only put in two miles before I stopped her, so I have another three to go before I turn around.

When I come back past her house, I glimpse the top of her head moving back and forth. I realize she's on an erg. I wonder if she just likes the rowing machines for fitness or if she's like me and rows. I've been a rower since I was in high school.

I don't have time anymore to be out on the water as much as I'd like, but I go out in my single as often as I can. Being on the water is peaceful to me, and rowing by myself is one of the few times when I'm alone and no one asks anything of me or reports any shit that's going wrong. I keep going, but the woman is on my mind the rest of the day.

I can't explain what it is about her that intrigues me. She's definitely attractive, and I wouldn't have minded more time to ogle her. But there was intelligence in her gaze and kindness in her smile. It's not that I'm lacking intelligent company. It's just I see kindness so rarely outside my family. My sisters didn't move to America until after I'd been here for nearly two decades. My sister-in-law, Margherita, has been battling cancer for a few years now. It's in remission, and she's doing better than she was. For most of my adult life, she was one of the few sources of kindness. It's not that she's unkind now, but she doesn't have the same optimistic air she did for years.

The treatments exhausted her, so she spent a lot of time at home. During that time, my brother didn't travel nearly as much for work as he has in the past, which meant I often did. It gave me less time to be around them, and I regret that.

"*Tío*, are you listening?"

"I'm thinking."

I don't need to tell Alejandro I'm not thinking about whatever he's talking about. I don't have a clue what he's talking about. I'm still puzzling over Elodie.

"The O'Rourkes are expanding into Eastern Europe and usurping the Kutsenkos' territory. It means they need more product, and they aren't buying from us."

"Do they have more labs?"

"That's what I'm thinking." Alejandro turns his computer toward me and has a map pulled up.

It's one I commissioned of the Amazon, a place with most of the cocaine labs spread out over hundreds of miles. Already marked on there are our production sites and ones we know for certain are where the Mancinellis, the Kutsenkos, and the O'Rourkes have most of their labs. We leave them alone because it's not worth wasting money and men trying to shut down their operations. If we do, it'll antagonize them too much. They'd partner with rivals I already have down there.

Only the other major New York syndicates get a pass. Anyone else who tries to grow or make anything in Colombia or the surrounding countries goes through me.

Alejandro points to a couple of locations. "We suspect this is where they are."

"That's creeping awfully close to our principal source of cocoa."

"We know. We believe they're trying to buy black market resources already promised to us."

"It wouldn't surprise me. I want to know for certain before we act. It's one thing for the O'Rourkes to fuck over the bratva. It's another for them to bite the hand that feeds them."

They're there because I allow it.

"*Tío* Luis is supposed to call me in an hour."

My brother is two years younger than me. We've lived apart for large chunks of our lives, but it was never by our choice. He's my best friend, closest confidant, and my conscience—which is saying something since he's back in Colombia right now to deal with a man who's been far too talkative.

Alejandro is one of our four shared nephews. We have two younger sisters, and Alejandro is our first sister's only child. Our second sister has three sons, and Luis had two. My heart's still torn when I think about that. Among my siblings, there are five young men in their early thirties. I have no children and need none since Luis's older son, Pablo, is my heir.

"Make it a three-way call. I want to hear what *maninto* knows." *Hermanito*—little brother. *Manito* for short.

"If he's on his way back, do you want me to go down there?"

"Let's wait a little longer."

We exchange a look, and we both know it has nothing to do with needing more time to investigate. Margherita goes in for more tests next week to ensure the cancer's still in remission. I'll move heaven and earth—truly because I will blow shit up—to be sure Luis is back here in time for those appointments, so I pray he's already on his way. I don't want any of my family away when we find out the results.

We've been discussing the situation in my home office, so Alejandro and I work at our computers on projects we each have until his phone rings. He holds up the screen, and I can see it's Luis. Alejandro answers it and puts it on speaker.

"*Manito, ¿qué pasa?*" Little brother, what's going on?

"*Demasiado que decir por teléfono.*" Too much to say over the phone.

Considering I have jammers at my house, and Luis has them at his home in Bogotá, something went so sideways he won't risk anyone circumventing our protections.

We continue in Spanish since Luis won't say anything he fears somebody in Colombia shouldn't hear.

"Are you on your way back?"

"Yeah. I'm leaving for the airport in ten minutes. I wanted to let you know I'm on my way. How's Margherita? She won't tell me the truth. She always says she's fine."

Margherita could lie to God, and he wouldn't know the truth. But she only does it to protect family. Otherwise, the woman's a devout Catholic who obeys the ninth commandment. She just maneuvers around the truth when she has to. Protecting family means protecting the Cartel, so she has no problems lying about what any and all of us do.

She normally never lies to Luis, but any time he travels, she says nothing worse than "fine." She admits it doesn't make Luis stop worrying about her and the family, but at least he doesn't know details to obsess over.

"She's still tired, but she's not as pale. *Tres J's* and Alejandro stay with her at night when Pablo can't. She's well taken care of. Our sisters are there so much during the day, I think your wife wants you home just for some quiet."

Tres J's—Joaquin, Jorge, and Javier—and Alejandro spend the night when our work keeps her son away. She insists she doesn't need a man in the house to sleep well at night. With the shit that's gone down among the top syndicates the last few years—especially after the shit my family's played a part in—no one wants any of the women alone at night, especially not my sister-in-law when she's not at full strength.

"They are exhausting."

Alejandro snorts and rolls his eyes, but it's good natured. He knows neither Luis nor I would allow him to utter a disparaging word about his mother or aunts.

"Do you need to see me as soon as you get back? Or can you take a few days with Margherita?"

"Come by in the morning, and I'll brief you on what's most important. I'll fill Pablo in on the rest when he's here. You can sort it out with him."

"Does Alejandro need to pack?"

"Not yet. Maybe next week."

I look at my nephew. If we didn't have a private jet, the poor guy would be in the multi-million-miler club with any airline. He claims he doesn't mind traveling so much, but I know he's growing tired of the constant travel. If going down there more often were safe for *Tres J's*, they'd split up the duties. But growing up there means they have a history that makes it better for those they left behind not to see them. Pablo has too many duties here in NYC for him to risk flying down there more than a couple times a year. So, the burden lands on Alejandro. It's a good thing he has the broadest shoulders in the family.

I'm about to wrap up the call when Luis continues. I clench my jaw since the first word tells me everything. *Hermano mayor* is big brother. *Mano* is just easier. He's been saying it since he learned to talk, and I know what each tone means.

"*Mano*, you won't like what you hear."

Chapter Two

Ellie

The man is hotter than any I've ever met. I've never had a type, but dark-haired guys outnumbered blonds in the past. However, I spent twenty-seven years married to a guy who started out blond. The asshole's mostly white now. Those men in the dusty part of my memory were nothing like Enrique.

He just ran past my driveway, and he's a sight to behold. Holy mother. The man's built like a god. I don't know if it's natural and working out keeps him that way, or if his fitness routine makes him that way. He's run past my house every day for a week. There's a park at the top of my street that marks the end of my neighborhood. From the speed he runs, he must take at least one loop around it before turning around. It doesn't take him forty-five minutes to come back because he's a snail.

Even from my garage where I'm working out, I can see the muscles in his thighs and calves bunch and release with each step. His shoulders are thick and broad. It took all my effort not to stare at the divide between his pecs that was noticeable through his t-shirt the other day.

I'm not one who loves tats, but his arms have detailed works of art. The one starting low on his neck makes me want to investigate what's under his shirt. I don't know if he saw me watching him yesterday, but he was a house up from mine when he pulled up his tank top to wipe his face. The man's abs—fucking-a. They are *chiseled*.

Today's workout included Pilates instead of weights, so I was on my reformer. If he glanced over here, he probably thinks I'm nuts. My feet were in the straps above me, and I did shit that likely looked like I was trying out for Cirque du Soleil to anyone who doesn't know Pilates. From a distance, I probably looked like they wouldn't even take me as an understudy.

I might have turned my rowing machine around before I started working out this morning. I might be facing the direction he'll come from on the way back. And I might be praying today's the day he runs past without a shirt on.

As much as I find myself daydreaming about him, once I start my erg workout, I'm focused. I wish I was on the water, but the closest place is still a bit of a drive from here. If I'm not swimming, then any kind of rowing is my happy place. I focus on nothing but my breathing and my rhythm. It clears my mind. It's also passing the time before I recognize the speck at the top of the hill.

I catch myself before I wipe my forehead on my shirt, but as I look down, I realize I'm pretty much in a puddle of sweat, anyway. There's not much dry on my shirt to use. I grab the towel I laid on the weight bench, dry myself off as much as I can, and snag my keys from where I left them. I get to my mailbox just as he becomes recognizable beyond the red shorts he's wearing today.

"Hi."

I turn toward him as I pull the envelopes out. I'm still breathing hard, and he looks fresh as a daisy. He didn't pant that word, but I fear I'll barely choke my response. My heart's racing, and it's only partly leftover from the workout.

"Hey. How're you?" I think I sound normal.

"Hot."

Yes. Yes, he is.

"Looks like you had a good workout, too."

He grins at me, and I want to melt into the ground. He thinks I'm a sweaty mess. I shouldn't have come out here like this. I feel like an idiot.

"I did. The weather's perfect."

"I noticed your erg the other day. You're a rower, aren't you?"

"Yeah." I guess I don't look in shape enough to be a Crossfitter.

"I can tell because you actually know what you're doing on it." His grin broadens, and he could be on a toothpaste or gum commercial. Did his pearly whites just twinkle?

"If you know it's called an erg, you must be a rower, too. I've been rowing since high school, but not the entire time."

"Same. I wind up going a few weeks at a time without being on the water."

I went a few years at a time without being on the water, but I don't want to explain.

"Is there anywhere near here? The closest I found is Van Every Cove, which isn't too bad, but it's still forty minutes away."

"That's where I go. It's the only place that's big enough to keep from rowing in circles."

"Is the boathouse the only place to put in at?" I can hold my own, and I'm not embarrassed to be lapped by the high schoolers. It just gets crowded.

"There are a few other places, but they're private entry. If you ever want to—I can get you passes."

What was he going to say?

"That would be nice. The kids are polite enough, but some of them are oblivious with their oars. They're too busy talking or texting."

"Does someone need to mention it to their coaches?"

His gaze hardens just enough for me to notice, but most people wouldn't. Is he being defensive toward me, like I'm insulting someone he knows?

"Elodie, you know as well as I do how dangerous that can be and how expensive if anything gets damaged. I know a few people there. I can mention it if it's a problem."

"No. I've heard the coaches correct them. I'm still really new to the area, so I don't know my way around yet. That's the only place I'm familiar with."

"Are you new to this part of Jersey?"

"I'm new to Jersey all together. I lived in New England for a long time, but I'm originally from DC Proper."

Let Virginians and Marylanders say they're from DC. You're not unless you've had a license plate that says Taxation Without Representation or a DC driver's license.

"New England's gorgeous."

"It is. But I'm understanding why New Jersey's called the Garden State."

"Did you assume we're just New York's landfill?"

I curl my teeth around my lips, trying not to laugh. I hold up my hand with my thumb and index finger close together.

"I might have a bit, but that was before I dated a guy in college who grew up not too far from here."

"You picked the pretty part of the state."

I glance around the neighborhood then back to Enrique. "I did."

And by pretty part, I'm thinking about the hot guy who runs past my house every day. I can't believe I didn't notice him before he helped me with my gutters.

My phone vibrates in my pocket, and I slip it out to peek at the screen. "I'm sorry. I have to take this. It's my son."

He looks at the house before looking back at me. "Does he need a ride home from somewhere? My sisters drove our mom nuts with chauffeur duty when they were teenagers."

I tilt my head before I shake it. "My boys are in their twenties." I slide my finger across the screen. "Give me a moment, please."

I put the phone to my chest as I shift the mail in my other arm.

"It was nice talking to you again, Elodie."

"Enjoy the rest of your run."

He takes off as I turn back toward the house. I glance over my shoulder to see him one more time. "Hey, Will."

I glance at my watch and hook the leash onto Constantine's collar before heading out through the garage. I punch in the code, and the door shuts just as I reach the street. Out of habit, I glance back to make sure the door closes all the way, then I set off. I hope to be toward the top of the hill by the time Enrique catches up with me. I don't know for sure he'll be running while I'm out for my walk, but he's been timing his runs pretty consistently since we met a week and a half ago.

They've deviated a little here and there, but never more than by about twenty minutes. I haven't lived here long enough to know if this is a usual habit of his or if it's anything different since he walked up my driveway. Part of me would love for that to be the case, but the realist in me says there's no chance of that.

I want to "coincidentally" be at the top of the hill for another reason. I'm in good shape, but I don't need him to hear me panting while I try to speak as we go up the incline together. My days of running are long over because I've torn my calf muscle twice, and I'm terrified of doing it a third time.

It also means to avoid straining them, I take longer to get up hills than I'd like. I'm putting way too much thought into this. He could run right past me and not even think twice about stopping to say hi. He's waved the last few times he's passed me while I've been working out in the garage.

I've had to go out to run some errands and for a meeting over the past week, so I haven't been home every day he's gone by. Twice, I've waved to him as he's leaving the neighborhood, and I'm entering it. I don't know where he comes from since I already figured out he doesn't live around here. At least not in my neighborhood.

I live on the street that runs the length of it, and I'm toward the top. I'm far enough into the neighborhood to enjoy privacy and for it to be quieter than it is for those people who live near the gate. It makes me wonder how he can get in and out of the neighborhood if he doesn't live here. The community's fairly young.

Most houses are only five or six years old, so perhaps he's been running through here since before they built these homes. If that's the case, then maybe the guards who work the gate already know him and just let him through.

I'm having a long conversation with myself, trying to occupy my mind as I crest the hill. It surprises me when I see him headed toward me. It's not that I've been staring out my window to watch for him specifically, but I've been outside working in the garden for a while. He slows until he stops in front of me.

"Good morning."

"Morning, Enrique."

"Did you finish your flower bed?"

He must have seen me while my back was to the street. "That one. I still have a couple more to go."

"You have quite the green thumb as you work on your garden. It's more than what the previous owner had."

"Yeah, I have the time these days. It's something I've always wanted but hasn't come true until now."

"Are you and Constantine just setting off for your walk?"

He pats my dog between the ears. Constantine approves of Enrique. He barely made a sound when he saw Enrique stop at the mailbox the other day. Since then, he's passed me while I've been playing with Constantine in the front yard. I have freshly laid sod in the back, so he's not allowed out there right now.

"Yeah, we're going to do a long loop today before it gets too warm. It's been unseasonably hot here, hasn't it?"

"Yeah, this is definitely June temperatures rather than April."

"Do you think it'll stay this way?"

"I hope so. I prefer it hotter than cold, but that's what I've always been used to."

I want to ask him about his past because I want to get to know him better. He definitely has a strong accent that tells me he grew up speaking Spanish before English. It's not a New York or even a New Jersey Spanish accent, but I'm not sure we're ready to jump into a background check when we're just chatting about the weather right now.

"Have you gotten out on the water this week? I thought I saw you pulling in the other day with your single."

He must have gone for an evening run on Tuesday. That was one of the few days I didn't see him.

"I did. It was beautiful. I caught the last of the light just before the sun started to set. I'm getting to know my way around the cove and figuring out what workouts I enjoy."

"Do you come up with your own, or do you use an app?"

He sounds genuinely interested, but Constantine tugs on his leash. He's normally super well behaved, so that tells me he needs to go to the bathroom. Enrique notices too and smiles, turning in the direction I'm facing. I guess that means he's coming with me. I set off, and he walks beside me to the left, keeping me closer to the curb. We continue to chat as Constantine waters the next five trees we go past.

"Did you say you'd been rowing for a while?"

He looks over at me as I stop again with Constantine, pulling a plastic bag loose from his leash. Fortunately, we're close to the top of the road and the park where there'll be a trash can nearby. Not exactly sexy carrying around a bag of dog shit.

"Yeah, I started rowing when I was in high school. Then I rowed in college as well. I coached for a bit right after college and rowed masters but was too young to compete with them. By the time I was old enough to qualify for masters, I'd already had my first son, and my family didn't live close enough to a lake, a river, or the ocean for me to go out on the water easily while still having a young child at home. When I was ready to go back out on the water because I had somebody who could babysit him in the morning after my husband—ex-husband—and I left for work, I was pregnant again. That pattern stayed the same through a third son."

I watch him from the corner of my eye to see how he reacts to all of that. I'm used to speaking of my former husband as my ex-husband most of the time, but it still feels a little odd to call Tim that when I talk about the past related to raising kids together. Or rather me raising them, and him floating in and out of the house whenever he felt like paying attention to us or work allowed.

Enrique doesn't seem fazed by me mentioning I was previously married. He already knows I have adult sons, though I could be way overthinking this, and it's of no interest to him at all.

Maybe it doesn't matter to him if I'm single. I haven't seen a ring on his hand or any shadow of shame—a wedding ring tan line on guys who slip off their rings to pretend they're single. For all Tim's faults, he never cheated on me except for the emotional affair he had at the end, but I encouraged that.

I'm lost in my thoughts, and I almost forget what we were talking about. Thankfully, Enrique pulls me back to the present.

"So, you had a few years off while your sons were young?"

Yeah, more than a few years. Try closer to two decades.

"I've just gotten back into it seriously over the last couple of years. I had to get my sea legs under me when I first started going out in a single. I hadn't done that since just after college. When I was in high school and college, I rowed in eights, fours, and quads, so it was never just me balancing the boat and making sure I didn't end up in the water."

He cocks an eyebrow and shakes his head. "I haven't had more than a few months off at a time since I first started rowing, and I tipped last week."

"You did?"

"In all fairness, I got waked." Someone's boat cast a big enough wake to flip him.

"Oh, that's obnoxious. How fast were they going?"

"Way over the speed limit."

"Was that five where you were?"

"Yeah, they had to have easily been doing ten in a bass tracker."

"That is obnoxious. Did they at least stop to see if you were all right?"

"No, they didn't even bother to slow down." He's still smiling, but there's that hard glint in his eyes I saw the other day when I mentioned going to the boathouse and some teenagers being careless.

It makes me wonder if he's plotting their demise. Maybe that's pushing it a little far, but he's definitely still pissed, even if he's trying to pass it off as no big deal.

"Did you play any other sports growing up?" I think steering the conversation away from him capsizing is probably a good idea right now.

"I swam, so rowing was sort of the logical progression, I guess. I love being on the water."

"Same. I injured my rotator cuff from overuse as a swimmer, but it never bothered me when I switched to rowing."

"I also grew up playing soccer." He watches me as though he expects some type of response from me. Some quip with a stereotype?

"Me too. I was a total tomboy growing up. I was usually the only girl out on the field playing soccer at my elementary school. I'd be out there before school, after school, lunch recess, morning recess. Any chance I had, but swimming was my real love."

"See, soccer is mine. I still play when I can with my brother and nephews. I played in college when I rowed just for fun because I couldn't commit to two seasons. Each year, I only had the time for a single season sport."

Rowing is both a fall and a spring sport with different lengths and styles of races, but it's a year-round commitment for academic athletes that isn't always easy to keep.

"Do you still play soccer?"

I shake my head and frown. "No, not in a long time. I tore my right calf muscle twice several years ago, so I don't run anymore. I'm too nervous I'll tear it again, and the third time will be the charm with me winding up in surgery."

"That's a shame, but I understand. You could always play keeper."

"Yeah, but I've never enjoyed those kinds of—"

I catch myself before I say what I'm thinking. I definitely don't know him well enough to make off-color jokes.

"What were you going to say?"

"Nothing. It's not important."

"I'd like to know." He sounds genuinely curious.

I laugh and shake my head. "No, I don't know you well enough for you to hear that kind of humor."

"Was it something about balls in your face?"

I can't help but laugh as I nod. I look over at him, and again, his smile is so bright against his naturally tan skin I wonder if he ever modeled. He could've been in those toothpaste or gum commercials. Hell, he could still be on a billboard in Times Square.

We keep chatting as we finish a loop around the park and head back to my house. The conversation was never stilted, even though we talked about sports we play and even ones we enjoy watching the whole way.

Chapter Three

Ellie

I was in the middle of work the last two days when Enrique went by my window in the morning. I couldn't pull myself away because of a deadline. He didn't go for any evening runs while I was out with Constantine, but I've walked with him every morning for two weeks now.

I've run into him on the water three times too. It was exciting to see him glide across the lake's surface, his body in perfect harmony with his oars. We didn't do more than chat like we do on our walks when we *happened* to take breaks near each other. We chat about plenty of things, but neither of us is ready to reveal anything too personal.

I don't want to be nosey, even though I'd love to know more. But if I ask, then I'll need to reciprocate. There's too much I don't want to talk about with a virtual stranger. It's a catch twenty-two: I want to know more, but I don't want to share more, so I'll never get to know more.

I've finally finished everything I need to do for today, so I'm headed out for my long walk with Constantine. I have an hour before it gets too dark. The sun is setting a little later, so I can get more done before heading out.

"If I didn't know that all it takes is a pat on the head to tame your wild beast, I might fear running up behind you."

I nearly jump out of my skin. I'm unprepared for Enrique's appearance. He isn't sweating like he normally would be at this point in his run. I'm just heading up the hill at my snail's pace.

"He'd give away where I hide all my silver and jewels for a biscuit. But don't let that get out. He's the biggest dog on the block. He has a reputation to protect. Otherwise, that little yappy chihuahua over there—" I point across the street, "—will think he can step to Constantine and do more than just bark."

"I doubt your dog would do anything besides sit on the little ankle biter."

"You're not far off. His size is intimidating to anyone who doesn't know him, but he's the least aggressive dog you'll likely ever meet."

"That's because nobody's tested him. I'm certain if he felt you were threatened, he'd have a very different reaction."

"I suppose you're right. Nobody's ever approached me in a way that's concerned either of us."

"I'm glad to hear that."

We're quiet for a moment before I wonder about something he said the other day.

"You mentioned you play soccer with your brother and nephews. It sounds like there must be a lot of them."

"I have a younger brother and two younger sisters. Among the three of them, there are five guys in their early thirties, so they keep me on my toes."

"There's seven of you all together. That doesn't make for even teams."

"Yeah, we take turns reffing, but if either of my sisters plays, then two of us switch sides."

What? That makes no sense.

"I'm not following."

"The team that doesn't have my sister gets two extra men. We rarely let them play together because one of us always ends up injured for at least a week."

"They're that good?"

"Oh, yeah. They both played Division One soccer. So did a couple of my nephews, but my sisters're fiercely competitive, especially protecting any of their sons who are on their teams. It doesn't matter how many times we say no slide tackles or shoulder checks. If they think one of their boys is about to go down, Mama Bear comes out. So, it's two of us to each one of them. We've played two on four and two on five before, and they've smoked our asses."

"Really?" I can't help but think he's exaggerating, but he stops and points to a massive bruise I didn't see on the back of his calf.

"That's from my second sister, Luciana. Last week, she subbed in for two of my nephews, neither of whom is her son. When I got a little too close to one of them, she made sure I understood."

"And your nephews are in their early thirties?"

"Yeah, but my sisters will always be their moms."

I glance away, but I can't hide my laugh unless I want to sound like I'm choking. I shake the hand that doesn't have the leash in front of me. I don't want him to think I'm laughing at him.

"I'm just like your sisters, to be honest. I've only gotten more competitive with age. Most of the time these days, I just compete against myself with work and my workouts. But I'm also a fiercely protective Mama Bear, too. I get how your sisters must feel. My boys rarely want to do anything competitive against me because, even though they've been bigger than me for years, I still put them to shame because my competitiveness makes me wily."

"That's what my sisters say. I'd invite you to play one of these days if you didn't have calf issues. It's a shame."

"It's tempting, but I tore it the second time kicking a ball around with my youngest. I still remember the feeling of tearing my calf both times. It's not one I feel like repeating, even for a game as good as that one sounds."

I caught myself before I said, *even if it was for you.*

23

"Maybe we could go out on the water together one of these days."

I didn't expect him to offer that alternative.

"That would definitely be nice. I still don't know my way around the adjoining cove. I don't know if there are any parts of Lake Hopatcong I need to avoid. I pretty much stick to the same route each time I go out. I just vary the workout."

We walk for a few minutes in companionable silence. He suggests we work out together, but he doesn't suggest a day or time. I guess he just tossed that out there.

"You know I come from a huge Latino family. What about you?"

I knew that question was coming. It doesn't mean I want to answer it.

"It's just been me the last twenty-nine years. My older brother died in a car accident when I was twenty, and he was twenty-three."

"I'm sorry for your loss, Elodie. I know it never gets easier, even if you get used to it."

I look over at him and wonder who he's lost as he speaks from experience. He must read my thoughts.

"My sisters didn't move to America permanently until well after my brother and I did. The younger of the two—the one with the three boys—didn't come here until they were teenagers. It was four years after her husband died."

"Oh, I'm sorry to hear that. It must have been horrible for them to lose somebody so important and then make such a massive change afterward."

"Yeah, it was rough for them."

He doesn't sound like he wants to offer more explanation, which is fine because I don't want to explain how my brother died. It was a car accident, but there was a lot more to it than just a head-on collision.

"You said your sisters didn't move here until after you and your brother did. Did you all move here as adults?"

"Yes."

He hesitates for a moment. I'm not sure why, since he opened the door to that.

"Luis—my brother's two years younger than me—and I went to different prep schools in New England, so we started coming to America when we were very young. We went home during all our school breaks and for the summers all the way through high school. Then he and I each moved here for college and considered America our home, even though we kept going back to Colombia during most of our breaks. After I graduated, I split my time between Bogotá and New York for several years."

"Have you been in Jersey for very long?"

"Yes. About eighteen years now, so this is definitely home."

"Have you been in the same area the whole time?"

"Mostly. I lived in the city for a while during the week and would come home to my place a couple miles from here. Eventually, I sold that house and moved into the one I'm in now permanently."

He kept a place around here as well as in the city, and he went to prep school. He comes from even more wealth than I suspected. I definitely don't own multiple properties. I never have.

"How long have you been in Jersey?"

"I just moved here when I bought the house. I've been in it for two months."

"What made you decide to live here?"

"I wanted a change of scenery. I wanted to be close to the city where I have friends, but also not that far from DC where I grew up until I was ten while my dad went through med school, residency, and his specialty training, then I came back for college. It's easy to get to Europe from New York, so that makes life easier. I'll even settle for flying through Newark."

"Sometimes that's simpler than LaGuardia or JFK."

"Yeah, I discovered that over the years, but both are still better than trying to fly in and out of most of the airports in New England during winter. Can't tell you how many flights I've had grounded trying to get out of Logan."

Boston isn't the only city with an airport in New England, but it's certainly the hub for all major flights in and out of the area.

Our conversation pauses for a few moments, but it's not uncomfortable silence. When the house comes back into sight, Constantine tugs a little more.

"Heel." I give the command, and he obeys immediately. I know he's ready for some water, but he still rarely pulls. That's twice today. It's not that hot, but who knows exactly what dogs think.

"Other than your garden, what other changes do you want to make?"

"There's not a whole lot to do. The place was pretty turnkey, but I want to paint in a couple of places, particularly my office and the kitchen."

"Are they a color you don't like?"

"No, they're white, which is fine by me. I don't know if they were something different before the last owners sold, but I just have a thing about having yellow kitchens. I have for as long as I can remember. I don't mean highlighter yellow, but something bright and cheery makes me think of sunshine. And even though I don't bake as often as I did when I was much, much younger, bright sunshine and fresh baked goods go together in my head. I know it's ridiculous."

"It's not. If that's what makes you feel at home, then go for it. It's your space to do with as you want."

"It is. That's why I'd also like to paint my office something like a soft misty green. I had a studio when I was in college, and my kitchen was yellow, and the main room was a light fawn green. I loved it. I've had white walls ever since then in most parts of my house. Otherwise, the few that were painted were much darker than I would've picked."

I don't want to get into how I came home from a trip with my boys to find Tim had painted the dining room almost chocolate brown. It made the space feel tiny, even though it wasn't. I hated it from the moment I walked in till the moment we sold that house. I learned to live with it and didn't think about how much I disliked it all the time. But as we were moving out, I remembered.

"I also just got new sod in the backyard, so I want to plant some flowers around it."

"Oh, that's why you were playing with Constantine in the front yard the other day."

"Yeah. When the weather gets too cold, I'll move my workout equipment to the basement, which I'm finishing as well."

"That's a lot to lug around."

"Well, when I say I'm moving it, I mean my three strapping young sons will move it for me. Then I'll have them move it all back up next spring. I like the fresh air, but it'll get too cold to have the garage doors open. I don't enjoy working out in there if I can't have them open. I'd rather be in my basement then."

We get to my driveway, so the conversation ends there. As we say good evening to each other, it's the same as every time we part. I wonder if I'll walk with him or see him on the water again.

It's another two days before I see Enrique. He's coming back from his run as I set off for my walk. I got a call I had to take, so I started later than I wanted. He hints he'll be away for work for the next week. It's as though he wants me to know that's what he's doing rather than maybe think he's avoiding me. I appreciate the heads up because I would've feared I did something wrong if he stopped walking with me.

"I shouldn't be away too long, Elodie. I hope we can plan for a walk."

Together.

It's a silent prayer.

"Mom, we can take Constantine out for you."

"Thanks, Will, but I could do with the fresh air. I want to get my steps in for the day."

"It's not like you wear a watch that tells you to get up and move around. You only track it on your phone. Nothing's telling you to go for a walk."

"I know that, Steve, but I know I haven't gotten my steps in after the brunch you guys took me out to this morning. Plus, there are those steaks you're about to grill. I need to get up and move around, or else you'll be rolling me up the stairs to bed."

"I highly doubt that, Mom. You've never looked better.

"Thank you, Hunt."

I appreciate that. It's not like I've worked out to get a revenge body because I couldn't give two shits from Sunday what my ex-husband thinks about how I look. I'm not interested in having a relationship with anybody, though it has been nice flirting with Enrique. At least that's what I've been trying to do. I don't know about him. I'm not sure if that's what he's doing, too.

He's been gone for nearly two weeks, so I'm hoping today will be the day he's out again, but maybe he's with family since it's Mother's Day. He's said nothing about having children of his own. If he has kids, maybe they're with their mother. Maybe they do something altogether. I don't know if his mom is around. If he's back in town, maybe he's doing something with his sisters. I have no idea.

It's wonderful having my boys here with me today. It's only since they've been adults that they've paid attention to Mother's Day and tried to make it nice for me. After they got too old to make things for me at school, it became pretty much nothing. Tim never pushed them to celebrate the day, even though I always made sure they had something for him on Father's Day.

That was the sad song of my life for years. I, like so many other women, only had gifts I bought myself or that I picked out, then wrapped myself. For years, if I didn't do that, I had nothing to open on Christmas if it didn't come from a friend or was mailed to me by my parents. My former husband never took the boys to get me gifts. He barely knew how to order anything online because I always took care of it for him.

Today's an extra special day, so it's not that I'm trying to ditch my boys, but it would be perfect if I got to see Enrique. I really enjoy our walks and our brief moments together on the water. Any chance to see or talk to him makes my day.

"I'll be back in like half an hour. I won't do a full loop in the park. Just enough for Constantine and me to stretch our legs."

I pick up the leash, and Constantine trots over to me, pushing between Steven's and Hunter's legs. He ignores my middle and youngest sons. He has no fucks to give if somebody's standing between him and a walk. I'm barely off my driveway before I hear Enrique call out to me. I'm certain at least one of my boys can see him walking up.

The grill was already going, and Will was headed outside with a plate of meat. He'll hold off putting the steaks on until I get back, but in the meantime, he'll make some burgers for himself and his brothers. It'll be their appetizers. They're in their mid-twenties and still have appetites like they're fifteen. They have the metabolisms to get away with it.

"Hi. Welcome back."

"Thank you. I hoped I'd catch you this evening. Are you having a nice Mother's Day?"

"I am. It's been really enjoyable. My boys took me out to brunch. They're at the house now. They're going to grill tonight and hang out with me for a couple more hours before they each have to take off.

"Do they live near here? Do you get to see them often?"

"My middle son, Steve, lives in Connecticut just outside the city, but my other two sons are still in New England."

I don't want to get much more specific than that because as much as I enjoy talking to Enrique, we haven't even exchanged last names yet. I'm kicking myself for telling him even one of my son's names.

"How was your trip?"

"It went well."

Is that all he's going to say?

"I bet you must be glad to be home."

"Yeah, it was nice to get back to my own bed."

"Did you go anywhere interesting?" I feel like that's the next natural question, but it's like pulling teeth.

"I had to make a couple of stops, but it was all for work. So, just meetings. Nothing exciting."

Clearly, he wants to talk about his trip about as much as I want to talk about my boys and about my past. I'd call him cagey if I weren't evasive, too.

"Elodie, I missed our walks while I was gone."

I look up at him, and his expression is so tentative. I suppose that's the easiest way to describe it, as though he's not sure whether he should have admitted that.

"I missed them too, Enrique. I'm glad you're back. Constantine's great company, but he's not much of a talker."

We grin as we approach the park. We have some companionable silence now that we've admitted we missed each other. The quiet isn't bad, but it's a little stilted compared to usual. He makes up for it when I turn to look at him.

"Would you have time to go for a walk tomorrow morning?"

"I'd like that, but I always feel bad when you catch me on your way out for your run. I feel just as badly on days when you double the distance."

"A little extra fresh air and activity is good for me. I don't have to run every day to stay in shape, so I'm not too worried if I walk rather than run some days."

"All right, I'd like that."

We linger for a moment, looking at each other. We say goodbye before it gets awkward. I head into the house through the garage, and I've barely stepped into the kitchen before my boys confront me. They're all leaning against something, one foot crossed in front of the other, their arms crossed against their chest.

"You learned that from me, so it's hardly intimidating. I don't care if you're all a foot taller than me. I'm thirsty." I turn toward the cupboard to get a glass, but they close ranks.

"Mom, who was that?"

"A friend."

"Mom—"

"Steve, you get that tone from me, too. You cannot intimidate me when I've been using that tone of voice on all three of you since the days you were born."

"Look, we're not upset you went for a walk with someone."

Will isn't always the peacemaker, but he's trying today. He hands me a glass of water I down while he continues talking.

"We're glad you're making friends in the neighborhood. We just didn't expect it to be a guy who looks like he could snap you in two."

"That's your reaction to seeing him? You think he'd hurt me?"

"No, we just don't know him. That's all. Are you guys dating?"

"No, we're walking."

"That sounds like something out of one of your books, Mom." Steve jumps in, and I'm not enjoying them being adults as much as I did this morning.

"I didn't say we were walking out together. He's not courting me."

"What do you know about him?" Hunt won't be left out either, and he can be the most dogmatic of them.

"His name's Enrique. He doesn't live far from here. We're both rowers. We both grew up playing soccer. He's got a lot of guys in his family who aren't too much older than you, and he was traveling for work the last few days."

"That's it? That's all you know about him?"

"Am I supposed to know much more than that?"

Will shoots his brothers a look, and they back down.

For now.

"We just want to make sure you're safe. No one wants to see you happy more than we do. You deserve it, and if you enjoy his company, cool. We're just not used to seeing you talking to a guy you might date."

Will wraps his arm around my shoulders, and I lean against him. I'm not completely used to having adult children.

"Let this run its course. Do nothing unless I ask."

I don't need a dossier on the guy, which is what I'll get if I let the boys do what they want. That or Enrique will never speak to me again.

"Ellie, I can't go on our walk this morning because I have an early meeting. I didn't want to just not show up."

"I understand."

Enrique's standing at the foot of the driveway with me, and his expression says he's disappointed—but not heartbroken. I try to hide how much this bums me out after he was gone for two weeks.

"I plan to go out on the water tomorrow. Would you like to join me?"

"I'd love that."

"Great. I'll meet you at the boathouse at six, if that works for you."

"Perfect."

I watch him run back toward the bottom of my neighborhood, and I can't stop thinking about tomorrow morning until I fall asleep. Then it's the first thing on my mind as I open my eyes.

Rowers are early morning athletes. I've always loved it because I start my day on the water, and I'm done with my workout before most people finish their first cup of coffee.

I have most of my equipment unpacked and staged. I'm standing on the lip of my car with my driver's door open as I lift my single rowing shell off the car rack. I hear someone behind me, then heat spreads across my back as long tan arms reach past me.

Enrique's body brushes against mine as he takes my boat from me. I'm unprepared for the boat's weight to disappear as he steps back. It puts me off balance, and I nearly fall. Enrique presses his chest to my back, keeping me from lurching backward. I grab the side of the door as an arm wraps around my waist, lifting me off my car and setting me on the ground. I know he has the shell resting on his head like rowers normally do to carry them, but we usually don't carry a person along with it.

"I'd never let you fall."

His lips are beside my ear, and his firm hold around me has me pinned to him. I feel all his muscles against my back. I know what I feel against my ass, and I'm tempted to rub against his hard on. I've wanted to believe he might feel even a sliver of the attraction I do. If his cock is like that because of me, then it's a yes.

He doesn't let go as he takes three steps back, getting us clear of my open door. I push it closed and turn to face him. I reach up to take the boat from him, and that squeezes my breasts together. I'm wearing a sports bra and tank top that cover me modestly, but he still has a full-frontal view.

My mind flashes to him running his tongue between them. To looking down and watching him sucking on them. To feeling his hands on them. His gaze drops to them for a moment, but it's so brief I think they don't impress him. But as he lets go of me, his hand definitely trails over my ass even if it's only a mere second.

"Thank you."

We work in silence as we assemble our rigging and walk along the dock. Neither of us says anything about whether we're sticking together. I assume so since he suggested we meet here, but I don't know. I don't want to slow him down.

"Do you have any favorite drills to warm up?"

I nod. "A few."

As we get in and shove off the dock, I tell him what my workout usually includes. I worry I sound weak and out of shape. He grins at me as I speak.

"I'll need a nap after this. How long do you work out each day?"

"A couple hours. I have the time now, so I do. I feel better for it."

I expect him to ask me why, but he doesn't. I'm not ready to delve into that. I don't want to discuss my ex-husband or that relationship's shortcomings.

We work through the drills I suggest then decide on the distance and pace we want to row and take off. His body is the definition of muscular grace. His muscles flex and release as his boat glides over the water. I do my best to maintain my concentration and stay on course, but he's mesmerizing and mouthwatering.

We only speak when we take breaks. I enjoy the companionable silence we often have together. We pick up where we left off each time we slow or stop, sharing memories about teams we were on and regattas we went to. We attended the same ones, but not at the same time since he's nearly ten years older than me. We move on to stories from college, which include some nights we should probably forget.

Two hours pass, and it feels like a couple minutes. I'm sweaty and parched by the time we get back to the dock. I accidentally flick water at him as I pull in one of my oars. He scoops up a handful that sprays across my lap. I fail to stifle my shriek since the water is freezing. I give as good as I get, ensuring he gets a healthy splash to his chest. His shirt's already sticking to him, and that soaks it. Fuck, he's fine.

He helps me put my shell back on my car, and we stand closer than usual as we say goodbye.

"I'd like to spend more time with you out here, Elodie."

"My schedule's flexible, and I like it out here in the morning and the evening. Let me know what works for you."

I observe him for a moment before I take the plunge since he just told me he wants to spend more time with me.

"I'd like to walk with you more, too."

"If I run in the morning, and you do your workout in your garage, maybe we could walk in the evenings."

"I'd like that. Tomorrow?" Do I sound too eager?

"Tomorrow."

We go our separate ways once we're ready. We avoided talking about work, and we said little more about our families. It's fine with me since I don't want to be evasive or lie. I like him too much to do that, and that's a real problem.

Chapter Four

Enrique

"Me importa un culo. Ese culicagado que te den." I don't give a shit. That ass shit can get fucked.

I'm fucking pissed. *Culicagado* doesn't translate well. It means ass shit—slang that combines two of the most versatile words in any language. But I mean someone who doesn't know enough to be running their mouth. That would be Sean O'Rourke. *Cabroncete.* Little fucker.

"Enrique, you know that. I know that. We all know that. But it doesn't change how Sean's figured out our cypher or that he's now got our offshore bank account behind so many firewalls and passwords I'm not sure it still exists."

Luis's voice remains calm, but his expression tells me he's as pissed as I am. I'm at his place along with his son and our nephews. Margherita's upstairs napping. It's the only reason we're meeting right now. As important as this is, I wouldn't pull my brother away from his wife the first morning he's home after being back in Colombia for six weeks.

"*Tio,* let them keep the account in Belize. It doesn't have much in it despite what they think. Unless they withdraw cash—which means they find someone they trust to do that or one of them goes down there—and there's little chance of that—they'll have to do a wire transfer. I'll keep an eye on any and all money leaving the country."

Jorge's our CPA. He doesn't just track our profits and losses, he's also a forensic accountant. Each of the Four Families has one. Jorge is superior to the rest. The other families think they have the best, but we actually do. Jorge's more discreet with how he manages our money, even if the O'Rourkes believe they've secretly stockpiled more than any of us know.

Jorge's brother Joaquin heads up our intel gathering and is a hacking genius. No one bought his way into MIT. He's cultivated an image of being the most blasé of their generation, but it's because he's painfully shy. He's a complete introvert who's learned to navigate an extroverted world. His couldn't-give-a-fuck attitude masks his aversion to being in crowds or making small talk. It lets him avoid those situations.

Since he's such a home body and is the most inquisitive of all my nephews, he creates computer programs that run circles around the other families. He built one that allows Jorge to monitor international transactions, especially any connected to Latin America. That means any large transactions get flagged. He'll let me know the moment anything pings.

No one brings drugs in or out of this hemisphere without my consent.

That makes me think of Ellie—Elodie. She has no idea who or what I am. To her, I'm just Enrique. She doesn't know my last name, so I'm sure she hasn't looked me up. If she had, she wouldn't come near me. If her dog knew what a threat I pose to her, he'd have chewed me apart by now. I shouldn't spend time with her, but she intrigues me.

I joined Luis down in Colombia for two weeks, but I've been in New Jersey the rest of the time. I've admitted to no one that part of the reason I've stayed up here is to be with Ellie. I keep thinking of her like that. We've been going for walks and out on the water for more than a month now, and I treasure every minute of it.

I've seen her all but three days in the past month. The only reason I missed those days was because I had a couple of my men make some poor decisions. They needed reminders they worked for me not the other way around. Once I was sure they couldn't forget, I made sure they couldn't breathe again.

I consider what Jorge said about the sheltered account in Belize and what to do about the O'Rourkes.

"Fine. But I don't want too much moving out of that account before we act. I don't want them thinking it took us long to discover what they're doing."

"I can be in Bogotá tomorrow and out to the labs by tomorrow night. I can check on everything. *Tío—*" Alejandro looks at Luis, not me. "—you didn't have time to go out there again. I can find their labs and get photos or video. No one will be any the wiser."

Despite Alejandro being the biggest of all of us, he's a fucking phantom. Even in daylight, the man moves with such stealth it's unnerving. He's been that way since he was a toddler. He'd disappear before anyone realized he was on his feet. Used to scare the shit out of my sister and brother-in-law. It's why they stopped after one.

"Let me think about it. In the meantime, *manito*, what happened with Miguel?"

"That *cabrón* thought he could set up his own import company. He didn't expect me to stop by." Asshole.

Miguel Rojas is one of the most notorious murderers in Colombia and has been in prison for twenty-nine years and is facing life in there. He worked for my uncle and was the one who was supposed to carry out the hit that killed my father. *Tío* Humberto—that fucking flaming sack of shit—wanted what his older brother had and what I have now. The role of *jefe de jefes*— boss of bosses. I heard about the plot, so I made sure Miguel went away. For the first twenty years, he was an ideal inmate. I'd say jump, and he'd ask how high. But a few years ago, he found his *huevos* again.

Every time he does, I kick him in the balls. Calling them eggs makes much more sense, considering how fragile they are. I make sure Miguel remembers I'll take him down to his knees if he reaches too far. Right now, "import company" means he's bringing drugs into the prison without my permission. I'm not getting my cut, and he bragged about that. Luis went down there to shut his operation down.

"How'd you make the connection between him and the O'Rourkes?" That's at the heart of this, and what I need to know.

"This shit he was selling is as dirty as what we send in, but the formula was different. I traced it back to Bolivia. That's when things slowed down and why I was out of touch the last two weeks. Fucking no reception in that part of the jungle."

The first two weeks Luis was down there, he was wrapping up some deals we made with rivals. Those deals meant they pay us a tariff to import *and* export, and we let them live. He spent two more weeks in the prison with Miguel. He checks in and out of prisons in Colombia like they're Hiltons. Sometimes he gets himself busted, and sometimes, he just walks in and pays for a cell. Depends on who he's visiting and what he needs to do.

He's known as *el Espíritu Santo*—the Holy Ghost or Holy Spirit—because everyone knows if he's coming for you, your soul's about to leave your body.

This time, he wanted to teach more than just Miguel a lesson. No one crosses me without facing me or someone in my family. After neutralizing Miguel, Luis went into the Amazon for some recon. That's where Alejandro will pick up from.

"What's so different about the O'Rourkes?" Pablo's the scientist in the family. He majored in chem and minored in bio.

"They're adding phenacetin."

"Where the fuck are they getting that? It's been off the market since the seventies when they discovered it's a carcinogen."

It's a local painkiller in the same family as acetaminophen—Tylenol—but with side effects like cancer.

Luis looks at his son and shrugs. "I don't know where they get it. I didn't have time to find out. They haven't been using it long enough for it to have done any harm yet. But it's making their product stretch further since they're cutting it with that. It's addictive, but not as powerful as cleaner formulas. It's got the inmates begging for more, which made Miguel a lot of money, which led to him running his fat mouth. He got really talkative when I put his *huevos* in kitchen tongs and held a torch to the metal."

That's not a new tactic, but we all shift in our seats. No guy wants to think of that happening to their nuts.

"How is that cost efficient for them? If they're using something that's not readily available, they're spending money to get it or to make it. That doesn't make sense." Jorge isn't tight-fisted, but he'll take his last penny to the grave if he can.

"¿*Mi amor*?" The meeting ends when Margherita's voice floats down to us.

"*Si preciosa.*" Yes, gorgeous.

My brother's been calling his wife that since the day they met. Luis was dumbstruck when he saw her for the first time. It was two weeks before their wedding. Margherita's father forced my hand, and I arranged the marriage. It was an alliance with her family or lose my hold on Colombia. I needed their backing against my uncle, whom I'd just had extradited from the U.S. back to Colombia. Her father refused me since I was *jefe*, and he didn't want his daughter to be a young widow. I clearly lived and have been *jefe* for more than thirty years. But it worked out because they fell in love during the first year they were married. If she and I married, I'd be the one going to check on her. I wouldn't be looking forward to a walk with Ellie.

I noticed the same car parked two houses down from Ellie just before I met her. It's there now that I'm back in town. The owner never parks in a garage or driveway, which is weird for this neighborhood. I've spotted it in the morning a few times, so I thought it might be a household employee. But then I saw it still parked there yesterday evening, and it's there now.

I haven't seen anyone in it, so I have no faces to make me suspicious. But I've survived this long because I'm wary by nature, and I trust next to no one and nothing. It's why Ellie is such a surprise. There's an openness between us most of the time that's refreshing. When she gets evasive, it's to protect her family. Even though we're spending more time together, she's cautious not to give a man she doesn't know well too many details, especially since it was easy to realize she lives alone.

I glance over my shoulder as I jog toward her house. She's just closing the garage door as I reach her driveway. She's got tight workout shorts on, which isn't what she's worn in the past. They've always been looser, not clingy. Rather than a tank top, she has an over-sized t-shirt on. It covers her ass, but it also covers her tits. I'm not thrilled about either of those.

"*Hola, chiquita.*" Hello, little girl.

Where the hell did that come from?

I haven't used an endearment for a woman since I divorced the woman I was eventually forced to marry. The few endearments I used were as forced as my wedding vows. This slipped out, but I mean it.

Her smile improves my day. The meeting at Luis's wasn't that bad, but my day went to shit afterward. The bratva's running most of the docks these days, and they're strong-arming me for more protection money against customs inspections. Alejandro and Pablo came over to my place so we could strategize. I wound up in an argument with them. They're intelligent and experienced, but sometimes they forget my memory is longer than theirs. Their suggestion was a short-term solution to what could become a much longer-term problem.

"*Hola.*"

She's definitely not a Spanish speaker, but her bubbly response is cute. The way she greets me with that smile feels like I'm coming home from a hard day of work to a warm welcome. Except we're standing on the street, and we don't share a home.

I want nothing more than to wrap my arms around her and taste her. I want to know how it would feel to press my dick against her cunt. I want to know how her tits would feel in my hands. I want to squeeze her ass and grind her on my thigh. I want her ass against my cock like I did at the lake the first time we went rowing together.

I've had these thoughts since we met. I jacked off to them while I was away. I've been doing that more often than I have since I was fourteen. I wonder if she thinks the same things about me. Could I be on her mind if she gets herself off?

"How was your day?" I need to get my mind out of the gutter.

"It went well. I'm ready to stretch my legs though. Way too long at the computer."

She tilts her head in one direction, then the other. I hear the cracks, and it tempts me to carry her inside, strip her, and give her a massage.

I'm in my fifties, and my dick doesn't lead me anywhere. I've never let it. I've been with enough women over the years to prove I'm no monk. But I master my libido; it doesn't master me.

Until now.

Fucking hell.

I've kept my dirty thoughts to a minimum when I'm with Ellie, so she never thinks I'm a stalker perv. But my mind's in overdrive this evening. Maybe it's because she's more covered up than usual. It's not like she's ever scantily clad, but my imagination's working overtime, picturing what I know is under that damn t-shirt.

"How about you?" She looks over at me as she rolls her shoulders back.

"Long day too. But the worst is over."

Her eyes drop to my lips, but they dart back up to meet my gaze. Perhaps she is thinking the same thoughts I am right now.

I always sneak glances at her while we walk. I love her profile. But today I'm likely to fall over my feet because I can't look away. It's not just the t-shirt that's different. Something's off. Some-

41

thing's bothering her, and I can tell. It's why I want to hold her even more than usual.

"Did something happen today, Elodie?"

She stops while Constantine sprays his favorite tree. She hesitates for a fraction of a second before she shakes her head. I know I didn't imagine her discomfort, even if the average person couldn't notice. I've spent more than four decades drilling secrets out of people. I started young. I know every sign there is when someone's hiding the truth.

"No. I was busy today, and I still have a few things left to get done."

I step closer to her as we reach the bottom of the hill. I put my hand on her arm, and it's the first time I've touched her since the lake the first time we rowed out together. As I turn us to face each other, I glance back toward the car parked on the street. I shouldn't have stopped us so close to it, but I did.

"Ellie, you don't have to tell me anything you don't want to. But I know something's bothering you. If I can help, I will."

She twists her arm, and I think she wants me to let go. But she rests her hand on my forearm, her thumb sweeping over it twice before she stops herself.

"Nothing's wrong, but thank you. I appreciate the offer. It's kind."

I don't slouch, but I straighten to my full height and lean in to whisper to her. "I told you, you don't have to tell me anything you don't want, but don't lie to me, *chiquita*. I know when you are. Tell me you don't want to talk about it. Tell me it's none of my business. But if you lie, I'll think you're guarding yourself against me finding out something. It will only make me more determined to know if something's wrong, if someone's upset you. Do you want to change your answer?"

I step back, and I watch the cords in her neck strain as she swallows. She doesn't appear frightened of me. Just the opposite. There's curiosity and temptation to challenge me. She wants to know what I'll do next. It's not to pick an argument. Just the opposite.

I think she wants to challenge me, so she gets more of the same dominant personality I'm showing now. While she's been easy-going so far, I didn't get the feeling she's submissive. That's how I've liked to play in the past, but it's not a requirement for me. It piques my curiosity even further. But I could be wrong.

"I had to talk to my ex-husband today, which isn't something I do often. We lead incredibly separate lives, considering we only finalized the divorce eight months ago. But he needed to find some documents I left for him. He insisted they were nowhere to be found. I insisted on where they were, but he refused to believe me. He kept going on and on about how I lost them, or I put them somewhere to screw him over on purpose. It was way too long a conversation that didn't make sense most of the time. In the end, I swapped it over to a video call and made him go through the stack of documents where I said they were. Lo and behold, that's where he found them immediately. I know he didn't look closely because he's too lazy. And he's too lazy because he still assumes I'll do things for him. But that's not my responsibility anymore."

She pushes hair out of her eyes as the wind whips the wispy strands across her forehead. It tempts me to tuck them behind her ear.

"I don't even have the documents to do what he needed, so it pissed him off to realize he's got to take care of himself like a grown-ass adult. It pissed him off even more that I was right about where they were. It bruised his ego all the way around. And in the meantime, I had to listen to him go off on me about it. It tempted me to hang up. But I wanted this over and done with, and I knew it wouldn't be until he found the paperwork. It was still just easier to bite my tongue like it has been for the past twenty-seven years. That put me in a foul mood. On top of that, I had a really frustrating call with someone I hired to take care of a couple of business matters."

I turn toward the direction we were going, but I don't move even when she takes a step forward. She looks back at me, her brow furrowed again.

"How did the conversation with your ex-husband end?"

She offers me a half-hearted smile. At least she doesn't appear upset, which could be a well-practiced mask after many years of hiding a dysfunctional relationship. When she opens her mouth to respond, I step forward, and we continue our walk.

"The way it usually does. Neither of us saying goodbye. We stop talking, then we hang up. He can't be bothered to greet me properly on a phone call. When I call, he's answered with 'yeah' or 'what' for ages. Now that's how I answer his call, which I know didn't set the best tone from the get-go. But I simply don't care about his feelings any longer. And because I don't have to live with him, I don't really care if he's pissed off at me. So, the call ended the way it started. Neither one of us wanted to talk to the other. I've moved on.

"Do you think he's going to do anything because you argued?"

"He can try. But there's nothing he holds over my head. This house is mine. Paid for in cash with my half of the proceeds from the house we sold together. I'm self-employed, so he can't interfere with an employer or put me in a position where I have to quit. I'm not financially reliant on him for anything. He can piss and moan all he wants, but he's got no whipping boy—or rather whipping girl—anymore."

"Do you think he'll tell your boys about this?"

Her laugh is anything but humorous. "That would involve him reaching out to them, which he doesn't do because he's pissed they don't reach out to him. He has never seen that as the first adult in the relationship, he should have led by example. He was disengaged for years, so the boys just don't really factor him in too much anymore. They say they're not bitter or anything like that. He's just a non-entity in a lot of ways. He didn't speak badly about me to them when they were kids. But if he were to call one of them or all three and bitch about me, they'd likely just let him ramble because his attitude toward me wouldn't be anything new. It didn't come as a shock to any of them when I filed for divorce. I was there for as long as I was for their sake. I waited to make sure all three were settled and on their feet. I know they're all self-sufficient and fine. So now I'm on my own."

She looks straight ahead and keeps walking. She doesn't look down as though she's ashamed or regretful. She doesn't look away as though she's embarrassed or avoiding anything. She merely looks like she's accepted everything for what it is. And that saddens me for her. She's shared enough of her personal life. More than she ever has, so I won't press her any further about her day, but I'll listen if she wants to say anything.

Even though it might've been easier if I'd asked about work rather than her private life, I appreciate what she's shared. It's given me insights I didn't have. I get the feeling what she left unsaid about staying until her boys were on their feet was that she couldn't afford to support them and herself. That seems contrary to what anyone would guess, considering the home she's in. But she said she paid cash from the settlement.

Maybe he controlled her all those years. Or maybe she sacrificed a career in order to keep her family together. That story sounds far too familiar.

"Well, tomorrow brings a new day."

I tried to sound optimistic, but I fear I sound phony. She looks over at me and grins. This time, she means the humor in it.

"Okay, Orphan Annie, the sun will come out tomorrow."

"I suppose it will. And whatever else you have going on, tomorrow is another day."

She laughs out loud. "Well, you've gone from Orphan Annie to Scarlet O'Hara."

My brow furrows. *"Gone with the Wind?"*

"Yeah, that was her line. 'After all, tomorrow is another day.' Sounds like a plan to me since I may have to let somebody go in the morning."

I cock an eyebrow, and her smile falters. She observes me for a long moment before she carries on.

"Yeah, I have a publicist I hired for a project, and we aren't in agreement. I may have to let her go if she won't compromise. She's patronizing as fuck."

She shakes her head and rolls her shoulders back, pressing them down, forcing herself to relax.

"If you know what's going wrong, then you must know what's right. Why hire a publicist then?"

She looks up at me, and her gaze sharpens. It's her professional business side I'm looking at now. Her chin notches up, and there's true defiance in her gaze.

"I'm not beyond learning new things when I need to learn them. The woman doesn't get that just because I hired somebody to do a task for me doesn't mean I don't know how to do it. It means I don't have the time or the built-in connections in that area. If I wanted to be patronized, I wouldn't pay for it. The woman is good at what she does, but she believes she knows more about this particular niche than I do. I thought that was true. That's why I brought her on. Turns out she doesn't. So, I won't pay good money hand over fist for somebody's mediocrity. I'm not risk averse. I just like my risks to make me money. I'll take the tasks back on myself until I find somebody competent. Then I will farm them out and move on to the things only I can manage in my business."

Our gazes are locked as though she dares me to disagree or to think she's foolish. Or worse, incompetent. Instead, I think she's never looked hotter, and my balls ache to pump my cum into her. It's a good thing I'm not trying to run with this hard on.

"Sounds like the decision I would make, and so would most people. Hopefully, the conversation goes smoothly, and you get what you want out of it."

She relaxes, and the tension eases away from her. I don't know if she expected something else, and she's relieved. Or if that was what she wanted me to say, and that's where the relief comes from. But either way, she's not as tense as she was a moment ago.

"I think you probably had a better day than I did, considering I dealt with an ex-spouse and maybe firing somebody. Am I right?"

If only she were. After my meetings with my brother and nephews, I dealt with a few more annoying matters and a trip to the out of business bodega we own in Queens. It's not just a closed little corner grocery store. The basement doubles as our place where we handle the more unfortunate side of our business.

I had questions, and Pablo tried to get the answers. It was an exhausting waste of time since, as good as Pablo is at getting information out of the most recalcitrant, this guy was bratva and trained never to squeal. Except I made him sound like a stuffed *cerdito*—little piggy. I still have a few tricks up my sleeves even my head enforcers, Pablo and Alejandro, don't. Pablo has fewer limits than Alejandro, but he still has some.

I have none. That's not something Ellie can ever discover. I need to come up with something to say rather than the truth. It's one of many lies I'll tell her if we continue to become better friends—preferably something even more.

"I had a meeting with a business associate who thought he could out-negotiate me, and it turned out to be a waste of time. He had more to give than I did, and he wound up giving in. He just took forever to do it. We could've finished in five minutes if he'd cooperated."

"Sounds quite a bit more familiar than I think either of us imagined."

She's being sympathetic. If only she knew how far off the mark she is.

"If you have a publicist, what are you trying to get publicity for?"

She doesn't strike me as a social media influencer type, but maybe she is. I don't know any, so I really shouldn't make any assumptions. Her entire expression relaxes, and I know she's happy to talk about whatever she does.

"I'm an author."

"What types of things do you write? Self-help? Business? Finance?"

She laughs. "No, I write psychological thrillers."

"That wasn't what I expected you to say."

"I don't come across as the bloodthirsty murdering type?"

"Hardly."

"I write some historical ones, but a lot of them are contemporary."

"A lot of them? Do you have many published?"

"I do. This is my full-time job now. It has been for about ten years."

"Wow. How long will it take me to read through your catalog?"

She looks at me sideways, unsure if I'm serious.

"I don't just work out, Ellie. I do read, and it's not all for my edification."

She nods. "I have one hundred and ten."

I think my mouth hangs open. That's hardly what I expected her to say either.

"A hundred and ten in ten years? I thought you might say fifty —sixty—but I didn't think you'd average eleven a year."

"Some years it's been more than that. Some years it's been a little less, but I love what I do. So, that old saying that 'it's not work if you love it' actually is true. I always thought it was a pile of bullshit. Work is work, and your job is a job. You might enjoy it, but not always. As an adult, you get on with it, and you pay your bills. But I realize there is truth in that. I just wasn't doing the right thing before."

I furrow my brow once more, unsure what she means, since I got the feeling she might've been a stay-at-home mom. But perhaps I totally read that wrong. I've been wrong all evening.

"You look nervous to ask me what I did before I was an author. I was an accountant, and I enjoyed it. I specialized in forensic accounting. I like puzzles and mysteries, hence the mystery and suspense parts of psychological thrillers. But it wasn't as rewarding as being in my imagination all day, which is a much better place most of the time than reality. Or at least it was the escape I needed for the last decade of my marriage."

"I guess I figured you did something other than that."

"You thought I was a stay-at-home mom because of what I said about sticking around for my boys."

"Not that accounting doesn't have its challenges, but I can't imagine a harder job than being a stay-at-home parent. But I also think it's probably one of the most rewarding experiences."

"It can be, and there were certain periods over the years when I was, but not my boys' entire childhoods. I worked outside the home for a long time, then there were also several years where I had a home office. I'm glad now that I travel even more for this work, I'm not leaving my boys behind. They're young men who fend for themselves. It's given me freedom back."

We've taken our loop around the park, and we're back at her driveway. She's revealed more to me than I expected, but I love it. I know I'm going to have to do the same for her, or she'll feel taken advantage of. It'll make her vulnerable and close off to me, and that's the last thing I want.

"Should I start with your very first book, or is there one you recommend over the others?"

"You could start with the first one. It's not my best, but all the series connect to each other, and the books within each series connect to each other. If you're going to jump into the world I created, you may as well start at the very beginning. Hopefully, you don't think I'm too twisted once you get an actual glimpse of how my mind works."

I wish I could tell her there's not a chance in hell she's more twisted than I am. I grin instead. "What name do you write under?"

"Elodie McCann."

"I'll be filling my digital library when I get home. I shall blame you if I get no sleep tonight because I'm up reading the whole time."

Her smile falters. "Enrique, you don't have to flatter me. I've been at this long enough to know I can't please all the people all the time. At best, I can please some people some of the time, so it's all right when people don't like my books. It won't offend me if it's not your cup of tea."

"I'm still going to read at least one, Ellie."

She watches me for a moment, and I know she caught the other time I called her that, but she hasn't said anything about that, or the two times I called her *chiquita*. Her hesitation makes me wonder if she's thinking about inviting me in. She let Constantine off his leash, and he's sitting in front of the garage. But she doesn't, and it crushes my soul a little.

"I won't ask you tomorrow what you think. I'll know by your expression. So don't worry. I won't put you on the spot."

I smile and nod, but it's not true. She'll never know anything I'm thinking that I don't want her to. I'll only give away what I want, never all of who I am.

"Have a good night, Ellie."

"Night, Enrique."

I head back to my place after we say our goodbyes. I snapped a picture of the license plates as I jogged past the car still parked across the street from her. They come back as fake. Not stolen, not mismatched, but fake.

They're not in the system at all. That sounds all sorts of alarms in my head, even if it has nothing to do with Ellie and isn't a direct threat to her. Something shady is going on near her, and I don't like that. I arrange for two of my most trusted and discreet guys to stake out her place.

I often have bodyguards with me, but the route through her neighborhood is in a gated community and close enough to my home that I enjoyed the time to myself. Now I enjoy the privacy of being with Ellie without an audience besides Constantine.

My men set themselves up in two separate spots in wooded areas near her house. They're on private property, but no one will know they're there unless they make their presence known. Alejandro trained them.

I stay up all night reading her first book. I'm entranced by the end of the second page. The story completely sucks you in, and it is pretty fucking twisted, but it shows she's as brilliant as I imagined. It takes a lot for anything to surprise me when it comes to human nature, especially in books and TV shows. I usually predict the ending before I finish the first quarter of the book, but this one blew me away.

I can honestly admit I did not see that ending coming. It

wasn't like she pulled it out of nowhere, and it made no sense. It made perfect sense, but completely surprising. I even flipped back to different parts of the story to see if she'd foreshadowed anything or planted any red herrings, but she truly hadn't. The complexity of the story seemed so smooth when I came to the end until I stopped to think about what it must have taken to craft that story.

If I didn't know better, I'd think she ran a criminal organization because there're few other people I know who could plot something like this and make it entirely plausible. I read a lot of psychological thrillers. Maybe it's a constructive outlet after what I do, blurring the lines between reality and fiction.

No, that's a pile of bullshit. I never blur those lines. It's not escapism from everyday life. Just the opposite. Many of the books mirror the truth too much. I suppose it's familiarity that makes the genre interesting to me. That's an entire psychopathy I don't need to examine.

I get the first report back from my guys at five a.m. It was too dark to see who got in the car and left an hour earlier, but the same car is back now. However, my guys are certain it's different men who went into the house. One of my men sneaked out and spotted a dash camera pointed toward Ellie's house, so away from him.

I'm headed there now to slip a note under her door before the sun's up. I'm telling her I'll be away for a couple days, but I won't be. I want to give her some space to see who these people are and what they're up to. If I'm a threat to her, then I need to know, and it'll mean walking away for good. I hate that thought, but I won't endanger her.

Even if I'm not the reason for it, I want to know anyway, so I can put protection in place for her. When I get home from that errand, I get cleaned up and head to my office. I downloaded five more of her books before I got out of bed. Now it's time to dig a little more into Ellie McCann and find out who she is.

I've been working for the past two hours, and I'm no more informed about Ellie than I was when I started. Her name links to next to nothing except the publishing company, which isn't a well-known one. It's an anonymous LLC, which makes me question why there're no names linked to it, not even hers.

There're only three states where you can file an anonymous LLC. Delaware—which is a place plenty of people file regular corporations—New Mexico, and Wyoming. She said she grew up in D.C. and lived in New England, but this LLC is registered in New Mexico.

In order to have an anonymous LLC, there still has to be a Registered Agent. Someone who can receive mail and sign contracts. I struggle to find that, so I'm growing more alarmed by the moment.

Why does she need this anonymity?

Is Ellie McCann her real name?

I assume not, since there's not a single record that matches up with her. Not a birth certificate. Not a social security number. Not a marriage license, a divorce decree, nor birth certificates for her children. Nothing. There're a few mentions of her at book signing events, and her books are listed all over the place. But there are no official documents.

Does she have a stalker? Is there more to her ex-husband than she admitted? Did that motherfucker abuse her? Is she in WITSEC? Witness Protection, as most people call it.

There's a reason for this, but I don't know what it is. And while she said she likes puzzles, I hate them.

I look down when my phone buzzes on my desk.

"Hey, Martín."

It's a guy I have watching her place.

"*Jefe,* nobody's come out of the house since those men went inside, but another car's driven past three times already. There's nothing that makes us think it belongs to somebody here on the street. It went up past the hill, but wasn't there long enough for anybody to have bothered with the park, even if they were meeting somebody, then left. I don't know why they've driven by a third time in the last two hours. They're coming back down the hill now. Do you want us to do anything?"

"Get pictures if you can, but don't engage. I don't want anybody to make you."

This isn't cool. I've spent all day at this, and now it sounds like my *chiquita* has some kind of stalker. It nearly kills me, but I wait two hours until it's completely dark out before I head over to her house.

Chapter Five

Ellie

I peek through the spyhole, shocked to find Enrique on the other side of the front door. I open it.

"Hi."

"Elodie, let me in."

"What?"

"Let me in, Elodie. Now."

Neither his tone nor his expression says I should ask questions. I step back, and he slips inside the door, pushing it shut and locking it behind him.

That should terrify the shit out of me, but it doesn't. We stare at each other for a moment, and then he's spinning me, so my back's against the door as he devours me.

Holy motherfucker.

This is better than any of the things I pictured while getting myself off with my vibrator. Over and over and over again. Definitely better than any porn I've ever watched.

He lifts me, and I wrap my legs around his waist as he carries me to the sofa. His hands grasp my ass and guide me to ride his cock. Our fucking clothes are in the way, but neither of us wants to stop kissing long enough to do anything about it. My hands run through his hair and over his shoulders and his chest as one of his hands slides up my back and around my ribs to grab my breast.

He's kneading and squeezing. It's arousing as hell. It's everything I've been missing for years.

When he pulls away, he yanks my blouse over my head. Then he twists to lower me onto my back and holds down my bra cups so he can feast on my tits. He sucks and nibbles, making me arch my back, longing for even more.

"Please."

He understands, biting the nipple he has between his teeth now while twisting the other. I moan, and my fingers grasp his shoulders. He reaches up and takes my hands, lifting my arms over my head. This is the most erotic thing I've ever experienced.

I grasp the armrest and hold on, widening my legs to allow him to fit between my thighs. He grinds his dick against me, and I want nothing more than for us to both strip naked, so I can get fucked the way I've wanted since long before I even met him. I haven't been with anybody since Tim, and even that was monumentally disappointing for most of the marriage.

Maybe this seems so spectacular based on the shit I have to compare it with, but I don't think it's that. I think it's amazing because it's him.

He kisses along my neck, up to my jaw, and behind my ear.

"Ellie, what are you doing to me? I have no self-control around you. I want every single bit of you."

"I want to give you every single bit, Enrique. I have no self-control either."

But my lust haze evaporates as he pushes my pants down, trying to get them over my hips. It's when I lift them that I come back to reality. I press against his chest and shake my head. Immediately, he pulls away.

"I'm sorry. I didn't mean to take it too far. I'll stop. Sorry."

I feel horrible about how guilty he looks. I sit up and follow him as he moves away from me. I adjust my pants back into place, then go back to straddling his lap.

"Enrique, this is new to me. Nobody has seen me naked besides one man in nearly thirty years. I don't look the way I did the last time a man other than my ex-husband looked at me or touched me. It's a little daunting."

I feel so embarrassed. I got myself into this. My common-sense disappeared the moment he walked in the door. There's a big difference between daydreaming about this and then actually letting it happen.

"*Chiquita*, can you not tell I want you just the way you are? You obviously turn me on."

"Yeah, but there's a big difference between what you might think is under these clothes and what actually is. I have a scar I rarely think about. However, it's one I really don't want anybody to see and—oh, fuck me—I haven't waxed in years."

I spit that last bit out entirely humiliated now.

He eases me forward to lie against his chest, pressing my head to his shoulder. He kisses my forehead and runs his hand up and down my back. I can't help the shuddering sigh as I relax against him. He wraps both arms around me, and it's the first time a man's comforted me in years. It's not half-hearted or perfunctory. I feel cared about. He kisses my forehead again, and my eyes drift closed. Would that I could just stay like this forever.

"*Chiquita*, I've wanted to do that since the moment we met. But I would have waited years—though that might've killed me—if you weren't ready for a kiss."

I laugh. "That was more than *a* kiss."

His chest rumbles beneath my cheek when he laughs, too. "I want you, little one. I want to feel you and taste you and bring you pleasure. But that's not all. I enjoy your company. I look forward to it. When you shared your day with me, I wanted to share your burdens. We'll go at your pace, *chiquita*, whatever it is."

"I don't know what that's going to be. I'm not scared of you, and I'm not scared of sex. I'm just self-conscious right now. I'm fine with clothes on, but—well—you're you." I lean back and gesture up and down as I look at him. "And I'm just me."

He tenses, and his hands slide to my ass. He holds on to me so tightly it hurts. I love it. He keeps squeezing until my hips rock forward, my ass having a mind of its own and wanting to escape his vise-like grip.

"I *will not* ask what you mean because I understand. It'll only piss me off to hear you put yourself down again. You will learn I am not a materialistic man. I don't need to acquire possessions to prove anything. But what is mine, I take care of because it's precious to me. You, little girl, are mine."

His hand goes to my throat, resting heavily on my collar bone. His fingers press against the back of my neck, urging me forward. He sits up and presses his lips to mine. Both hands move to cup my jaw, and I feel like I'm in a movie love scene. Everything about the way we kiss is perfect. I've never felt this desired. Not by my ex-husband when we were dating. Not by the men before him. I'm breathless and in a haze when he sits back.

"Ellie—"

"Why do you call me that? No one shortens my name to that."

"I think Elodie is one of the most beautiful and feminine names I've ever heard. I think Elle is sophisticated. But Ellie is just mine. It's soft and light, which is how I want you to feel. Not like you have the weight of the world on your shoulders like I've sensed. I want to make you happy and take care of you."

"That's the second time you've said that. What do you mean?"

Does he want a kept woman? A mistress? Does he think I can't take care of myself?

"I call you Ellie and *chiquita*, but I don't think you're a child. You're independent, and I know that's important to you. I'm not suggesting I put you in a situation where you're reliant on me. I don't want to just come over to fuck, then leave. I mean as a partner."

Oh. Shit. Um.

"Enrique, I can't give you that. I never want to be in another committed relationship. I never want to be accountable to someone else or have to hold anyone else accountable. I don't want—"

I snap my mouth shut as I realize how I truly feel. I've said what I just did to plenty of people, especially ones who've tried to reassure me I'll find love again. I don't want it.

Accountability only scratches the surface. It sounds like I want freedom to do whatever I want. There's some of that, but that's not all of it.

"What don't you want?"

I shake my head. This is pawing at a wound that's scabbed over but not healed. I'm too exposed, and that's part of why I don't want a relationship.

"Ellie?"

"It's nothing."

I squeak as I reach for his shoulders, unprepared for him to lift me off his lap and lie me face down on the sofa. He spanks me. Hard. Several times. After the surprise that comes with the first one, I press my hips up. I want the spanking. I want his dominance and my submission, which is ludicrous. It's the perfect opposite of what I want when he isn't spanking me.

"Enrique, that hurts. Ow!"

"I know it does. It's supposed to. I told you never to lie to me. I told you to tell me something is none of my business. To tell me you don't want to talk about it. But do *not* tell me, little girl, that something that's obviously important to you is nothing. Everything that's important to you is important to me."

"All right. Stop. Please. I'm sorry." My voice trembles, and I feel like utter shit.

He scoops me up and cradles me this time. I don't like it. I can't hug him like he's hugging me. I shift to straddle him a third time.

"Shh, Ellie. It's done."

"I pissed you off. That's disappointing."

"I'm not pissed off, *cariño*."

I know that means sweetheart for a man or woman. I shudder as I burrow into his chest. I feel raw. I want to run from it, but I want to run to Enrique. That makes no sense.

"I'm not disappointed in you or this conversation. I want you to understand you aren't alone. I want you to understand you're important. The things you think. The things you do. The things that happen in your life. I'm not trying to control you or demand to know every little detail. You can keep your thoughts to yourself. Just don't diminish them or yourself. You're too special for that."

"That's hard to believe, and it's going to take me time to accept that. I know I'm hiding, but I understand now why I never want a committed relationship again. I never want to rely on someone again and be that deeply disappointed again. It would crush me."

"If you let no one near you, no one can hurt you."

"Yes."

He tips my chin up and gazes down at me. He kisses me again, and it's so tender a tear slides down my cheek. The other ones tonight have been passionate and possessive. I loved them. This—this gives me hope I don't want. Because the other side of hope is disappointment. I can't take more of that.

But, God, how he tempts me.

His voice is soft as his hand runs up and down my back. His other one cups my ass.

"*Chiquita*, we have a lot we need to talk about that could make all of this moot. But before I tell you why I came over here—no, it wasn't to ravish you—I want you to know what I said earlier hasn't changed. If you want anything between us—romantic or platonic —we go at your speed."

"You make me want to trust you, Enrique. And that's fucking terrifying."

He closes his eyes and tilts his head back for a moment. When he looks at me, there's regret in his eyes. I pull away, but he holds onto me.

"Let me say what I have to say. If you want me to let go of you —if you want me to leave—I will. But I need to feel you in my arms while I tell you things I've told no one else."

What the hell is he going to confess?

His expression is so earnest, but it grows more vulnerable the longer I watch him. I'm unprepared for it after the man who just spanked me. He's dreading what he has to say. I grip the front of his shirt but sit up. I press my pussy against his semi-aroused dick.

60

It lengthens, and I nearly moan. He pulls me close, and I have this urge to sit on his cock. Not for sex. Not to edge either of us. It's as though I need that physical connection to prepare me for whatever emotional shit's about to come up.

"Before we go any further, you should know my last name, too. It's Diaz."

"Enrique Diaz?"

Oh, holy fucking shit on a shingle.

"Yes. Do you recognize the name?"

Do I lie?

"I've heard it before."

He stares at me for a moment. I haven't moved. Some of it is shock, but nothing makes me want to bolt.

"What have you heard?"

Do I lie?

"I know you're one of the wealthiest men in the world. I know you have business connections everywhere."

He's watching me intently enough to make most people squirm. I'm not most people.

"Anything else, *chiquita*?"

"There are rumors and speculation I've read in articles. What do you want me to know about you, Enrique?"

"Do you believe those rumors now that you know me?"

"I believe you're capable of those things, but so are millions of other people. It doesn't mean you've done what they've accused you of, but maybe you have."

"Do you think I run a drug cartel?"

"Do you?" I notch up my chin.

Shit got real, real fast.

"Yes."

Well, that sure was blunt.

"Will someone kill you if you don't?"

"Yes."

"Would someone have killed you if you hadn't taken over?"

"Yes."

"I'm glad you're alive."

61

He waits for me to say more, but I think that speaks volumes. He watches me, and I know he's trying to tell whether I mean it, whether it's bravado, whether I have some twisted bad boy complex.

"You aren't kicking me out."

"Do you use your product?"

"Never."

"Will you expect me to?"

"Never!" He's shocked I asked, but how could I not?

"Good, because I've never even smoked a cigarette. Do you or your nephews deal on the streets?" From my tone, he knows I know the answer.

"I won't lie and say none of us have. But that hasn't been my role for more than thirty years. My nephews are too senior for that now. What about the other things you've read about me?"

"The violence?"

"Yeah."

"Nothing about a single interaction I've had with you makes me think you'd *ever* bring that around me intentionally. I don't fear you losing control and hurting me. It doesn't thrill me to know the lengths you'd go to protect illegal products. But I get that it's not as simple as what you import and export. You can't get out and stay alive, so you're in this for life. What you do protects your family and people who depend on you. Maybe you're a horrible person, and maybe so are the people who work for you. But there are innocent people who depend upon you, too. Maybe the ends justify the means. I read once that you inherited the position from your uncle. You were born into this, and so were your brother, sisters, and nephews. If this is all any of you've ever known—if what you do isn't just about the money but about protecting your family—then I will never disapprove of what you do. There are no limits to what I would do to protect my sons. None. I won't fault you for being the same."

"You don't think I'm a murderer? You don't think I'm a criminal? You don't think I'm—"

"Have you raped a woman?"

"What? No! I can't believe you'd—"

"Do you abuse children?"

"No!"

"Do you abuse animals?"

"No!"

"Then you haven't crossed the line of what I can't accept. I'd love to be idealistic enough to believe ethics are universal. Life isn't that simple. A lot of times, ethics are situational. Is it wrong to kill? Usually. If it's between kill someone or let my child die, I will put a bullet through that person's head before my next breath. If I'm responsible for a multi-billion-dollar empire that ensures people have roofs over their children's heads, food in their children's stomachs, and clothes on their children's backs, then I'll do what I have to provide for those who rely on me. Duty is duty. It's rarely glamorous."

"That's very philosophical."

"That's very real for me."

"It's why you stayed."

I don't need to say anything because it isn't a question. He gets it. If only he knew the extent of it. But it's not the time for all my secrets to come out. Or maybe it is, but I'm not ready.

"This brings me to the reason I came over."

He waits for me, but I only raise my eyebrows. I won't freak out until there's a reason to. I won't waste the emotional energy if I don't have to. Another coping mechanism. That's what they used to call it. A trauma response is what they call it now. Who knows what the next term will be? Whatever the hell it is, it's how I get by.

"Ellie, being with me—being anywhere near me—comes with a level of danger we need to discuss."

"That's not surprising, Enrique."

"But you need to understand what I mean. This isn't just a passing comment."

"It's not like I think you're some movie gangster, but I'm also not naive to what goes on. I see the news."

"*Chiquita*, that's only a fraction of reality. There's so much

63

that never gets reported. Many of the stories you read or hear are only an abridged version. I came over tonight because there's been a car parked on your street the last few times I've been in the neighborhood."

I look toward the living room windows, but I already closed the curtains. As soon as the sun dips, I always close them, but the moment the sun is up, I open them. I love natural daylight, so most of the time, anybody could look in my window. I return my focus to Enrique.

"The car looks out of place, not because of make and model, but simply because it's parked on the road when everybody else in this neighborhood parks in their driveway or garage. I've never seen anybody get in or out of it, but it's been there, and it's close enough for someone to watch you if they're in that house. I didn't want to make something out of nothing, so I assigned two men to watch the car."

"Two men to watch the car or two men to watch me, Enrique?" There's an edge to my tone, and I know it.

"To watch the car, but that also means watching you."

I narrow my eyes, and his left hand goes to my waist. He strokes up and down my ribs to reassure me. While the gesture normally would, knowing he's had men report to him makes me suspicious and uncomfortable.

"Ellie, the car has a dash camera."

"What?"

"My men spotted a dash camera pointed toward your house, not toward the one the car's parked in front of. My men only started watching the car yesterday. They haven't seen anything else unusual except this evening another car drove past your house four times. That's when one of my guys called me. He said the time spent at the top of the road wasn't long enough for anybody to do anything at the park. It sounds like they merely turned around and came back down your street. I don't know if they're looking for something. I don't know if they're trying to intimidate someone on your street. It could be completely unrelated to you, but on the mere chance it is, I don't want you here alone."

"Do you mean tonight, or do you mean permanently?"

"We'll start with tonight until I can investigate a bit more."

I observe him, and there's something else.

"Enrique, what aren't you telling me?"

"The plates are fake. I ran them, and nothing came up. They don't belong to a different car. They don't belong to some law enforcement agency. Nothing. They've never been registered."

That sends a chill down my spine. What the fuck? Could this be connected to me? Could it be someone doesn't like Enrique spending time with me? I don't know what to make of that, since I live in a gated community.

"No one's allowed to drive into this neighborhood without either a resident sticker or being logged as an approved visitor. How is a car with fake license plates coming in here?"

"I don't know. It's something I need to investigate."

"How are you able to come in the neighborhood? I know you're on foot, but they stop pedestrians, too."

"Ellie, my company built this neighborhood. I've been coming here since I bought the land."

"You built—What?"

That's a lot for me to take in. This home was previously owned, so I know very little about the developers. This is a substantial-sized community. The homes all have varied floor plans that don't look like ticky-tacky boxes all in a row. It doesn't look like an obviously planned community. It's one of the things I like most about it. I don't feel like my home is cookie-cutter.

"I bought the land seven years ago. I own a development company and a construction company. I have a team of architects, builders, and various other people needed for a project this size. You live in an upper-middle-class neighborhood where plenty of people could buy custom homes and not just the interior fittings. The first-time owners all worked with the architects to design houses how they wanted them."

"Was this project a cover for something else?"

"No. I have plenty of legitimate, above-board businesses, and this is one of them. I'm a venture capitalist, among other things. I legally invest in plenty of companies."

"That you then sell at a profit or break into shell corps."

"Sometimes, not always." His brow furrows.

"Enrique, I told you I was a forensic accountant."

"I hadn't thought about that. But the above-board businesses mean I pay taxes on all of those things. It keeps my nose looking clean."

I cock an eyebrow.

"I told you I don't use any of my products. I never have."

"All right. I already told you I know you're one of the wealthiest men in the world. I didn't want to consider how you gained it. There's nothing flashy about you that gives away just how much you have."

"Because I can only live in one home at a time. I can only drive one car at a time. Do I have multiple properties? Yes, but I use all of them. Do I have multiple cars? Yes, but none of them just sit in a garage idle. I don't need to spend every penny I have. I'd rather reinvest the money and make sure I can provide for the people who come after me. The people who depend upon me."

"Do you have children?"

"No."

"Have you been married before?"

"Yes."

"Could it be her?"

"No. She died."

I didn't expect that. I blink several times before I rest my hands on his heart.

"No, *cariño*, it's not what you think. I'm not a widower. The marriage was arranged several years ago, but it didn't last. We weren't happily wed, and when the alliance fell through, it was as good a reason as any to end it. She remarried someone back in Colombia and was unfaithful. He found out."

I swallow, and he shakes his head.

"I told you, I don't abuse children. I don't abuse animals. I've never raped a woman. I don't abuse women either. Call me old-fashioned, but women aren't supposed to be pawns in men's business. They're to be protected and kept away from this life as best as we can."

"But that doesn't always happen, does it?"

"No. But I've never hurt a woman, and I never will. She wasn't faithful to me either, but she survived our marriage without a hair out of place."

I nod. Taking in all of this information is a lot to process. I think I'm doing a pretty fucking great job not losing my shit.

"If this car that's parked across the street and the one that went by tonight are connected to you, what does that mean?"

"That depends on what you want, Ellie. Do you want me to leave you alone?"

"No!"

I blurt that answer, and I don't have to think twice.

"Enrique, I don't want you to leave me alone. I want to know how we deal with this together."

"*Chiquita*, there's no dealing with it together. I have to deal with it, and I need you to trust that I can."

"I don't doubt for a moment that you can. This isn't a life I know here, so I'll take your advice on how to handle everything. But I still want to know what's going on, Enrique. I don't want any surprises, and I need to know if a man approaches me, whether he's somebody to trust or fear. You need to be honest with me about at least that much."

"I will. I will always tell you as much as I can. I will never lie to you about how I feel and what I want with us. But there are plenty of other things I won't tell you. Plenty of things I'll lie about. It's not just protecting me. It's protecting you. It's protecting my family. It's protecting all the people who rely upon me."

"And that makes perfect sense to me. But I need you to be forthcoming whenever you can be. I won't live fearing every stranger I see because I don't know who to trust."

"I don't want that for you. I want a safety detail parked

outside. If this isn't about you, then it won't matter to whoever this is. If it's about me, then they'll know I'm aware."

He doesn't need to say anything more than that. If they're aware, they know he'll react to anything he perceives is off.

"Won't that raise suspicion too? You said it's unusual for someone to park a car on the street. Now there'll be two."

"Would you allow them in your driveway?"

I can just imagine what my boys will say if they come over and see a strange man parked in the driveway. Fucking hell.

"What if I said no to the detail?"

"Do you have to answer a question with a question?"

"Do you?" I lift my chin again, my gaze unwavering.

"You know you make it hard to concentrate when you make me want to fuck you even more than usual."

I have another one of those beached trout moments—I sit here just blinking.

"Ellie, I love your independence and how you challenge me. But your safety is a topic that's non-negotiable. If we're together in any way—friend or dating—you will obey everything I tell you for your safety. If you don't, I'll bare your ass and spank you. Earlier will feel like taps. I'm asking you to accept the detail, but you'll have one regardless of your answer. If this has nothing to do with us, then it'll be temporary. If it's about us, especially if our friendship becomes more, then the detail is in place permanently."

"You mean until I die or until things end."

His dark eyes bore into my soul. I don't know what he's thinking because he doesn't want me to. I've only known what he wants me to. He's a man with more secrets than the Vatican.

"I'll accept just friendship from you because you said you don't want a committed relationship. I'll accept being a fuck buddy if that's all you'll offer. But I want to be with you romantically. I want to see if we can have a lasting relationship. I wouldn't want that, and I wouldn't agree to anything else, if I didn't mean for the definite future."

"Definite? How long is that?"

"Definite as in there's no question we have a future together."

I want to hold on to that. Sink my nails into it and cling to it for dear life. I want companionship, even love. But not more than I want to avoid disappointment. It's cowardly, but I don't give a shit. Dress me up as a lion and call this fucking house Oz. I don't want to depend on Enrique for anything, certainly not my emotional fulfillment. I told him I'm not risk averse, but that's in business. I'm one-hundred percent risk averse to getting my heart broken.

"I'm spooking you. You're ready to bolt. Let's just deal with whatever's happening with the car."

"I'm not scared, and I'd walk you to the door if I didn't want to be around you. I'm working through all of this. I won't give up the friendship we're building. That's not in question. I'm brave enough to have sex with you as long as you're in front of me. I'm not brave enough yet for you to see the parts of me I dislike the most. I'm not ready for anything more than casual dating. I admit it. If I want to run, I want no strings attached that'll tie me down."

"Do you want to date in general?"

"I've thought about it, but I'm not on any apps and haven't gone out with a goal to meet somebody."

"Do you want to date more than one person?"

This is wading into shit I don't want to discuss. My emotions are contradictory, and I'll sound like a bitch.

"Ellie, you can tell me anything."

The fuck I can.

I wait too long because I watch him retreat.

"You won't open up because there are things I won't tell you. I know it's not fair I—"

"What you can or can't tell me isn't a factor."

"Then what is? Do you want to date other men?"

"Not particularly."

"Do you want to be alone?"

"Yes."

My deadpan response surprises him.

"I spent nearly thirty years being lonely in a marriage. I'd rather be alone than lonely with someone there."

"And you assume that's what would happen with us? That I wouldn't give you what you need."

"I don't know you well enough to know. Even if you did, I don't know that I ever want to give up my freedom again. I don't want to *have to* consider a partner's feelings before I decide. I don't want to *have to* put someone else ahead of me for the sake of keeping the peace. I've spent nearly thirty years doing my best not to be selfish. I've compromised—or rather, told myself I'm compromising but never gotten equal sacrifice in return. I've given up doing things—given up even considering doing things—for someone else's sake. I don't know if I'll always feel this way. I don't know how long it'll take me to stop feeling this way if I ever do. I need to breathe. I need to feel like I can fill my lungs rather than always being suffocated."

I pray he understands what I'm muddling my way through because I sound like an utterly selfish bitch right now. I sound petty and immature to my own ears. Maybe I am.

"I don't want to play the field, Enrique. I don't want to date a slew of men. I'd like to fuck. I want to do that a lot. As in how strongly I wish to do that and how much I want to have. I'm not looking to rack up a body count. I want to make up for lost time, but not indiscriminately."

I'm sitting on the lap of the hottest man I've ever seen. I don't have my shirt on, and my bra is back in place, but my breasts are half hanging out. If I hadn't lost my nerve, we'd be fucking right now. I tell him I want to fuck, yet when I had the chance, I stopped us. I make no fucking sense to anybody but me because I'll sound shallow as fuck if I admit why I feel the way I do.

"And if I'm happy to fuck you as often as you want to be fucked?"

"Can you accept being a fuck buddy?"

"I already told you I can."

"You're practically grimacing."

"Because you know I want more. But I can't force you. Ellie, I will lose my fucking mind if I know you're sharing your body with someone else. Can you agree to sexual monogamy?"

"Yes. I told you, it's not like I want to sleep with a ton of guys. You spanked me earlier for what you considered me speaking poorly about my body, but it doesn't change how I feel. You are the most attractive man I've ever seen. In front of an average guy, I might not be so self-conscious. In front of a guy I might only want to sleep with a couple times, I might not be so embarrassed. In front of you—" I shrug. "Look. I know what I don't want, but I'm not really sure of everything I do want. I want to spend time with you like we have been. I'd like to do more than just walk my dog or go rowing. I want to have sex with you. I don't want to sleep with anyone else, and I'm not eager to date anyone else. I just can't promise I'll ever want to be in a committed relationship. You said you wouldn't bring me into this world if you didn't want something more definite. I never want you to feel you wasted time with me. I know that feeling far too well."

I've said what I've said more than once. Enrique's let me get all of it off my chest. He's let me muddle through it. He's let me rehash it. He did that and listened. He hasn't looked bored. He hasn't accused me of attacking him when all I want is to share how I feel. I didn't intend for any of this to be a test, but he passed.

What the fuck happens if I fail?

Chapter Six

Enrique

Her piece of shit ex-husband had two-and-a-half decades to break her heart. To wear her down and leave her feeling shitty. She's got miles-wide walls around her because she's scared. They're so high they're taller than the Tower of Babel, but even that didn't reach heaven. There was a top to that and a top to her walls. I'll have to climb until I can get over to the other side.

I hate knowing she fears anything. Especially something I can't protect her from. I can't change what's made her so gun shy. But I can do my best to show her I'm not the man she was married to. That I won't take her for granted. That I won't ignore her needs and wants. There will be times I can't give her what she wants, but I'll always give her what she needs. I'll fucking move mountains to do that.

Her ying and yang are strength and fragility. She has to be strong because she's so fragile. She's so fragile because she's had to rely on her strength until it's worn thin.

I didn't think my heart was malleable enough to break. Maybe it's so brittle it's snapped. But my chest aches as I listen to her work through what she'd only partially acknowledged or understood. She trusts me to hear this, and she trusts me to support her choices. She says she never wants to rely on anyone ever again, but she'll rely on me to ease her back into the dating world. That's a start.

"*Chiquita.*"

I cup her face and lean in for a kiss. I keep it light, not wanting to pressure her after what she's divulged. But I want her to know beyond just my words that I accept her. My hands roam over her body, letting her know I enjoy every inch, but without coming on too strong. She cups my cheeks, and it's erotic as fuck.

When we pull apart, I watch her. Our gazes lock, then she dives in for another kiss. This one is passionate and aggressive. I let her lead for a few swipes of her tongue, but that's only while I unfasten her bra and pull the straps down her arms. She tugs at my shirt, and we pull apart, so I can take it off. I lift her and turn, so once again, she's lying on her back.

"I won't expect anything to be different between us in the morning." Even if it is. "I won't pressure you for more than this. But you agreed to sexual monogamy. Do you still agree to it?"

"Yes." She's breathless, but she's focused.

"Your heart and your mind are yours. But your body belongs to me now, *chiquita*. It's mine to pleasure and deny however I want."

Hurt flashes in her eyes before a mask falls into place. Fuck.

"Ellie, when I say deny, I don't mean reject. I mean tease, edge, master, leave craving more. I won't ignore your needs, but I may not always give you what you want. But that's about delayed gratification. About knowing I'll take care of you, even if it's not the way you want or ask."

I can practically feel her uncertainty as though it were a tangible barrier between us. I watch as she battles with herself, finally letting the part of her that wants this win. I've chipped away at countless men's defenses. I've fooled them into lowering their guard. I've convinced them to rely on me when they never should have. I've controlled them merely because I can.

That's not what I'm doing now because none of it has malicious intent. Just the opposite.

I kiss along her neck as I shift back, making my way to her magnificent tits. These are the breasts of a mature woman. It wouldn't surprise me to know she nursed her sons. They aren't perky. They aren't unblemished. I see the faint lines on them. I see the enlarged areolas.

I see tits I want to bury my face between and never leave. I see tits I want to suck and fondle until my last breath. I see a woman who's lived life, given life, nurtured life. She's spent years taking care of others. It's her turn to receive.

I lick around the darker skin, laving her nipple until it tightens. I swirl my tongue around it before sucking. She presses the back of my head, wanting more. I give it to her, but I draw her hands away, crossing her wrists and holding them in one hand. She tugs against my hand, and I release her. I'm about to sit up when I watch her keep them crossed but raise her arms over her head like she had them earlier. She arches her back with a moan that shoots straight to my cock.

I go back to sucking on her tits as my right hand tugs at her pants' waistband. I shift, leaning my weight on my left forearm, so I can pull her pants down. She freezes. She doesn't move her hands, but her body tenses.

"I'll stay in front of you."

"I haven't—I'm not—Fuck me."

"I plan to."

"No. I mean—"

"You told me already. I don't give a shit whether you wax, shave, or nothing at all. All my dick cares about right now is being inside you. My hands want to touch your skin. My tongue wants to taste you. And I want to see what's mine."

I push back to kneel and yank her yoga pants and thong down with one hard tug. She may not wax or shave, but she's ladyscaped. I've seen nothing more inviting than her pink little pussy. I pull her clothes the rest of the way off, and she's finally naked. I toss them aside before leaning forward to kiss her forehead, her temple, the tip of her nose, her cheek, her lips, her jaw, down her neck, her shoulder, between her tits, all over her belly, and finally inside each hip joint. Then I'm at the promised land. I hook her thighs over my shoulders and get my first taste.

Fucking hell. I may never leave.

She's so damn wet I nearly abandon this, so I can strip and thrust into her. My *huevos* ache, so I wrap my hands around her waist and lift her up the sofa, allowing me to stretch out enough to press my cock into the cushions. I give myself a moment's relief as I grind against the edge of the sofa. But if I keep doing that, I'll come.

I focus on Ellie with the next lick. I work her clit like I did her nipples. I flick, suck, swirl, and graze my teeth over it. Her heels find enough space on the couch to lift her hips. I pull back and slap her pussy.

"Thank you for the offer, but I will take what I want when I want. I told you your body is mine. I decide."

She watches me for a moment before her legs fall open even wider. She licks her lips, thinking about something.

"Yes, sir."

Her chest and belly don't move. She's holding her breath, waiting for my reaction. Her hesitancy tells me she's not used to saying that phrase. It's not just uncertainty about my response.

"That's right, *chiquita*."

I tweak her nipple as I thrust my tongue into her cunt. I let my hand glide down her ribs before thrusting three fingers into her. She easily takes them, and I work her, plunging in and out of her. I find her G-spot and press on her belly from on top and from within. My thumbs rub her clit and just below it.

"Sir, please may I come?"

"No."

"Enrique!"

"No, *chiquita*. You will come when I'm buried inside you. I'm not done tasting you yet."

I pull my fingers out, but I replace them with my tongue as she moans her disagreement. I keep working her clit, bringing her to the edge, then pulling back. I want her to want me as much as I do her. I want her mind to only focus on her need for me. Even if it's just tonight. Even if it's only ever just to fuck. I don't care. I want her as desperate as I am.

"*Please.*"

There's a catch in her voice. When I gaze up at her, I see tears in her eyes. She's reached a limit I didn't expect so soon. I scoop her into my arms and stand. She wraps around me as I kiss her. She grimaces but doesn't pull away. She doesn't like her taste as much as I do.

"What's wrong, little one?"

I walk up the stairs, holding her tightly against me. Her pussy rubs against my cock, and the pressure's painful. I'm getting a dose of my own medicine.

"Oh, God. I've already revealed so fucking much tonight."

She buries her head against my shoulder.

"I wasn't ready for how intense it felt being fingered *properly*."

Oh.

That sack of shit didn't even fuck her well.

I get to the top of the stairs and look around. She lifts her head and twists before pointing to the end of the hall. I pass two bedrooms with their doors open. The rooms are furnished but clearly aren't lived in. I know the house has a finished basement with what could be a bedroom down there. There's also an ensuite downstairs that I noticed is her office. She has space for her sons to visit, but she lives alone. I'm glad it means no one's likely to walk in on us, but it also means I worry about her safety even more now that it sinks in how empty this house is for one person.

Constantine barely lifted his head when I came in the door, thumping his tail twice on his bed. But now I hear his paws on the stairs, then a disgruntled huff when the door closes in his face. Ellie looks over my shoulder and laughs.

"He's not used to another guy in my bed."

"I don't share."

Her gaze doesn't waver as we stare at each other.

"Neither do I."

We agreed not to have sex with anyone else, but I sense she means more. I won't push her since I know how confused she is by all of this. Words *and* deeds. That's what she needs. That and time.

I put her down once I've walked to the far side of the bed. Habit and an intense need to protect her prompt me to keep her away from the door and to have my back to it instead of her. If anyone finds us in here, I'll be the first target. It also means I can get to the door without having to move around her.

I'm unprepared for her arms to wrap around my waist. There's a reason I moved her hands earlier.

"A gun?"

I observe her as she assesses me. She nods, moves her hands to my chest, and pecks my lips. She lowers her eyes and moves her hands behind her back. It's barely noticeable, but she's biting the left corner of her top lip. She's not used to this. I want to pounce.

"Are you a submissive?"

"I wanted to find out, but never got to."

"Do you think I'm a Dom?"

"Maybe. You're definitely dominant."

I hope she never believes that shifts into domineering.

"I have been in the past. That's not what I want with you, Ellie. I don't want a D/s arrangement. That's not what I want out of you as a fuck buddy. Are you into kink?"

"Again, I wanted to try but never got to. But I'm certain I'm into at least some stuff."

I swallow a frustrated sigh. As pissed off as that makes me on her behalf, I thrill at knowing I can introduce her to this.

"You understand the difference?"

"Yes. I've written a few books with varying degrees of those dynamics. I just haven't lived it."

"Do you want to?"

"No. I don't want to be a sub, but I want to try being submissive tonight."

Plenty of people wouldn't see a difference between the two. Me being dominant but not being a Dom or her being submissive, but not a sub. You can be into kink without needing the true power exchanges that come with a D/s relationship.

"Um, I have condoms." Her cheeks flush.

"Good. I don't carry one with me, Ellie. It's not like I expect to randomly hook up."

"I have them just in case. It's not like I planned to bring guys home."

"And that's smart."

She walks to the bathroom. I don't know if she realizes I can see the entire length of her. I see the scar she means, and I see another fainter one. She probably had a Mommy Makeover, but something went wrong with part of the incision. I've inflicted enough wounds and seen enough of them to know what it is. She had a burst seroma, which usually aren't stitched. They're a hole that has to heal from the bottom up. It leaves uneven surfaces. I get why she wouldn't want someone to see it. I won't point out I have, but I'll make sure she knows I like the view, nonetheless. Her ass...

I unfasten my pants, pushing my jeans to the floor. I leave my boxer briefs on, stroking myself through the material as she returns. She watches me as she puts three condoms on the bedside table. Her lips twitch. I snag her around the waist and pull her close.

"I plan to send you back for more."

I lift her again, and she wraps her legs around my waist. I'd kept her legs higher not to touch my gun earlier. Now they rest more naturally atop my hips. I crawl onto the bed. She holds onto me as I lower her to the mattress, but the moment I stretch out, she lifts her arms over her head a third time.

I kiss behind her ear, then tug at the lobe. I move down her neck as I brush hair from the other side. I cup her jaw as I whisper to her.

"You have no idea how badly I want you. If I'm too rough, tell me. I never want to harm you."

"I know, sir."

"Enrique. When we talk about how we want things between us, we're equals. Always."

"Thank you."

I kiss behind her ear again.

"I'm going to fuck you all night, *chiquita*. I'm going to show you what it means when I tell you your body belongs to me. I'm going to make you beg. I'm going to make you scream. I'm going to make you come until you can't take more—then I'll do it again."

"Yes, please, sir."

I lift my head, and she turns to see me. I smile and wink. She returns the smile before she drops her gaze. It's not entirely submissive. She wants to see what I'm doing as my fingers run down her mons and slide into her. She's still so fucking wet. I can't wait any longer. I roll to her side and push my boxer briefs down. She wraps her hand around my dick but does nothing.

Fucking tease.

She watches me, and I realize she's waiting for permission. I stifle a groan as she slides her hand up and down me with a twist. She does it five times before she lets go. I think she wants me to move on, so I'm not prepared for her to swipe her fingers through her cream, then rub just below my balls.

Holy fuck. That's hot.

She does it two more times, and I'm ready to blow. When she pushes on my shoulder, I roll onto my back.

"Sir, may I?"

I hadn't planned to wait at all before sliding into her. But I'll let her lead for right now. We're getting to know each other's body and what we like. If she's offering to suck me off, I sure as fuck won't say no. She kneels beside me, moving her hair out of the way. She licks me from root to tip, flicking the underside of the head, then sweeping her tongue over the slit.

But when she sucks the top before inching her lips down my cock, my eyes cross. I grab the sheets. I'm the one submitting right now. Fuck. She knows what she's doing.

She takes as much of me as she can. It tempts me to press her head down farther, but I let her remain in control. I want to see what she's going to do too much. She wraps her hand around the part she can't take comfortably. She sucks, licks, and teases me. But when her other hand moves between my legs, and she rubs below my balls, I can't take any more.

I sit up enough to wrap my hands around her waist and lift her, making her straddle me. She drops onto my cock, and we both moan. I don't recognize the sound coming out of me. I don't recognize this level of bliss. I thought I'd felt good cunts before. But this is sublime.

It's her. It's her body. It's her mind. It's her soul. That's the difference. I care about Ellie.

"Enrique." She sighs my name.

"I know, *chiquita*. Nothing's felt better than this."

"Yes, sir."

I guide her to ride my cock. She grinds on me, leaning over. I knead her tits before lifting my head to suck on them.

"Sir, I'm close. Please?"

"Yes. Come for me, *chiquita*."

She moves faster, and I suck air in through my nose, focusing on not coming. I want to get her off more than I want to finish. I master my body.

"I'm so close, sir."

"Come, little one."

"I'm almost there. Don't stop."

The house burning down around us wouldn't get me to stop. I watch her; the look of concentration on her face is fucking sexy as fuck.

"Oh, God. What're you doing to me, Enrique? So intense."

She tightens around my dick and threatens to squeeze the cum from me. Intense seems too mild a word. Mind blowing. Earth shattering. Coming might kill me.

"I'm coming, sir."

My hands grip her ass and move her harder and faster, grinding her clit against my pubic bone. She explodes again, her entire body tenses. She was grasping the pillows, but now her left hand clings to my shoulder. She circles her hips before she flexes her pussy muscles. I wonder if she'd twerk for me. I picture sitting in a chair, stroking myself, while she leans forward with her hands on her thighs and shakes her ass.

That's distracting me in a way that makes me leak. I focus on the here and now. She draws out sitting back, pressing against my chest until she's upright. Her expression is pure siren. She puts her hands on her hips, arches her back, and rises on her knees. Then she eases down my cock. It's excruciatingly slow. I inhale, prepared for her to tease me. I'm unprepared for her rise and fall with a speed that shatters my restraint. She circles her hips each time she drops and Kegels when she's at the top.

The woman fucks like a goddess.

I buck beneath her, but it's not enough. I flip her before I kneel. I lift her hips and pound into her. I have a fingernail hold on my self-control. If I completely let go, I'll hurt her. But she tempts me. I've never been so wholly consumed by someone or something. I'm oblivious to all else.

"May I come again, sir."

"Fuck yes."

I thrust and grind as I watch sweat bead on her forehead. I feel it sliding between my shoulder blades. She presses her heels into the mattress, rolling her hips despite how I try to hold them in place. I can't wait.

I lean over her, kissing her as I blow my load. She moans, and I know she's coming too. My arms shake by the time I'm done. I open my eyes as she does, too. We stare at each other, panting. We're both struggling to breathe.

I'm about to roll away, but she wraps her arms and legs around me. The moment she realizes what she did, she lets go. A look of embarrassment flashes across her face. I lower my body to hers. I kiss her again, and she sighs. She wraps herself around me, and I love it. I love the feel of her holding on to me, her entire body pressed against mine.

I slide my arm around her and roll us together. I know she thought I was pulling out, and she didn't want our connection to end. I feared crushing her. I don't let go of her as she sprawls across me. My hand rests on her ass as the fingers of my other hand trail up and down her spine. She settles and rests her head on my shoulder, drawing her legs up.

I turn my head to kiss her forehead. I'm not used to feeling affection. I've done this very thing before with subs as part of aftercare. But it always felt perfunctory. Right now, my heart aches to take care of her. To make sure she understands how much this means to me. How much I want to give her everything she could ever need. That I want to keep her beside me for the rest of time.

I'm a man who makes irrevocable decisions in seconds. I rarely have the luxury of minutes. I sure as shit don't have hours or days. I don't think it's ever taken me a week to decide something. I know what I feel from instinct and a lifetime of assessing situations in a heartbeat.

Ellie isn't used to that. If I tell her how I feel, she'll run for the hills. She'll bolt like a scared animal. I keep my thoughts and feelings to myself, but she will know she's mine. Not just her body. But all of her. I'll give her my heart and soul. I won't settle for anything less from her. She just doesn't know it yet.

Chapter Seven

Ellie

That was surreal. I would call it an out-of-body experience if I hadn't just felt every bit. My mind alternates between whizzing among memories of what we just did and restful silence.

Peace.

That's what it is. When my mind is at rest, it's at peace.

It's a foreign feeling to me, but it's one I'd very much like to get used to. We're both way too hot, and neither of us can catch our breath while pressed together. I roll toward my side of the bed, always sleeping closer to the door since I had my first baby, but Enrique stops me and shifts me to the other side. I let him, not giving it much thought. My head lolls to my right, and that's when I see the bedside table.

Oh, fuck.

I don't move, not responding to Enrique rolling onto his side, wrapping his arm around my waist. He follows my gaze and sees what I do. He pushes up on one elbow and gently nudges me to look at him.

"I'm clean, Ellie. It's been a while since I've had sex, but I'm always testing regularly."

I nod. I'm still shocked by what we did. It all moved so fast. That's why I'm without words.

"Ellie, are you not on birth control anymore? If you're worried that we might have—"

I shake my head.

"I had a hysterectomy years ago. I'm just surprised at how fast everything happened. That's all. I'm clean, too. Not just because I haven't been with anybody other than him, but because I double-checked."

He kisses my cheek and settles beside me. If this had happened five years ago, I'd be in a panic. But now, I'm fine since the baby ship not only sailed but sank.

We share a series of brief kisses before we both close our eyes and doze off. It's only an hour later when I wake, needing to go to the bathroom. I sit up and reach for a t-shirt at the end of my bed.

Most nights I sleep naked, but I changed clothes today, and the t-shirt is still there where I left it. It's long enough it'll cover my ass when I stand. I lift it to put it over my head, but I feel Enrique lean around my body, his arm around my waist. I twist to look down at him.

"What are you doing, *chiquita?*"

"I was just going to go to the bathroom."

"No, why are you putting on a t-shirt?"

"Because I already told you, I'm not comfortable with you seeing the back of me. I know you did when I went to get condoms. I realized that once I was in the bathroom. That doesn't mean I want to do it again."

"Do you know what I saw when I watched you walk away?"

I force myself not to grimace. I'm sure he's going to say something meant to be reassuring.

"I saw an ass I plan to fuck many, many times, and the first time will be tonight. I saw an ass I want to hold on to, hips I want to grab as I plow you from behind. I saw a muscular, elegant back, shapely legs I love having wrapped around me."

Shapely? If he means two bratwursts, then I guess that's the shape he sees.

"Ellie, I know whatever you're thinking right now isn't gracious appreciation for sincere compliments. I told you your body belongs to me now. You haven't said no. I will see and touch whatever part of it I want, and I want to see and touch all of it. There's no part of you I don't desire. If I'd found it a turnoff, would I have been so hard when you came back from the bathroom?"

I shake my head.

"Let me enjoy what I already love looking at, *chiquita*."

He sits up and kisses my shoulder all the way up my neck. I toss the shirt aside. I muster my courage and stand, but it's only long enough to turn around and climb back onto the bed.

"I was only going to freshen up." I wrap my hand around his lengthening cock. "But I don't think there'll be much point."

"There won't be any point all night. I expect to see it dripping from you. I'm going to keep filling you with my cum. You will know when you finally stand up and walk to that bathroom that I've fully claimed you because it'll drip between your thighs from your little pink pussy to your tight little ass."

We lie on our sides as we kiss, our hands trailing over each other slowly. He eventually rolls me onto my back and eases into me. What we did earlier wasn't kinky. It was just rough. This is strictly vanilla. It's so incredibly gentle and languid it moves me just as much as the first time we had sex only an hour ago. We watch each other throughout, kissing when we can't hold back.

"Ellie, you're the only drug I've ever taken. I'm already addicted, but I'll never get enough."

I cup his jaw and nod. "Same, Enrique."

We kiss as we come together. We doze off, but this time we wake to his phone ringing. He rolls off the bed and answers it. I don't speak Spanish but can usually follow along somewhat. But the conversation is moving too fast for me to know what's going on. I'm not sure if he's speaking it and hoping I don't understand, or if that's just his regular preference.

The only word I recognize is little brother. Will took Spanish in school, and he'd call Steve and Hunt that when he wanted to annoy them.

I don't bother pulling the sheet over me as he slides his boxer briefs back on then his jeans. He's about to fasten the button when he hangs up the call. I continue to watch him, saying nothing. I wish he wasn't leaving, but I won't ask questions he can't answer. I won't complain about him leaving. I'll just accept what he can offer me because that's all I can offer him. At least, that's what I thought at the beginning of tonight. He sits on the edge of the bed beside me.

"You can tell I have to go, *chiquita*, but believe me this is the last thing I want to do. I don't want to leave this bed. I don't want to leave you. But something came up that I need to deal with. I'm not sure how long it'll take."

"I got your note, but I didn't think about it earlier. You already told me you were going out of town, but then you showed up tonight."

He mulls over what he wants to say, and I'm not sure what his response will be. Will it be the truth or a lie?

"When I wrote that note, I knew I wasn't going anywhere. I didn't want you to think I was ghosting you, but I wanted time to find out whether whoever's across the street was there because of us or some other reason. When I found out a car drove past your place four times by the time I got here, I knew I wouldn't stay away. But I really have to be away for a while. I don't know how long it will take, but there's a good chance I won't stay in New York. If that's the case, I want that security detail with you around the clock, Ellie. I want a car parked in your driveway. If you go anywhere, I want at least two men with you."

I know he won't budge on this, so I don't bother arguing. I merely nod. His expression morphs to one of sadness, or maybe that's guilt.

"I'm okay. I'm not agreeing out of resignation. It's not like I feel you're bullying me into this or something. I'm agreeing because it's the right thing to do, and I don't want to be any type of distraction or worry when you're dealing with whatever it is you have to do."

"Thank you, *chiquita*. If I'm going to be away for more than a week, it's because something went really wrong. I'll send one of my nephews to you. I'll make sure you know that before anyone shows up at your door. I don't want to be away from you for that long, but if I have to be, then I want to ensure you're as protected as can be."

"I don't know any of your family, Enrique. I don't even know your men who'll camp out in my driveway."

"I know, little one, but we'll sort it out if it comes to that."

"All right. I know you need to go, so I don't want to delay you."

"You aren't a delay, little one. I may have to deal with something, but it's not more important than this conversation."

"Thank you."

We kiss once more, and I watch him walk out of my bedroom. I can't hear the door close downstairs, but my bedroom looks out over the front yard. The motion sensor light at the front door flicks on. I don't want to watch him walk away, so I finally pull the covers up.

It takes me ages to fall asleep, but when I do, I'm passed out until morning. When I head outside for Constantine's morning walk, there's a car parked in my driveway with a guy sitting in it. I approach the passenger side and lean forward. He winds down the window, and we stare at each other for a moment.

"Good morning, Ms. McCann. *El jefe* assigned me as your guard for today. I'm Andrés. My partner, Carlos, is across the street tucked away in the trees. That car is still parked with a camera pointing toward you."

I don't straighten, but my gaze darts in the car's direction. I'd seen it, but I hadn't given it much thought. I'm not a nosy neighbor, even if I am aware of what goes on around me.

I nod. "Did Enr—*el jefe*—say anything about whether I can still go for walks?"

Andrés smiles when I catch myself, uncertain how informal I can be. Obviously, this guy knows Enrique and I are involved. If he was staked out here last night, then he knows how long Enrique stayed.

"*El jefe* said we're to watch out for you while you keep your routine. If you need to go anywhere, then we go with you."

"All right. Thank you."

I can be gracious, even if I don't like this arrangement. I'd rather not have anybody monitoring my coming and going. But it seems like somebody may already be doing that. It's reassuring to know at least some men are on my side.

I take Constantine to the top of the road, but I don't go into the park. There are too many blind spots. I'll run if I have to. But what if I were to injure myself and get stuck barely able to hobble? As I walk up my driveway, I pull out my phone and tap on the group text I have with my boys.

ME

I'm sending you a link to a video call in five minutes. Unless you're doing something for him you will get on this call.

My boys know who I'm talking about. They also know it's rare for me to demand anything of them these days. I put out food and water for Constantine before heading into my office. I didn't open the curtains or the blinds this morning. I leave it that way. I set up the video call and send out the link before I hop on. I make sure the signal jammers are on, so no one's monitoring my calls. Enrique's not the only one with more secrets than the Vatican.

Hunt's the first one to join me. "Mom, what's going on?"

"Let's wait for your brothers. It's not an emergency, but it is urgent."

A moment later, my other two boys appear on screen.

"Mom?"

"It's all right, Will. I'm not dying, and neither is anyone else. But I need to speak to you guys about something. Did you go digging when I asked you not to?"

"No." All three of them answer at the same time.

"Are you having me watched instead?"

"Mom, who's watching you? What's going on?"

Will jumps in, but he's no more overprotective of me than the others. I'm certain that's what they all want to know.

"I noticed a car parked a couple houses down that isn't usually there. I haven't seen anybody coming and going from it, but there's a dash cam pointed toward my place. So be honest. Are you watching me?"

"No." Steve answers for all three.

"Are you watching Enrique when he comes and goes?"

"No. But should we? Is he the reason why?"

Will's voice hardens, and he gets the same stubborn gleam in his eyes he's had since he was a toddler.

"If it's not you, I don't know yet. That's what I'm trying to find out."

"You told us not to be nosy, and we've respected that wish, Mom. But now you're making it awfully hard to stick with that."

"I know, Hunt, but there's no reason to panic until there's a reason to panic."

"You always say that, but by the time you realize you should panic, it's usually too late. That's the whole reason people panic."

Steve has never appreciated that logic, but I've stuck with it for years.

"Look, I don't know why the car's there. I thought maybe you guys were being overprotective. I don't think there's any reason to believe this is about me. It probably isn't even about Enrique. I don't know whether the dash cam is on, even if it's pointing toward my place. I'll just keep an eye out and see if I can spot who's coming and going from the house and who gets in and out of the car. If there's anything that worries me, then I promise I'll let you know."

"But if it isn't about you, Mom, is there something about Enrique we should know?" Steve's the quiet one, but when he speaks, it's best to listen.

There's a shit ton about Enrique they should know, and at some point, I'll wind up telling. But not yet.

"He's a wealthy man, so who knows who might be curious

91

about him? Nothing's shown up online, but for all I know maybe it's paparazzi." I laugh, trying to ease the tension that has inevitably grown during this call.

"Mom, is there something about Enrique that would make Tommaso suspicious?"

"I don't know whether he pays attention to me anymore."

All three boys stare at me through their cameras as though I've lost my mind.

"Fine, I'll call him next."

"Are you going to tell Dad something's going on?" Will looks ready to choke over his words.

Now it's my turn for my expression to harden. "No, and neither are you. You know how I feel about him being involved in my life now. I'm fine seeing him at family events. I'm fine talking about him, but no one's bringing him back into my life in ways he doesn't need to be. That's the point of divorce. If he finds out, then it better be through Tommaso and not through any of you. Do you understand?"

"Yes, but he can watch out for you, too."

"Hunt, that is the very last thing I need or want. You know that. And don't you dare bring him into this."

"All right, Mom, if that's what you want, then we can agree to that." Hunt doesn't like it, but he offers a compromise.

Middle child Steve has always been the conciliatory one. But for now, Hunt, the baby of the family, tries to keep the peace. But he has always had an ingrained sense of self-justice. He's always been one to let most things go, but if someone wrongs him... If he thinks I'm wronging them by not listening to their suggestion, he'll dig his heels in.

"Mom, Hunt's not wrong."

As the oldest child, Will has always been protective of his younger brothers, even when they haven't always liked each other or been best friends. I never expected them to be best friends, though I always wished they had been. They were always free to have whomever they wanted as friends, so they drifted in different circles. But now that they're adults, they've come back around and are closer than they used to be. I'm certain the divorce played a large part in that.

"All right, Will. Let me let you go, and I'll call Tommaso."

"Should I be on that call too, Mom?" Will sounds anything but excited.

"No, let me deal with this. I don't want to make it a bigger deal than it has to be. If he's not involved, then I don't want him asking questions he doesn't need to. I'll keep you guys posted."

"All right, Mom. Love you."

"Love you."

"Love you."

Hearing all three say those two words at the same time will always make my heart overflow.

"I love you too, boys."

I end the video call. I can only imagine the call they're having amongst themselves now. I grab my phone and tap a contact.

"Hello, Elodie."

Fuck my life.

"Hey, Frank. Is Don Tommaso around?"

"Yeah, he asked me to answer for him. He's just coming out of the kitchen. Here you go."

"Hello, Elodie."

"Morning, Don Tommaso."

It's never a good morning when I have to talk to the Boston don.

"Elodie, cut it out. You haven't called me that in decades. You didn't even call me that when you worked for me."

"Yes, worked. Past tense, Tommaso."

"What's going on? I don't care for that tone, Elodie. What're you accusing me of?"

"What tone? Are you asking because you feel guilty?"

I must be on speaker because I hear two men laugh.

"You know, that's not an emotion I generally feel."

"I know. I'm all too familiar with that. But you are suspicious by nature. Are you keeping tabs on me?"

"What makes you think I might be?"

"Tommaso, you and I have known each other a long time. We can run circles around each other for days. But in the end, the result is always the same thing. I last longer than you do. So just be honest with me. Are you having me watched?"

"No. Somebody's watching you?"

His tone changes immediately. I know his fake concern from his genuine concern. He's worried.

"I'm not sure. I thought maybe somebody was. But I can totally be wrong. Before I do anything about it, I wanted to check with you."

"No, it's not me. Do you want me to find out who it is?"

"If I'm being paranoid, then I don't need more eyes on me than I already think there are."

There's a pause, and the longer it draws out, the less I'll like whatever he says next.

"I'm glad you called, Elodie, because I was actually going to call you this week."

"No, I'm retired. I don't do that anymore. You know the deal."

"You're the only one good enough to go."

"No, find someone else. I don't care who it is, but it's not me."

I refuse to get sucked back into a life I left when I left my husband.

"So, you'd be fine with one of your boys?"

Stronzo. Asshole.

"You promised me, Tommaso. Thanks for nothing."

"Elodie—"

"I was done with any obligation I had to you. You wrote it down, and Tori notarized it. You're going to break your word to your sister? Maybe you'll break your word to me, but you don't do it to her."

"It wouldn't surprise her if I did."

"But it sure as shit would disappoint her."

"Maybe so, but she understands business comes first."

"Tommaso Vizzini comes first. That's what you really mean. There are other people who can do what I used to."

"I need you to do—"

"No, I don't need to hear you out to know I'm certain I won't like it. I'm not doing it."

"All right, never mind. I'll have Steve go to Brazil."

My hand clenches around the armrest. I'm barely containing my anger. It's rapidly moving to rage.

"I will never forgive you, Tommaso. You and I *will not* be good. You know what that means. If you're willing to send me down there, it's because you know I have no limits. If you send my son, I'll have no limits toward you either.

"I figured you'd see it my way, eventually."

"What do you want?"

The foul taste in my mouth is one I haven't had in nearly a year. That's the last time I spoke to Tommaso Vizzini, the Boston Mafia don. My old boss.

"The Kimuras withheld payment for product sitting off the coast. I refuse to bring it ashore without them paying. They've already received payment from their buyers. However, they're crying foul to them, saying we're the ones holding out and not bringing in the goods like promised. They think they can keep their own money while also keeping their customers'. They want us at odds with their buyers, so I'll give in to them to keep the peace. I want you to go down there and look at their books."

He wants me to use my forensic accounting skills to find out where the money is and where it's going. If only he needed a pencil pusher.

Oh, no.

There's a reason they say women are a better shot than men. I can prove it every day of the week and twice on Sundays. That's how I wound up in this fucking shitstorm.

"How many do you think it'll be?"

"Start at the top of the pile."

"You cannot be serious. You want me to go after Ignacio? How the hell am I supposed to get out of there if I carry out a hit on the most senior leader of the Rio cartel? Every *donos* will be after me."

The Brazilian structure is looser than the Italians and some of the other syndicates. Ignacio Kimura must be out of prison if

Tommaso is sending me down there. He oversees a cadre of *favela* leaders—*donos*—slum lords. They're the ones who'll be after me.

"Cut the head off the octopus and the tentacles no longer move."

"In this case, the octopus will sprout another head. Benicio's a fucking psychopath. Do you want me dead? Is that what this is about?"

Benicio Kimura's nickname is Pato. Not because he looks like a duck or swims like one. It's because he can hold his breath under water long enough to drown a man four times his size. That's how he earned it.

"Of course not."

"Then why are you putting me in this position, Tommaso? You know there's a greater likelihood I won't come home if you send me down there."

"You've always come home from every other mission. That's why we're having this conversation."

"Yeah, and you know how much I fucking resented that."

"Well, you also know once you're in, you're in for life, Elodie."

"Men. That applies to men. I am not a Made Man. Your grandfather swore the Vizzinis would never have Made Women. I was never supposed to be part of this. You promised me, Tommaso, that I was retired."

"Your retirement was too early. You're going to do this, Elle. You're going to do it with a fucking smile on your face. There'll be a big old cash deposit waiting for you when you get back."

I'm fighting a losing battle, and I know it. It fucking sucks, but he can hold my boys over my head. He has been for years, but now all three of them are old enough and trained well enough that he could send them on missions far more dangerous than they went on when they were in high school and college.

I want to think Will is now senior enough Tommaso wouldn't send him on something like this, but he will if he can punish me by doing that. That's how fucked-up things are when you're a family in the Mafia.

"All right, send me the details. I'll make it work. When do you want me to leave?"

"Day after tomorrow."

"That soon? I have other obligations."

The fuck am I going to tell Enrique? How am I going to tell him when he's not around? If this were a pre-planned trip, I would have said something when he told me he was going to be away. If I make it sound like something's just come up, he'll worry and want to know what's going on.

"Rearrange your schedule."

Well, I'm used to doing that. But I can't say something so snarky aloud. I have something else to say instead.

"How many people is it? Because the price went up. Every *dono* is two mil, and Ignacio is ten mil."

"That's ridiculous. No way."

"Yes way. If you're asking me to do this, it's not because I'm disposable and you don't care what happens to me. You're sending me because you know it's something no one else is likely to accomplish. You're going to pay me accordingly, or I'm going to take a vacation on the beach in Rio."

"You have an awfully high opinion of yourself. You always have."

"I do, and I've earned that opinion of myself and the reputation I have. That reputation is what you're banking on."

"Fine. Pull all of it off, you'll get exactly what you demand. Don't accomplish it all, you won't get a damn thing."

"Regardless, this is the last time I'm doing shit for you, Tommaso. I'm serious, and if you try to hold my boys ransom like this again, I'll take you out at the knees. You better hope Rocco is ready to lead because once you're kneeling in front of me, I'll put a fucking bullet through your head."

"Don't threaten me, Elodie. No one does that and lives."

"What're you going to do? Kill me? You're going to pay me close to twenty-million-dollars because you need me. It sure as shit isn't for shits and giggles. I won't threaten your sons like you did mine. I'm not fucked-up like that. I will punish you if you do something to my boys. There'll be no stopping me. There's a reason your sister and I have been best friends since I was a teenager."

"Yeah, you were fucking tiny tyrants together."

"And you and Frank learned to keep your mouths fucking shut, didn't you?"

Tori is ten years older than me and started babysitting me when I was five. I wanted to be her. Once I was in high school and had more in common with a woman in her twenties, we became thick as thieves. From the first time she came over to babysit me, I was a mini her, so we always ran roughshod over her brothers. I got started young.

"I thought you'd mellowed with age."

"These are my terms. Figure out how to live with it, Tommaso."

I wait for a response, but it's not the don who snaps at me.

"You're not worth the bullshit that goes along with dealing with you, Elle."

"Frank, I'll stand right here and remember that the next time you get froggy, thinking you'll force me to carry out a hit. Send me the info."

I'm usually not rude enough to hang up without everyone saying goodbye, but I want the last word.

I glance toward the window and brace myself. I hate what I have to do. Not just the trip to Rio. I hate the situation this puts me in with Enrique. I've been dreading this conversation for the past two days. I head outside with a smile I don't feel plastered on my face.

"Andrés, how do I get a message to Enrique?"

Over the past couple days, I've gotten to know the guys who guard my place. They never ask anything of me. They relieve each other every few hours, never getting out of their cars, never asking to use the bathroom or get a drink of water. When I walk by, they nod with a smile. They're always polite. I'm certain it's on pain of death if they aren't.

"I can pass it along to his brother. He'll know how to get in touch with *el jefe*."

It was too much to hope I could keep my message private. I definitely don't want to discuss this with my guard before Enrique knows about it.

"Actually, is there any way I could speak directly to *el patrón?*"

I'm guessing at what Enrique's brother goes by. But I don't know for sure if his brother is his second-in-command or his heir or what. He might be the cartel equivalent of *consigliere* rather than underboss. He might be Enrique's top advisor, and one of his nephews could be the equivalent of his underboss. I can't ask those things without giving away that I understand even a little about syndicate hierarchies.

Andrés calls somebody and hands the phone to me. "It's *señor* Luis, his brother."

"Okay, thank you."

I accept the phone and straighten, taking a step back from the window. Andrés takes the hint and winds it up.

"Luis?"

"Hello, Ms. McCann."

"Hello, Mr. Diaz."

"No, it's Luis."

"It's Elodie."

"It's Ms. McCann until my brother says otherwise."

I want to roll my eyes, but this is hardly the hill to die on. Considering what I dealt with the other day on my call with Tommaso and Frank, I'll take all the chivalry I can get. It may be the last for me.

"I didn't get to tell Enrique I already had a trip planned, and I'm leaving in a few hours for about a week. It slipped my mind since I haven't had a way to get in touch with him. I hoped I could tell him myself that I won't travel without letting somebody know."

There's a protracted silence before Luis responds.

"Where are you going?"

"On a trip with some friends. Just a little getaway."

"If you'd like to use our family's jet, it's at your disposal, Ms. McCann."

There's not a chance in fucking hell I'm using the Cartel's jet. I'm not telling them where I'm going either. They aren't taking me there, and they sure as shit won't be watching me while I'm in Brazil.

"No, that's not necessary. I already have flights arranged."

In the Vizzinis' jet.

"I wanted to let you know I'll be away, so if you hear from Enrique or he gets back, I don't want him to think I just took off."

That's exactly what I want to do.

"I'll make sure he knows. Andrés and Carlos can take you to the airport."

I'd rather take an Uber or Lyft.

"I appreciate that. Thank you."

"*Buen viaje.*"

Nothing about this is going to be a good voyage.

Chapter Eight

Enrique

It's been a hell of a week. Leaving Ellie in the middle of the night to go deal with some bratva bullshit wasn't how I envisioned our first time together. When I went over, I had no expectation of what would happen besides letting her know of the danger she faces being with me.

I didn't know I would confess as much as I did. I didn't expect her to share as much as she did. I didn't expect us to fuck or to—dare I say it—make love. It wasn't just vanilla that second time. I've had plenty of non-kinky sex in my life, and it wasn't like that. It's never been like that.

I've never felt so connected to somebody in my entire life. It has never felt that intimate before. It left me feeling raw—not a feeling I'm opposed to.

I could get used to it if I know I'll have Ellie in my arms at the end. That she shares the same feelings I do. From the look in her eyes, I believe she did. And that's part of why I miss her so much. I don't recall the last time I missed somebody during one of my trips. I miss the fun of being around my family. I've missed the familiarity and comfort of being with them. But I don't recall missing a person the way I do Ellie.

I've already gotten used to the sight and sound of her. Her floral scent that often wafts to me while we're walking. Now I'm already used to her feel and taste. She's a sensory overload. One I'll happily enjoy once I see her again.

First, I've got to deal with this meeting.

"Luis, I don't know what the hell is going on with the fucking bratva. But they've got a hard-on for causing us problems right now."

"Yeah, that's not anything new. Their *pequeña pollas* are always doing jumping jacks to fuck somebody else over. Just happens to be us this week." Little dicks.

"I know, but it's been a while since they've done any business with Ignacio. As a courtesy to Pasha's wife, they've kept her family out of it. But now they're up to their greasy little palms with the Brazilian nuts they're sucking."

"Rather than sending Alejandro down to Colombia or Bolivia, our best bet is to send him to Rio. Ignacio owes us that product. We've already put the down payment on it. Alejandro will get him to either cough up the shipment or get our deposit back."

"And that'll fuck over the Vizzinis in the process. I don't need anybody in Boston breathing down our necks right now."

"That's too fucking bad, Enrique. That's their problem, not ours. We've got people in our neighborhoods who'll look elsewhere to get what they want."

And that's exactly what the bratva's counting on. They're going to cause a problem at the top of this food chain. And let it trickle down, so they can step in and save the day in neighborhoods that are ours.

"Luis, you're not telling me anything I don't already know. It's not like this is news to anybody. We need to come up with a solution no one has in the past."

I sit back in my desk chair as I watch my brother do the same in the armchair across from me. Our mannerisms are so similar that from a distance people often confuse us. But his hair is several shades lighter than mine. Too many extended stays in Colombian prisons leave him a solid fifteen pounds lighter than me. He may be thinner than me, but he's no weaker than I am. My money will always be on my brother. Not only is he strong, he's scrappy.

"We could've dealt with this sooner, *mano*, if you hadn't been distracted."

If anyone else spoke to me like that, even my nephews—who wouldn't dare—they'd be scraping their own shit off their kitchen floor. I'd scare it right out of them.

"I can focus on more than one thing at a time, Luis. Keep her out of it. You know as well as I do the bratva has been working on this for months."

"And we missed the extent of it. We only scratched the surface of their plan."

"And that falls on all of us." I gesture between the two of us.

"But we could have acted sooner if you were attending all our meetings the last couple of months."

"The last couple of months? I've been gone for an entire week dealing with this shit. I didn't plan that trip to Colombia for the pleasant weather. Never mind the two weeks last month that I was down there."

"Before that, then. When you aren't out for your walks with her, you're thinking about her."

"So, you don't think about your family during the day? I have never called them a distraction."

And I haven't. I never called Margherita a distraction when they were newlyweds, and he couldn't keep his hands off her. I've never called her a distraction during all of her treatments. I never called his son Juan a distraction when he was royally fucking everything over for our family and nearly brought us to our knees.

"I'm not *el jefe*."

"You're not, but you're still my second-in-command in Colombia. You know you have the authority to decide when I'm not around. You do it down there all the time. You do it when it's necessary if I'm away from here. What is it? What do you have against Elodie?"

"*Mano,* there's something off. I don't know what it is, but she's hiding something. You told me you couldn't find any records of her, even when you had Joaquin hack police records from all over New England. That's weird, don't you think?"

"It is, but there's bound to be an explanation. There always is. I'd say—"

Saved by the bell when the doorbell rings. But a moment later, Pablo steps into my office. He's a replica of Luis at that age, even down to the similar scar they both have on the back of their right hands.

"Welcome back, *tío.*

"*Hola, sobrino.* Have you found out anything in the Heights?" Hello, nephew.

Jackson Heights is our hub. It's in Queens in what's always been a heavily Colombian community. We run a lot of our operations out of there. Even though Luis and I live in New Jersey, the boys—that's Pablo and our nephews—all live in the city—Manhattan.

"Just people complaining when their stash runs low. It's good business when the dealers can have it."

Scarcity's driving up the street price, so our kickbacks are bigger. But it won't be long before everything runs out.

"We've got the warehouse in Parsippany that has enough to float us for another month."

Luis shakes his head at my suggestion. "But we wanted to sell that in the Netherlands."

"I know, but with the cost of shipping and customs over there, we'd make more keeping it here. Go ahead and distribute that."

Pablo looks at his dad, then me, as he nods. I look at Luis, then Pablo.

"Out with it. What did your father tell you to do?"

"He didn't tell me to do anything."

"Fine. What did your father allude to that you took the hint and did on your own?"

"I didn't entirely work on my own."

I drum my fingers on the desk, and Pablo barely contains his shiver. He just turned thirty-six, but that one gesture still strikes fear in his heart. He knows I'm moments away from losing my temper. That always bodes poorly for anyone in my sight.

Pablo sucks in a breath before he speaks. "You know, after what happened the last time, can you blame us for being concerned and cautious?"

He means my ex-wife, Daniela. That bitch was loyal to nobody but herself. She sold secrets I purposely planted to test her. Once I knew she was cheating and scheming to make money any way she could, I ensured the alliance with her father fell through. I set it up so he suggested the divorce, and she filed the paperwork. But it was my doing all along. Needless to say, my family doesn't want a repeat of that.

We all knew Daniela was trouble from the start. I'd hoped we could at least have a peaceful marriage and maybe develop some affection. But that would never have happened. If a woman I could barely stand caused that much trouble, my family's concerned about any woman I could care about.

"You think I'll turn a blind eye to her, or I won't see the red flags because I'm infatuated with her."

"Those are your words, *mano*, not mine."

Luis tries for conciliatory now, but too little, too late.

"I'm just saying what you're thinking, aren't I?"

Luis doesn't have to say anything. His expression tells me all I need to know.

"What did Joaquin find?"

"It's what he didn't find. He hacked the FBI and the DOJ. He came up with nothing for her name. We got a set of prints off her."

"You did what?!"

I really am going to lose my shit.

"We got a set of her fingerprints off her—"

"You invaded her privacy—touched her belongings to snoop—without asking me first."

I look between my brother and nephew, stunned by this revelation. It's not as though they haven't taken these steps before, but they knew each of those times it was what I wanted. They have to know this is not, *not*, NOT what I wanted.

"We got the prints off her mailbox. We didn't go in her house or anything like that."

"Her mailbox? You got clear prints from that when any mail carrier could have smeared them or covered them."

"We got a few different prints we identified. The set of prints that must be hers didn't trigger anything in the system. That's more than just suspicious, *tío*. That's practically impossible. Even our fingerprints come up, and we make sure half the shit they've charged us with never sees the light of day."

"Could she be in WITSEC?"

"No. Joaquin hacked that system as well. There's nothing about her in the U.S. Marshals database. And I paid our informant to do a manual check at the WNRC."

Washington National Records Center is part of the National Archives. That makes me raise my eyebrows. My nephews were thorough.

"Not only that, we looked for any flight or car rental reservations out of Newark, JFK, and LaGuardia. There was nothing. So, we expanded the search, and still nothing came up."

"Private jet?"

Luis shakes his head. "She's in a nice neighborhood, but she doesn't have that kind of money if she's living there."

"Or maybe she does because she paid cash for that house. She doesn't strike me as someone who needs anything flashy, but she enjoys comforts that don't come for free."

"Are you saying her furniture and decor are expensive?"

I glare at Pablo. It's not a secret where I left from or what time I left when I made my impromptu trip to South America. However, it's entirely different for Pablo to come out and ask about anything in Ellie's home. I say nothing because I know I'm defensive about her. They don't need to know the extent of how I feel. It's unreasonable considering how little I obviously know about her and how little time I've spent with her despite seeing her most days for the past two months.

My visceral reaction is to tell him to tread carefully since he's speaking about his future aunt. I definitely am not saying that aloud. They'll flip the fuck out if I do. However, they must have some idea I see potential for Ellie and me. I told her I wouldn't bring her anywhere near this world if I didn't want something long-term. They must know that too.

She might not agree yet. But after the other night and what we shared, I think she'll either run for the hills on her own or come around to my way of thinking.

That doesn't mean I want to divulge any of this to anyone in my family.

"She's doing just fine for money from what I can tell."

That's as much as I'm willing to give away. Luis knows his job is to play devil's advocate. But he also realizes this is one topic that could put him on the path to hell with one wrong word. He's quieter when he speaks this time.

"Could she have flown on somebody else's private jet?"

"That's entirely possible."

When I look at my brother and nephew, I know what they're thinking, but we're not in a committed relationship. If she already had a trip planned with someone else, then she's free to travel with them, whether it's a girls' trip or a romantic trip with someone else. I have no hold over her, though my mind screams I have a claim on her.

She's mine!

The questions are going a mile a minute as I fight to remain calm, my suspicions screaming in my head as loudly as my claim that *she's mine.*

If she's on a romantic getaway, then she lied about whether she wants to be involved with anyone else and what she wants out of a relationship.

Could she have lied to me?

Did she say all of those things to push me away, then temptation got the better of her?

Did she say all of those things to push me away, knowing she already had plans with someone else?

I suppose anything is possible. I look at my brother again.

"So, what do you propose I do? Walk away? Never go back in that neighborhood? Never see her again?"

He practically snorts before he responds. "Like there's a chance in hell you would do that. Once you have your sights set on something, no one's getting in your way. Mama's said it was that way since you were in the womb. If you wanted to jump around and stretch, that's what you did. You made sure she knew when you were hungry."

"You say when I have my sights set on something. Elodie is not a thing. I'll wait until she gets back and speak to her about this. I'll know if she's lying. Until then, if we can't find her, there's nothing any of us can do but wait. In the meantime, let's get Alejandro down to Brazil and set up a meeting with Ignacio. Find out what the fuck is going on with them."

I can't force her to want to be with me, even if I think that's what she wants. Even if I've made it clear to her, that's what I want. It's up to her in the end.

"*Tio*, Ignacio's disappeared somewhere into the jungle. Nobody's seen hide nor hair of him in two weeks. He's hiding from us, but I think he knows as pissed as we are, the Vizzinis are even angrier. It wouldn't surprise me if Tommaso put a hit on the piece of shit."

I'm staring at Alejandro on a video call with the computer in the center of the table, so my other nephews and brother can see too.

"What are your informants telling you?"

"That's as much as any of them know. He took off on his own with only two of his personal guards. He told no one where he's going. Benicio's been silent. That *chismoso* brags about everything. The *cabrón* thinks putting all their family news out into the world intimidates people. All he does is piss off his father. But since he cleans up all of Ignacio's mistakes, there's not much the father can do about the son short of killing him."

Cartel King

Disgust drips from Alejandro's words and all of us nod in agreement with Alejandro's assessment, since Benicio is a gossiping asshole.

"*Tío*, do you want me to track him down or wait until he comes back to Rio?"

"Do we have the resources in place yet for you to look? Or is your time better spent in the city?"

"I think it can go either way, *tío*. There's plenty to learn here in the city, and I can stir up plenty of shit. But whatever is going on is serious enough to make Ignacio turn rabbit."

"And we all know what a fucking warren the jungle is. Unless you have solid leads, you'll go in and find nothing, or you'll wind up finding somebody who doesn't want us looking. We don't have time to deal with that right now."

"Fine. I'll stick around in Rio for a couple more days and see what I hear. Like I said, I suspect the Vizzinis sent somebody down here to put a hit on him. They won't leave until the job is done. He can't stay hidden forever unless he wants Benicio to run the business into the ground."

"Then wait him out a few more days. Keep your informants well paid in Rio and São Paulo. Have the drones go out over the areas we know he's set up labs in the past."

As I hang up the call, Luis's phone vibrates on the coffee table. He picks it up, and his brow furrows. He slides his finger across the screen, unlocking it. I assume it's a text since he takes a moment to read, then scrolls up and down before looking at me. I see his head tilt slightly toward the guys. I jut my chin toward the door, and they know they're dismissed.

"Keep me posted on anything else. Find out what Pasha's up to. I'm certain he's the one helping Ignacio hide."

"Will do, *tío*."

Javier is already tapping his phone screen as the guys stand up. We exchange a round of *"te amo"* before they leave.

My mother and father insisted we always say "I love you" before we leave because, in this world, you never know when it's your last chance to do that. Since Luis and I went to boarding schools in New England and our parents lived in Colombia, we went long periods without seeing them. Luis and I went to different schools, so it's not like we saw each other every day, either.

It wound up being a good rule to live by because I got a call that my father was dead an hour after I hung up with him. The one person I've never said it to in my immediate family is my *Tío* Humberto. That piece of motherfucking shit is the reason my dad's dead. I've never loved him. He's rotting in the Colombian jail I made for him. I gave him a luxurious home he hasn't left in nearly thirty years.

Luis was my first call after I found out. I had to tell him, and with my little brother, we told our sisters and mother. That life lesson taught us never to take for granted the opportunity to let our loved ones know they're important to us.

"It's Andrés. He got a text from Elodie. He screenshot it." Luis stands and crosses a small space to my desk handing me the phone.

ELODIE

> Sorry to bother you but I hope you can pass this message along to el patrón and he can pass it on to el jefe. I just wanted to let him know that all is well and I arrived safely. I'll be back in a few days. I also wanted to let el jefe know Constantine misses him.

I hand the phone back to Luis, keeping my expression neutral. I don't want him to know I'm equal parts giddy to hear from her and hurt that she's still away on this mystery vacation she forgot to mention to me.

She doesn't have my number, and since she didn't call Luis, she doesn't have his number either. My brother explained the other day that she spoke to him on Andrés's phone. She had his number as her bodyguard in case she needed him for anything.

"She checked in with you. Do you think it's a guilty conscience? Does she feel badly that she's on a trip with someone else?"

"Maybe."

"Do you think she's trying to distract you from what she's really doing?"

"No, I think she's considerate. She hasn't heard anything from me either. I'm guiltier than her. I haven't contacted her."

"I'm certain you told her there'll be times when you have to go out of town and can't tell her where you're going. Why couldn't she tell you where she was going? How is that such a secret?"

"We don't know each other that well, Luis."

Even though I bared my soul to her, and I thought I did.

"Yeah, well, it's strange no one's finding records of her."

"If you step back from this for a moment, can you blame her for not telling a guy where she went when she barely knows him?"

"I'd say you know each other pretty well, don't you?" Again, Luis is the only person who could get away with saying something like that to me.

"You know damn well what I mean. Tread lightly, *manito*. You know you can say anything to me, but that doesn't mean you need to say everything."

"Fine. There's no need to point out the obvious, anyway."

"Exactly. So don't make me remind you she owes me nothing."

"Yet."

He stresses that one little word, and I stare at him. We both know she's mine. Inevitably, she'll come to accept that. But first, I need to know who the hell this woman I fell for is.

Chapter Nine

Ellie

"Ignacio, you're wasting my time, and you know I'm not as patient as I pretend. You thought your disappearing act would save your ass. All it did was piss me off, having to track you down. At least you have the good sense to have a decent place as your hideout."

The ten-thousand square foot home would do Pablo Escobar proud. Ignacio has a veritable compound out here, and it's fucking invisible with the canopy cover. You'd never guess, flying over, that all these buildings are down here. It took a shitload of money for me to convince a helicopter pilot to bring me out here. Then it was a twenty-minute horseback ride to get to the gates. It took me five minutes to convince the guard to even tell Ignacio I was here. That was after wasting four days trying to find his sorry ass.

"Well, you are certainly persistent, *senhora* Messina."

Emelia Messina is one of many personas I've had over the years. It's the one I use in Brazil. I have a different one for Colombia, and a third for Bolivia and Uruguay. That doesn't even scratch the surface of all the fake identities I have for Europe and Asia. I have three that I use in South Africa alone. It's fucking mental jumping jacks on some trips to remember who I am on any given day of the week.

But it's been like that for twenty-seven years. Tommaso has sent me on these little excursions all over the world. My complexion and features allow me to blend in most places. I mastered various accents as a kid and used to do impersonations. If only I hadn't found that so much fun and hadn't shown off too many times to Tommaso and Frank. Now I collect money no one else can find. That's what I'm doing here.

"Ignacio, I should charge you a fee for every day you've wasted my time to track you down."

"*Senhora* Messina, that's not how it works."

"Ignacio, you don't make any rules with me. We do things the way I say, or I make one call to Tommaso, and you can say goodbye to all of this."

"We took your phone and your tracker, *senhora* Messina."

"You don't think I sent him a message before I came knocking at your door? I suggest you figure out how to make all of my wishes come true, or this will cost you more than what you owe Tommaso and my service fee."

It's going to cost him a shit ton more than he realizes. But that's a secret I'll keep to myself for now. I put my hand out and flap my fingers, waiting for him to hand over a thumb drive.

Fucking prehistoric system keeping any financial information on a thumb drive, even if it's a backup from a cloud. I slide his computer in front of me. There's not a fucking chance in hell I'd ever use my computer, whether it's really my personal one or the one Tommaso gave me for work.

From his hesitation, I know he's put something on this thumb drive he doesn't want downloaded onto his computer. I'll have to work fast before it clears out the data. I access files that would look like nonsense to most people. But I already know his encryption system.

When one of his men shifts to stand too close to me, I glare at the guy and raise an eyebrow. It's a harsher version of the look I'd give my boys when they got in trouble. The toned-down version was enough to make them apologize without me guessing what they'd done. It makes this man give me a wide berth.

I type rapidly, pulling up a connection to a cloud where I safely upload all these documents I need. Then I hurry to wipe any traces of what I did. I barely finish before the screen goes blue. I spin the laptop toward Ignacio. Then I pick it up and hurl it against the wall.

"You fucked around, Ignacio. You're going to find out. I saw enough to know what you did, even if you haven't provided all that information to Tommaso or Enrique like you should have."

Yeah, that was a motherfucking shock to discover the customer waiting offshore for Ignacio's product was Enrique. I may be doing a job for Tommaso, but maybe Enrique'll look at it as a gift when he inevitably finds out.

That's laughable. I doubt I'll be lucky enough to leave here, let alone survive whatever Enrique will have in store for me.

Everyone in the room looks at the shattered computer before turning their gaze to me.

"Be glad it's only the computer I broke. You really fucked yourself over this time, Ignacio. Pay Tommaso what you owe him, get the product to the customers, and maybe I can convince him not to send somebody down here."

"Maybe you shouldn't leave, *senhora* Messina."

"You know I'm walking out of here just fine since I already sent my location off. If anything happens to me, Tommaso will burn your fucking labs to the ground. He'll do that before his hitman puts a bullet between your eyes. He'll make sure you see everything he's taken from you. Don't kill the messenger, Ignacio."

The man sits back and crosses his arms. He doesn't intimidate me. He looks like a petulant child instead of a grown ass cartel kingpin. But I don't put it past him to slice my throat.

"And if you make any trouble for me between here and Rio, I'll make sure Pasha Kutsenko knows you went after a woman."

"You're fucking fair game, *senhora*."

"No, I'm not. I'm an accountant. I handle the books for foreign deals. The only women who're fair game are mercenaries.

You had your guards pat me down thoroughly. I had no weapons on me."

"Maybe you stashed those wherever you stopped to send Tommaso a little love note."

"Believe you me, love is not what Tommaso and I share. You need me as much as he needs you." I lean forward, elbows on the table. "What I report to him will determine what happens next. I'm certain from what little I saw, you'd prefer I not give him the full story. So, that service fee I mentioned before went up. It was a million. I'll cut you a pretty deal at one-point-five."

"That's insane, *senhora*. There's no way I'm paying one-point-five million dollars for your silence."

"All right, then. Take your chances by killing me or having me talk. See what happens. The lesser of all the problems is for you to go along with what I'm saying. So, you decide how hard and how expensive you want to make this for yourself."

I remain quiet, giving him time to supposedly think. But everyone in this room already knows what the only answer can be.

"Very well, *senhora* Messina, you'll get your money. You're lucky you're a woman, otherwise I might not take to your negotiation strategies as well as I have been."

"I seem to have a special touch."

I push back the chair and rise. Ignacio and the other men sitting here who've remained silent throughout the meeting stand when I do, too. At least some manners are so deeply entrenched they almost come across as civilized.

"I expect the money in unmarked bills at the drop point. Make sure you don't tell your son."

I lock gazes with Ignacio, and he knows exactly what I mean. The young man is fucking psychotic. He's a terrific enforcer because he has no boundaries. He loves to torture, but he's got a big fucking mouth. If Ignacio wasn't paying off all the law enforcement in Rio and half the politicians in this country, his son would not only be locked up, but Ignacio would be out of business. The guy has no discretion at all.

"If I hear even a whisper of what's going on from anyone

outside this room, I'll know where it came from. It won't please my boss if there're more complications."

"Please your boss?" Ignacio snorts. "Since when have you ever considered Tommaso your boss?"

"He sent me here to do a job. I did it, and he's going to pay me for it. Sounds like he's my boss to me."

"Come now, *senhora* Messina. That's a pile of shit even you can't shovel."

"Regardless of whether I'm a free agent, self-contracted, or an employee, I work for Tommaso Vizzini, and he will have his money. Since you've made my life more difficult than it needed to be, I will have my money. The drop place tomorrow."

I walk to the door, not bothering to wait around to find out if any of them would shake my hand. There's not enough hand sanitizer in the world to stop feeling scuzzy after touching any of them. When I get to the front door, I stare at the armed guard. He opens it, but I look over my shoulder to where I know they're holding the two men who accompanied me. I tap my toes and cock an eyebrow.

Sometimes you've got to play like you've got the biggest pair of balls in the room, even if you don't have any at all.

The guy in front of me gestures to someone I didn't see, but the second guy goes down the hallway and knocks. The door opens, and they speak Portuguese. The two men step aside, and my escorts come out. They flank me, and we walk past the guard at the door. None of us say a word. We keep walking until we get to the gate. It's not until we're on the other side that my escorts get their weapons back.

All three of us check the horses we rode out here on. They didn't come through the gate with us. Instead, we had a local man hold on to them. One of my escorts pays the villager, who swears no one came near the animals. We still examine underneath their saddles, their bridles, and all their hooves. None of us can afford for a horse to go lame while we're trying to get out of this part of the jungle. I ride well enough to get by, so I mount on my own, then we head out.

The three of us remain silent since none of us trust there aren't cameras in the trees. Maybe they're only infrared, but they could pick up more than just that. It's not until we get to the landing zone and the helicopter touches down that anyone speaks.

"Are you all right, *signora* Messina? They didn't do anything to you?"

My guards are Tommaso's men, so they use the Italian honorific. But they know not to use my real last name.

"No. Luca, I'm fine. They wouldn't dare."

No one believes that as we board the helicopter. I fully expected to die, and I still very well may. I played a dangerous game I couldn't guarantee I'd win. I'm exhausted by the time I return to the hotel where I'm staying. There's extra security for me here.

It's not unheard of, so I don't stand out too much with guards outside my door and my window. I trust no one to provide me with anything to eat or drink. I brought all my own bottled water and non-perishable foods. While the cuisine in Brazil is excellent, and I wish I could enjoy it, it's not worth being poisoned. I'm certain plenty would call me paranoid, but I've seen enough counterparts die from something as simple as accepting a bottle of water from hotel staff.

I kick off my shoes and slip out of my cargo pants and blouse. Once I have the pillows adjusted, and I'm comfortable leaning against the headboard, I suck in a deep breath and turn on the portable signal jammers I always travel with. I'm using burners, and all of my boys have them, too.

It didn't go over well when I explained where I was going. It was much easier when they were younger, and I just told them I was going on a work trip. They'd ask where, and I'd lie, since that's all they wanted to know. My ex-husband would corroborate that story.

When they got older and started asking for more details, my truth-stretching got more creative. I did my best to keep the lies to a minimum, but they were unavoidable. Once my boys were teenagers and started doing odd jobs for Tommaso and Frank, they figured a lot of shit out. By the time they were in college, they knew who and what I really am.

A mercenary.

They still hold a boatload of anger and resentment about that. They'll always direct some of it toward me because I'm not the mom they thought they had. But most of it is toward their dad for not protecting me and keeping me out. The rest of it is toward Tommaso for sucking me in and digging his claws in.

Steve and Hunt are Mafia-adjacent. They still go on missions when Tommaso insists, but that's extremely rare. Sometimes they do an odd job here and there for him, but they keep their noses clean.

Will wasn't as fortunate as the oldest. The don—Tommaso—and *consigliere*—Frank—lured him in, and Tim did nothing to stop it. Fortunately, Will created a reputation for himself early on as a wrestler, then bare-knuckle boxer. Very few take him on.

He got my ability to look at numbers, sort them out, and just know what they mean. I'm faster at mental math than anyone I know except for Will. He's a stockbroker on paper, but he handles the Vizzinis' investments. I've worked alongside him to make sure the creative accounting doesn't draw too much attention from the SEC and the IRS.

ME

Fine

I send one word to the boys. I won't risk a longer message than that. For now, they know it means the initial meeting went fine. When I'm on the plane, and I'm over international water, I'll send another one.

I expect no response from them, so when nothing comes in, it's not unusual. I swallow my disgust as I dial a phone number I always hate remembering. It rings twice.

"Elle."

"The meeting's done. I'll have what I came for tomorrow morning."

"What about the rest of it?"

"It'll be done by the time I said it would."

"How much are you skimming off the top?"

"It's not skimming off the top when it's a separate negotiation and deal. You'll get yours. I'll get mine."

"You've always been sneaky like that."

"Is this really the conversation you want to have when I'm about to have all your money and could go anywhere in the world with it? It's not wise to antagonize me right now. Believe me, I'm in no hurry to stay here any longer than I have to. The moment I'm free to leave, I will."

"Good work."

I roll my eyes. Compliments from Tommaso are few and far between, and rarely are they genuine. I'm certainly not foolish enough to think he means those two words. I end the call and toss the burner on the bedside table.

I chose the clothes I packed with a purpose. I glance over at the closet and see the second pair of black cargo pants, the black turtleneck, the black hoodie, and the black boots on the floor beneath my pants. That's tomorrow night's ensemble. For now, I'm going to get whatever sleep I can when I refuse to close both eyes.

"Is that Ignacio's man?"

I jut my chin toward a shady-ass looking guy. I have two different escorts today from the ones I had yesterday. Tommaso lined it all up for me, and these are guys from back home who speak Portuguese. They've traveled with other Vizzinis down here. They blend in as well as I do, but I'm never seen with the same two men two days in a row. The same men would make me too memorable.

We're in one of the roughest *favelas* in Rio. It's not somewhere I enjoy hanging out, but it allows me to stay in the car because nobody would think twice about a woman not wanting to walk along the street.

"Yeah, that's him. He's not at all suspicious-looking, is he?" My driver grins.

Anywhere else the man we're watching would stand out, but he doesn't look any different from the strung-out addicts around here. The guy is twitchy as fuck, but it's from fear, not from the street drugs Ignacio's family provides most of the city. We watch as the messenger bumps into a man, and it almost appears natural when they make the handoff.

I know what I'm looking for, but most people wouldn't since they're carrying identical bags. I made sure the one my guy passes to Ignacio's errand boy has everything we need. When my guy returns to the car, I check the bag. I thumb through all the money. No dye packs. I pull out a loop and check. It's all unmarked, and none is counterfeit. It's all there.

We follow the messenger at a safe distance. He never looks back to see if anyone's following him. When he gets to the outskirts of the shantytown, he finally looks around and bolts. The moment I'm certain he's far enough away from anyone's home, I reach into my pocket and press the little clicker.

A miniature Fourth of July show goes off right before us. The guy never checked the bag to see what he got in return. That's on him, and it's on Ignacio if he thought this guy would live to tell the tale about this deal. This is a little reminder in case Ignacio thinks to pull this shit again. I giveth, and I taketh away.

We head back to the hotel until it's dark. Now's the most dangerous part of this mission. It's when I work with only one guard. Tonight, he's my scout and will help me locate my targets. Once they're locked on tomorrow, there's nothing he can do except get the fuck out before anybody guesses he's connected to the shitstorm that'll blow through.

I'm in all black with a ball cap that allows me to tuck my dark hair underneath along with a bulky coat. I can pass for a man. I'm a little on the short side, but not unreasonably.

I know my partner's moving parallel to me across the street. We don't acknowledge each other as we wind through a nicer part of Rio. I have a gym bag with me that nobody would guess weighs a fucking ton. I have it pinched close to my side with my other hand in my pocket. My fingers wrap around the butt of my pistol. My head isn't on a swivel because that would only gain attention I don't need. However, my gaze sweeps the area, looking for anybody who not only appears out of place, but anyone who appears to fit a little too well. This is a more touristy part of the city, not one locals prefer to frequent.

It takes an hour before I spot what I'm looking for. A peek at my guard confirms it when our gazes meet. I ease around the side of the building, ensuring I remain in the shadows. I watch my guy who's still across the street inch closer to the five men who're meeting at a table on a restaurant's outside patio. One of them is definitely Benicio.

That's pretty fucking ballsy since it makes all of them easy targets. Tonight's about gathering information and making sure I know who my targets are. If the opportunity strikes, I'll take it, but I need to follow the plan I created. Impetuousness rarely pays off when you commit a capital crime, then need to disappear.

I watch the men for thirty minutes before they all rise. There's one who stands in the shadows. His build is familiar. It reminds me of Enrique. I inch closer, maintaining my cover. I can't see the man's face, so I can't be sure.

Is Rio where Enrique went? Are we both here at the same time? I know in my bones I'd recognize Enrique from anyone else. The man may remind me of him, but he's not Enrique. I'll send Andrés a text that hopefully he'll pass along to Luis who'll pass it to his brother. Or maybe Andrés can share the message directly with him.

The meeting breaks up, and the men go in separate directions, none coming toward me. My escort and I slip back to the hotel.

"All you have to do is head out on the tarmac and keep your back to the windows. I'll make sure nothing happens to you. Nobody can see your face. They need to believe you're me."

"And if I do this for you, you'll pay me?"

"Yes."

I have on a sun hat with a huge brim, Audrey Hepburn sunglasses that cover half my face along with a nondescript gray sundress and black ballet flats. I look wealthy enough to fly in a private jet. This woman works at the airport. It's a lucky coincidence we're the same height and build. I hand her a dress to change into in the bathroom.

"I'll hold on to your uniform, so you don't have to worry about it."

"All right. And where do I meet you after this?"

"Come back to this bathroom, and I'll be sure you get your clothes back, and the money I promised you."

"All right."

She's reasonably skeptical about my request. Once she's dressed, she leaves the restroom, and I'm close on her heels. We go in opposite directions until I double back and change into her uniform. I fold my dress and stick it under my shirt and down my pants. I slip through the security doors I need her badge to open. I'm certain there's someone waiting for me when I'm supposed to get on the Vizzinis' jet.

I creep out of the building and tuck myself away in the spot I already selected this morning. I grab my binoculars from the gear bag I hid and scout the area. It takes me a few sweeps before I see what I'm looking for.

Discreet but not invisible. It only takes me a handful of seconds to assemble my rifle. I roll onto my belly and set it up on the tripod. I set my scope on the man who's got a gun pointing at the woman. I watch him home in on her as she heads toward the private plane I should be boarding.

Everything around me dulls except for what's through my rifle scope that sharpens like a blade. Everything's crisp. I adjust my position until I'm comfortable. Then I wait.

Come on, fucknut, get this over with.

The longer we're both out here, the greater the chance someone will discover either of us. Ignacio's mercenary is well hidden, but not as well as me. I recognize the guy. He's got a solid reputation and isn't cheap.

I suppose it should flatter me Ignacio chose him for the job, clearly expecting me to be a hard target to pin down. The assassin lifts his rifle and wraps his finger around the trigger. The moment that finger moves even a fraction, I pull my trigger.

Blood explodes from his head, twisting his body toward me with the force. It opens his chest as a perfect target. I put two through his heart just to be on the safe side. If the bullet to his brain didn't kill him, then the two through his heart did. I'm on my feet, disassembling the rifle as people scream.

The assassin's bullet hit the decoy woman, but I timed it, so my shot knocked him off balance. The bullet only winged her. I couldn't guarantee such good luck, but I took my chances, and it paid off. People run to her as I slip back into the building. I duck into the restroom where I met the woman earlier. I change back into my clothes and fold up hers. When I leave, I nod to a woman across from me.

She's one of our informants and has been for years. I hand over the clothes and the money I promised the woman who pretended to be me. My informant will help ensure she gets the medical treatment she needs and can disappear along with any family she wants to take with her. She'll make sure the rumor spreads that I died out there on the tarmac.

Ignacio will think the hit was a success. He'll accept the money's gone even though I'm positive he's sent somebody to ransack my hotel room. I checked out this morning. It's a matter of waiting around until it's dark, so I can finish the very last of this job.

The hours crawl as I hide at another informant's house. This woman was my guide the first time I came to Rio nearly thirty years ago. That was purely for vacation. At the time, she worked for a resort. We struck up a conversation and hit it off. She warned Tim and me about the cartels and which areas to avoid. There was something in the way she spoke that gave her away.

She knew more than just passing information or the rumors

and history most residents know. The second time I came back five years later, I sought her out and tested the waters. She's been an excellent partner ever since.

"The restaurant's back door leads into a storage room. My brother'll make sure it's unlocked for you, and you can wait there. There's already a spyhole cut into the wall. It's one Ignacio had put in."

"And you're certain he won't have anyone there?"

"He definitely won't because the man he's meeting with will have already had the entire restaurant swept. He won't go inside if Ignacio has anyone hidden."

"Do you know who this man is? Could he be the one I saw last night? The one Benicio's met with?"

"I haven't found out his name. No one has. The only people who seem to know him are the ones he met with last night."

"Ignacio wasn't there, so I don't know if he's back in Rio."

"I have it on good authority he's supposed to attend tonight, *senhora*."

"I'm counting on that."

If he isn't, then it'll be a long fucking night while I track him down and try to keep anybody from finding me.

Like I did last night, I slip out once it's dark. I'm wearing the same clothes I did yesterday, keeping me inconspicuous and easily blending into the shadows. My escort strolls across the street from me, blending in like a local. He falls back a block as I approach the restaurant. I recognize the man smoking beside a door.

"Hello, *senhor* Sousa."

He greets me as the man I'm pretending to be. My response is a nod as he gestures at the building.

"I'll be out here if you need me. I've got the van waiting. Engine's already on and idling. The moment you come out, I'll have the door open and waiting for you."

Again, I say nothing. I merely nod. He eases open the storage room door, and I look around, but it's pitch black. I shrug out of the coat I'm wearing over the hoodie and backpack. I slip the strap off one shoulder. I pull out a headlamp and adjust it as I put it on.

It sits just above the brim of my baseball cap. It provides enough light while the brim refracts some of it. I sweep my gaze around the storage room, satisfied with what I see.

"It's right there." The man points to my left and closes the door once I step away.

I flick off my headlamp before creeping toward the wall. I run my fingers over it until I find what I'm looking for. There's a piece of tape on the wall at someone's eye level. I stand on my toes. Of course, this was cut into the wall for a man.

I open my backpack all the way and pull out everything I need. It would shock most people to realize rifles can break down into small enough parts to fit in an oversized hiking backpack. I pull over a crate I noticed earlier and pray it can bear my weight once I'm on it. I step up, peel off the tape, and put my eye to the peephole.

There are two men sitting at a table with their backs to me. There're still six seats open at the table. I climb down and put my ear to the wall. Since it's dark in the room, anybody who looks in the peephole's direction won't realize it's there since no light will shine through it. I don't need anyone spotting my white eyeball against it.

The wall was thin enough to cut the peephole, so it's thin enough for me to hear some of what's going on. Chairs scrape across the floor as more men join the two who were already at the table. I count each chair as I believe it moves.

When I'm certain all of them are taken, I step onto the crate and peek to ensure I'm right. Ignacio is at the head of the table, which puts him facing me. I inhale silently, keeping my breathing even. I focus on my heart rate and not letting it spike. Despite how many of these missions I've been on or how high my body count is, there's always a moment of apprehension knowing everything could go sideways, and someone could discover me. I'm not in the mood to die today, so I must remain calm.

I hear the voices as the meeting starts, but I don't understand what anyone says. I speak no more Portuguese than I do Spanish, though I can follow along in Spanish fairly well. I'm fluent in

Italian and Sicilian along with English. The first isn't a language I grew up with. It's one I learned out of necessity. I have a fair amount of Russian and Polish as well, and some Chinese and Japanese.

I haven't learned Spanish because I'm always with Vizzini men who speak the language when I'm anywhere I need it. I don't trust interpreters for any other language because they're rarely any of Tommaso's men. Some of the men who've traveled with me are my boys' ages, and I've known them their entire lives. I trust them to get me home to my sons.

I pull out my phone, which is already on dark mode, and shield the screen. I tap on the translation app and hold it toward the peephole. I watch the words appear across the screen.

"Ignacio, you played a foolish game, and you didn't win. The woman Tommaso sent—it sounds like she put your balls in a vise and squeezed. Did she make them pop?"

"I'm at a meeting here with you. I'd say I still have the balls to do that."

"Fair enough. They just shrank, but they're still there. Did you pay the Vizzinis the money you owe them?"

Ignacio doesn't respond. The man who's speaking has a hint of a Spanish accent, but his Portuguese sounds fluent to me. I could be wrong, but he sounds more than just proficient. I keep reading my phone screen.

"Yeah, we made the drop this morning. Then I made sure the bitch didn't leave the country."

Good. He thinks I'm dead.

"Did you get your money back?"

This is met with more silence. Ignacio hates admitting any of this didn't go his way. Certainly the part about all the money he couldn't get back.

"Aren't you concerned it'll piss Tommaso off that his accountant isn't coming home?"

"He should've sent a man to do a woman's job then."

There's laughter all around, and it makes me want to punch the fucker in the face. There's no reason for him to be so obnoxious. I thought I was being extremely reasonable during our meeting. I could have done far worse. I should have put a bullet through him when I had the chance.

They may have frisked me when I arrived, but I put up enough of a stink about one of his guys getting too handsy with me, they missed the small pistol I had on me. It was very dainty and remained hidden in my pocket. What they didn't know, in this case, didn't hurt them.

I continue to read my phone screen as they go back and forth. They're still shooting the shit, and this young man puts up with Ignacio and his men's bullshit. I read the translation throughout their dinner, hoping something'll come out of this conversation that's useful for Tommaso. The guy with the Spanish accent works for somebody out of Colombia, but I don't know who. His back is to me, so I can't see if I recognize him. His voice isn't familiar.

When I hear the dessert plates being carried away, I know there'll be a dessert wine coming next. I've already assembled my rifle, so I pick it up and put the barrel to the peephole as I peer through the sights. Just as the men lift their glasses to toast one another, I squeeze off rounds, putting bullets through all the men's heads except for the Spanish speaker and Ignacio.

I make sure Ignacio sees everything that happens. All that's taken away from him in a heartbeat. Once I'm certain the other men are dead, I shift my target to him. At the same time, I pull the trigger to kill Ignacio, the Spanish-speaking man turns in my direction.

Motherfucking son of a bitch. He is a near replica of Enrique. It has to be one of his nephews.

Fucking hell.

I can't shoot him, but if I don't get the fuck out of here, he's going to find a way in here and will shoot me, then ask questions. I barely pull the rifle back in time before he shoots at the wall I'm hidden behind. I jump off the crate, ducking low to the ground as I disassemble the rifle, shoving it into my bag as I head to the door.

It swings open, and I whip out my pistol. I didn't expect my informant to be there, but he is. He must have heard the shouting that started with the second bullet. I'm through the door and launching myself into the back seat of the van, pulling the sliding door shut as my guy hops in the driver's seat. I peek out the window as the tires squeal. The sound of bullets hitting metal warns me we barely got away in time.

I lift my head high enough to peek out the back window and watch Enrique's nephew point a gun toward me. I drop flat on the ground as the back window shatter. There's a solid metal divider between the back seat and the front seat for things just like this. A bullet won't pass through to kill the driver.

I hold on to anything I can grab since I can't sit up and put my seatbelt on, and the roads are rough. We're going way too fast for how narrow they are, but I trust my driver knows where to go and what to do.

We head directly to the airport where my escorts already wait for me. This time I board the plane with no one trying to kill me. I left Enrique's nephew a block away from the restaurant. The plane's engine is already on and idling just like the van had been. We're wheels up before I catch my breath. I sit in my seat with my eyes closed once again, focusing on my breathing, calming myself.

I look out the window into the night sky. When there are no longer any city lights beneath us and only a dark abyss, I know we're over the Atlantic. I pull my burner phone from my backpack and pull up the group text for my boys.

Again, it's only a one-word message.

Off

It means I took off. I'm on my way home.

It's an hour before I trust the plane won't explode right after takeoff. There's no guarantee somebody didn't tamper with it, but I recognized the pilot and co-pilot. This isn't a luxury flight, despite how nice the plane is. There's no flight attendant offering me drinks and moist hot towels. There's nothing for me to do during this leg of the flight, so I recline my seat and close my eyes.

We'll make a stop in the Cayman Islands, so I can deposit the money in one of Tommaso's offshore accounts. No one wants me traveling back into the U.S. with this much currency.

I'm exhausted after running off adrenaline and fumes for the last few days. I swear to all that's holy, if anything goes wrong between now and when Tommaso gets proof his money's safe—if I survive it—he won't.

Chapter Ten

Enrique

"What the hell do you mean somebody shot him and Benicio and four of their men? How the hell did you make it out alive? Are you all right?"

I can't fucking believe what Alejandro just told me.

"Yes, *tío*. I'm fine. Whoever the mercenary was knew me or figured out who I was because they shot everyone else at the table except me. The speed at which this shooter worked was unlike anything I'd ever seen. It wasn't rapid fire. It wasn't some spray of bullets. They picked off each man with precision either straight through the top of the spine or dead smack between the eyebrows. They took out everyone, saving Benicio for second to last. Ignacio was this person's ultimate target. Whoever they were, they wanted Ignacio to have the time to recognize what he was losing and a moment to see his son die before he did. Either that's how the hit was commissioned, or it was something personal."

"You're absolutely certain you're fine, *sobrino*?"

"*Sí, tío*. You don't have to worry about Mama knocking down your door to come after you because I got a hair out of place."

"Good. Your mama isn't too fond of me right now, and I don't need her having an excuse to fillet me in my sleep."

My sister got pissed like a shaken hive when she discovered where Alejandro went. She knows he's a fluent Portuguese speaker, but she still doesn't like it. He blends in, which is a blessing and a curse. It means he can pass for a local and doesn't stand out in a crowd. However, because he can pass for a local, it's easy for anyone to assume he's in a cartel. They just don't know which one. They wouldn't know he's in a Colombian one, not a Brazilian one.

When he travels to Colombia, everyone knows who he is between the reputation he's earned for himself and how much he looks like me. He could pass for my son rather than my nephew. It only takes one look to know we're related. That makes him untouchable in the countries we do business with down there. However, Brazil's cartels don't have the same hierarchy as those in Colombia. His rank within our cartel doesn't have the same significance to them.

Incarcerated men lead most of the Brazilian cartels. *Donos* pay insurance money to them for protection outside the jails. The men in prison have far longer reaches than those who are free. They're the ones who can keep people safe.

There's no *jefe* at the top of their food chain. There's no equivalent to Alejandro, either. That makes my sister understandably worried and unhappy when he has to go there, which fortunately is infrequent.

"*Tío*, I caught a glimpse of the person as they pulled the van door shut. It was someone young. I couldn't tell any specific features about the guy, but whoever he is has been trained well and has practiced a lot in the short time they could've been working. I'd guess they're younger than me."

That would put whoever this is in their mid to late twenties. It's not impossible for a mercenary to have the skills Alejandro described at a young age, but very few can not only shoot that well, but break down their gear, be out the door and into a vehicle as fast as Alejandro described. That part takes the longest to master.

Luis is listening to the call as well since we're in his office this evening. Margherita wasn't feeling well today, so I came over instead of expecting him to leave his wife.

"What do you want me to do, *mano*? Do we look at this as a blessing in disguise?"

"Hardly. Tommaso'll be blowing up my phone by morning, expecting me to thank him for fixing a problem he created. Alejandro, get to the airport and come straight home."

"All right, *tío*."

It pisses me off that he's leaving empty-handed. He's not coming back with any of the money, and he doesn't have any of the product either. I've been working on the latter, and I didn't fully expect the former, but it would have been nice.

Luis, Alejandro, and I say our goodbyes with our round of "*te amos*" before I hang up. I look at my brother and sigh.

"Do you know who this shooter could be?"

Luis frowns and shakes his head. "No, but I want to. They should be on our payroll. I'd rather they work for us than one of us taking a bullet from them."

"Have Joaquin find out who it is and strike up a deal. I doubt this person is Brazilian. My guess is American, English, or Russian."

"Do you think the bratva discovered Ignacio's fuck-up and cleaned house?"

"No, I don't think it was them. But it could be an unaffiliated Russian who's just work for hire."

"If that's who it turns out to be, how do you want to handle it with Maksim?"

I consider that for a moment. "If we get this person to work exclusively for us, then there's nothing to say to him. If this person refuses, then they're a threat to us. We don't tell Maks anything. He can go fuck himself. We take this person out, so there's no next time around. I won't risk them not sparing one of our boys."

"All right." Luis is already shooting off a text as he speaks.

It's late, and I'm exhausted, so I head home. I'm about to pull into my neighborhood when I get a text from Carlos.

> She's home.

My lips twitch, and so does my cock. I want to turn around and head to my *chiquita's* house, but she's probably exhausted too. I don't know that she wants a reminder I have men guarding her, which means they're watching her. If she thinks they report everything she does to me, it'll freak her out.

But I have an overwhelming need to see her. I don't want to wait until tomorrow morning. Part of me wonders though, how long it will take for her to ask Andrés or Carlos to let me know she's back.

I pull into my garage as my phone pings again. I live in a gated community and on a gated property. I'm still waiting for the garage to shut all the way before I turn off the engine. I unlock my phone as I hit the ignition button. It's a screenshot, much like the one Andrés sent me last week.

> Can you please tell el jefe I'm home and I'm safe and sound?

I glance at my watch as I walk into my house. It's nearly two in the morning. It's an odd time for her to get home. I can't think of too many flights that would arrive after midnight if they were coming into Newark or JFK, and LaGuardia stops inbound flights around eleven.

Perhaps she flew into a private airfield. Maybe she had to drive back several hours, and this is when she got in. I have so many questions and not nearly enough answers. I text Carlos back.

> What's her number?

He sends it to me immediately. I don't hesitate before I tap the numbers in and hit call. It rings four times before I'm certain she sends it to voicemail. She doesn't know my number. I tap out a text to her instead.

> That was me, chiquita. I'm going to call back.
> Answer me. Carlos already told me you're home.

I give the text a moment to go through before I hit the call button to redial.

"Enrique?"

"*Sí, chiquita.* It's good to hear your voice."

"Oh, Enrique, it's so good to hear yours, too. I—I—Fuck it. I missed you, Enrique."

"Was that so hard to admit, little one? I missed you, too."

"I don't want to sound clingy or anything."

"You don't. I'm glad to hear that's how you feel because it's the same way I do. I missed you, and I can't wait to see you. I heard Constantine misses me too."

She chuckles, and the sound goes straight to my cock.

"I didn't think you'd be awake right now. I hope having Carlos text you didn't disturb you."

"No, I'm still up."

If only she knew how literal that was.

"Are you—" She pauses for a moment. "—up for a visit?"

Is she inviting me over to fuck?

"If you want me to come over, I can be there in five minutes, little one."

"I don't want to drag you out of your house in the middle of the night. I don't want to be an imposition."

"Ellie, you know you're not an imposition, and if you believed I'd say no, you wouldn't have asked. You know I want to see you. If you hadn't just arrived home, and if it didn't matter to me about you being out again in the middle of the night, I would have suggested you come here. But I'm happy to meet you at your place."

"All right, I'll be ready for you."

I wonder what that means. I only have five minutes until I find out. I turn around and head back into my garage. I ensure the car's locked before I hit the button to open the garage door. The moment it's up high enough I don't fear I could poison myself if it jams or something goes wrong with my ignition, I turn the car on. It feels like the door taunts me and is moving even slower than usual, but it's only a few seconds before I'm backing out. The men who patrol my property barely notice since I come and go at all hours of the day, any day of the week. The guy at my gate nods as he opens it.

It's the same as I leave the neighborhood. The guards who work there are all mine. They work for the community's property manager ostensibly, but really I employ them. When I arrive at Ellie's community gate, I don't recognize the person working there. That immediately makes me uneasy. It's not my men who work here, but I know almost all of them.

I've met them all from running through the neighborhood and most have worked here since I built the community.

"Good evening, sir. Which home are you headed to?"

I stare at him for just a moment before I give Ellie's address.

"Oh yes, Ms. McCann just called to say she's expecting you."

The guy says nothing else even though I feel suspicious about him.

Something's off.

As I approach Ellie's house, I notice the car that was parked on the street for weeks is gone. I got an update while I was away that it left and didn't come back. My men tried to get photos the few times anyone went near it, but it was always far too dark. I ordered it followed, but the trackers stuck to the vehicle disappeared, and the drivers know how to lose my men.

I know the owners of the house the car was always in front of since they're the original ones. I know they aren't connected to any syndicates, and they've been abroad most of this spring. I learned they didn't rent out the house; it's supposed to be empty. The car's an anomaly I'm still trying to sort out, and my men's failure is something that won't go unpunished.

I pull into Ellie's driveway and nod to Carlos. He and Andrés are the two most discreet men outside of my immediate family. They're brothers and second cousins to Luis and me. That's why I trust them most with Ellie. They won't gossip about me coming over or how long I stay.

Part of me wants to send them home to increase our privacy, but after not recognizing the guy at the gate, I'm uncomfortable without somebody watching the house while I'm—shall we say—distracted. I shoot off a text to my brother before I get out of the car.

> Find out who's working the gate in Ellie's neighborhood. I don't recognize him.

I stick my phone back into my pocket and hurry to the front door. It opens the moment my knuckles touch the wood. Then she's in my arms, just like the only time I've been here before. I twirl her around, her back against the door now. We can't get enough of each other. Our lips meld as our bodies press together.

Her hands roam over me for a couple of minutes, then I take control once more. I lift her arms over her head, pinning her wrists together in one of my hands, but she pulls away and shakes her head.

"Not yet. Please let me touch you."

Her tone isn't begging, but her expression is. She needs this as much as I do. I let go, and she cups my face as we come back together for another cataclysmic kiss. I love it when she does that. I lift her, and she wraps her legs around my waist. Now that she knows who I am, I don't fear her feeling the gun at my lower back.

Her leg presses against the top of it, but she doesn't react. It's one thing to know it's there, but another to not seem to notice. In the back of my head, that strikes me as strange, but it's not enough to make me stop what I'm doing. I squeeze her ass as I carry her to the sofa. The moment we're seated, we're pulling our shirts off. She unfastens her bra and flings it halfway across the living room. We pause long enough to laugh for a moment before diving back in.

We're like two people lost in the desert who find an oasis. I sweep my tongue against hers and the satiny inside of her cheeks. Nothing has felt more life-giving than this. She tastes sweet, and I can't get enough. She continues to cup my jaw while my hands move over her tits and back. When I tweak her nipple, one hand drops to my shoulder, squeezing to where it's almost painful, but I relish every moment of knowing her desire matches mine.

Then both hands sweep over my pecs and up and down my abs. She moans with pleasure, and it does things to me. I unfasten her jeans and slide my hands down the back to her bare ass.

"*Chiquita*, I missed this. My hands have felt so empty every moment I haven't held you."

"Enrique, it's been such a long ten days. I don't mind traveling, but it's been a while since I've been this happy to get home."

I kiss along her neck up to behind her ear. "I hope the next trip either of us takes is a getaway together."

Where the hell did that come from? It's way too soon to suggest something like that. I'm probably going to freak her the fuck out. However, when she leans back and our gazes meet again, she smiles.

"Can we go today?"

"The idea of traveling with me already doesn't raise every red flag a woman should have?"

"It likely would if it were any other man, but for better or worse, I trust you, Enrique. And I can't think of anything better right now than getting away somewhere that can just be the two of us, so we can get to know each other better without the outside world intruding. But I also understand after you left the other night that no matter where we go or what we do, there's always the chance you'll have to leave with no warning. I get that, and I'm okay with it."

I watch her, and something in her tone and her gaze makes me suspect she's used to that. Did her ex-husband have an affair and make excuses about why he wasn't around? Did he have some type of job, like being a doctor, where he got called away unexpectedly? It's not resignation, so I don't fear she already resents that possibility, but it is acceptance. And not merely she thinks she's okay with it but will later discover she's not. It's more something she's already used to.

"Enrique, I can practically hear your thoughts whirling through your head. My dad is a trauma surgeon. He often got called away even when leaving the family was the last thing he wanted. While he chose the occupation, and you didn't, he did important work just like you do. So, I couldn't fault him for helping other people when they needed him the most. He missed holidays and school events and vacations because of work, but I could appreciate it because of his altruism."

"Do you see me as altruistic?"

If she can wrap her head around that and believe it, I should nominate her for sainthood because she's the most forgiving and accepting person I've ever met.

"I think you prioritize duty and loyalty to your family above all else, and to protect them means protecting the people who depend upon you. So, your loyalty and sense of duty extend to everyone beneath you. The movies might make it seem like all that syndicate men are after is money and sex, but that's a naive way to look at a community. Syndicates aren't just a transactional organization. They're communities, and that means people depend on you who don't directly work for you."

She fucking gets me.

"I'm certain some of your men must have families who rely upon the money they make working for you. And businesses can only survive when they make money, and it's reinvested into them. That's why I can reconcile the things you do because of other people's needs. I get I'm making excuses, but to me it's also an explanation."

"There are parts of me and of my life I will never share with you, Ellie. I can't. It's not safe for you, but it's also a part of me I never want you to see. It's the monster in me."

She studies me for a moment before reaching back and pulling my hands away from her ass. My heart sinks until she laces our fingers together.

"Enrique, tell me the truth, and I will know if you're lying to me. Do you do those things because you crave it? I don't mean the satisfaction you might get when you dole out a punishment or justice to someone who threatens your way of life. Or do you do those things because someone trained you to?"

"No, I have no innate compulsion to do these things, but I've accepted my role, and I do what I must."

I've accepted it makes me a monster with psychopathic tendencies.

She squeezes my hands.

"I understand vindication and justice. Sometimes that comes in the form of vengeance."

I wait for her to say more, but she doesn't.

"Have you always been this philosophical, *chiquita?*"

"I don't know that I'd call it philosophical so much as merely practical."

"Most people would condemn me for what I do."

"And it would be easy for me to do that, but I also know there are no limits to what I would do to protect my sons. There's no limit to the violence I'd willingly inflict for their sake. There're also no limitations to what I would do to protect my parents and extended family, but the visceral need for vengeance isn't the same as it is when I think about my sons. That's merely my reaction as someone who prioritizes family. Being trained to exact vengeance isn't something I would wish upon you or anyone else, but if it's kill or be killed, then I can't fault you for doing what you must to survive and to protect your loved ones. There must be thousands of people who rely on you not just in New York, but all over the world."

"Ellie, did you google me?"

"No, but I told you the other day, I've heard of you. I don't know all the ins and outs of your business, but I know you're pretty important."

That's certainly one way to put it, but I won't tell her how much of an understatement that is. I kiss her cheek, and she leans against me. It's a moment of affection I'm not accustomed to. However, I want to grow used to it. I want it to be something I experience every day and not just with anyone. Only Ellie.

We sit silently, just enjoying each other's company. I sweep my gaze around her living room. The last time I came over, Constantine didn't bark. He didn't even get up. He just thumped his tail when I looked at him.

"Where's Constantine?"

I don't know the guy at the gate, and her humongous dog isn't around. I'm glad I didn't send Carlos away.

"My youngest son, Hunter, has him."

"He didn't bark or anything when I came to the door the other night."

"I said your name and sent him back to his bed before I opened the door. Once he saw it was you, he was fine."

"Would he normally react if a stranger walked in?"

"He doesn't bark when someone knocks or the doorbell rings. He goes to the door and waits for me. If I send him to his bed, then he won't get up unless I tell him to. If I don't send him away, he'll sit and wait for my command. If I don't know who's on the other side of the door, I usually won't answer. If I answer, just seeing him is a deterrent. One flick of my hand, and he'll stand next to me. He gets rid of solicitors before they say anything. But I told you, he's basically a pacifist. For a biscuit, he'd tell you where all my jewelry is."

"Do you have an alarm? You didn't set one the other night, and you haven't set one tonight."

"You've distracted me with your kisses both times. Enrique, what's going on? Why are you asking me about my home security?"

"When you called the gate guard, did you recognize his voice or name?"

She stares at me for a moment before looking toward her door. Her expression shutters as she stands. I watch her go to a keypad and punch in a code. She activates her alarm before she grabs her cell phone off the coffee table. I can't tell what she's doing, but I think she's sending a text. She looks at her living room windows before returning her attention to her phone. She's definitely sending a text now. She locks the screen and puts it face down on the table.

"I didn't call. I was about to, but I saw the headlights flash from my driveway. I checked, and it was you. I figured you knew the guard, and they let you in."

"He said you called to say I was coming."

"Could one of your guys have done it?"

"No. The guard specifically said you let him know."

Her phone vibrates, but she ignores it. If she sent a text, isn't she expecting an answer?

"What did he look like? Did you see a name tag? Maybe I know him."

"His uniform said Mark. He was about five-eleven, sandy-colored hair, with blue eyes. The light above the stable-style door made it easy to see him."

She shakes her head as her phone vibrates again. This time with a call. She watches me for a moment before grabbing her phone. She slides it unlocked and puts it to her ear.

"*Que se passe-t-il?*" What's going on?

Does she assume I don't speak French like I assumed she doesn't speak Spanish? I understand everything she says.

"*Tu l'as envoyé?*" Did you send him?

She listens to whoever's on the other end. I can't hear anything.

"*Trouve qui l'a fait.*" Find out who did.

Whatever the response is, it's brief.

"*Je t'aime... Toi aussi...Gros bisous. Fais de beaux rêves.*" I love you...You too... Big kisses. Make beautiful dreams—sweet dreams.

That sounds more like she's talking to one of her sons than a lover or friend. I wait for her to hang up, and when she does, we stare at each other. I know she's evaluating what to tell me. She comes back and straddles my lap. We both like it when she sits that way.

"Enrique, I obviously live a very comfortable life here. I told you I used my portion of the house sale after I divorced to pay cash for this home. I work my ass off to write and publish my books, and with ten years under my belt, I've got a solid income every month."

She shifts, bringing her body closer to mine. She's not doing it to distract me. She wants more physical nearness as she shares information she fears will push us emotionally apart.

"This is an extremely modest lifestyle compared to what I could've once had. My sons benefited by getting superior educations and having their undergrad degrees paid for. Two have already paid for their graduate degrees. All three got high salaried jobs on their own. All three are on their way to being independently wealthy. With that money comes resources. They worry about me. They don't know you, and they didn't enjoy learning you can come and go as you want in this neighborhood. My oldest son has a friend who owns a security staffing company. I wondered if he put his friend up to getting one of his guys hired here, so my boys could keep an eye out for me."

"Did he?"

"No. My son didn't know what I was talking about. I told him to find out who got the guy the job. He'll reach out to his friend, who'll call the security company. I've known my son's friend since they were in high school together. He'll ask some discreet questions. If he learns anything concerning, he'll tell Will."

There's more to this she's not telling me. She knows I know that. She's bracing for me to demand an explanation. I could order her to tell me, but I have something else in mind.

"*Chiquita,* I'm certain you're safe here. Between the alarm system, my guys, and me, you're well-guarded. But does it bother you enough that you want to go to one of your sons?"

"No. If you say we're safe here, then I believe you. Besides, one of my boys is in New England, another is in Connecticut, and the third is staying with a friend in the city while he pet sits Constantine."

I tuck a lock of hair behind her ear. It's not that our lust is no longer there. We both feel it crackling between us. But we know there's more we need to talk about, and it wouldn't hurt for us to slow down a little. I try an easy question.

"How was your trip?"

"It was good, but it's always nice to be home."

Evasive.

"How about you?"

Now it's my turn.

"Productive, but you're right. It's always nice to be home."

I cup her cheek, and she leans forward. Our lips brush.

"I really missed you, Enrique. I didn't think I would that much."

"I hated not knowing how long either of us would be away."

This kiss is languid as she melts against me. There's a depth of emotion I know she's not ready to admit. It's one that unsettles me.

"Little one, I know it's unfair that I can't tell you about where I went or what I did. But I'd love to hear about your trip."

Once again, she watches me as though she's evaluating whether I have an ulterior motive for my question. She never takes more than a couple seconds, but I recognize it because I do the same thing.

"I got to see some folks I haven't in a while. When I wasn't thinking about you, the time flew. When I was, it dragged. The weather was nice."

"Where'd you go?"

"The Caymans."

"Beautiful."

"It is. Usually, I wish I could stay longer and enjoy more of it."

"You said you wouldn't mind if we went away for a little while. Had more time to get to know each other without distractions. I know most—people don't travel together so soon. But it's a good way to get to know if they're compatible."

I caught myself before I said couple, but the moment the word compatible came out of my mouth, I knew I fucked up.

"I think we already proved we're pretty compatible. I think we were about to remind ourselves of that."

I stop her as her hands trail down my chest toward my abs. I wrap my hands around her wrists, and she pulls back from leaning in for another kiss. We may as well have it out since it's only going to linger over our heads.

"Ellie, you know what we shared was far more than what fuck buddies do. It meant more to both of us."

"It was the best sex I've ever had. I hope it's always like that for us. Of course, it meant more because we learned the sexual tension between us was worth it."

I tighten my hands. "Bullshit, Ellie. Why're you downplaying it?"

She yanks her hands from mine, and I let her go. She stands and backs away, shaking her head.

"Don't do this, Enrique. I told you what I could give. You said you could accept it. Don't ruin what's starting."

I stand and step forward, but I don't crowd her. "And I told you from the start I want more. That I see us being more. *We are more.*"

Tears well in her eyes, and I rush forward. I no longer care whether I crowd her. I pull her into my arms, feeling her shuddering breath.

"And you had to leave in the middle of the night. I didn't lie. I understand it, and I can accept it. But it doesn't mean I wasn't scared for you. It doesn't mean I didn't worry. I told you I never want to be emotionally reliant on anyone ever again. If you push this to become more, then I'll fall for you."

"And you expect me to disappoint you. You expect me to fail. I'm not your damn ex-husband."

"No. You're more likely to die. That's even worse."

She clings to my shirt. From her rigid body that's usually so pliable against me, I know she doesn't enjoy admitting this. It makes her uncomfortable because she can't control this. Not what could happen to me, nor how our feelings have exploded between us.

I sweep her into my arms without a word and carry her upstairs. I go straight to her bedroom and kick the door closed behind us. I put her on her feet in the middle of the room, then move to the end of the bed and sit.

"Strip."

"Enri—"

"Strip. Do not make me say it a third time, *chiquita*. Your sexy ass won't like the spanking I'm ready to give you."

"Spanking? I haven't done anything wrong."

I rise and prowl toward her. When I'm standing toe to toe with her, I grab the front of her thong that's exposed by her open jeans. I tug as my other hand rests lightly on her throat. She doesn't balk, so I put more pressure on it without squeezing.

"You're disobeying me, little girl. You say you want control over your life, but you feel out of control because you want something you refuse to admit. It's overwhelming you. What you need is a break to clear your mind. You need someone else in control, so you're not worrying about what comes next beyond how I'm going to make you come. Take your clothes off before I rip them off. I will shred them."

I give her a gentle push back as I step away. Her hand flies out and fists my shirt. She tugs and goes onto her toes. She offers a kiss that nearly steals my resolve to play out this scene.

"Yes, sir."

She pushes her jeans down as I go back to the bed. Her fucking panties need to go. I struggle to maintain all the restraint my father and uncle drilled into me. I want to maul her.

She kicks her jeans away as she watches me. She must see how much I'm enjoying this torture because her back straightens and her shoulders inch back. She lifts her chin, and the expression that enters her eyes is pure seduction. Her hands glide from the outside of her upper thighs over her hips and along her ribs. She watches me for as long as she can as she turns away from me. In a thong, I have a spectacular view of her ass.

She hooks her thumbs into her thong's waistband and playfully moves it up and down a couple inches, but before she pushes it down, she twists to look back at me.

"No. Face away from me while you take it off. I love your tits, but I'm fucking your ass tonight. I want to see what I'm going to take."

"Enrique, you know I don't feel comfortable with you seeing my scar."

"You're going to feel even more uncomfortable when my hand lands across your ass."

I walk over and slide my arms around her. I slip my fingers down the front of her thong and press them into her pussy.

"You're already so fucking wet, little one. You feel how hard I am. That won't go away until I'm inside you, and I can come. You might be unwilling to give me your heart, but you've given me your body. It's mine to enjoy however I want, Ellie. I'll never lie to you about how I feel about you. I'll never lie about how attracted I am to all of you. I'll never lie about how badly I want to fuck you in every position we can come up with. I want to bend you over that bed, fill my hands with your ass, and plow you until you beg me to stop because I'm too rough. I want to give you a moment to catch your breath, then take my cock that's covered with your cream and fuck your ass. I want you to be a sloppy, dripping mess with proof of how much I want you. You agreed you wanted to try submitting to me. You will obey me now."

Her breathing's rapid and shallow. Halfway through my declaration, she reached back and grabbed my pants as though she feared her legs would give out if she didn't have an anchor.

"Take your thong off and give it to me."

I kiss the crook of her neck, then move to give her room. She rushes to follow my command, turning toward me before shimmying it off.

"Which drawer has your underwear?" I walk to her dresser.

"The top one."

I reach for the dresser, giving her a moment to stop me in case there's anything she doesn't want me to see. She does nothing but watch. I open the drawer and pull out a pair of bikini panties. I take my knife from my pocket and flick it open as I observe her. Her eyes widen for a second as she watches my hands, then her gaze darts to me. I say nothing, so her attention returns to my hands.

I slice a slit into the cotton, then rip it apart. When it's in two pieces, I drop it on the floor. I do the same to two more pairs. I close the knife and drop it back into my pocket. I sweep up the rest of her underwear and drop them on the floor. I push the drawer shut and walk through the strewn panties. When I get back to the bed, I sit with my hands clasped between my open thighs.

"Throw them all out."

"I can't go commando all the time." She's indignant.

"You will. When I want your cunt or your ass, you will *not* hide either of them from me."

She assesses me, considering what I'm saying. I know she's dissecting what she believes is dirty talk and what's serious. She'll learn I'm dead fucking serious about all of it.

"Come here."

She moves slowly, but it's not with hesitation. She wants to regain some control. If she wanted it all back, she wouldn't move. She's obeying me, but she wants it on her terms. I can accept that.

When she reaches me, I stand then spin her away from me. I pinch her ass hard enough to leave a mark for a day or two. I move her hands behind her back. Once I cross them, I use her thong to bind them. I fist her hair, pulling her head to my chest, but careful not to jerk it too hard. I bring my lips to her ears.

"Pick a safe word, *chiquita*."

She licks her lips. I can't help but steal a kiss.

"Mushrooms. I hate them. I would never ask for them."

I wrap my hands around her waist and lift her as I turn. I put her on the bed, guiding her to kneel with her shoulder pressed into the mattress. I drop to my knees, spread her ass cheeks, and lick her. My tongue travels the length of her pussy and up to her asshole. I stop just before it since I don't know how she feels about that. I don't want to ruin this by taking it a step too far.

I knead her ass cheeks as my tongue dives into her, swirling inside her cunt. I pull her toward me, making her flex her hips. I nuzzle her before latching onto her clit. I work it until she's panting and moaning. She's fighting the urge to move, catching herself each time her hips rock. She's doing her best to obey my silent command. That effort turns my lust into something akin to a wildfire. It's unpredictable, roaring uncontrollably.

I continue as my right hand glides up her ass to her hands. I wrap my fingers around the material between her wrists. The heel of my other hand rubs her pubic bone before I slip three fingers into her. I ease just the tips to the first knuckle, teasing her until she whimpers. I thrust to the base of my fingers. I stroke her G-spot, and she can no longer master the need to move. Her hips rock as she pulls away from the intense pressure, then rocks back, needing more.

She cries out when I let go, but it's only long enough to strip. Then I'm inside her with one push.

"Fucking hell, *chiquita*. I'm going to come."

I fight the need because she hasn't gotten off. I pound into her, reaching around to rub her clit, desperate to make her come.

"I'm close. Don't stop, Enrique."

My balls might shrivel up and die if I stopped.

"Fuck. You feel so good, Ellie. I can't last much longer."

My dick is working on its own schedule. It wants what it wants, and it wants it right now. Blessedly, her inner muscles contract around me. I watch her arms straighten, her triceps straining. I see her fingers move, and I realize she's reaching for me. I lean my body over hers and thrust once more before blowing my load.

I want to collapse, but I'll crush her if I do. I rush to untie her wrists, then I lift her off the bed as easily as I put her on it. I can carry all of my nephews, and there's not a light one in the bunch. She's a feather compared to their two-fifteen, two-twenty asses. I sink onto the bed with her on my lap. I engulf her in my arms. If I turn her, I'll have to lift her off my dick. I don't want to break that connection.

Her hands run up and down my forearm as she tips her head to rest against me. She turns her face toward me, and even though it's a little awkward, we share a kind of kiss I only share with her. She stands, but only so she can sit on my lap with both legs hanging over my right thigh. I wrap my arm around her back and brush away hair that's sticking to her temple. She gazes up at me, and the ice that's encompassed my heart since I was ten and stabbed someone for the first time cracks a little more.

"Let me take care of you, Ellie. Let me give you everything you need. Let me try to give you everything you want." *Let me love you.*

"You are taking care of what I need. I needed that with *you.*"

"More than that. Let me do more things like cleaning out your gutters. Let me keep you company when you aren't walking your dog. Let me in."

"Don't do this. Please."

"We want to spend more time together. We're growing closer. You just don't want to acknowledge it."

I should've kept my mouth shut. I watch her withdraw into her protective shell. I realize too late she's probably heard promises like these before. She believed them, and then she lived with the disappointment for years. I want to rail at her and tell her I'm not him. That I won't disappoint her. But she's scared.

"You keep pushing me, and all it does is make me want to run. Then I feel shitty because the only place I want to run to is you. You make me feel safe because I know you'll do your best to protect me from anything. But I'll resent you putting me in a position to need you like that. Please don't make it come to that."

She makes it sound like an emotionally manipulative cycle. She's not wrong. It's not what I want or intend, but that's what I could wind up doing. But I hate how she refuses to accept what we both know is there.

"I told you I wouldn't lie about my feelings for you. You might not lie about trusting me to protect you. But you're lying about the other half of what you feel. You're pushing yourself away. You're distancing us because you don't want to admit you want something more with me. You're too scared to admit it."

She scrambles off my lap, evading my hands as I reach for her. She shakes her head, then points to the door.

"I know I'm scared. I've admitted as much. I don't need it thrown back in my face. Leave if you don't like what I can give you. Find it somewhere else."

"You know I won't. I can't. That's the whole point."

"It is. So, accept what I can give you or go without."

Chapter Eleven

Ellie

I refuse to ever cry over or in front of a man ever again. I nearly did downstairs, but I caught myself. I will *not* give up control of my emotions, and I will *not* give up control of my relationships. I'm doing my best to meet Enrique halfway, but he wants all of it. I'm a fucking coward, and I know it. But I'm too fucking gun shy—ridiculous choice of words—to trust him completely.

I'm ready to kick him out then run after him.

I'm so fucking damaged. What's worse is it's self-inflicted. I could've walked away from my marriage years ago, but I didn't. A small part of it was spiritual. Marriage is a sacrament and a covenant I didn't want to break. But almost all of it was a fear that life would be worse for my boys. I traveled, but it wasn't all the time. I was home far more than I was gone.

But each time I left, I worried about whether the boys would bathe since Tim refused to help them, even when they were young enough I feared them slipping. I worried they'd never have dinner, since I'd come home from my regular job at eight-thirty some nights, and he hadn't made them dinner. I worried he'd ignore them because he was more interested in his sports video games and the people he played with online.

I worried that if I left him, he'd remarry. Then some other woman would mother my children. That last bit was entirely self-centered, but I still feared it would be worse rather than better if he brought another woman into their lives. What if she had her own children and mistreated or neglected mine?

I worried all the fucking time.

I don't want to worry about whether Enrique's feelings will dwindle. I don't want to worry about whether he'll show a different side of him when the newness of this wears off. I don't want to worry that it'll leave me in another emotional vacuum.

"Ellie, you want the benefits of being a couple without a label."

"I want the benefits of being alone right now. Go."

"No."

I stare at him, only blinking. He said it so matter of fact.

"Fine. Stay."

I walk to the door, and I know he watches me. I leave my bedroom and go down the hall to one of the guest rooms. I walk in, close the door, and lock it. I'm naked and afraid. I'm not even going to win any money from this like on that survival show. I grab the blanket off the foot of the bed and wrap it around me as Enrique jiggles the knob.

"You really locked yourself in?" He sounds aggravated now.

"No. I locked you out."

Did he just chuckle, then clear his throat?

"You're being stubborn, but I can be patient. I can wait you out, Ellie. If nothing else, the room isn't an en suite."

I'll have to come out to pee. Fuck that. I'll hang my ass out the window and water my plants first. Yes. Yes, I am that stubborn. I did it once in college. I was visiting my high school boyfriend at the beginning of freshman year, and he was pledging a frat. I wasn't supposed to be in his room overnight. He went to see who was around and left me in the room alone. I had to pee so badly I couldn't wait. I looked around the room, then out the window. I opened it, pushed my ass out, held onto the walls, and peed. That was thirty odd years ago, but if I did it once, I can do it again.

I hear what must be him sliding down to the floor and leaning against the door. I smirk as I pull down the covers and climb into bed. I grab the remote off the bedside table and turn on the TV. Now I'm certain he laughed.

Let him.

I get through three half-hour episodes of a sitcom I've seen all the way through at least four times. I wouldn't let myself look at the door, but I know he's still there. I know if for no other reason than the alarm hasn't gone off, which it would if he left without disarming it.

"Ellie, come on." He knocks twice.

I have nothing to say that won't be hurtful or won't dig myself in deeper. I just stare at the door. I hear something against the knob, then the door opens. I should have fucking known. He has what I do. A lock picking set. How much shit can he hide in his pockets? I didn't hear him get up to go to my room where his clothes are. Though he might have grabbed them before following me down here.

He steps into the room, but he doesn't close the door. Instead, he steps beside the wall. We watch each other.

"*Chiquita*, I'm sorry."

I push back the covers and nearly fall out of bed in my rush to get to him. Fucking hell. So much for my resolve.

"Please slow down, Enrique. Please don't leave because I don't know yet whether I can get to what you want. Give me time to try."

I'm in his arms again, and I take my first deep breath since our argument started. He's still naked, and I let the blanket fall to the floor. Our bare skin touching is so fucking intimate, even though I've stood in this position with other men. I feel him harden as we kiss. He lifts me, and his cum that's still inside me makes it easy for him to slide in. He walks to the bed and climbs on with no effort. He moves to lean against the headboard. We just sit together, joined and peaceful. As I lean against him, he strokes my ass.

He's taking care of me, and I know it.

"I'm sorry too, Enrique. Please hold me."

"For as long as you want, *cariño*."

Sweetheart. He's called me that before. He has four nicknames for me, and I have none. I won't use any Italian ones because that opens me to more questions I don't want to answer. I think about a French one. *Doudou*. It sounds horrible in English, but it means cuddly toy. I think the irony would be funny. But I love these hugs we share. I enjoy cuddling with him.

Mon minet. Mee-nay. Sounds far better in English.

"Thank you, *mon minet*."

He hesitates for a breath, then laughs so hard his body shakes. It rumbles through his chest, and his abs rub against me as they contract and relax. I suspected he spoke French.

"Your pussycat?"

"I like to make you purr." I grin and waggle my nose.

"There's only one kitty purring in this house." He grinds me against him.

"You remind me more of a lion or tiger." I run my hand through his dark hair. "Jaguar. But you're sweet with me, too. I don't think you're like this with many people. It's special to me, so I want a name for you like you have for me."

"I don't think I've had a sweet side since my nephews were preschoolers. You're my haven, Ellie. I can let my guard down around you in a way I can't even do around my family. My mind will always have a low hum because my responsibilities are always there. But you let my mind quiet. You let me breathe easier and enjoy the moment. You let me be who I'd be if I weren't *jefe de jefes*."

"Boss of bosses. You're truly one of the most powerful men in the world, and I just called you pussycat."

"You said you didn't google me."

"And I haven't." Because I don't need to.

"Do you speak Spanish?"

"No. But I know what *jefe* means. I've watched TV. *De* is 'of' in Spanish and French. Easy to figure out the meaning or the significance. I may not have known your title, but I suspected your power."

"And you still accept me?"

"You wouldn't be buried inside me if I didn't." I need to tell him the truth.

"Is that part of your hesitation?"

"No. Enri—*mon minet*—I'm certain my guesses only scratch the surface."

Even with what I know about this life, I'm not lying.

"I know some of it, but I'll never know all of it. You explained that, and I accepted it. I know that's one side of you, but it's not the one I've ever seen. I can differentiate between the two and reconcile they both exist within you. You don't flash your wealth and power. I wouldn't be interested if you did. I've been around the excesses of obscene wealth, and nothing about you makes me think that's you. Maybe I'm wrong because I haven't seen how you live. But that's not the impression you've given me."

"Are you worried that if we were a couple, I'd expect you to be seen with me?"

Yes. "No."

He doesn't believe me.

"Enrique, you're the hottest man I've ever met. That alone is enough to make me want to drag you down the street to show off. 'Look at what I have, bitches. He's mine.'"

"Get dressed. We can head into Manhattan right now if you'll claim me like that."

"I know law enforcement could see me as guilty by association. I don't fear for myself if we were together. I fear them using me to get to you."

"I fear them insisting you know things I will never tell you. I fear what they'd do to you."

I'm going to have a hell of a time explaining this when the truth eventually comes out and likely rips us apart.

"My middle son, Steve, is an Assistant U.S. Attorney. He can't make everything disappear, but I'm certain he could deter some colleagues from coming after his mommy."

"Are you afraid of what your boys will think about us?"

They're going to lose their ever-loving shit when they discover which Enrique I'm fucking.

"It won't please them."

"Would they try to stop you from being with me?"

"Yes, but last I checked, I'm the parent. Not the other way around."

He gives my lips a peck. "Part of me fears you, and part of me wants to get in trouble just to see how you'd punish me." He waggles his eyebrows.

"I cannot see you letting me spank you."

"Haha. Maybe not that. But I'm certain you'd get creative."

"I could edge you."

"That's not punishment. That's torture. I'm certain there's a line about that in the Geneva Convention."

A narco-king and a mercenary jest that kinky edging is a crime against humanity. That's the opening line of the shittiest joke ever.

"*Mon minet*, can we agree to slow down? Don't push me, and I'll be more open-minded about what you want."

"That's fair. You know what I want, but I'll take you on whatever terms you can give me. I want you too much not to."

"I'm suddenly so exhausted I can barely keep my eyes open. Will you stay and sleep next to me?"

"I wasn't going to leave until you told me to again."

I wince. "I'm glad you didn't listen to me."

He swings his legs off the bed and stands. "Come, *chiquita*. Let me tuck you in."

"Good morning, *mon minet*."

I stretch and roll over as I feel Enrique brush his cock between my ass cheeks. We made it to my bed—barely—before fucking again. The movement of me on his dick as he walked down the hall got us all hot and bothered. It's ten a.m., which is ridiculously late for me to be in bed. But I didn't get to sleep until nearly four. Then we woke up twice to have sex again. Now we're ready for another round.

He rolls me onto him, and I guide him into me. We've had bursts of passion where we're clawing at each other. But we've also done it like we are now. We're slow, savoring each movement. As I gaze into Enrique's eyes, I know he's won me over. I don't want to admit defeat, but I also don't want to fight my chance to be happy.

I need to put my big girl panties on and cowgirl up.

It would be self-sabotage to run from my feelings and what he wants to offer. I'd cling to the misery I've lived with rather than let it go.

We move together, and I feel my orgasm creeping up. I ride him with one hand pressed on his chest and one on my hip. My tits bounce, and he appears fascinated. I graze my nails over his pec before pressing against it again as I come.

"I'm yours."

He freezes for a moment before flipping us. He pulls my legs up, hooking his forearms under them. He watches me as he thrusts. He understands what I mean, but he's claiming me to be sure I understand what I've agreed to.

"Mine!"

He roars as he comes. When he's done, he lowers my legs. I wrap them and my arms around him. He brings his chest to me, and I smatter kisses across his face.

"Why the change of heart, *chiquita?*"

"I'm not sure. I just woke up knowing I don't want to hold on to my anger and bitterness like a badge of courage. I don't want to be a coward. I don't want to go through life missing something because I didn't have the tits—since I don't have *huevos*—to accept it."

"You have the most magnificent tits."

I don't agree. I've nursed three kids. I've fluctuated in weight.

I've wanted a reduction, but the insurance refused. I wanted all three boys to start grad school without debt already looming over them. That was more important to me than perky tits. So, I'll take Enrique's compliment because it isn't one I'd ever give myself.

"Thank you."

I'm quick to respond. I don't want him to think I wasn't a gracious receiver and wind up with another spanking for not thinking well of myself. From his quirked brow, I know he was thinking the same thing.

"Do you have to get Constantine?"

I didn't expect that.

"No. Hunt will hang onto him until I fetch him. Constantine adores all three of them since they helped train him. But Hunt's the animal whisperer."

"Do you have to go anywhere?"

"No."

"Good."

Someone knocks on my door, and Enrique grins. I watch him roll out of bed and grab his jeans. I push back the covers and try to get out of bed, but one look and a shake of his head makes me stop.

"Wait here. If you're naughty and peek, I won't be pleased."

"Peek at what?"

"You'll see."

He disappears down the hallway. I hear men's voices, but I can't make out what they're saying. The door closes, and I listen to Enrique on the stairs. He's carrying three medium-sized boxes that are all open. He comes to my new side of the bed—the one away from the door—and puts the boxes on the floor. He pushes back the flaps of the top one, and my eyes widen so much they hurt.

"Did they see what's inside?"

I don't know if he spoke to a delivery driver or one of his men, but I'm mortified and horrified as he lifts out three vibrators of varying sizes. Beneath those is a box of Ben Wa balls and another package with butt plugs in it.

"Of course not. Andrés was nearby, but he couldn't see what's inside."

"You checked them before you brought them in the house. Do you expect a bomb or niacin?"

"I don't expect it, but it wouldn't surprise me. I know it's an invasion of your privacy, but from now on, someone opens your packages before they come in the house."

This again.

I merely nod.

"Ellie?"

"I understand. I want us more than I'm worried about your men seeing the toothpaste I order."

Is Fredrick's of Hollywood even still a thing? I guess I'll be going to a store to get lingerie rather than ordering it online.

"If there are things you really don't want opened, you can ship them to my house. Everything gets x-rayed, so no one has to open them unless they're suspicious."

"You didn't order this stuff to your house."

"Because I ordered it while I waited outside the guest room and had it overnighted. I'm here to receive it."

"You were that certain I'd give in?"

"I was that optimistic. Otherwise, I would've been hiding in the bushes to grab the packages before they wound up on your porch. Then I would've tucked tail, gone home to mope, and returned it all."

He flashes me a grin before lifting out three riding crops of varying lengths. He moves the first box aside and empties the second and third ones. By the time he's done, there are floggers, crops, handcuffs, vibrators, butt plugs, Ben Wa balls, gags, blindfolds, lube, sanitizer, and a few other things laid out on my bed. The *pièce de résistance* is the swing. It needs drilling into the ceiling, so he promised we'd do it at his house if I agreed. I told him I was ready to get a drill and stud finder.

"Before we play, let's get you fed. I'm starving, and you must be too. You'll need the sustenance to keep your strength up."

He takes my hand and tugs me off the bed. I wrap my hand around his jeans covered cock and squeeze.

"There's something I'll keep up."

He playfully gobbles at my neck, and it tickles. I never imagined this side of him. Not from the rumors I've heard over the years. Not from how serious I've sensed he is. I love it.

I grab a t-shirt and shorts and lead the way downstairs. I'm tempted to go naked. If I'm going to do this, I may as well be all in. But I don't want to splatter anything on myself if we make bacon or sausage. We move around my kitchen together with ease. I point to where things are as I mix the ingredients for a quiche. He cuts up fruit and makes toast before setting the table.

Once the quiche's in the oven, he pulls me into his arms. I rest my hands on his biceps and smile. I slide them up his shoulders and wrap my arms around his neck.

"I refuse to question this now, *mon minet*. I want to be happy with you. I want to make you happy."

"You do."

He pushes down my shorts and lifts me until my tailbone's on the kitchen island. I've always hated it and planned to take it out. It takes up too much space, but now I think I'll appreciate it. I kick the shorts free, and he pulls my hips until I'm nearly off the edge. His hands disappear under my shirt as he lowers himself to bring his mouth to my cunt. The things this man can do with his tongue.

"Fuck, Enrique."

"I'm too hungry to wait, little one. I want my peaches and cream now."

I put my hands behind me to keep my balance, but a moment later, my right hand pulls up my shirt and tucks it under my chin. I want to see everything.

"God. I'd forgotten how good this is."

I wince. I didn't mean to say that out loud. Damnit. Enrique pulls back and looks up at me.

"I don't compare everything you do to Tim, but I can't help it. This is all so new, and that's all I had for so long. It's all so much better that it amazes me. I promise I won't do it forever."

"I've understood since the beginning. But what do you mean you'd forgotten? You haven't been divorced that long."

My cheeks feel like they're on fire. Another reminder of my past. One I am firmly shoving behind me as of now.

"He stopped doing this a few years after we got married. He spent more time expecting me to blow him than he did pleasuring me. I knew he wouldn't do it, so I stopped expecting it. I'd do what I had to until we were having sex. I never pushed the issue because I didn't want to feel like he was doing me a favor or that I was a chore before he got what he wanted."

I feel so fucking middle-aged. I don't think all marriages wind up like mine did. But I can't be completely on my own, can I?

I press the back of Enrique's head to my pussy. I don't want to talk anymore. When he sucks on my clit, I brace myself again with both hands. Holy hell, this is divine. My body reacts in ways it had forgotten or never knew it could. I ache for him. Between his lips and fingers, he arouses me to the point of an aching need.

"May I come, sir?"

"Mhmm."

He doesn't lift his head. He drives me wild, and I have to lean back on my elbows. I feel the sensations build from my pussy into my lower belly. Then it's there. I sit up to grasp the edge of the counter, fearing I'll slide off as my body goes entirely lax.

"Mmm. Just the snack I needed."

He hands me my shorts and lifts me down. When I reach for him to reciprocate, he stops me. Shit.

"*Mon minet*, I don't want you to think I'm doing this because I feel obligated or because I assume you expect it."

"I know. But I wanted to do something for you for no other reason than to make you happy."

I pull my shorts on, and we wrap our arms around each other. I don't enjoy tasting myself, but I love the kiss we're sharing. His hands cup my ass, and he pulls me onto my toes.

"Mom!"

Chapter Twelve

Enrique

Ellie and I pull apart, and I push her behind me as I spin toward the man's voice.

Shock.

It's what I feel, and it's what's clearly on the man's face.

"Enrique Diaz? That's who the fu—hell you're dating?"

Ellie tries to step around me, but I hold out my arm. That makes her son lift his as though he'll reach behind him.

"William Vizzini is your son?"

What the fuck is going on? Who the hell is the woman I'm sleeping with? The one I've fallen for? Is this Daniela all over again?

Pain stabs through my chest.

The betrayal.

"Stop. Both of you."

Ellie pushes my hand out of the way and steps around me. She walks to her son, and he gives her a quick hug. She walks back to my side, watching me, nervous.

She should be. But I also hate that she fears me. That's not what I want. She stops in front of me, our gazes locked.

"Will, you didn't know until just now, did you?"

"Of course not. He wouldn't be in your kitchen, and he sure as shi—shooting wouldn't have been kissing you."

He catches himself twice. He doesn't swear in front of his mom. Good.

"Have I told you anything about him beyond his name's Enrique?"

"No. Last I heard, you didn't even know his last name. Did you before I said it just now?"

"Yes."

I don't like the insinuation, but Ellie's expression warns me to remain quiet.

"Will, didn't I tell you not to dig around?"

"Yeah. Did you tell us that after you knew who he was?"

"No. I didn't want you boys prying into anyone's private life."

She's going to hate learning how much digging I did into hers.

"Enrique, what do you think my name is?"

"Think?"

"Yes. What's my name?"

"Elodie McCann."

When Will shifts, and my gaze flies to him, she whirls around, stepping in front of me.

"I'm not shooting him if he's not touching you, Mom. You really haven't told him anything, have you?"

"No. Why do you think he's so shocked a Vizzini's standing in my kitchen? Why do you think you're so shocked a Diaz is standing in my kitchen?"

"He was doing a lot more than standing, Mom."

"Get used to it."

She doesn't quite snap at him, but it makes him jerk his chin back. The oven timer goes off, and I'm closer. I grab oven mitts while Ellie walks up to her son again. I can't hear what she whispers, but he nods.

"We wanted to be sure you got home safely."

I barely hear Will, but I catch what he says. Five minutes ago, I would've thought it was the normal question you ask when you know someone was traveling. Now it probably means something entirely different.

She doesn't keep her voice down now, and she looks over at me before turning back to Will. I set the quiche on a trivet and put the mitts down. I want to wrap my arm around her again and stake a claim. But that's utterly prehistoric and likely to cause a war with the first battlefield in Ellie's house.

"Will, what are you doing here instead of Boston?"

"I have a meeting." He stares at his mom.

Probably Salvatore Mancinelli.

"Don't say anything to Tommaso yet. I haven't fully debriefed him, and he definitely knows nothing about this. At least, I don't think so. Did you learn anything about the gate guard?"

"My friend did some digging first thing this morning. He doesn't know who the guy is. He's not one of ours."

I know far more about Will than I want Ellie to realize. He knows way more about me than I wish he did. I'm lucky I'm breathing after he caught me kissing his mother. Most sons would've put a bullet through my skull.

"Are you going to tell Steve and Hunt, Mom?"

"Of course. I'd hoped to tell you all together."

"When was that going to be?"

"I'd hoped to go a little longer, but—" She looks at me. "—it can't wait. I was going to tell Enrique over breakfast. I planned to have Hunt bring Constantine back, and we'd video call you and Steve."

"I think I better tell them. Tommaso will lose his mind. Dad'll—"

"Dad'll do nothing."

The steel in Ellie's voice makes Will back down. I see it in his eyes even if nothing else changes about him. It's not fear—at least not of her. He doesn't want to hurt her.

"I should tell him, though."

"No. You are not telling your father about your mother's romantic life. Let Tommaso or Frank."

The penny drops. Her ex-husband is Timothy Vizzini. He's

one of Tommaso's most loyal *capos*. It tempts me to pinch the bridge of my nose. Ellie has a shit ton of explaining to do.

"Do you want to stay for breakfast, Will?"

He doesn't shift his gaze from Ellie when I ask.

"Not today. I came to check on you, but I'm headed out to golf. I have a one o'clock tee time. Next time."

This time, his hug is much warmer. He glances at me, but he focuses on Ellie. She turns her head, and I can see her smile. Her entire expression is relaxed. There's nothing better for her than hugging her boys. I can tell.

"I love you, honey bear."

"I love you, too, Mom."

They kiss each other's cheek, and Will looks at me. He steps around Ellie, and she wraps her hands around his arm. He walks to me and sticks out his right hand.

"Hurt my mother, and you'll know how I earned my reputation. I'll take it all from you, and I'll make you watch. Then I'll lock you away where even God can't see you. I'll throw away the key and leave you there. Much better than killing you. That ends it too fast."

Our handshake is a test. We both squeeze. Ellie knows what we're doing, and she finally gets scared. I release his hand immediately. He turns to look at her.

"Stop protecting your mom like that, and that's when we'll have problems. Whatever happens between Tommaso and me, your mom comes first."

"Always. I'm glad we agree on that."

"Always."

Ellie gives him another quick hug before we both watch him leave the kitchen. She doesn't turn around until the front door closes. It's at least a minute before she faces me. I know I should be outraged, but I'm not. I move toward her. She doesn't shy away. She braces herself. It's just as bad. She expects me to yell at her. When I open my arms, she rushes into them.

"Ellie, what has Tommaso made you do?"

She could be a statue in my arms. Not a bit of her moves.

"*Chiquita*, you're living under an assumed name, or at least your pen name. It explains why my nephews couldn't find any records of yours."

She pulls away. She lifts her chin, defiance radiating from her.

"I get why you have to be cautious of anyone new coming near you. You told me about your ex-wife. But I didn't google you, Enrique. Not even after you told me who you are."

"Obviously, you didn't need to."

"But you had your nephews dig. Did you suspect me of something?"

"I didn't know what to think. Your home's owned by an anonymous LLC. You have no fingerprints under Elodie McCann in any system. You disappeared on a trip that you've been evasive about."

"When were you going to confront me about this?"

"I wasn't. I hoped you'd tell me when you were ready."

"And your brother and nephews were fine with that?"

"Not particularly. But not finding your past didn't change how I feel about you now and what I want in the future."

"Didn't. Not doesn't. So, it changes everything."

"No. Don't put words into my mouth and don't misconstrue them. Ask me."

"Like you did with me?"

This is potentially insurmountable. We've broken each other's trust, and that single fragile thing has been the barrier between us since the start.

She inhales and blows out the breath loud enough for me to hear. She rubs her right eye before glancing at the quiche behind me. She's unsure of herself, but she reaches out her hand. I take it, and she leads us into the living room and to the sofa. She's even more unsure. She doesn't know if I'll stay. Normally, I wouldn't sit until she does, but I do. She looks at my lap as my hand tugs her forward. She straddles me, and we gaze at each other before she closes her eyes.

"I've used Elodie McCann as a pen name since I started writing. I couldn't have people digging into my past and discovering who I was. Because you can file copyrights under pen names, I always did that. I started an anonymous LLC and made an accountant I know who lives abroad my Registered Agent."

She opens her eyes and looks at me.

"I'm certain you know that since you mentioned the LLC. When I divorced Tim, I knew it wasn't enough to legally change my name. I didn't want a paper trail if I did that. It would defeat the point. My driver's license and car registration are the only things that have my real name. I carry them in a pocket under the driver's seat in my car. If I get pulled over, I have the legit ones to give them. I have a fake driver's license for when I know it won't get run."

Her thighs flex against mine. She appears relaxed, except for that tell. This is a woman used to lying with ease.

"If you look up my real name, you'll find everything you wanted. I'm Elodie Vizzini."

The name tickles a memory, but I don't know why.

"You've heard it before, haven't you?"

"I think so."

"I've known Tommaso, Francesco, and Victoria since I was a toddler. Tori used to babysit me. We always got along, and I adored her. She always said I was the little sister she would've traded Tommaso and Frank for. Once I was fifteen and she was nearly twenty-five, we became more like peers. She was about to get married, and she made me one of her bridesmaids. When I got to college, she and I were best friends. We still are. She's going to be the most pissed about this. Not because she'll disapprove. She'll be the first one to congratulate us." She points between us. "She's going to throttle me for not telling her."

She smiles, but it droops a moment later.

"Since I grew up around them, Tommaso and Frank know me better than most. Frank and I are close in age. I used to do impersonations because I was a snarky kid. I'd do them of all the adults we didn't like. It didn't matter where they were from. I mastered all the accents I heard. I knew Tim because he's their second cousin, but I didn't pay attention to him because he and Tori weren't close. I didn't hang out with Tommaso and Frank much once I got to middle school. Tim and I dated in college, then got married a week after I graduated. Two weeks after he did. I told you I'm an accountant."

She watches me expectantly. It's my turn to close my eyes for a moment.

"Brazil. That's where you really were. You stopped in the Caymans on the way home. You didn't lie. You just didn't tell all the truth."

She nods.

"Did you volunteer?"

"Hell no. I never volunteered for any of the jobs Tommaso sent me on."

"What?"

She sighs, and it's soul deep.

"I promise you've heard of me. I'm *that* accountant."

"The Ball Buster?"

"That's what you call me?"

"That's the nicest thing everyone calls you."

That spews from my mouth before I can keep it to myself. She grimaces.

"Wait. You were supposed to have died two days ago."

"That's what Ignacio was supposed to think. I didn't die, but that persona did. I've died at least twenty times."

"You have a unique identity for each job."

"Sometimes I use the same one more than once. Ignacio knew me as Emilia Messina."

I run my hands through my hair. This is a lot to take in.

"You're why the deal went through. You knew I was the customer."

"I didn't until I got to Rio. I hoped that when you found out—because I knew you would—you'd see it as a gift not a deception."

Her shoulders round as she leans away. My hands on her hips pull her closer to me.

"You're lucky Tommaso has someone watching out for you. How'd you find a decoy?"

"I banked on finding someone at the airport who'd want to make a little extra money, and I did. The woman agreed to wear some of my clothes and board the jet. I knew Ignacio would send someone. The bullet grazed the decoy woman's arm, but Tommaso's men at the plane spread the word I died. She's somewhere with her family with enough money to start over."

"Thank God Tommaso sent enough men with you. Someone killed the hitman."

Her gaze doesn't waver as she stares at me. It's intense. It's even more than when we talked about her letting her publicist go. She was all business then. Now...

"Ellie?"

"I killed the man sent to kill me. Enrique, I didn't know which one he was, but one man at that table was your nephew. Nothing could have made me shoot him. He would've shot me before I could do that to you."

My ears buzz. My head feels like there's cotton wool between my ears. I can't process a thought. I think I might be sick. I suck in air through my nose as a lump rises in my throat. My heart hasn't raced like this in years.

Ellie says nothing. She watches me. Cautious but unrepentant.

"You're the mercenary no one's ever found. Alejandro thought you were a young man."

"I wore all black with a bulky coat to go over my backpack. I didn't get the coat back on before I left the storage room, but the van was waiting for me. From a distance, I probably looked like a skinny guy in his twenties."

"He could've killed you. He would've if he'd been closer."

"I know."

"You spared him."

"I told you I didn't know which nephew he is, but I knew he's one of them. He could be your son—you look so much alike."

"You killed seven men at that table. Alejandro said each was a clean shot. You picked them off, saving Benicio for second to last.

You made Ignacio watch everything slip away before you killed him."

I think for a moment.

"Did you train your son to threaten people that way?"

"No. I didn't have to. All my sons think that way." She frowns. "They get it from me. Tim's not a forgiving man if someone wrongs the family. He has plenty of blood on his hands. But he just gets on with it. His size intimidates people enough. If you know him, then you know Will's built the same. So are Steve and Hunt. I've never had the size to strike fear in anyone, so I use my words and my expressions. My sons use all three. They want to make sure people understand their righteous indignation, their justification for righting the wrong."

"Were you there to kill Ignacio all along, or did you decide after the hit on you?"

"All along. I'm certain Ignacio expected Tommaso to send someone for him. He wanted me dead to get the money back. He was probably pissed about the money but satisfied to have me out of the way. He didn't know Tommaso sent me for both jobs."

"You've worked all over the world then. You're the one nobody's ever found. The one who only worked for the Vizzinis."

"Yes. There isn't anywhere I haven't been."

"Is the story about Antarctica true?"

"I've heard various renditions of it. They're a sliver. I threatened to divorce Tim and take the boys with me after that one. He knows I can disappear, and he knows I would do the same for our sons. It's the one time he put his foot down and forbade Tommaso from sending me on another job like that. It was the first and only time he acted like a Mafia husband was supposed to. He didn't keep me out when Tommaso came knocking. He didn't stop him once we had Will. Having Steve then Hunt wasn't enough for him to stop Tommaso. Three sons weren't enough to stop Tommaso from demanding I work for him."

"What did Tommaso have over you?"

"Everything. One word, and Tim would be dead. He could've stripped me of everything. He could've dumped me somewhere, and I would've never seen my boys again. He could've taken them from me."

"You believed he'd do that?"

"Between Tori and Stella, no. I believe they would've stopped him. But the chance existed that they couldn't. When he made the boys train, then go on missions, it became even more imperative I obey. I didn't want a whoopsie, then me standing over a gravesite."

If anyone can make Tommaso come to heel, it's his wife. Stella Rizzo is the Chicago don's sister. She married Tommaso while her father still ruled the Mafia there. Tommaso is ruthless like me. Stella's his conscience. She's like Ellie from the sounds of it.

"There's more, Enrique."

Of course, there is. How could there not be?

"My dad's Pauly Luigiano."

That name's enough to send a chill down my spine. By day, he's a trauma surgeon, like Ellie told me. But he's a butcher by night. If Tommaso wants to exact the slowest, most merciless torture, then he calls Pauly.

"My dad's the one who taught me to shoot. My mom's nearly as good as me, but she'd only do it out of self-defense. With what he does for Tommaso, he's feared someone would go after my mom or me. He insisted we know how to protect ourselves. When I was seventeen, my dad took me to the range. Tommaso and Frank, and their uncle, Don Manfredo, were there. I outshot everyone. I had no idea I should've held back. I wasn't boasting. I just did what I thought I was supposed to. Manfredo took notice. Creepy old fucker. You know he was supposed to marry Stella, right?"

I nod. The man was beyond twisted. He reminded me of the old bratva leader. The one who trained Maks, his brothers, and their cousins. Manfredo had a plan to murder Stella and keep the dowry. He'd already killed two wives. Tommaso and Stella fell in love while he was her guard before the arranged wedding. It's what kept her alive.

"The first time Manfredo propositioned me, it was for sex. I told my dad. He dealt with Manfredo. I don't know what he said, but Manfredo never looked at me like that again. Instead, he wanted me to go with Frank to some horse race and deal with a bookie who wasn't paying out like he was supposed to. My dad refused to let me go. Once Manfredo was gone and I married Tim, it was different. My dad tried to stop it, but I gave in to Tommaso because I wanted to make Tim happy. It all went downhill from there."

"Nobody's heard about you in a couple years. Not as the accountant or as a mercenary."

"I was supposed to be retired."

I look at her as though she grew a second head. There's no such thing as retirement.

"Don't look at me that way. There aren't supposed to be Made Women. They're few and far between. Female mercenaries are just as rare in the Boston *Cosa Nostra*. I was never supposed to be part of the men's business. Tommaso even signed a letter with plenty of witnesses that I was out. Once I left Tim, he had no hold over me except for my sons. He threatened to send one of my boys down there this time. They've been on plenty of missions where I didn't intervene despite how much I wanted to. But Ignacio and Brazil were different. Not with Benicio around. I wouldn't risk it. But it cost Tommaso and Ignacio a shit ton of money. The hits didn't come cheap, and I forced Ignacio to pay me for wasting my time and for me smoothing things over with Tommaso. Or so he thought. Even if I didn't need to deposit the money for Tommaso, I still would've stopped in the Caymans to deposit mine."

She looks around her living room before focusing on me again.

"I can't take the money to the grave, and it's all blood money. I haven't touched any of it in the nearly thirty years Tommaso's been paying me. It'll go to my boys when the time comes. They can decide what they want to do with it. Until then, it's my rainy-day fund. This was my last job for Tommaso. It was the last time he holds my boys' lives over my head. If he does it again, that'll be my true starting over money. I'll need it because Rocco and Dante won't stop until they find me and punish me for killing their father."

If she doesn't kill me in my sleep, I'm marrying Ellie.

Chapter Thirteen

Ellie

He's taking this way better than I expected.

For starters, he hasn't dumped me on the floor and stormed out. He's listening to me, and I think he's reserving judgement. He hasn't flipped out and sworn to bludgeon Tommaso. I count that as a win. There's so much more I could tell him—want to tell him —but I can't.

I no longer feel any loyalty to Tomasso, but I'm a Vizzini, no matter what my last name is. I was one when I was still a Luigiano. I'm still one now that I go by McCann. My family's always been Mafia. I worked for the organization. There are things I'll take to the grave before betraying my family by blood and by bond.

"*Chiquita*, what'll happen when Tommaso finds out?"

"He can go fuck himself." My lips purse. "He'll have plenty to say. I mentioned the car with the camera, and I believe he doesn't know about it. But I could be wrong. He might already know about us."

"I don't think so. He would've confronted me about it. He wouldn't have sent you on a mission where you could've fucked him over to help me more. He would've known I'd gut him for suggesting you go."

"True. I need to tell my other boys, and you need to tell your family. How will they react?"

"It'll piss my brother off. Alejandro'll feel guilty he tried to kill you. And you'll impress my other nephews."

"Should you tell them alone?"

"No. I want them to meet you and see who you are. They can read people as well as I can. I admit I didn't guess you were a mercenary, but I've always known how loyal you are to family. I can hear it and see every time you speak about your sons. It's no surprise there're no limits to what you'll do to protect them."

"Won't they fear I'll tell Tommaso anything I hear? That I'll try to kill all of you?"

"Probably."

I wrap my arms around myself, putting a barrier between us and guarding myself. He pulls them apart, putting my hands on his heart.

"You've done everything to separate yourself from the Vizzinis. It explains why my family couldn't find anything about you."

"Or they'll think I'm still an active mercenary, and I'm living in plain sight to distract from who I am."

"They might."

Nothing he says reassures me. I'm growing more anxious by the word. I want to retreat. Just when I let myself think I have a future with Enrique, reality kicks me in the teeth. I shouldn't have let my guard down.

What was I thinking?

Everything about my past screams, "don't get close to anyone else." As though my baggage from my marriage wasn't trunks rather than suitcases, my history with the Mafia fills fucking storage tubs.

"*Chiquita*, don't run away. Can you trust me to make my family come around?"

"I'm more likely to cause a massive argument. I knew I shouldn't have agreed to anything."

His gaze hardens, and I wish I'd kept that to myself.

"You are mine, Elodie. Either you and my family can accept that without a fuss, or I will make you all understand it."

"Don't call me that. I don't need scolding."

"But you could use a spanking for arguing with me."

I stare at him for a moment as guilt threatens to pull me into its undertow.

"You know it's not that simple. I *will not* cause friction in your family. I refuse to get between you and anyone else in your family. I'm not w—"

"I dare you to finish that sentence, *chiquita*."

He cuts me off, and it's probably just as well. He's giving me a chance to save my ass from that spanking. Of course, who am I to use common sense?

"I'm not worth the trouble, Enrique."

He snarls as he rises from the sofa. He hefts me over his shoulder and pulls down my shorts. He spanks me all the way upstairs and into my bedroom. He pulls the shorts off and hurls them across the room. He puts me on my feet and grabs the front of my plain blue shirt. He rips it apart, pulling it off me. His hand comes down on my right breast.

"Mine."

He slaps my left one.

"Mine."

He pushes me to lean forward on the mattress and grabs a cat o' nine tails. He flicks it across my ass five times, the sting painful but not nearly what he could inflict.

"Mine."

He nudges my feet apart until they're more than hip-width apart. He takes a crop and strikes between my legs, nailing my clit. That one I can't keep from crying out after.

"Mine."

He pulls me up from the mattress, spins me so fast I nearly lose my balance, then devours me. He nips at my lower lip, then thrusts his tongue into my mouth. I tangle mine with his before sucking on his, rhythmically reminding him of what I can do to his cock. He coils my hair around his right hand while his left rests heavily around my throat.

"All of you is mine, Ellie. Mine to protect. Mine to pleasure. Mine to worship. You don't want out because of who I am. You want to hide *in case* something goes wrong. You're a stronger woman than that."

That punches through the flood gates.

"I don't want to be strong! I'm tired of it. Why do I *always* have to be the strong one for *everyone*? Why can't somebody else be fucking strong *for me*?"

Enrique pushes everything out of the way and gently lifts me onto the bed. I reach for him, but he pulls away. The tears that started as a dribble now cascade down my cheeks. He pushes off his jeans, then hurries to get on the bed beside me. He's still hard from when I sat on his lap. Whenever I touch him, he seems to be in a permanent state of arousal. Is being this dominant what gets him hard? Or is it me?

He lifts me like he always does. I'm not a light woman. I'm a straight up heavy one. But he makes me feel delicate and petite when he does this. That's why I don't object. He positions me and guides his cock into me. Then he eases my head to his chest.

"Shh, *chiquita*. I'll take care of you. Always. Just let me. Please."

I want to believe him. I want someone to take care of me for once. I want to feel safe for once. Even though I left Boston and the Vizzinis, I didn't feel entirely safe. Finding out there's a car with a camera pointed toward my house freaked me out more than I admitted to even myself. Having his men nearby helped, but I only felt safe while Enrique was here, and that didn't even last an entire night the first time. We've argued, and he was just punishing me, but I'm safe. He was punishing me because we're into kinky shit, but also because he wants me to think better of myself.

He wants me to see myself as he sees me.

"Baby girl, will you let me take care of you?"

His accent does something to me. And the way he said baby girl... *Dios mío.*

"*Sí, papí.*"

Where the fuck did that come from?

His hand stroking the hair down my back pauses for a moment before he holds me tighter. The hand on my ass—one always seems to wind up there—squeezes.

"Are you learning Spanish, *chiquita*?"

"No. I don't know where that came from."

"You don't mean it as the slang, do you?"

I try to shake my head.

"No, Daddy."

There I said it. Every atom of tension in me seeps out. Not even a speck remains, and I feel boneless as he holds me. I'm suddenly so relaxed, it's like I'm weightless. Nothing feels heavy anymore.

"Ellie, do you know what a Little is?"

Oh, shit!

"Enrique, that wasn't what I had in mind when I said that. I—I'm not—I feel every fucking bit of my forty-nine years. I doubt I can ever be as carefree as I was as a child, and that's a level of control I won't give up. If that's what you're into—Is that why you call me *chiquita*, little one, little girl, and now baby girl? Is that what you've been hinting at?"

"No. Not at all. I want an equal at my side who I can talk to about anything that's safe. Now that I know you're part of this world, I know I can share more than I would with a woman who wasn't. I am *not* a Daddy Dom. Never have been, and I never want that with you. But I've felt protective of you since the moment I saw you on that damn ladder. I've wanted to take care of you since I saw you straining to do a job someone taller than you should have. You are shorter and smaller than me, and you're younger than me by nearly ten years. I've asked you to let me take care of you several times. I think you feel safe with me, and I think you're finally letting your guard down enough to let me take care of you beyond getting you off. I want to stand by you and support you in all things."

"I think that's why I said it. What you just described. I don't need nor want a replacement for my father. I don't have daddy issues either. But I love that you're bigger than me, stronger than me, protective of me. You make me feel special in a way I haven't in far too long. I'm still scared this will all go up in smoke. Not because either of us wants to walk away, but because life will pull us apart. That's overwhelming and terrifying now that I see happiness around the corner, and it could literally all blow up. When I'm with you like this, it's like I'm invisible. You're a shield around me, and you won't let anyone pass."

"I will *always* be that shield, Ellie. There will be times when I can't put you first. I hate knowing that, and I feel guilty about it already. But I will always want to put you first. Whenever I can, I will. With your safety, I won't budge about you being my top priority. You letting me take care of you in a way I do with nobody else makes me feel like more of a man than anything I've done up to meeting you."

I sit back and pull his hands from around me then lace our fingers together.

"I've always loved how *papi* sounds, especially with a sexy *ay, papi*. Since it's slang, would it be weird to your family if I used that around them when I'm not Latina or a Spanish speaker?"

"No, especially since I intend to teach you Spanish. Ellie, I need you to understand enough to know if someone's a threat. There are twenty Spanish-speaking countries in Latin America, plus Puerto Rico. I'm respected but not well-liked in any of them. I'm feared in all of them. You need to know enough to get by in case someone takes you or you overhear something. How do you not know Spanish?"

"Because so many other people do. On most missions, Tommaso sent a couple of men with me, even if we weren't together after the flight. They were around in case I needed extracting. When I was in Latin America, he had men who could interpret for me. Since I'm fluent in French, Italian, and Sicilian, I can follow along mostly if people don't speak too fast. I'm fucked around Argentinians and Cubans. My problem is I don't have the vocabulary to respond. I speak enough Russian, Japanese, and Chinese to get by. I have a strong translation app on my phone, so that helps. That's how I understood what was going on during Ignacio and Alejandro's meeting."

He nods, and I wonder what he's thinking.

"Daddy, I—" I'm not sure if he really likes that, or he just agreed for my sake.

"Sí, *chiquita*."

"Daddy, I can't do anything that'll endanger my sons. And I will put them ahead of anyone else, anywhere, anytime. Will didn't get a choice, as I'm certain you know. He does what he has to, and I'm loyal to him. But beyond keeping my sons safe, I have no loyalty to the Vizzinis. If we're together and plan for this to be permanent, like you say, then my loyalty is to you and to your family. I have faith you'll never coerce me into working for you or going on missions for you, but I will. Now that you know who I am, you know what I've done. You know what I can do. I don't know who your accountant is because I've never needed to. If they ever need anything, I will do what I can. If you need my other skills, you have them."

I think I stunned him from the way he's looking at me.

"Are you pledging fealty to me, Ellie?"

"In a way, I suppose I am. You told me you'll make me your top priority when you can. I know you have to put the organization before your personal wants. I don't have to do that anymore. No one owns me anymore. I choose where I give my time and talents. I choose to put you ahead of anyone but my sons. If that means helping your organization to help you, to protect you, then I will because I can."

I don't know if he's worked through all that it means to be with me yet.

"Enrique, I want to be the one you come home to. The one you can be yourself with. You never have to be *jefe* with me. I want to give you a reprieve from who you have to be, but are you

183

prepared to be with someone who's done far worse than most of your narcos? Tommaso may have stripped most of my choices, but I got paid for each job. I'm a killer for hire."

If I have to murder anyone, I prefer being a sniper. But that hasn't always been the best method—hasn't always been an option. Enrique knows that. Enrique knows I'm morally gray. When he kisses me, I know he's fine with that.

His right hand releases mine, and he cups my jaw. It still feels like I'm watching a love scene from a movie. It's fucking erotic as hell. I move my hips, and he groans.

Talking is over.

Fucking isn't.

I rise and fall, rolling my hips as we break apart, and he sucks on my tits. I put my hands on the top of my headboard to brace myself. My ass and cunt clench when his hand lands against my left ass cheek. I hear a moan, and it surprises me to realize I made that sound. I'm so enthralled with each sensation, I don't realize my reaction.

When he bites my nipple, the headboard shakes from how I pull it as my instinct is to escape the stab of pain. But then I'm leaning into it, wanting more. I arch back, offering him whatever he wants.

"Daddy, I'm close. May I come, please?" I'm breathless and pant each word.

"No."

I whimper. I recognize that sound because I need to come so badly I feel like my entire body's vibrating with it. My pussy ached for him while we talked. Having his cock pressed against me tested my restraint downstairs. I wanted to dry hump him until I came. He rolls us and pulls out. My hands fly forward to reach for him.

"Hands over your head, *chiquita*."

He kneels between my legs, his cock glistening. He grabs a set of nipple clamps and rips the package. When he holds them up, I realize there's a chain that attaches a clit clamp too.

"Do you have any experience with these?"

"I have a pair, but I haven't worn them in ages. Even when I did, it was only a couple times. It was short-lived."

"You will always tell me when it gets past the point of hurting and will harm you."

"Yes, Daddy."

"I'll make these snug, but I won't tighten them to what I think we can work up to."

He clamps each nipple, turning the little dial. I breathe through the initial pain, having always enjoyed my nipples being bitten and tweaked. I inhale and hold my breath as he attaches the clit clamp. He leans forward and kisses my neck.

"Breathe, baby girl."

I flinch as he tightens it one turn. My fear is worse than the actual pain. I relax, and I consider the sensation. It's not as intense as I expected. However, I nearly spring off the bed a moment later when he sucks what's exposed of my clit.

Holy motherfucker!

I reach for him, unsure if I want to push him closer or push him away.

"Kneel facing the headboard again."

I do as I'm told. I hear packaging ripping once more, then he lifts my arms over my head. He guides me to bend them with my elbows up, bringing my hands behind my head like bunny ears. He snaps handcuffs around my wrists.

"Stay still, *chiquita*."

"Yes, *papi*."

"This isn't a punishment, Ellie. This is purely for pleasure."

He shifts from behind me to beside me. I close my eyes, waiting for whatever'll come next. I try not to clench my ass, knowing how that looks. But I can't help it. His palm rests on one cheek, his fingers dipping into the division, and I swear I hear him sigh. I think he's an ass man from how he's always touching mine. Though he seems pretty fond of my breasts, too.

When I open my eyes, I can see him when I look in his direction, but I can't see his left hand. I shiver when the cat o' nine tails' leather thongs trail down my back from my shoulders to my ass, then swish over it. It almost tickles. Then I hear the snap before I feel the sting.

My hips jerk away before I press my ass back. He does it twice more before I lean forward to rest my elbows on the headboard. It allows me to bend and push my ass toward him. I breathe through the increasing burn as the whip covers my lower back, ass, and upper thighs. I'm unprepared for his hand to travel up the length of my inner thigh, his arm resting between my swinging tits. He flicks the clit clamp, and I howl. Then I beg.

"Please, Daddy. More."

I don't know how much more I can take, but I intend to find out.

Fuck my life.

The moment I beg, he pulls his hand away. He rests it on my pubic bone. So close to where I need him, but a million miles away. My head falls back toward my hands, and I'm ready to clench my hair in burning frustration. It's been decades since I ached to be fucked like I do with Enrique. The need to feel full pulsing between my thighs.

Nothing is little about Enrique. The man's proportional *everywhere*. The man is a work of art. His body is sculpted perfection. If the story were about a man, he'd be Henry of Troy. He has the face that sailed a thousand ships. He fucks like a god.

I much prefer Enrique to Henry. It's way hotter. It's—

"Pay attention, *chiquita*. No letting your mind drift to handle the pain. If it's too much, safe word."

"Yes, Daddy."

How'd he know?

"I've been a Dom for a long time, Ellie. I can read you."

I'm glad he knows what he's doing. I trust him to take me places I've never been before.

His fingers graze the inside of my thighs again, making them quiver. If I were standing, my kneecaps would shake. I moan with need, not risking a word. My head lolls to my right arm, and I feel sweat bead on my forehead.

"Do you need me to stop, Ellie?"

"No!"

I straighten, not wanting to give him the impression I can't take this or don't want to. I'm just getting used to it. He rewards me by slipping his fingers into me. Blessed relief.

Finally.

Of course, it's short-lived. He isn't ready for me to come. He controls my orgasms. His fingers are inside me, but they don't move. They don't thrust. They don't stroke my G-spot. They don't rub near my cervix. They're just there. It's not comforting like when I sit on his dick while we talk. I can't stop my hips from twisting when I shift my weight from knee to knee. I'm antsy.

"You need to get off, don't you, *chiquita?*"

"You know I do, Daddy."

"I could...But I don't want to."

"Will you ever?"

He chuckles, and it's about the sexiest sound I've ever heard.

"Maybe. Why should I let you when I'm having so much fun toying with you?"

"I don't know."

I don't. It's getting hard to form a coherent thought. I breathe through the nearly unbearable pain that's a coalescence of several overly sensitive parts of my body. But the more I relax to bear it, the more my mind eases. I'm not letting my mind wander. I'm living in it. Basking in it.

I've never experienced so much physical sensation. He can do whatever he wants as long as he doesn't stop. It's my turn to sigh. He senses the change in me because he strokes my G-spot for a moment before pulling his fingers out. I don't complain. I accept it. They're only gone long enough for him to remove the clamps. He drops the whip as he shifts around me to suck my throbbing nipples as the blood rushes back into them. Since he can only reach one, the other's left longing for his ministrations. His fingers bury into me, and his thumb rubs my clit.

I yelp when I feel the riding crop's rapid tapping. He lightly swats me in fours as he moves the crop in an unpredictable pattern across my ass. He's not inflicting more pain, just keeping the burn going. He pulls away from my breast and straightens.

"You're so much stronger than you realize, little one. But you don't have to be in control all the time. Let me do it, and just let your mind rest."

"Thank you, Daddy."

He stops spanking me. While he continues to stroke me, I feel him reaching for something. It's the handcuff key.

"Move your arms around. I don't want your shoulders sore, only your ass."

His thumb rubs slow circles on my clit, and it's soothing now. A few minutes ago, it would have taunted me.

"Hold onto the headboard again."

I follow his command, and he moves to kneel behind me and wraps an arm around me. He pulls my hips back as he thrusts into me. His arm keeps me from falling forward because my arms are too tired to brace myself. He thrusts until he doesn't. I didn't keep count. He draws my ass to his lap. I yelp at the contact, but then I settle. His hands knead my breasts as I rock with him inside me.

"There is nothing more beautiful than your submission, Ellie. Your body is more than I ever dreamed of. It's feminine. It's strong. It's carried and given life. It's a temple to be worshipped."

He kisses each shoulder.

"I've never genuinely belonged anywhere. My position has always kept me apart from everyone else, even my family. But I belong inside you."

"How're you so sure, Enrique? We've never been on a date."

"How long does it take you to pull the trigger at the right moment?"

"I just know."

"Because you've made those life changing decisions in seconds for years."

"Yes."

"That's how I've known since the moment you looked down at me from that ladder. And I consider each walk and our time on the water as dates."

"Me too."

I turn my head, moving my arm out of the way, so we can kiss. That hand moves to cup his head because I'm not ready for the kiss to end. I want it to go on forever. I rise and fall on his lap as his left hand trails down my soft belly until he's rubbing my clit again. His lips brush mine as he speaks.

"Come for me, *chiquita*. Come for Daddy."

"I'm so close."

"I know. I feel you contracting around me. I won't last much longer."

My free hand releases the headboard, and my arm reaches back and wraps around him.

"Lean on me, baby girl."

There's so much more to that than my head on his shoulder. My eyes slide shut, and I do as he says. The moment I accept I'm where I belong for the rest of my life, my orgasm explodes. I kiss him again, my hand fisting his hair. His arm tightens around my waist, pinning me in place. Pinning me where I belong.

Chapter Fourteen

Enrique

Ellie's surrendered to me.

I feel it.

Will she finally let herself feel for me what I feel for her? It's not love. Not yet. But it'll build to that if she doesn't put any more walls between us. We need time together. We need to do normal couple things.

I withdraw, and neither of us like it. But we shift to lie on our sides facing each other. She inches into my embrace, and we bask in our afterglow. Her fingertips trail over my back absentmindedly, and it's comforting and arousing all over again. I don't remember the last time my jimmy's done this many jumping jacks. I'm insatiable with her. It's not like I've been a hit it and quit it kinda guy, but basically. My partners have always known I have no emotional attachment beyond lust, then enjoying the physical fulfillment after a good fuck.

When I've been a Dom, I've enjoyed the aftercare. But it was never sentimental. It wasn't perfunctory either. It just never had the overwhelming peace I feel with Ellie. It had no tenderness and fondness. It was praising and comforting. Never loving.

I watch as her eyes grow heavy, and I fight the urge to sleep because I don't want to miss watching her. But I'm exhausted too.

I love seeing Ellie bound to her dining room table. She's spread eagle on it, her arms and legs secured to the table legs. I roll the Wartenberg pinwheel over her nipple before circling it three times. I leave a trail of pinpricks between her tits as I move it to circle her belly button. The sensation follows as I travel over her right hip bone and down the inside of her thigh all the way to the arch of her foot. It twitches. I shift to the left, lingering behind her bent knee. Then I'm arriving at the juncture of her leg and hip. I run it over the crease. I'm careful as I move it along the outside of her pussy lips, not wanting to pinch.

"You've been a naughty *chiquita*, haven't you?"

"*Sí, papí.*"

She tests the phrase, and my cock's ready to abandon me and find its own way into her cunt.

"Why am I edging you?"

"Because I came this morning when you didn't give me permission."

"That's right. Who does your body belong to now?"

"You, Daddy."

"Who decides when you come?"

"You do."

"Then what made you think you decided?"

"I couldn't help it. It just happened."

"You thought I couldn't tell. You thought you'd get some relief then carry on. You thought you could fool me. Why can't you?"

"Because you already know me."

I lean forward and nip at her belly, grazing my teeth over the flesh before sucking. I've marked her all over her body since we woke up from our nap yesterday. We've had round after round of kinky sex since then. I've tied her up all over her house. We've used everything I bought except for the swing.

I watch her as I straighten, then continue to draw the pinwheel over her in an unpredictable pattern. Goosebumps rise on her arms and legs, both from anticipation and her natural response to the light pricks. I've been edging her for the last half an hour.

She's done so well with everything we've tried over the past two days. I've offered her all the things she's asked for, and she's been open-minded, trying all the variations I suggest. Every moment we share like this, we rebuild the trust that cracked and continue to make a solid foundation for a relationship I no longer have doubts about.

It was hard not to question myself as I learned about the past she didn't want to share. She's told me a little more, and if I weren't committed to spending the weekend with her, I'd be in Boston beating the shit out of Tommaso and Frank. As is, once they know I'm with Ellie, they're going to owe me a shit ton to make up for what they did.

I don't care if it was years before I met her. Just sending her on the mission last week is enough to make my blood boil. Rather than stew in anger, I keep my focus on the woman tied to the table in front of me.

"Do you think you deserve to come yet?"

"I don't know that I deserve it, but I'd really like it."

My lips twitch. She has a colorful sense of humor, a quirky sense of humor, a sarcastic sense of humor, and a dry sense of humor. I've seen all of it this weekend. It's only made me want her more, and it's made it easier for me to open up to her.

I slip my fingers along the outside of her pussy lips, then twist the vibrator that's running on high with the little arm turned away from her clit, rubbing the smooth strip of skin. I bring it back to her clit, and she tries to arch her hips off the table, but she has no leverage since her calves hang over the end.

This position leaves her pussy resting at the edge. I put the pinwheel aside and merely watch her as the vibrator makes her tremble. I observe how her body tenses until she's straining to get off. She wants it so badly right now. She'll risk another punishment just for momentary relief. I withdraw the vibrator and put it on the tablecloth we laid for this express purpose.

I lower myself until I'm kneeling between her legs. I lick and groan at her sweet, musky taste. I've never minded eating out a woman, but it's never been my favorite thing to do. However, with Ellie, it's like nectar from the gods. I think some of it's knowing I'm the first man to do this in so long. It's almost like I'm actually her first. At our ages, it's practically impossible to try anything we haven't somehow done with previous partners.

As I dip my tongue into her, I twist the plug I put in her ass this morning. We started with a medium-sized one for a few hours yesterday while we watched a movie, and she warmed my cock. She offered, and I said yes. We spent the first half of the movie with my cock in her mouth. It was divine torture for me. Then she sat on my lap, continuing to warm it, flexing her pussy every so often to keep me hard.

Now I bring her to the edge as I spin the largest plug. Her eyes are closed as she moans over and over. I know how sensitive she is after all of this tormenting. I don't want to go from hurting to harming her. I'd never trust myself again, and this isn't something I want to give up sharing with Ellie.

Just the opposite. I hope this intimacy continues to grow.

I slide three fingers into her, rubbing her clit in between flicking it with my tongue. I planned to leave her needy even longer, but I don't have the heart to do that.

"Come for me, *chiquita*. Let me taste how much you love my mouth on you."

"*Sí, papí.*"

Those two words make my heart feel three sizes too big in my chest and my cock about ten sizes too big in my boxer briefs. After her son walked in on us yesterday, we decided going naked wasn't a good idea. We settled for a tank top and little shorts for her and my boxer briefs for me. That's less traumatic if anybody walks in on us than her in nothing except maybe a bra, since I refuse to allow her to have her panties back. In fact, I laid a fire and symbolically burned the ones I slashed, the rest I threw in the trash.

"I'm so close, Daddy. Just keep going, please, a little more."

Her wish is my command.

"Yes, yes, just like that. I'm coming. I'm coming, Daddy!"

That word's never been my thing before. I've never asked a woman to call me that. I never even considered it. It's something I haven't shared with anyone other than Ellie. I guess we have a first, after all.

Her cream coats my lips, and her taste is still on my tongue as I stand. She watches me as I lick my lips and grin. She opens her mouth and turns her head to the side, her invitation obvious. I untie her legs and move her up the table, so her head is at the far end, able to tip back off the edge.

I don't rebind her legs, so her feet come up onto the tablecloth. She pushes back a bit more until she's comfortable. As I drop my boxer briefs, I realize our precautionary minimal clothing is moot since we're both naked now, and she's tied to a table. It was a placebo thought because it would traumatize any of our family to walk in on us like this. Hell, it would traumatize Ellie and me if anyone saw her like this. But it makes us worry less when we aren't in the middle of sex.

When we live together, I question whether I would give keys to her sons like they have to this house. I'm already picturing her sharing a home with me. We'll have to implement the same rules for my family as we'll have with hers. They need to call or text as they arrive in the neighborhood, then call or text again as they come through my gate. That way we should have ample time to get Ellie dressed since I intend to keep her naked as much as I can.

I stroke my cock three times, then tap her lips. She opens for me and sucks my cock practically down her throat. She works it in a way that tempts me to think about her past and the clear experience she has doing this. But I refuse to allow ghosts to share this time with us.

I lace my fingers through her hair, helping support the weight of her head as it bobs.

"Ellie, you're going to make me embarrass myself with how

fast I come. Fucking hell, *chiquita*. You're going to swallow all of me, aren't you?"

She hums, and the vibration nearly does me in. I intended to fuck her throat, but she's the one fucking me. I can't get enough of her. Everything about her lures me in like a siren.

"Ellie, if you don't want to swallow, snap."

Her hands flatten on the table. I don't hold back.

Considering how many times I've already come, it shocks me there's still any left. I know how the male anatomy works, so that's an exaggeration. But it defies understanding, since every orgasm is so intense.

When I withdraw, she licks her lips just like I did. Her grin matches mine. I hurry to unfasten her arms and help her sit up. I rub and move them around. She promises she's not stiff anywhere from the many times I've restrained her.

I've spanked her enough her ass remains a deep shade of pink. I noticed the beginning of a bruise last night. I stopped immediately. That's not my goal. I like her ass cherry red while I'm spanking her. And I love seeing how pink it still is. But I don't want to mar her with bruises.

I'm about to carry her upstairs when I remember what's at the other end of the table. I guess her son really has me spooked because I don't want to leave anything behind. I grab the vibrator and the pinwheel along with the pillowcases and sheet I used to bind her to the table. She holds out her hands to make it easier for me. I pass her everything as I stoop to gather them, then I lift her off the table and into my arms.

"I can walk. I don't think my feet have touched the floor since yesterday morning."

"Why should you walk when I prefer to carry you? I enjoy having you where you belong."

"And where is that?"

"In my arms."

"You say the sweetest things, Enrique."

She kisses my cheek and rests her head against my shoulder as we make our way to her bedroom. What I have in mind next involves a mirror. I place her on the bed before I grab the full-length mirror on a wooden frame that lets it tilt up and down. As I lay it on the floor, I know she's watching, wondering what I'm doing. I'm certain she can guess part of it. I set it up in front of the rocker recliner she has in her room. I grab the lube from the bedside table before I offer her my hand. She takes it without hesitation.

"You're letting me walk somewhere?"

"For now, little one."

I guide her over to the chair and mirror. We put a foot on each side of the mirror.

"Lean forward."

She grasps the arms of the chair. I twirl the butt plug again, gliding it in and out. Sometimes all the way to the tip. Sometimes barely enough to notice.

"Do you think you can take me, Ellie?"

"I've known I can the whole time. You're the one who insisted on stretching me."

"Because I don't want to harm you. I never want that."

"I know, Enrique, and I've never worried you would. You'll always be careful with me and always mindful of your size and strength. I know if you were thoughtless and harmed me, you'd never forgive yourself, and we wouldn't do this anymore. That would be an epic tragedy."

"Epic?"

"Yes. Of the greatest proportions."

"You really are a little kinky."

"A little? I thought I was showing you I'm pretty fucking kinky all the time."

It's not like we haven't had vanilla sex. That was partly to let her body rest. But it was more about sharing something neither of us is ready to say. It was practically a spiritual experience. It was like the first time we did it slowly. We watched each other the whole time, and I didn't want that connection to end. I don't think she did either because we both fought to hold out for as long as we could.

I ease the plug from her and let it fall to the floor beside my foot. I snap open the cap and pour lube over my cock. I let a stream dribble down her ass to the place I haven't visited yet, but I will soon claim.

"What's your safe word, little girl?"

"Mushrooms."

I use the tip of my cock to spread the lube around, pressing into her enough for it to dribble farther inside her.

"Look down, Ellie. Watch us."

We peer into the mirror together. I've had sex in rooms with mirrors on the ceiling. I've had sex standing in front of mirrors.

But I've never done this. The view is mesmerizing as I sink into her over and over again.

"Enrique, I don't...I didn't know...Holy fuck."

"I know, Ellie. I feel the same way."

We continue to observe ourselves. I'm not a young man anymore, but I feel like a horny nineteen-year-old around her. It's not like I've ever needed a little blue pill to get me up or keep me hard. But it's been a long time since I could have round after round of sex as fast as I do with Ellie.

It's almost like I'm making up for lost time. All the years she wasn't in my life. All the years I wish she had been.

"How are you doing, little one?"

"Don't you dare stop."

I chuckle as I obey her command. But when I know I'm close, I reach past her into the box where we placed all our new toys and implements last night. I snag another vibrator that's even wider than the one I used downstairs. I turn it on and slide it into her pussy.

"You take it, Ellie. Do what you need to."

"Thank you."

The two words come out on a moan. My hands grasp her hips as I move faster. The gliding rocker pulls her away as I thrust, then supports her as I pull her back. I drive into her over and over as she moans, begging for me to keep going.

"God, Enrique. Everything's so tight and so full. Don't stop."

"Don't worry, little girl. I'm not. My balls would never forgive me if I did."

"Enrique, yes...Yes...I'm coming. I'm coming."

I don't hold back as I shoot my load into her. I groan and tilt my head back. When we both come back down to Earth, we look in the mirror. As I pull out some of my cum drips from her ass.

"Enrique, if I wasn't completely yours before, I am now."

"Nothing will keep me from you. *Chiquita*, I will move heaven and earth for you, and I'll burn it all down if anybody stands in our way."

"We're going to have to face the real world soon, *chiquita*."

"But I don't wanna."

She playfully pouts, and I chuck her bottom lip before giving her a kiss. We're walking into her living room where we're going to jump on a video call with her boys. We set it up for this evening because we want to go into the new week with everything out in the open. Plus, she's understandably concerned that the longer we wait, the greater the likelihood Tommaso will find out on his own. Then he'll tell her other two sons. She also doesn't enjoy expecting Will to keep a secret from his brothers. She suspects he probably already told them.

However, she won't assume that, and she doesn't want him to bear the responsibility of being the one to tell them. It would only come across as though she's hiding from them. That's not what she wants.

She heads into her office, and I can see her from the living room. She unplugs her laptop and brings it over to where I'm standing by the sofa. When we sit, she positions it so the camera will allow her sons to see both of us. She already texted them the link to this call. They're waiting for her when we hop on together. Her brow furrows as she looks at the three young men.

I've only met Will. I haven't seen the other two besides the photos I've noticed in her house. I barely know their names. I was aware Will had brothers, but they weren't men I'd ever met or had any interaction with.

"Hi, boys."

She tries to keep her tone airy, but their scowls deepen, knowing there's nothing light about this conversation.

"Will, did you tell your brothers?"

"Of course I did. What did you think was going to happen when I found out you're involved with a *jefe de jefes*? When you wind up with your head cut off and the rest of you is hanging from a bridge, we need to know who to go after."

"William." She snaps his name, and anger radiates from her.

I remain quiet, though I have plenty I'd like to say.

"For starters, you know as well as I do Enrique is Colombian, not Mexican. Don't use recycled stereotypes unless you want me calling you all Guidos as though Mafias are interchangeable from Boston down to the Jersey Shore."

"That's not fair, Mom, and you know it."

"Then don't sound like a petulant child."

Will clams up, but it's easy to tell he has far more he'd like to say. Since we can see Constantine nudging one of her sons, I know he must be Hunt. It's Steve who speaks next, and I can tell he's the peacemaker in the family.

"Mom, we thought you wanted as far away from syndicate life as you could get. And rather than run from it, you've run right back to it. You couldn't pick somebody more entrenched than Enrique Diaz."

"That's just the way life worked out. It wasn't like either of us planned this."

Hunt's eyebrows shoot straight up, and he glowers at me. I feel it's time for me to speak up.

"I did not target your mother. I didn't know who she was until yesterday morning when William showed up. Your mother has done an excellent job protecting her anonymity. I never would've guessed, and she never gave a hint."

She jumps in when all three of her boys open their mouths at the same time.

"You know I disappeared, and you know how well I can stay hidden. If Enrique and his family didn't discover who I am, then it means I did the job properly."

"But do you really believe, Mom, that he didn't know who you are?" Hunt pats Constantine's head before gently easing the dog away from him, so he can lean back and cross his arms.

"Do you believe I'll give away family secrets to Enrique? Is that what this is about? You're worried what I'll tell him?"

All three boys shake their heads.

"So, you believe he'll torture me to get information from me?"

Three sets of eyes dart from their mom to me before looking back at her. None of them react beyond that.

"What would Enrique have to gain by doing that? If he'd discovered who I was sooner, he would've just recognized my reputation sooner. He would know I'm not telling anybody anything I don't want to. He also would've known I haven't done any jobs for Tommaso in quite some time. So, anything I might have to tell him wouldn't be very current."

"There are old family secrets you could divulge."

"Hunter, do you really believe I would give away a single bit of our family business knowing how that would endanger you if I did?"

"He could force it out of you."

Her expression hardens as she looks at her boys.

"Nobody's ever gotten anything out of me, and nobody's going to. It's not like people haven't tried."

"Ellie, what're you talking about?"

I turn to look at her rather than the screen. I haven't seen any questionable scars, so that makes me wonder, are there invisible ones? What have men done to her?

She puts her hand on my thigh where the boys can't see it and squeezes. She turns to offer me a reassuring smile.

"If anything horrible had happened to me, nobody would've let me live to tell the tale. The reputation I cultivated as the accountant meant people knew Tommaso would avenge me. You said yourself my nickname was 'The Ball Buster.' I didn't know that, but that should be some reassurance."

"Hardly."

My voice overlaps with her three sons, and we scowl at one another. This conversation isn't progressing as well as I'd like it to.

"Look, boys, I understand what an unlikely match we are. I understand the position it puts you guys in. Don't you think it's going to be even harder for Enrique?"

"Not if this has been his plan all along, and his family knows about it." So much for Steven being the peacemaker.

"If Enrique were going to do something to me, don't you think that would've happened the moment he found out who I am, so he could keep me from speaking to any of you?"

"Or maybe, Mom, he's planting things he thinks you'll repeat to us."

"So, you expect me to betray all of you?"

She lifts her hand, her index finger pointing up as she circles it.

"That I would betray the three of you by giving away Vizzini secrets and endanger you. And you think I would betray Enrique by giving his secrets to you? That's how little honor you believe I have?"

All three boys grimace.

Questioning anybody's honor and loyalty is an invitation to a duel.

"I know this isn't easy for anyone, like I said. But I'm happy with Enrique."

"You barely know him."

Hunt snaps. His miniscule patience is gone. He throws his hands up in the air, fully exasperated at his mother. Constantine's head nudges his arm, and the dog looks toward the camera as though he wishes to get between Hunt and us.

"Maybe we will get to know each other better and realize we're not as compatible as we thought. Then we go our separate ways."

"You really think he's just going to let you walk away?" Will leans forward as he glowers at me.

"And you really believe I would harm your mother?"

"It wouldn't be the first time your family targeted women."

"And every time someone in my family thought to take it upon themselves, I punished them."

"Obviously, you didn't do an outstanding job if it happened more than once."

He's not entirely wrong, but many of the times my nephews acted questionably with the other syndicates' wives, it's been us or them. And as much as they didn't want to target women, they still put our family first. But I don't need to explain myself or them to anyone.

"You saw me yesterday morning with your mom. You heard what I said about protecting her. However any of you feel about me and about this relationship, it's your mother's decision what happens. I won't walk away. It'll either be her leaving me, or us staying together for good. I won't end it. That means I need all three of you to forgive your mom for the slight you think she's giving you because I need to know you'll never hesitate to protect your mother."

"*Eres un verdadero pedazo de mierda si crees que no protegeríamos a nuestra madre solo porque está con un gilipollas como tú.*" You're a real piece of shit if you think we wouldn't protect our mom just because she's with an asshole like you.

"Steven!"

She probably didn't need to understand all of that to recognize words she wouldn't want them to say about me or in front of her, considering how Will caught himself before he swore in front of her. That was not just him. I believe that's a rule they all have from the flash of guilt on Steve's face before he goes back to glaring at me again.

"Steve, I don't think you'd begrudge your mother your protection. But I need to know that no matter what happens, she's the first person on your mind. That none of us assumes someone else is there for her unless we see it with our own eyes.

"She's more likely to protect you than you are to protect her."

Steve's hunch isn't wrong about that. But I never want Ellie in that position. I pray it never comes to that. However, I'd be a fool not to know it very well could.

"Boys, you know how unhappy I was for so long. You knew what it was like for me. It's the opposite of what it was, and I have the chance to be happy. I was fully prepared to give that up and let it pass me by because it terrified me that someone would disappoint me again. But hopefully I have many years ahead of me. And even though I told myself I wanted to be and would be fine on my own, that's not really what I ever wanted. I told myself that to justify not having another failed relationship, to avoid that kind of hurt ever again. But I want to be with someone who makes me happy. Somebody who understands me. Somebody who can accept my past and not resent me for the things I can't tell him. There's so much of that, and there are not too many men who would be okay with that. Their suspicion would be an assumption I'm unfaithful to them or that I don't care about them the way they care about me. I don't have to make excuses with Enrique. And that means I have a chance again that I haven't had since I was twenty years old."

She pauses to look at me again, and I hate she's in the middle of this. But as she looks at me, even though she's speaking to her sons, I feel like I'm the only person in the world to her.

"It's a chance I never believed was possible. I know Enrique isn't who you want me to be with, but are you going to begrudge me finding somebody who cares about me and will take care of me the way I'd always hoped someone would?"

"Couldn't you find somebody else—anybody else? Even a Mancinelli?"

I grit my teeth at Will's suggestion. That is not a family I ever want to picture Ellie with. Not that I want to picture her with anybody but me.

Ellie snorts.

"And who in that family would I wind up with who isn't an infant? There's not an unmarried man over the age of twenty-five.

You know I would never cheat, and they never would consider it either. I know this isn't what you want from me. And I understand that. I already admitted I also understand the position this will put you in. But I'm asking you again to at least give us a chance to see whether we have something that will last. I'm asking you to give me the opportunity to have something I never thought I would."

Steve goes back to being the peacemaker again. "Mom, none of us want to see you unhappy. Just the opposite. You deserve the chance to find someone who will treat you the way you always should've been treated. But none of us'll think that this is a good idea. That anything good can come of this. No one would call Enrique naive, but that's what this seems like. If he's not naive enough to think this could work out, then there must be something else at the heart of it. You can't blame us for being skeptical."

"I don't blame you for being skeptical at all. But you will not insult him. You will not cause problems where there don't need to be any. We'll have enough problems from Tommaso without you guys adding to it."

"Enrique, what about your family?" Will seems to have cooled off the most.

"My family knows I care a great deal for your mother. They know I wouldn't bring any woman into my life if I didn't see potential for it to be permanent. They also know after the problems I had in my first marriage, I'm wary about bringing in anyone who could sabotage my family. They'll have the same concerns and complaints as you. There's just more of them."

"Do you believe they can accept Mom, or will she always be an outsider?"

"That's a fair question, Hunt. I know and trust my family. It'll take a little while for Ellie to gain their trust like it'll take me a while to gain yours. They trust my judgment. I've been leading this family since I was younger than any of you. They know I'd never do anything to risk their lives and what I've built. So, they know I don't enter this lightly. I'm not with your mom on a whim. If I were using your mother, my sister-in-law would never forgive me. Her opinion of me matters a great deal. My sisters wouldn't forgive me either, and they terrify me."

That garners a chuckle out of all of them. Hunt's eyebrows rise as he speaks.

"So, in other words, they'll get along with Mom like a house on fire."

"Your mom'll fit in perfectly, especially once she learns Spanish."

Will jumps back in and ends the moment of needed levity.

"What type of protection are you putting in place for her? I saw the guy in your driveway. He stopped me. If I didn't look enough like my mom for it to be obvious I'm her son, he wouldn't have let me pass because I wouldn't have told him my real last name. I wondered who he was and whether he was private security Mom hired. Then I saw you together, and it made sense. One man in the driveway and one man tucked away in the trees aren't nearly enough protection for our mom."

"I agree, it isn't. Once we go out in public, it won't be a secret we can keep. So, from here on out, your mom will have two regular bodyguards. She'll also have a man from my family."

Will shakes his head. "Your brother travels too often. He disappears all the time. What happens if he's on the schedule and suddenly has to take off?"

Will's concern is valid.

"I never planned to put Luis on the rotation. It'll be my nephews. There are five of them. There's no one I trust more with your mom's safety than them. No one outside my family, except for you three, will ever be good enough for me to trust entirely with Ellie's life. So, it will always be at least one of them if she's not with one of you. I understand why you might not appreciate me insisting one of them join you if you're out with your mom. I won't insist upon that. But, besides you three, she will always have a Diaz with her."

"Mom?"

Hunt tilts his head as he watches Ellie. I can see us on the screen, but I look toward her when her youngest son speaks.

"Are you all right with this? You've never had bodyguards with you at all times."

"I know, but I haven't been in this position before. As senior as Dad is, it's not like he's the don. Stella always has one of the guys in the family with her. I see this as being no different. I appreciate Enrique wants me to have that level of security."

"Before you accuse me of assigning them so I can spy on her or control her—"

"No." Steve interrupts me as he shakes his head. "It's obvious from the way Mom started leaning against you when we began talking about her protection that not only does she trust you, but it's obvious relief on her face. Mom's no fool. It's one thing for us to hear her say she trusts you and that we should too. It's another to see it. She was never this relaxed around Dad. From the way you've wrapped your arm around her waist, you're being discreet, not wanting to rub this in our faces. But you're supporting her, and she deserves that. It'll take us a while before we're absolutely certain. We know you don't blame us for being suspicious. It's obvious how different things are between you and what our mom has known for so long. None of us wants to begrudge her finding somebody who will take care of her the way she deserves. Who won't just expect her to give and is only willing to take."

"Just because your mom can defend herself and take care of herself doesn't mean she should have to."

All three of them visibly relax when I say that. They don't like that I'm me and all that I bring with me. But I think they'd be just as concerned about another man taking advantage of her.

Ellie and I remain quiet as we observe the boys looking at each other through the computer screens. It's obvious how close they are and how they've learned to depend on one another in situations where they can't speak. Some agreement passes between them before they look at us again.

As the oldest, it seems to fall on Will's shoulders to pass the final judgment.

"Like I told you yesterday morning, do anything to hurt our mom—disappoint her even in the least—ruffle a single feather—

and you'll learn why I deserve my reputation. And my brothers may not be Mafiosos every day like I am, but don't underestimate them because none of us will forgive you if you do anything we consider even a smidge wrong. One word, one thought, one anything, and we won't care who you are, what your title is, or who could come after us. We won't forgive you."

"I believe you. And like I said yesterday, the moment you stop being that protective of your mother is when we'll have problems."

"Can you live with this, Mom?"

"Yes, this is better than I could've hoped for."

Will sighs. "I don't envy you having to face your family, Enrique, when there's only three of us and six of them."

"Nine. There're my five nephews, my brother, my sister-in-law, and my two sisters. There's no way any of them won't have an opinion on this."

Ellie looks over at me. "When will I get to meet them?"

I squeeze her hip as I look at her.

"Tonight."

Chapter Fifteen

Ellie

All things considered, the conversation with my sons went better than it could've. It was tense at times, but it didn't explode into an argument. I don't think they're going to say more once I'm alone, and Enrique can't hear. They don't approve, but they're closer to accepting it. For now, I'll take that.

I knew where Enrique's house is, but I've never been here.

Holy fuck.

So, this is how the other half lives.

I lived in a three-thousand-square-foot home and felt it was more than big enough for five people. We all had space, which was great. We also had plenty to clean. Tommaso, Frank, and Tori all live in homes like the one I did. Theirs are a bit bigger than mine was. But the houses around me are bonified mansions. They'd swallow my current house and my old house in one bite. They must be seven- to nine-thousand-square-feet homes.

I can't imagine rattling around in such a humongous house on my own. But as we arrive at the gates, and I see the driveway more clearly, I realize why. There are four cars in the driveway.

I'm not feeling anywhere near as confident as I walk into

Enrique's home for the first time. We've taken more showers
together than any two people need in two days, but shower sex has
never been that good. If he didn't already carry me around whenever he wants, it would've terrified me the first time he picked me
up with the slick shower floor. He swears he can carry all his
nephews and that Alejandro—who I've seen—is the biggest. I
don't want to know if he's practiced carrying them or needed to. I
won't ask.

But while Enrique finished our last shower alone—much to
his disapproval—I stared at my closet, hating everything. I finally
settled on a pair of capris and a floral top that covers my ta-ta's
completely. I don't need anyone thinking I'm inappropriate with
my clothing. I'm already that because of my family.

"*Cariño*, you look beautiful. I won't leave you alone with
them. I promise."

He kisses my cheek, and I force myself to relax. No matter
how many times I've faced death, this is the worst. It's not one
person gunning for me. It's nine. It's a fucking firing squad.

"Thank you, Daddy." I whisper as I kiss his cheek in return.

He gives my hand a squeeze, then wraps his arm around my
waist as we head toward voices I think are in the dining room.
They're already here.

"Don't worry. If they don't remember to call before they arrive
from now on, I'll change the locks."

I love how when he smiles, creases form around his eyes and
mouth. It's sexy as all get out, and I'm certain it makes women wet
and men hard, but it reassures me. He pats my ass as we approach
the group.

I try to step away, not wanting to antagonize anyone by
walking in with Enrique's arm around me, but he pulls me to his
side. His lips come to my ear.

"No one will stop me from touching you whenever and
however I want. I will not hide how I feel about you from my
family. This isn't about publicly claiming you, even though I will.
This is about me finally being with someone I share genuine affection with. Someone who makes me happy when I'm beside them."

"I don't want to anger them even more."

"That's for them to work through. My cartel. My home. My woman."

He's still smiling, but he's dead serious.

I can't react because we're stepping through the archway, and there are nine people staring at us. I offer as warm a smile as I can muster. I sweep my gaze over the people gathered before me, but when my gaze meets Alejandro's, his eyes widen. He shifts his focus to Enrique, and his shock morphs to anger.

"Alejandro, she could've shot you, but she didn't. Be glad she figured out we're related."

Mothertrucker.

That isn't the introduction I wanted.

"What?" An elegant woman pushes past two men to stand in front of Alejandro.

Marvelous.

"Catalina—"

"Mama, I was safe. But I nearly killed *tío's*—"

Alejandro looks away from his mom to Enrique to me, and back to Enrique. He doesn't know what to call me. I don't know what I am since we're in a committed relationship I swore I didn't want.

"*Novia.*" Girlfriend.

I know that one. Better than something like lady friend. That would make it sound like he's a widower, and I'm eighty.

Alejandro looks back at me, and there's something akin to wonder in his expression. I brace myself.

"I went in that room afterward. The angle was tight, and the hole was meant for an eye not a rifle muzzle. You must have stood on a rickety crate. Knowing that makes your accuracy even more impressive."

"Thank you." *I think.*

I'll take it as a compliment, but I'm uncertain that's what it was. Catalina, who must be Alejandro's mother, observes me. Judges me.

"How did you know who my son was?" Her accent is thicker

than Enrique's, reminding me she didn't move here until much later in life compared to Enrique and Luis.

"There was something familiar about him that reminded me of Enrique. He was never my target. When he turned toward me, the wall hid me, but I could see him clearly. They're two peas in a pod. It was like looking at a younger version of Enrique. There was no doubt who he was, even though I didn't know which nephew." I lift my chin, and my tone hardens. "I would never do that to Enrique."

I dare them to accuse me of something—anything—that betrays Enrique. I don't feel as defiant as I sound or look. That doesn't mean I don't speak the truth.

"You're a Vizzini."

I know the man who just spoke must be Luis. The family resemblance among all the men is uncanny. Luis and Enrique could be twins if Luis's hair was a little darker. There's another man standing beside a seated woman who looks tired. It's unquestionable that the younger one is Luis's son. It's like a look back in time for Luis and a fast forward for his son.

"By marriage, I was. My family's ties with the Vizzinis go back generations. Ever since my father's family came to America from Sicily. My mother's side of the family only goes back to the fifties."

"But you're not a Vizzini anymore?" Luis isn't wasting a minute to launch the Inquisition.

"You know I live under an alias since you couldn't find me. I could've changed my last name back to my maiden one, but I want the same last name as my sons. My father is Pauly Luigiano." I let that bomb explode for a moment. "My maiden name is probably more dangerous for me on my own than being a Vizzini."

The Vizzini name protects the bearer because they're close enough to the don's family to still have it. There're plenty who hold grudges against my father for what he's done to men who wronged the don's family over the past fifty years. The Luigiano name would paint a bullseye on me for anyone who wants revenge against my father.

"Let me introduce everyone before we dive into that, *manito*."

I guess *manito* is the diminutive for little brother. I'm learning already.

Enrique introduces me to his other sister, Luciana, and his sister-in-law, Margherita. Then I meet Pablo, his heir apparent. Is part of his suspicion that I'll have a son who'll usurp his position? He needs to know not only can't I have more kids, I wouldn't even if I could. Not just because Enrique is who he is. That phase of my life is over.

Javier, Joaquin, and Jorge look similar to the others, but not as much as Alejandro and Pablo look to Enrique and Luis. They must take after their father more. I know their mother is a widow, so that explains why Luciana is alone, but no one says where Catalina's husband is. She's wearing rings.

"The rest of this conversation with Ellie will take place in my office."

I don't like how Enrique summarily dismisses his sisters. If we're moving to his office, they're not invited. I turn toward him, and he realizes I don't approve.

"Tell me where to go, but I'm going to speak to your sisters first. Alone."

It's like the air is collectively sucked out of the room as everyone inhales a silent gasp. If he wants a partner of equals like he said, then I won't defer to him on everything in the privacy of our homes. I won't argue with him in front of anyone, but I don't take orders outside of sex and my safety.

"It's down the hall at the end. Please knock first." He kisses my cheek like he did earlier.

The men file out of the room behind them, leaving me with the three women. Javier, Alejandro, and Pablo hesitate. They fear for me alone with their mothers.

What the fuck did I just invite myself into?

I watch the men walk away until the door closes behind the last one. I join the women at the table and pull out a chair, hoping Luciana and Catalina will sit, too. Otherwise, they're going to stare down at me literally and figuratively. I relax when they do. It definitely feels like three against one.

"I don't know what the men would tell you if I left it up to them. I'll tell you all I can, and I'll answer whatever questions I can. I don't know if Enrique told you how we met." I pause, and Luciana shakes her head. "I was trying to clean leaves out of my gutters and was leaning way too far while standing too high on the ladder. I knew it wasn't smart, but the company I hired cancelled. I worried about the weather changing and the gutters getting clogged when it rains. He pretty much ordered me off the ladder then did the work himself. After that, we *coincidentally* wound up outside at the same time. I think he timed his runs for when I walked my dog. I started timing the walks when I thought he'd go by. I enjoy his company, and we chatted about different things, but we were both evasive about family and anything too personal in our past. I did *not* know who your brother is. Not until he told me his last name. I recognized it."

"Did you tell him your real one then?" Luciana definitely doesn't trust me.

"No. As much as I enjoyed our walks, I swore off relationships. My ex-husband never physically abused me. But there was a lot of emotional abuse. He'd tell me he wouldn't talk to me for an entire weekend if I said something he didn't like. He'd ignore me when I spoke to him if he didn't feel like answering. He wouldn't make friends with my friends and made me feel guilty when I built a life without him because he refused to engage in anything that involved our boys and me. He preferred gaming. For the first ten years of our marriage, he was so addicted to his video games I feared interrupting him. Friends would say I should just throw them out. I couldn't think of many things scarier than how he would've reacted to that. I was so scared of pissing him off if I bumped him in my sleep that I slept on my hands for years. He stopped asking how my day went within a couple months of getting married. It was one of the things that made me fall for him because none of the guys I dated before him asked."

I need a moment to push aside the resentment threatening to flare my anger into a wildfire.

"He'd belittle the work I did outside of the family business, even calling it stupid and pointless. He'd blame me for his boredom when he did nothing but laze around the house on the weekends and sleep because he had nothing better to do. There was always stuff he could have helped with—something to clean, a meal to cook, laundry to put away. If he did dishes, he needed a Medal of Honor. He complained about everything and everyone. I couldn't have a conversation with him if he was driving because he'd bitch about everyone else on the road. If we were on the phone, he'd cut me off mid-sentence to complain. I was so lonely in that marriage. I vacillated between hating him when we argued and not caring if he lived or died when we weren't. I stayed because of my boys. If we divorced, I feared they'd be worse off if they were with just him when they'd inevitably go to his place. I feared he'd remarry, and the woman wouldn't care about them. I worried and waited for years."

I swallow because I'm laying shit bare I haven't told Enrique, but I think his sisters—by blood and by marriage—will understand better, even if they've never been in this position.

"My boys are adults now. They have lives of their own, and they're financially independent. I had no reason to stay, so I didn't. Some of my wounds have healed, but they're tender when tugged at. Others are only scabbed over. I swore I didn't want another relationship because I wanted freedom. What I didn't want was my heart breaking all over again. I didn't want to commit to Enrique. We had a nasty argument because I wouldn't agree we're more than I wanted to admit. Because I didn't want to commit, I kept my secrets until I couldn't keep them anymore."

"You sound like you're more than a woman who married a Vizzini." Margherita's voice is soft, but her gaze is sharp as the blade she's ready to stick in me if I misstep.

"I've told Enrique this already, and he's probably telling your sons right now. I was Tommaso Vizzini's accountant. The one who handled the private books when other people messed up his transactions."

I stare at them because that's as close to admitting what I did when I extorted the shit out of people or coerced them into paying money they didn't want to or didn't have.

"Women are far superior to men in most things. Their egos are just too fragile for most of them to learn that. But Tommaso knows I have better aim than even an Olympian. When it became my life or my husband's, I learned to bend my morals. When he held my sons' lives ransom, I let my morals burn. Only one of my sons is active, but they trained the other two. When I left my husband, I made Tommaso swear in writing in front of witnesses that he released me. He reneged and held my sons over my head, so I did one last job. It put me near Alejandro. He would have killed me before I took your son from your family, Catalina."

"You would have left your sons without a mother?"

"I've taken other women's sons from them and not heard a peep from my conscience. But I couldn't do that to your family. I took my chances by letting Alejandro live. All I've ever wanted on those missions was to get home to my boys. The last time wasn't any different, but losing your parent is life's normal path. Losing your child should never happen. I will put my sons ahead of everyone, and Enrique knows that. But intentionally harming your family harms Enrique in a way I can't stomach thinking about. I believe he feels the same way about your sons and me. My sons will always be Vizzinis, and your sons will always be Diazes. Right now, I'm neither. I plan to move forward, not look back."

They listen to me, and like proper syndicate wives, I have no clue what they're thinking.

"Why not end things when you found out who my brother is?" Luciana's left eye narrows a sliver, and I know she wants to catch me in a lie.

"Because who he is doesn't bother me. I've been around men like him my entire life. I know better than most syndicate women what the men do and what their businesses are. I told Enrique the truth about why I can accept it without telling him how I knew I could. Enrique was born into his role. He carries a heavier burden than most people can imagine. The only one in this house who will ever know is Pablo. The rest of us can only guess or assume.

216

More than just your family relies on him. He's responsible for thousands of people. What he wants or doesn't want doesn't matter if it doesn't support the Cartel. His duty is to them before *anything* else. His duty is to you before *anyone* else. If your family is weak, then everything falls apart. If any of you walk away, you're as good as dead. You have to remain in this world to survive. I knew the day I filed my divorce papers I would make myself disappear. I'm a full-time author. It was easy to create my identity as Elodie McCann because I've been writing novels under that name for years. People already believed it was my real one because I couldn't let my readers discover I was a Mafia wife, daughter, and mother. When I go in public with Enrique, I lose that anonymity immediately. Between my past and Enrique's life, I'm in more danger than I've ever been. But your brother is worth that risk. I didn't think I could care about someone like this again. There's nothing I won't do to protect him and protect what we have."

I draw a breath. I revealed far more than I probably should have, but I want them to know I get it. I get the life. I get the danger I bring Enrique. I get the danger he brings me. I get I'm not giving this up now that I've accepted it.

"You're telling us more than our brothers, sons, or nephews would." Luciana assesses me, and I think the ice is chipping.

"It's nothing you wouldn't overhear in bits and pieces or figure out on your own. I'd rather just tell you."

"What happens the next time Tommaso wants something from you?"

I lock gazes with Margherita. "He knows I'll put a bullet through his skull before I do another job for him."

My gaze shifts to Luciana, then Catalina. It wouldn't shock me if these women have killed before. You wouldn't know it from how they were around the men. Not even when Catalina stepped in front of her son. But it's there in their eyes now.

"I'm not part of your family, and I don't know if I ever will be. But you're important to me because you're important to Enrique. My loyalty is to my sons before everything else. After that, it's to

Enrique. If it's between a Vizzini and a Diaz who's in this house right now, I pray you'll give me shelter when the Vizzinis come looking for me."

The women look amongst themselves before Margherita speaks on their behalf. "Your sons are under our protection, too."

"Thank you."

They'll kill for my children, and they'll make sure the men in this house know the price they'll pay if they won't kill for my sons too.

As I push back my chair, Luciana fires the parting shot.

"Fool us, and you'll wish it's *our* men who find you."

They won't kill me, but I'm not one of them.

Chapter Sixteen

Ellie

I tap on Enrique's office door and wait for him to tell me to come in. Instead, Joaquin opens the door for me. He strikes me as the shyest in the group. I'm certain he can have the machismo every syndicate man needs, but I don't think it comes as naturally to him as it does for others.

Enrique's office is far larger than I expected. It tucks back behind the building in a way the front exterior didn't hint at. He's seated behind his desk, much like a king on his throne, except there's now a chair beside him I doubt usually remains there.

No one's seated in it, and a muscular giant stands beside each of the other spots. Obviously, it's reserved for me. That screams a pretty fucking significant commitment to have me next to the *jefe de jefes* as though I have my own queenly throne.

La reina. That reminds me of the TV show about the Mexican narco-queen. It was a good show.

I never thought I'd have anything in my life that could make me resemble a narco more than I already did, but I guess life just had to one-up me. I walk over to the seat, and Enrique adjusts it for me. Nobody sits until I do. Chivalry isn't dead, I guess, after all.

Enrique sticks out his hand. At least he's not overly obvious about it, but there's no way the others don't notice. As our arms lie on the armrests, his hand is at the end of my chair's, so I don't have to stretch.

"Ellie, I've filled them in, and they know most of what I know."

That one word "most" makes me want to cringe. It screams secrets, and that's the last thing I want, but it's the first thing that's inevitable.

"What else do you want to know?"

I sweep my gaze around the room, keeping my tone even, hoping I don't sound defensive. Pablo checks with Enrique first, who nods before looking at me.

"How did you create an alias that has no records at all, not even falsified ones that match your fingerprints? There's nothing at all."

"I am whoever I want to be whenever I want to be. Elodie McCann is one of many identities I have. You've probably heard of me a dozen times over. I'm Yuliya Koritrova. I'm Elizabeth O'Donoghue. I'm Samira Abbas, Katarina Kowalski, Hanifa Soloman, and Angelina Rosati. I've been Maggie Sinclair, Madeline Garnier. I'm Rebekah Horowitz and Sarah Goldman. I'm plenty more people I've either killed off or retired over the years."

"You're Yuliya Koritrova?" Disbelief hangs in the air when Luis says that name.

That is my most infamous identity. It's the one that's done the most damage. It's the one that stole twenty million dollars out from under the Albanian *kyre's* nose a few years ago when his bag of shit son terrorized a woman who's now a bratva wife here in New York. He was so distracted he didn't realize what he signed over to the woman with the low-cut blouse, negotiating circles around him. To make my point at the end of the meeting, I shot each of the men he had guarding him at his house. I picked off the ones in his office with us. Then I conveniently hid around the corner from the office door and took out each additional guard as they entered.

"Yes, I am one and the same."

"And we're not supposed to fear you'll kill our uncle in his sleep?"

Pablo doesn't just have dark eyes. There's a darkness I think life has ground into him. It wouldn't surprise me if he and Alejandro are the chief enforcers in the family. But something tells me Pablo is the one who wages the psychological warfare that takes a toll on anyone after years at it. He's the one I should be most wary of, but he's also the one who needs the most patience and kindness.

What was that embroidered sign I saw once?

Children need love the most when they seem to deserve it the least.

If anyone fits that description, I think it's Pablo.

"If no one found those aliases, I was confident no one would figure out Elodie McCann since I went to even more trouble to make her a ghost than I did anybody else. If anyone makes me, then I have what I need to disappear again and start over."

"You hide in plain sight?"

"I suppose you could say that, but I hid out of sight so much over the years, people don't know who to look for. They wouldn't recognize me since I do my best not to be in those circles anymore to avoid people who might recognize me. At least until now, I did. But I don't regret admitting to you or your uncle who I am."

"Because you assume we'll protect you." Jorge is the family's accountant, so I imagine he has the strongest grudge to hold.

"All I wanted was a quiet life away from the family I belonged to. For the past year, I've had no contact with anybody in the Vizzinis except for my sons and periodically my ex-husband. And that was usually when he couldn't find something. How was I supposed to know a bossy man on a run would demand I let him clean my rain gutters? And that I'd find it endearing when my overgrown puppy wags his tail so hard he shakes every time he sees your uncle? We didn't know the truth about either of us until neither of us had the choice but to reveal it. I think we both would've maintained ignorance is bliss for even longer if we could've. But rarely does this life allow us to get all that we want, does it?"

Everyone remains quiet for a moment, then Luis speaks up. "What do you expect us to do when Tommaso's the one who puts a hit on you?"

I can't help my laughter. "Tommaso Vizzini would've killed me years ago if he could have, but he can't. My father is loyal to him and has been since Tommaso was a *capo* then the underboss. He was one of the first men to pledge his fealty to Tommaso when he killed his uncle and took control of the family. But he will be the first one to exact the worst kind of punishment on Tommaso if he ever ordered my death or approved it. That's also assuming any of his henchmen would come near me and survive. I trained half of them how to shoot, and I'm still better than them. They know they're more likely to die. There's a reason I've lived to the age I am after the jobs I've done. I'm damn good at what I do."

I look at Alejandro, and he nods when the others follow my gaze. I look back at Luis.

"I doubt Tommaso would believe Enrique would forsake me like that. Tommaso knows if he confronts me, I'll shoot him then disappear. And if it means I run for the rest of my life, so be it. He knows my bite is far worse than my bark. I'm one of the few people he knows not to push too far. And after sending me down to Rio, that's what he did. Honestly, if I weren't involved with your brother, Luis, Tommaso Vizzini would have lost a shit ton more than you as potential business partners."

I look over at Enrique, and our gazes lock.

"Once I realized you were the customers waiting offshore for the product, I changed my mind about the outcome. Since Tommaso sent nobody else down there with me except body-guards, I wasn't worried they would know enough to stop me. It wouldn't have been the first time a shipment that size went missing or got resold before I could get there. I've fucked Tommaso over enough times to feel vindicated, but this was going to be my magnum opus, if you will. That changed once I discovered Enrique was involved. I did what I had to for Tommaso, but it was mostly for Enrique."

"Did you do it to buy his good graces?" Luis won't let up.

"I'd hoped when he inevitably found out, he'd look at it as a gift. But I knew discovering who I really am—especially like that—was more likely to end everything than strengthen our relationship. I see it as nothing short of a miracle that Enrique didn't walk away."

"And that would have bothered you?"

"Luis—" Enrique's ready to jump to my defense, but I squeeze his hand.

"Would I have entered this house knowing how easy it is for any of you—including Enrique—to kill me and make sure nobody even knew I disappeared since I'm already a ghost? It's not like I don't know your family's reputation, Luis. It's not like I believe I'm untouchable because I'm a woman. I'm a mercenary. That means those rules don't apply to me. So yeah, your brother means an awful lot to me if I'm willing to face a firing squad after everything I've done. Would I really do something so illogical and irrational for your brother if I really wanted to ensure I'd live? I've put targets all over myself for the sake of being with him."

"And you didn't put more targets on my brother?"

"Well, I guess this relationship really is a two-way street, then, isn't it?"

"But—"

"Enough, Luis. You've made your point."

"Enrique, it's fine. Let them all say what they have to say. Today and any other day. I will always tell what I can. While I may still have plenty to hide, it's only what'll keep me alive and keep my sons alive. For the rest, I feel no loyalty left to the Vizzinis. Sending me to Rio was Tommaso's ultimate betrayal, so I feel no loyalty to him."

"What about the *Omertà*?"

I shift my attention to Jorge as I shrug.

"It's probably similar to whatever you swear in your syndicate.

But I'm not a Made Woman. I'm a gun for hire. I just worked solely for the Vizzinis. I didn't swear an oath. The men in my family did, but I didn't. I'm not bound by that."

"Do you think telling Tommaso's secrets will make us believe you won't tell ours?" Jorge is even more dogmatic than his uncle.

"I believe I've extended an olive branch in goodwill. I believe you're smart enough not to ask me questions I won't answer. And I believe you'll never tell me anything you fear me repeating. I can tell you how I feel, knowing you won't test me. If you did, you'd stand to lose as much as I do. Are you willing to take that chance?"

"If you have reasonable things to ask Ellie, then do. Otherwise, we're not going to go around in circles, putting her on the spot like this."

I look over at Enrique, then down at the chair, then up at him, and cock an eyebrow.

"Enrique, I'd say there's not a hotter spot to sit in your office right now than the one I'm in."

I don't whisper because that would be pointless, but I lower my voice and offer him a smile when I finish speaking. He rubs his thumb over the back of my hand.

"Fair enough. I didn't give you much choice about that one. I'm sorry."

The guys look at him as though he's sprouted a second head. I'm certain they're not accustomed to him apologizing to anybody outside their immediate family. That alone shows them I'm more important than they wanted to believe.

"It's fine, but it's awfully crowded on this side of your desk. Maybe you need more space the next time I'm in here."

I try to find the delicate balance between insinuating no one will shut me out when I don't need to be without coming across as presumptuous that they would now include me in conversations I never should be. I look at the other men in the room.

"I may be important to him, but you're his blood. If you can't accept me, tell me now, and I will walk away." I feel Enrique tense and suck a deep inhale. "No, Enrique, you won't stop me from what I'm going to say, and I don't need your permission to do it."

I shifted my focus long enough to pre-emptively halt his interruption, but now I focus on the others again.

"I will walk away because of how much I'm coming to care for your uncle, your brother. I will not come between him and his family. I wouldn't, regardless of his position, but I most certainly won't do it to *el jefe*. If you won't accept me, I'll leave. You'll have to make peace amongst yourselves, but if having me is just going to cause problems amongst you, then I'll step aside."

"Ellie, that's not their decision to make."

I don't turn my head toward him. I won't argue with him. I haven't changed my mind about that. But I will be an equal partner.

"Yes, it is, Enrique. You may be the roots of the tree, but they're the branches. Without their support, you're left as just a stump. Without you, they have no roots to tie them to lands you rule. You need each other to survive, and don't tell them otherwise when I'm not around because I will know. You can pick me before anybody who isn't in your immediate family, but you will *not* pick me before them because I will not knowingly endanger your life. Even if they continue to obey and follow you, the resentment will fester, whether or not any of you realize it. It will weaken their loyalty, even if it's subconsciously. I won't put you at risk like that. That would be worse than anything else because it would be unpredictable. If you need to talk amongst yourselves about this, I can step out."

"How did things go with my wife and sisters?"

Is there an edge to Luis's voice? Does he want to find out if they chewed me up and spat me out?

"I think it went well. They know what they need to know, which is more than any of you would've told them. We parted on good terms. If you believe nothing else I say today, know your mothers, wife, sisters are definitely far scarier than any of you can ever be. So, when they warned me, I took heed of it."

I look over at Enrique to ask if I need to step out, but all their phones buzz at once. I know what that means.

"Do you need me to do anything? Do you have a go bag I can get for you? Do you guys need food?"

They all pause from pulling out their phones to look at me. I didn't drop a beat when I made the offer. Enrique cups my face and gives me a quick, hard kiss before answering.

"No, *chiquita*, but thank you for the offer. You know what this means. I don't know when I'll be back. You can stay here if you want."

I know he'd prefer that, but I'm not ready for that yet.

"I need to get Constantine. Hunt changed his plans at the last minute to stay down here and has been teleworking out of his friend's condo in the city. But he's got to get back to Boston. He's already extended his time down here for my sake."

Enrique knows I mean so we could have our sex fest this weekend.

"All right, I want Javier to go—"

"Enrique, if all of you got this alert, you're not going anywhere without all of them with you. If you need to assign an extra regular guard, I'm fine. But an alert that goes off for all seven of you is serious."

"No, Ellie, I won't argue with you over this."

"I know. Don't push me on this, Enrique. This is exactly what I was talking about. You will not pick me over your family. I'll be fine. If anything, I can ask Hunt to spend one more night here, and he can stay at my house."

I don't intend to do that, but I can at least offer that reassurance to Enrique. He watches me for a moment as the other guys shuffle out the door. Luis closes it behind him as Enrique and I stand. He pulls me into his arms and devours me. I return the kiss in equal measure. I don't want to let him go, even though I have no choice. I remember going through this with Tim over the years.

In the beginning, I feared for him. By the end, there were times I prayed he wouldn't come home. But for Enrique, I'll do more than he can imagine to ensure he does.

"You have a habit of making me hard at the most inopportune

times. Your feistiness is arousing as hell. Then a kiss like that. Nobody in my family will doubt how attracted I am to you."

"Yeah, well, I'm not exactly thrilled you have to walk away while I'm all hot and bothered, too. So, misery loves company, Daddy."

I head into the living room with him and join everybody else. Luis is kissing Margherita. Alejandro is hugging his mom while Jorge, Joaquin, and Javier hug theirs. Then Margherita's wrapping her arms around Pablo, making a sandwich of him when Luis hugs them around Pablo's back. It's a touching family moment, especially when I watch the five adults embrace.

Well, I suppose the younger generation are adults, too. But I see them the same way I do my own kids. They're adults, except for when they're around their parents.

Enrique comes back to my side as he makes a call. It must only ring once, but his rapid Spanish is way too fast for me to follow. I catch Carlos's and Andrés's names, then three others. When he hangs up, he pulls me into his arms again, and I rest my head against his chest. I knew the significance when he left my house in the middle of the night. I know this time, too. My heart aches, fearing this could be the last time I see him. Not just alive but see him at all. If something happens, it's unlikely whoever this is will return his body.

I wrap my arms around him, wishing I could hold him forever. But it's only a few seconds before we pull apart. This kiss is so tender my eyes sting with tears. I refuse to shed any in front of anyone. I'll save them for when I'm alone with Constantine.

"I have three men coming. Two are our cousins. Luis and I have gone on countless missions with all three, so, I trust your safety with them. They've guarded my sisters before."

I love how he includes Margherita in that. She's not set off to the side as an in-law. She's as much one of them as Catalina and Luciana.

"You can stay here until the town car comes for you. My sisters know all three of them. Don't go with anyone unless they tell you it's safe."

"All right, I understand. Don't worry about me, Enrique. I'll be fine. I'll go home and watch some crappy reality TV. I'll also get some writing done. I'm falling behind on my deadline because this gorgeous man who insists upon ravishing me keeps pulling me away from the computer."

"Gorgeous, am I?"

"Absolutely. You know it, Daddy."

I whisper the last word, ensuring nobody can hear me except Enrique. A moment later, all the men are gone, and I'm left looking at three women who still don't know what to make of me, and I don't know what to make of them. Luciana walks up to me and shocks me when she offers me a loose embrace.

"You care for my brother more than I think even you realize."

"What makes you say that?"

"It's the way you stand together. It was that kiss. You two look like you've been together for years, not weeks. There's intimacy between you new couples don't have even during the early days when everything seems perfect. Your intimacy is the kind that usually takes time to develop unless you're with your soulmate."

I know what I see when I look into Luciana's eyes. She's lost her soulmate because the pain is clearly soul deep. I remember from what Enrique told me that she's been in America several years, but she probably wouldn't have come if she weren't a widow. All I do is nod and offer her a tight smile, hoping she realizes I understand, and I won't press for a more personal explanation. She gives my upper arms a quick squeeze.

"One day I will tell you that story, but not tonight."

That's about as much of an official welcome to the family as I'm likely to get. She's agreeing to tell me such a personal story, and she's telling me it'll be at a later date that she plans. She believes I'll be sticking around.

It's only a few minutes later when there's a knock on the front door. A guard materializes who I didn't realize was around. He checks the spyhole before opening the door. There's security at the gate at the end of Enrique's driveway and men patrolling the grounds in black utilities with bulletproof vests, Kevlar helmets, and rifles. Even with all of those protections in place the guy still double checks before letting anyone into the *jefe's* house.

Three men file in, and one of them goes to Catalina. I don't hear what they say, even though they look at me while they speak. Their kiss is quick and affectionate.

"Elodie, this is my husband, Matías. He is your head guard tonight. If you need anything at all, tell him whatever it might be. Nothing's too big or too small for our sister."

Oh, holy shit.

I did not expect to be called that so soon. Maybe I'll not only survive to tell the tale, but I might actually be welcome in this family after all. If the women accept me, then so will the men. When Catalina winks, I know she understands my thoughts.

Matías introduces me to the two other men, Pedro and Diego. It's not long before I'm climbing into a town car with Diego driving and Matías in the front passenger seat. Pedro is in a car that will follow us first to Hunt, then to my place. I've just sat back and buckled my seatbelt when my son calls.

"Hey, honey bear. I'm just on my way over to come get Constantine."

"Hi, Mom. I was calling you because I'm on my way to your place to drop him off. I have to go home. Cindy slipped and dislocated her shoulder in the shower. I've got to get back to her."

He's been dating this girl for three years. They need to shit or get off the pot. Not necessarily marriage, but at least admit they want to spend their lives together. When I think about them and how frustrated I've been with them and how ridiculous I've thought their relationship status has been, I realize the apple didn't fall far from the tree since that's all I was initially willing to agree to with Enrique.

"All right, I'll meet you at the house if you're still there. How close are you?"

"I'm about ten minutes out."

"I should get there just before you. I'll make sure the guards know. Let me let you go, so I can tell them before we head in the wrong direction. I love you."

"Love you too, Mom."

I hang up and lower the privacy glass.

"That was my youngest son. He's headed to my place to drop my dog off. His girlfriend hurt herself, so he's headed back up to Boston. We don't need to go into the city after all. Sorry about that."

"No need to apologize, *señora* McCann. We go where you tell us to go."

"Thank you. I appreciate that."

I don't raise the privacy glass before I sit back. I have second thoughts about it and feel like an idiot leaning forward again, but I realize they may want to discuss things I can't hear, so I put the glass back up.

When I close my eyes, it feels like it's only been a few seconds before the car shifts into park. I open them to find us in my driveway. Matías opens the door for me, and I head toward the garage, ready to enter the code. I look over my shoulder, and Matías steps next to me.

"Do you prefer me to go in through the garage or the front door?"

"The garage. You can wait in there while we sweep the house and be sure it's clear in there without leaving you exposed."

"Thank you."

That's what I expected to hear, but I question why I had to wait for him to walk over to me. He should have led the way. If I didn't want to come in this way, I would've corrected him. But as my guard, I shouldn't approach any doorway without someone ahead of me.

I cannot imagine no one trained them to do that. I'm immediately suspicious, though I tell myself to trust Enrique knows who to assign to me. However, it also makes me wonder if what Catalina said was a lie and that she put her husband up to this when they whispered together. I punch in the code, then I stand by my driver's side door. My keys are already in my pocket in case I need to lock myself in or leave. Matías doesn't enter my house until the garage door closes. Pedro went ahead of him, and Diego is by the garage door.

When Matías comes out and nods, I head into the house. I wait in the mud room, watching from there as the three men leave through my front door. I lock the garage door behind me out of habit and as a precaution now that I'm on edge. I hurry to lock the front door. I head into the living room and peer around a curtain as Hunt pulls into the driveway.

Chapter Seventeen

Enrique

I'm in the middle row of the SUV Jorge's driving. Alejandro's in the front passenger seat, and Joaquin is beside me. Javier is driving the second SUV with Luis and Pablo. I rarely ride in vehicles or fly in planes with Pablo. It's too great a risk to the organization and the family. Thinking about my nephew reminds me I need to explain to him that Ellie and I won't have children. I need to assure Jorge she won't tally the books over his shoulder. I know that's part of why both of them were chilly toward her.

Ellie handled herself beautifully until the part about her walking away. If we'd been alone, my hand and her ass would've had their own conversation. I'll address it when I go to her house after this is done. Nothing in the past tempted me to text a woman to say goodbye a second time. I want confirmation she got home safely. I also don't want to draw out the agony.

ME

Are you at her house?

DIEGO

Yes. Her son arrived fifteen minutes ago. Her dog watered every flowerbed in her yard.

ME

Anything unusual?

DIEGO

No

ME

Leave a message or send a text even if my phone's off.

If we have to go to our bodega, then we'll shut our phones off. We don't keep our location services on anyway, but it's an extra precaution against any calls or text being traced. We shut our personal and vehicle electronics down five miles from the store. The other syndicate families do the same thing when they head to their place.

Every family has a location they completely control. It's where we conduct the dirtier side of our business. It's somewhere no one can hear what's happening inside. It's where we can take our time with anyone who refuses to be forthcoming. It's where we punish, then dispose of bodies in a furnace or a vat of acid.

DIEGO

Will do

"*Tío?*"

I hear Pablo through my earpiece. We're all wearing our radios. Luis doesn't live too far from me, so we went to his house to get ready and strategize. We didn't want to do it near the women, and Luis didn't have his things with him. Javier grabbed my go bag from the hall closet while I said goodbye to Ellie.

We're all in our black utility pants, black turtlenecks, and black boots. We'll put our bulletproof vests on and pull down our balaclavas before we arrive, but both drivers already have their vests and helmets on. Our windows are barely street legal, so the tinting's dark enough we don't worry about other drivers wondering why ours look the way they do.

"*Sí.*"

Pablo continues in Spanish. It's *Tres J's*, Luis's, and my first language, but Alejandro and Pablo grew up interchanging it with English as toddlers. We lapse in and out of either language without thought, often in the same conversation.

"My CI says Pasha already broke into the furniture warehouse and took what he wants. He torched the rest."

"Fine."

There's often more in the upholstery than just stuffing, but we smuggled nothing that's in the warehouse right now. It's all legit, so I'll file an insurance claim and be done with it. That's assuming Seamus O'Rourke's wife doesn't spot it and decide she'll be the adjustor for it. She did that six months ago. Slowed down a construction site for eight weeks.

We're two blocks from our industrial park with our furniture warehouses. Technically, it's Catalina's warehouse since she's an interior designer, but that's a useful front that's not much of a secret among the Four Families. That's why Pasha Kutsenko went after it. He thought he'd steal some product from us, then leave nothing left we could profit from.

We pull up and can see our men working to put the fire out. It's not as bad as I feared. There's plenty that's still salvageable. I walk over to the warehouse manager.

"What happened?"

"The bratva. We lost two of our men, but fortunately most of the guys were already off the clock. They came back as soon as I made the calls."

"Thank you. Did they lose anyone?"

"The guy who started the fire trapped himself inside, so we don't think he made it. Besides him, I don't believe so. I hit one of their men, and Miguel shot at Pasha just before Pasha put a bullet through his heart."

"Was Pasha the only one there?"

"No. Misha was with him."

Of course.

They're mutual cousins of the four Kutsenko brothers who run the bratva's Ivankov branch. Misha's mother and the Kutsenkos' mother are sisters. Pasha's father and the Kutsenko brothers' father were brothers before the latter died in the Second Chechen War.

"Did they demand anything or leave a message besides the fire?"

"No. They were just in and out."

"*Mano.*"

I turn to Luis as he hands me his phone. The warehouse manager knows to give us privacy.

"Who is it?"

"Paco."

Our spy at the harbor.

"*Hola.*"

He speaks next to no English and doesn't need to living in New York. It's useful when he does minor jobs for us because there are plenty of street level men from the lesser syndicates who don't speak Spanish. He can't tell them anything they'd understand, and their threats mean little since he can't understand them either.

"*Pasha acaba de avisar a los agentes de aduanas en los muelles. Lo vi pasarle un fajo de billetes a dos agentes.*" Pasha just tipped off Customs at the docks. I watched him slip two officers a wad of cash.

I keep speaking Spanish as the others join me. "Did he pay for them to inspect our ship or to turn a blind eye while he boards?"

"I think both. The agents boarded the ship, but he and a dozen of his men are standing near the gangway. Hold on...Yeah, he just went aboard after the agents came back on deck."

"All right. We're ten minutes out."

"Do you want me to follow them if they leave?"

"Yes. Keep me posted if you leave the docks."

"Will do, *jefe.*"

I look at Alejandro as I hang up. I raise my eyebrows to our chief strategist. Of all my nephews, he's the one most like me. It pisses Matías off since people who don't know us assume he's my son. It shocks them to learn I'm not. It double shocks them if they see Matías. But they sound alike to a tee. The same pitch, inflection, cadence. All of it. It's nature, not nurture because it's uncanny.

"We can go to the docks, but likely show up too late. We can figure out where he's going next, or we can retaliate."

"Retaliate." Three voices blend into a single insistent one.

Tres J's particularly detest Pasha since he confused Jorge for Javier when he jumped Jorge in high school for supposedly breaking his football pads. It was that little shit Carmine Mancinelli. After he did it, he dropped a hint that made Pasha go after Javier, but he and Jorge looked too much alike from the back. Jorge wound up with eight stitches across his left shoulder blade from Pasha's knife. Pasha wound up with a concussion, two cracked ribs, and a nearly collapsed lung from Javier when he came to Jorge's rescue. The brothers are extremely close after what they endured growing up in Bogotá without a father.

"*If* we retaliate, what would we do, Alejandro?"

"We're assuming this is about Ignacio since it involves Pasha. Do you think he believes we put the hit on his uncle-in-law?"

"Possibly."

I brace myself for the inevitable.

"*Tío*, we should tell him it was Tommaso."

But I can't be sure it won't lead back to Ellie.

Alejandro watches my reaction. I give no outward one before he continues.

"From what I saw and heard in Rio, I think Pasha was behind the shipment delay that started all of this. He saw a way to fuck us over while he thought he was ensuring Tommaso had to give in to Ignacio."

"It wouldn't surprise me. Maks must have sanctioned this because that was a lot of moving parts to conspire and carry out on his own.

"Misha was with him, too." Pablo jumps in to point out, making us all scowl.

Alejandro stares into the distance as he thinks aloud. "That makes it a family affair. Kutsenko Partners are mid negotiations for the vehicle shipping contract with the *yakuza*. If they don't have a container ship at the Port of Long Beach because we stole it, then there's no contract. If we have two ships—ours and theirs—in the Port of Nagoya, then Nishida will accept our offer. The *oyabun* needs the car sales too much to turn us down. It fucks the Kutsenkos while putting the *yakuza* in our debt. It'll put a dent in both families' pride. Nishida still owes us for the Wo Shing Wo confusing our trucks for Nishida's in Taipei. That was a lot of fucking corn wasted on the side of the road. We barely made it out before the Three Seas Union discovered a Hong Kong triad and the New York Colombian Cartel were operating in their territory."

I consider Alejandro's suggestion about Haruki Nishida, and it has merit.

"It'll cost us to send two empty container ships across the Pacific, but they could be there in less than two weeks. If they sail with the next tide, the bratva wouldn't catch them before they're in the major shipping lanes."

I look at Jorge.

"Are you willing to spend?"

"If we make Tommaso deal with this, he's more likely to sell out Elodie to get back at us and to deflect his role, even if he's the one who sent her. It'd be better if you announced your relationship with a public appearance together than have a bunch of *chismosos* playing telephone about you and your girlfriend."

I look around the group, and I know the others agree. My gaze settles on Luis, who nods.

"Pablo, make the ships happen. We don't involve Tommaso in

that. In the meantime, I'm not satisfied Pasha will learn his lesson from that. I want something more personal."

Jorge's smug expression and folded arms haven't changed since he was five and beat Javier at *cinco huecos*. He tossed one more coin in the hole than his older brother and won. He didn't say a word. He didn't need to. He had more arrogance in his five-year-old body than most syndicate men possess at twenty-five.

"I found out where his rainy-day fund is. So much for Singapore ranking so highly for financial secrecy. I can move the money to a U.S. account, then report it to the IRS. It wouldn't bankrupt him, but it would make his day suck."

Pasha is the bratva accountant, so that adds an extra layer of *coma mierda*—go eat shit—coming from my accountant.

I nod and watch Jorge walk back to the SUV and open the back passenger door. He grabs his laptop bag and sits. He's plonking away at the keyboard before I turn around.

"How about Tommaso?" Joaquin's usually quieter than the others, but it's not because he doesn't pay attention.

It's a good question. My instinct is to wait to talk to Ellie about this, either to get her opinion or to warn her to stay out of the way. I can't involve her without compromising her safety. However, we don't have time for that.

"He's been on good terms with Salvatore ever since he helped Carmine and Gabriele rescue Misha's sister-in-law. I think that needs to end."

I look at Alejandro again. The things we've devised might seem simple, but there are swiftly evolving elements he'll oversee to ensure it comes together. He'll course correct if anything goes wrong.

"We make it look like he fucked the Torettas over by making a deal with the Lombardos or Randazzos. After what happened with Sylvia's family, Salvatore will never forgive Tommaso for betraying his wife's family. Even if he discovers we orchestrated it, he won't forgive Tommaso for falling for it."

"Tommaso won't go near them. How will you get him to make a deal?"

Alejandro flashes a frown and shrugs. "By making it look like Salvatore cut him off from everyone but the Lombardos and Randazzos. He can think it's Salvatore's retaliation for involving Elodie. To make it work, though, Salvatore needs to know about some of Elodie's past with Tommaso."

"No. I won't agree to that until I know what involvement she's had with the Mancinellis. If she carried out any hits on them, I'm not exposing her past to Salvatore. That's like waving a red flag in front of a bull. She was a mercenary. She's fair game for them to retaliate. I won't knowingly make her a target."

"Then Tommaso can think it's Salvatore's retaliation for doing a deal with us, even if it was indirect."

"That's better. How will you cut them off? The Vizzinis still have strong ties to Palermo."

"Make it known he did the deal with Ignacio as our middleman. If the Sicilian families think Tommaso's on the outs with Salvatore, they'll treat him like he has the plague. The only ones who'd do business with him are the Lombardos and Randazzos because they still hate the Torettas and have never forgiven them or Salvatore for his arranged marriage to Sylvia, then supporting Carmine and Serafina's marriage."

"Do you have enough men over there to make it happen soon? The rumor needs to buzz around the island fast before anyone can talk to Tommaso or Salvatore." I need to be sure it's workable before I sanction it.

"Yeah. Our guys'll lay it on just thick enough to be the juiciest gossip in years without being so over the top people'll question it."

It's dark now, so that's the only reason we've remained in the open as long as we have. There's not much more we can do. With the time differences, Pablo gave me the signal everything's in place to happen tonight in California. It's already the next business day in Japan and Singapore, so Jorge has things on the move. It's still early to start work in Palermo, but Alejandro will do it before dawn their time.

The guys head to the vehicles while Luis hangs back.

"Rather anticlimactic, *mano*."

"True. But anticlimactic means you go home to your wife, and the *niños* go home to their mamas. I get to keep breathing."

Little boys. None of my nephews, who vary in height from five-eleven-and-a-half to six-three and weigh between two-ten and two-twenty-five, are little, but I changed all their diapers. They haven't lived the things Luis and I have, and I pray they never do. *Tres J's* are the closest since they lived in Bogotá with only Luciana for a few years after Esteban died. Catalina moved to America before Alejandro was born because I promoted Matías, but Alejandro's seen some shit since he goes there as often as Luis.

"True. I want to get home to Margherita. The medicines made her sick today."

"Luciana's probably wearing a hole in my living room carpet by now."

When the street gangs started targeting her sons and trying to lure them in, she knew she had no choice but to move here. Luciana was too alone to protect her boys. Our uncle was no use. I allow him enough freedom to run things for me. He knows I'll kill him the moment he no longer obeys me.

Since I hold his balls in a vise, and everybody knows it, the street gangs thought they could work around him. He didn't help *Tres J's*, even though he could have. He knew I expected it. Luis beat him so close to death, it wouldn't have surprised anyone if he'd met the devil.

Tres J's saw things as kids Pablo and Alejandro have only seen as adults. It's Alejandro's job now to inflict some of the shit *Tres J's* saw way too young.

"Let's go."

We walk to the vehicles. When I get to Jorge, he spins his computer for me to see. I grin. The fuckery's started. I watch a money transfer process from a bank in Singapore to a bank in Mauritius. That money will probably go through the Bahamas before it winds up in Switzerland, then finally here. Either Pasha won't sleep tonight trying to stop this, or he'll have a rude awakening in the morning. Either way, the *pequeña perra*—little bitch—will remember my reach is longer than his.

I climb into the SUV and give Jorge directions to Ellie's. As soon as I turn on my phone, a message pings from her.

"I'm safe but we have a problem. Call me when you can."

"Jorge, hurry. Something happened at Ellie's."

I tap the screen, and Ellie answers on the first ring.

"Daddy, someone has photos of me."

Chapter Eighteen

Ellie

"Thanks for watching him for so long, Hunt."

"Not a problem. I would've been happy to stay down here longer, but Cindy needs me."

"I get it."

I'm certain I'm not imagining my son's hesitation to leave. I wrap my arms around his waist. Sometimes it still surprises me when I hug my boys that I'm hugging full-on men. Part of me still expects a little boy who leans against me, and my arms can go around him with ease. Now I rest my head on their chests, and they have to stoop to rest their head on top of mine. They're solid when I hug them. As much as I miss their innocence, I'm grateful for their support.

I'm ready to let go, and Hunt usually does the same as soon as I do. I know they're often indulging me. But this time, he doesn't.

"Hunter, what's wrong? Are you worried about leaving me here?"

"No. I just—It's nothing."

"What is it?"

He hesitates before running his hand through his hair. He

looks at the door, then his shoulders droop. This isn't my usual happy-go-lucky, everything-rolls-off-his-back-like-water-off-a-duck son.

"Seeing you with Enrique made me think about how things stand with Cindy. The way he looks at you—I don't think I've ever looked at Cindy that way. I thought I had, but now, I really don't know. How comfortable you are around him—you were *never* like that before. Your body language made it look like you've been a couple for decades not days. I don't know that Cindy and I will ever get to that."

That sounds like what Luciana told me.

"Hunt, why haven't you and Cindy moved in together?"

My son flushes, and I want to roll my eyes. It's not like I discuss my sons' sex lives, but I'm not an idiot living under a rock.

"Hunt, you're twenty-two, but you've been with her for three years. I'm definitely *not* advocating marriage at your age. In fact, I'd like to forbid all of you from marrying before you're at least thirty-three. I married way too young at twenty-two, especially to another twenty-two-year-old."

"I know you refuse to consider us actual adults until we're over twenty-five, so that means only Will."

"Despite what all of you have done, and how that's matured you, your brain hasn't caught up to your life experience. Thirty-three is a good age for having a fully developed brain *and* life experience. Even if I don't advocate marriage, I still figured you'd at least be talking about moving in after all this time."

"Are you hoping I'll hate living with her and will break up with her?"

My eyes widen as I shake my head.

"No. I like Cindy, and I think you love each other. But it's like you're in a holding pattern. Even if you're not talking about marriage, you never talk about what's to come. Not even three months in the future, and certainly not years from now. You never talk about anything beyond a few weeks down the road. Yet you've both told me you belong together, that you're perfect for each other. Is that what makes you perfect?"

"No. Hardly. One of us will bring up the future, and it's like a cue to the other to bolt from the room. We're not on the same page, so we don't talk about it. I feel like I'm treading water. I don't believe I need my entire life planned, but I feel like I'm still stuck in a college relationship rather than an adult one."

"Where's the disconnect? Does she want to settle down, and you don't? Or the other way around?"

"I don't know. We just avoid the topic."

"Is it our family that's holding you back? You'll have to tell her if you stay together."

"I know. That's definitely not something I want to discuss, but it's not even that. You haven't been on a date with Enrique, yet you just know."

"We haven't been out to dinner and a movie, but we consider our walks our dates. I know the here and the now. I know what I want for the future. But I don't know if that'll happen. More than anything, I know what I don't want. I remember Dad and I nearly broke up the night we got engaged. It happened a few hours after. I don't remember what we said, but I remember needing space. We were in Hawaii, so I went out to sit on the sand in the middle of the night. A couple months later, he came down to DC to visit me. I had a studio then, so it was tight with the two of us for two weeks plus the yellow lab I had back then. Rather than just tell me he needed a breather from being together the entire time, he insisted on going out to a bar by himself. I didn't understand why he'd want to do that if he was in town to visit me. It felt like he was ditching me and that anybody's company was better than mine. I questioned why he wanted to look like a single guy out at a bar if he wasn't looking to meet someone. I was so frustrated because he just wouldn't tell me why. It wasn't about sparing my feelings. He just didn't think he needed to explain. I nearly told him to go to the bar and not come back. But I kept telling myself relationships aren't easy. That for better or for worse meant not walking away just because I was unhappy. Things got better before he went back up to Boston, and I was excited about starting a life together. Things didn't go how I hoped."

I won't say more than that because Hunt lived in the same house as us. He heard the arguments. He saw us give each other the cold shoulder. He remembers how uninvolved Tim was for most of his life.

"With Enrique, it's like the weight I've carried for a lifetime isn't so heavy anymore. Sometimes it doesn't feel like it's there because he's willing to shoulder it along with me. I can talk to him about how I feel without him getting evasive or annoyed or belittling. Nothing about him makes me think that'll change the longer we're together. I had hints of what would go wrong before I got married. I'm more secure than I was when I was in my early twenties. I don't feel like I need to cater to Enrique or give in to him because I'm scared if I'm not perfect, he'll leave. I feel seen and understood without having to explain."

"That. The last bit. I don't get that with Cindy. There are times I look at her and wonder if we switched bodies with other people and have never met before."

"I'm sorry, honey bear. I'd make it better if I could. You need to think about what you want right now and what you want in the future if you think this relationship is for the long haul. If it's more a situationship, then enjoy it until it isn't fun anymore."

"It stopped being fun a while ago. Do you see yourself growing old with Enrique?"

"I didn't want to picture that. Or at least, I didn't want to picture growing old living with someone else. I thought I'd be happy with his and her lives that overlapped when we wanted to be together, then went back to being independent when we didn't. Once I let my guard down—or rather Enrique forced me to stop hiding behind it—I realized I want our life together. I don't know if it'll work out, but I want to try."

"Thanks, Mom. I'm going to help Cindy, and once she feels better, we're going to talk."

"If you need anything, let me know. Otherwise, keep me posted."

I never ask details unless they bring it up. I don't want to be a Smother Mother, so it's hard not knowing more. But I trust them, and they wind up telling me a lot of things on their own. I wonder if Enrique has a similar relationship with any of his nephews. I wonder if he ever regrets not having his own kids.

"I'll let you know when I get home."

I frown as I look toward the window. It's already dark. I'm glad it's only a four-hour drive on a major interstate and not winding country roads.

"Do you have to go back into the city, or are you getting straight on the highway?"

"I'm getting straight on the road. Are you going to be all right here?"

"Yes. I have work to do, then I'll veg until I'm ready for bed. I'll be here, writing for the next few days. When Enrique's back, I'll see whether those plans change."

"All right. I love you."

"I love you too, honey bear."

I get one last hug, then I watch him walk out to his car. I lock the door and turn toward Constantine, who's snoring on his bed in the living room. I walk past, and he barely opens an eye. But the moment I'm on the sofa with my laptop, he becomes a lapdog.

"I can't type around your head, you big love bug."

He merely sighs and gets comfier. I adjust him, my hands reaching the keyboard again. The next couple hours slip by, and I don't notice. It's not until my stomach rumbles that I look up. Constantine heads to the backdoor, and I follow him through the kitchen and let him into the yard. I sweep my gaze around the open space like I always do. Old habits die hard.

The moment I look to my right, I spy a manila envelope on the table. When I shift my gaze, I scrutinize everything I can see. I inch to the table, keeping my eyes searching for anything out of the ordinary. I grab the envelope with the corner of my shirt and call Constantine back inside. Immediately, I go to my office and get my testing kit out. I'm not touching this with my bare hands until I know it's safe. I may be burying this shirt in a bag or burning it.

I exhale. It's clean.

I rip the envelope open, glancing down at Constantine, who's looking up at me expectantly. I swear the dog thinks anything I open must be a treat for him. I pat his broad head, and it gives me a moment of calm before I pull out the contents.

Motherfucker!

What the fuck?

I spread photos out that show me doing all sorts of things. There are photos of me working out in my garage and kneeling to weed my flowerbeds. But it's not just my front yard. Oh, no. There are photos of me in the backyard—not flattering ones of me bending over. Whoever this is, I'll fuck them up just for that.

There are photos of Enrique and me on our walks in the park and farther up the street from my house. These aren't photos the dash cam could have caught. There are photos of Enrique coming in and out of my house and of the guards parked in my driveway. There are photos of them when they're staked out among the trees separating my property from my neighbors. They were invisible unless you knew what to look for.

Touching only the very edges, I turn them over, but there's nothing handwritten or printed on them. I hold them to the light, and I see no marks on them. I check inside the envelope again, but there's nothing else. Just two dozen photos. That's not meant to freak me out or anything.

How'd they get in my backyard?

I'm pretty positive a drone took most of these photos. Is it precise enough to drop the envelope propped up on a table? I don't think it would be. I don't know. The more reasonable explanation is someone's been in my backyard.

When?

It had to be within the two-and-a-half hours I was out with Enrique because I glanced out the backdoor before we left. I always check the doors and scan the front and backyard in case anything's out of place because of shit like this.

I let talking to Hunt distract me. I didn't look out back because I forgot, and I didn't check until Constantine needed to go out. Shame on me. I'm usually not this lax.

I pull out another kit and dust for fingerprints.

Gotcha fucknut.

There are prints where I didn't touch the envelope or photos. I can't run them here, but I'm certain Enrique has a way. I'm cautious as I tuck them back into the envelope. There aren't any nudie pics of me—yet. That's what I'm worried about. That's the next step. If they wanted to send photos of me away from the house, they would've. It's creepy enough they got pics of me in my fenced backyard. They don't need to send me proof of going to the grocery store. If they can invade my privacy more, then that's what they'll prove.

Thank God Enrique and I made sure all the blinds and curtains were closed before we had our sex fest.

I grab my phone and dial Enrique's number, which I got yesterday morning after we had at least six rounds of sex. I don't expect him to answer, so I leave a message. I don't want to panic him, but I need him here.

Who the fuck did this?

The most obvious is Tommaso, since the car with the dash cam was around before Enrique and I met. The photos of me working out and in the front yard are from before he walked into my life.

I'll call Tommaso, but I want to consider alternatives first. I start with Boston families since they're obvious.

The O'Malleys—those motherfuckers couldn't find their asses in a bucket with lights shining out of them. They've fucked up so much they don't sneeze without asking the O'Rourkes' permission. They targeted the woman who married the O'Rourkes' second-in-command. They're also connected to a woman who married one of the O'Rourke twins, and that ties both the O'Malleys and the O'Rourkes to the Montreal mob. The O'Malleys are keeping their heads down, so none of the O'Rourkes get froggy and pick them off one by one.

The Iglesias—the churches. Too ridiculous to even laugh at. Those shitbags are just puppets—violent as fuck puppets—of the Espinozas who run the *Culiacán* out of Chihuahua. The

Espinozas have ties to the Mancinellis through marriage. And they sure as fuck aren't crossing Enrique. He'll shut that entire enterprise down. I've heard the stories about his relationship with Jesus Espinoza. He does *not* like Jesus, who isn't particularly fond of Enrique, but understands his place in the Latin American pecking order. He's high, but nobody's above Enrique.

The Colombians have a presence in Boston, but they're more low profile. It's the Mexican *Culiacán* who are the poster children for cartels. From what I know, Enrique set it up that way since he doesn't have as large a Colombian community up there as he does here.

The Volkovs—their name means wolf. They do nothing but howl like the beaten dogs they are. Between the Kutsenkos down here—who don't let them off a short leash—and their ongoing overlords in the Solntsevskaya bratva in Moscow, they wouldn't reach this close to NYC.

The Solntsevskaya is the oldest and biggest modern bratva in Russia. We can thank them for the bratva arriving in America when they sent the original Ivankov over. They have ties to the Podolskaya, who are the Kutsenkos' mortal enemies from crap that happened in the motherland and here. It's why the Ivankov branch—run by the Kutsenkos—don't let the Volkovs do jack diddly.

There are the lesser syndicates like the Polish and Albanians. No one should overlook them, but they're at the mercy of the Ivankov bratva. The Kutsenkos chewed up and spat them out a few times. The Polish in NYC are *persona non grata* to the O'Rourkes, so the ones up in Boston tread lightly.

There are the street level gangs, but I had nothing to do with them. Tommaso didn't use me much domestically, and definitely not locally. The chance for someone to recognize me was too great. I refused once I had the boys. I refused to have them watch someone murder me at the park.

I stare at my phone before I hit Tommaso's contact. It rings four times.

"It's late, Elodie."

"Not that late when one of your goons left the photos on my patio table."

"Huh?"

"Wake the fuck up, Tommaso, and tell me the truth."

I hear Stella's voice in the background, asking what I want.

"Put it on speaker for her, Tommy." Only Stella can call him that, so it's a definite slight when I do it.

"Elle?"

"I'm sorry to wake you, Stella, but this can't wait."

"What happened?"

"That's what I want Tommaso to explain. Why did you have someone leave photos of me in an envelope on my back patio table?"

It may not be him, but I've learned to launch my attack with a bang. If I work up to accusing him of something, he has time to devise his lies. I've run circles around him for years, so I know I'm better off with the rapid-fire approach.

"I didn't have anyone send anything. You asked me about a dash camera before your trip, and I said it wasn't me." He's careful not to tell Stella anything that could endanger her.

"Yet, these photos of me in my front yard, working out in my garage, *bending over* in my backyard surface. There are photos of me going for walks with my boyfriend, Tommaso."

I brace for impact.

"Your what?"

I knew it would hurt Stella to find out this way. But when Tommaso explodes in a moment, it'll be good she's there to keep him from ordering an assassin at my door in the next ten minutes.

"My boyfriend. I started seeing someone a couple months ago."

"Who?"

Tommaso and Stella speak, and I don't drop a beat.

"Enrique Diaz."

Silence. Fucking crickets.

For five seconds.

"What the hell are you doing with that *stronzo*, Elodie? How could you betray me like that? Are you crazy? Do you have a death wish? Break up. Now!"

"Don't bellow at me, Tommaso. I don't work for you anymore. Consider this a courtesy for Stella's sake, even if I wish I could've told you first, Stella."

"If you've been together for a few months, why didn't you tell me yourself sooner?"

"Business got in the way, Stella. I'm sorry."

She falls quiet because she knows what that means, and I can practically hear Tommaso snarling.

"End it, Elodie."

"No, Tommaso. Be glad I'm involved with him, or things wouldn't have been so profitable."

I hear his muffled voice as he tells Stella he'll be back soon. He must be going to his office for the rest of this call. I already have my jammers on, so no one's recording this call on my end. I turned them on before calling Enrique.

"You will end this, Elodie. Your loyalty is to your family, not some guy you're fucking. He'll probably kill you once he knows about your past."

"He knows. I told him."

"You broke the oath?"

"I never took it. Remember? I'm not a Made Woman."

"You may as well have when you said your wedding vows."

"Which are null and void now. I didn't know who the guy I liked was when I met Enrique. He didn't know my past, either. Circumstances forced us to confess before either of us wanted to. I didn't tell him until after I got back. He told me before I left. I've been more loyal to you than you deserve. But my life is my own now. You aren't a part of it except for being my friend's husband. If you sent the photos to intimidate me into following orders, you wasted the paper they were printed on."

"I didn't order any surveillance on you, Elle. You've stayed out of sight, so I had no reason to. Clearly, I didn't know about your boy toy."

"Then who found out about me? Do you have a leak? Because someone's watching me."

"Could it be Pasha Kutsenko? Did he find out you carried out the hit on his wife's uncle?"

"Maybe. But the camera pointed at my house before I met Enrique and a long time before Rio. The car with it hasn't been on my street for a while. How would Pasha know about me before Rio or Enrique?"

"You've taken out their associates in Europe. Maybe they figured it out."

"Then that means others may have too."

Fuck me. I've always been so damn cautious.

"It's possible."

"Did you ever tell Salvatore about me? Could he be keeping an eye on me?"

"He knows I had someone better than any other syndicate, but he never knew it was you."

"Are you certain?"

"Yeah. If he'd known, he would have asked to borrow you, or he would've approached you to freelance."

Borrow.

Fuck him.

"What about one of his nephews?"

"I doubt it. I helped them a while back with a woman who was kidnapped. Turned out she was Misha Andreyev's future sister-in-law. I don't think it would be the Kutsenkos, either. They know I helped, and they don't target women."

I press my lips together. The saintly Kutsenkos aren't so saintly. They may not allow anyone to abuse or sell women, but that doesn't mean they don't catch them in the crossfire. They were the first family to all get married, so with that many women in their homes, they've only gotten sneakier. I put nothing past them.

"That leaves the Irish. Did you get too close to the O'Malleys? Or did you fuck them over too much?" I'm running out of obvious possibilities.

"They're a fucking mess, trying to regroup after what happened with Finn's wife's family and Sean's wife. They're in no position to come after someone like you. If they know who you are, then they know you're a Vizzini. They're fucking stupid, but not so stupid they don't know we'd avenge you. And if they have photos of you with Enrique, they sure as fuck aren't going near you enough to drop them off. They're too weak right now to risk him annihilating them."

"I doubt it's Marcelo since this started before I shot his father. He'll be too busy scrambling to hold on to his family's empire now that Ignacio and Benicio are dead. The Kimuras are weak, just like you wanted."

"Marcelo and I have a deal now that's far better for both of us than anything his buffoon father negotiated."

Small comfort.

"Moscow?"

"Maybe. It could be Tokyo or Osaka."

"Nishida? I've been nowhere near his family in ten years. Why now?"

"Because you don't have family close. That's my guess. I think it's someone foreign who's banking on your being alone."

"But they have photos of Enrique with me. That's what doesn't make sense. Who's willing to take him on? I can't think of too many people."

"I doubt staying with him will be good for your health. You need to end things, Elle. You're not a fool, but this is the most foolish thing you've ever done."

"I won't do that. You can't order me to, and whoever this is won't scare me into it."

"Then you have no one to blame but yourself. I wash my hands of it and you."

"Good. Then you won't call me for anything else. If you're playing me for a fool, and you're behind this, Tommaso, there will be no recovering from this. Don't make me put Will in that kind of position. Don't make me discuss this with my father."

"You've been doling out a lot of threats lately, Elodie. Most people don't survive even one. Yet, I've been putting up with your attitude ever since you called me about this the first time."

"If you really think my anger is misplaced, then you shouldn't have gotten me involved in this to begin with. You should've kept me away from Ignacio. You had to know this was the only reaction I'd have to you breaking your word of honor to me."

"The organization will always come before you or anyone else. I needed you to do the job I paid you for."

"About that. I'm still waiting on that payment, Tommaso. I haven't seen any change to my account since I've been back."

"It's the weekend."

"And your point? You know that doesn't prevent all transactions from going through. So, I expect to see the money in my account bright and early tomorrow morning."

"Or what, Elodie? What threat are you going to issue now?"

"I'll tell Enrique. So far, all of this has been just business between you and me. Push me harder, and you'll find out what it means to push me into the arms of the *jefe de jefes*. Is that what you want?"

"Bullshit. Don't say I'm pushing you toward him when you're probably on his dick right now."

"Tommaso!"

Stella's voice rings out in the background. She must have followed him to his office, or he decided it was safe enough to go back to his bedroom. Staying on the phone for them arguing isn't a good use of my time, but I'll let her chew him out for a moment before I interrupt.

"I'll ask one last time, Tommaso, so tell me the truth because if you don't, you'll be lying in front of Stella about me. That's one thing you haven't done. Are you responsible for these photos?"

"For the last time, Elodie, no. I don't even know what the fucking photos are besides what you told me."

I sit back in my desk chair.

Tommaso is like every other syndicate man who lies about any and everything. But he vowed to Stella a long time ago that with family—which she considers me—he'll either omit things or tell her straight to her face he can't talk about it. He wouldn't give her a bald-faced lie like he does about other things. It makes me confident he's telling the truth. If not for my sake, then for Stella's.

"All right, I choose to believe you. Don't let Stella down, Tommaso."

"Whatever, Elodie."

"Bye. *Va' con Dio.*" Go with God.

"Bye, Elle."

"Bye, Stella."

I hang up, leaving them to whatever conversation they'll have. I tilt my head back, wondering what the hell to do next. I don't think there's much I can do until Enrique gets here. And who knows how soon that'll be?

I turn toward my front door, where somebody's practically pounding it down. I sat staring off into space at my desk for an hour before I remembered I was hungry. I just made myself a bowl of pasta.

I check the peephole before opening the door.

"Oh, thank God, Enrique."

"Ellie."

His gaze sweeps over me before he does the same thing he did the first and second time he came over. He pushes the door closed and locks it as he spins me around and presses me against it. Our lips meet. The house could fall down around us, and we wouldn't notice. Everything feels right in the world again as he kisses me.

I feel safer, braver, stronger with him than I ever did on my own, which is saying something, considering all I've done over the years. I lean against him, cupping his face for a moment, then sliding my fingertips down his neck to trace the tattoo I've memorized and wrapping my arms around him. I hold on to him for dear life as though he might disappear if I ease my hold even a little.

When we're both breathless, we finally pull apart. It's my turn to sweep my gaze over him, assuring myself he's no worse for wear after his mission.

"Daddy?

"Yes, *chiquita*. I'm here."

"God, I was so worried about you, and now there's more for us to deal with."

"I know, little one."

"Are you hungry? I just made some pasta. I can get you a bowl."

"I'm starving, but in a little bit. Right now, I want you in my arms."

"All right, Daddy, if you say so."

I smile as he scoops me up and carries me to the sofa. I shift to straddle him and once again lean into his embrace. Having his arms around me—it feels so perfect. Right now, it's exactly what I need.

"Ellie, let me hold you for a while. This is too perfect to let go of. I need this to convince me you're safe. Your message scared the shit out of me."

"I'm sorry, Daddy. I knew even though I told you I'm safe, you'd still worry, but I needed you to know it's important."

"You didn't tell your guards about the photos."

I sit back. "Did you?"

"No. I asked if anything unusual happened or if you needed anything. Matías said he hadn't seen you since he left you in here."

I don't respond, which makes Enrique furrow his brow.

"What's going on besides the photos, Ellie?"

"The few times I went out while you were gone before I left on my trip, Andrés and Carlos would walk to the garage or front door ahead of me. Then they would sweep the house before I went in. When we got here, all three of your men got out of the cars with me. I was going to go to the front door but decided on the garage instead, so I wouldn't be as exposed while I waited. It was weird that none of them went ahead of me. Matías caught up to me when I looked back at them. Only then did they go ahead of me. Pedro went into the house first, and Diego waited in the garage with me. It made me feel uneasy."

Enrique watches me as I speak, and I grow more nervous by the word.

"Ellie, I know you're uncomfortable telling me that because he's my brother-in-law, but your safety is a higher priority than whether he gets his feelings hurt if I talk to him about this, which I will. There should've been a guy going in through the garage, a guy going through the front door, and one staying with you. That's why I assigned three men to your detail."

Do I mention Catalina whispered something to her husband before we left? It could be nothing at all. It could be something private between man and wife.

"Ellie, there's something else you're not telling me about this."

"No, I'm just trying to work out in my head if I missed something about all of that. Maybe I misunderstood how they'd planned to do the sweep."

"There's no reason for you to make excuses if you feel uncomfortable. If I find out you're keeping things from me that could affect your protection, you and I are going to have a come to Jesus, and it'll be my hand and your ass having the conversation. Which reminds me, we're going to discuss your ridiculous altruistic offer. I will work things out with my family no matter what we are unless we don't work out. And that won't be because somebody else got in the way."

He gestures between us when he says we. If only it were that simple. But I appreciate how convinced of himself he is. He grabs my hips and pulls me forward.

"Whatever you're not telling me has to do with that—not putting yourself ahead of my family. I'm doing my best not to lose my mind because I haven't seen these photos that were dire enough for you to call me and leave a message while I was on a mission. I'm trying to keep calm and greet you properly, but you're making it awfully hard, little one."

"I'm sorry, Daddy, but I'm still struggling with whether I should say anything."

I'm unprepared for him to unfasten my capris' waistband and hoists me enough for me to have no choice but to lift my legs and move them as he lays me flat over his lap. He pulls my pants down, and his hand lands across both cheeks. He creates a steady rhythm, alternating sides. I kick my feet because it stings so much.

"Enrique, please!"

He ignores me, and just as the sting turns into a burn, he alters the pattern. Now two spanks on each side before moving on. He covers my ass, including my horizontal crack.

"Enrique, I'll tell you. *Please* stop. It hurts."

"I know it hurts. It's supposed to. And I believe you'll tell me. This wasn't about getting an answer out of you. This is about you understanding I do *not* play games with your safety. I expect you to tell me anything that's even remotely questionable. If you even think twice about it, then you will tell me about it. Ellie, with your background, you can figure out and accept a lot that might intimidate the average person. If it's enough to bother you this much after it happened, then it's significant. You will tell me right now."

He lands an extra hard smack across both cheeks, then across my upper thighs. I howl with pain.

"It was something Catalina said to Matías. I couldn't hear it, but it just made me feel funny after Matías didn't walk up with me."

I burst into tears and sob. He rubs his hand over my ass, and it's so soothing. But I'm still upset. I continue to cry as he helps me to sit on his lap, his legs open with my ass between his thighs, so they don't press against me. But that isn't what either of us needs. We reach for his cargo pants at the same time. He unfastens them, and I pull his boxer briefs out of the way. He brings me down on his cock, and our gazes lock. We've resolved nothing, but things just got a little better.

"What do you mean Catalina said something to Matías?"

"I don't know. Luciana seemed pretty accepting of me when she said one day she'd tell me what happened to her husband. That was after she said you and I look like we've been together far longer than we have. That there's natural intimacy between us most couples don't share unless they've been together for a while. Catalina called me 'sister' when she explained I should ask Matías for anything I need, but now I don't know what to make of it. None of them really gave me any assurance they welcome me into their family."

"They will."

I shake my head.

"When Matías arrived, he went to say hello to Catalina. They both looked over at me before they whispered something to each other. It was while Luciana was talking to me. I just assumed it was a husband and a wife talking. I know it probably was, but I doubted it once we arrived. And then, when I found the envelope it made me suspicious all over again. Your men swept the house, so why didn't they spot the envelope? If someone placed it on the table while Hunt was here, then they should've been in place to see anybody sneak onto my property."

"I'm sorry, *chiquita*. I will find out what's going on. I know Catalina. I don't believe she had anything to do with this. I don't believe Matías would either. But I trust my sister more than I do him. I won't get angry at you for telling me this. I'm worried, too. You don't know them yet. Just like you have to build their trust, it's understandable they have to build yours. It doesn't come naturally in this world. I will find out what's going on."

"Please don't say anything to your sister about me doubting them."

"I won't, but I will find out why none of the men walked from the car to the door with you. Be honest with me, Ellie. If you went in through the garage, they would've closed the garage door behind you. How scared were you to be in there with those men?"

I don't want to meet his gaze. I feel like a coward considering all I've done. Yet, it spooked me being alone with them.

"I had a knife in my purse, but I didn't have my gun, Enrique. I had my keys out because I considered going in through the front door before I got out of the town car. They were in my pocket. If it had taken a moment longer for Matías to go in the house with Pedro or if Diego stepped away from the garage door, I would've gotten in and locked the car door. If any of them got any closer, I would've left."

"Ellie, that's a big deal, too. If you were apprehensive enough to plan an escape, something was seriously off."

"I should show you the photos."

"Yeah."

I stand, neither of us liking it, but I have to show him. I don't bother pulling up my pants. Instead, I kick them free. The last thing I want is that cotton rubbing against my skin. Since he doesn't insist I wear them, I step around them. He slides his hand into mine as we walk into my office. He sees both testing kits on my desk and pulls me to a stop.

"Did you find anything with the contaminant test?"

"No, they were clean. There's nothing on any of them, but I found fingerprints. I just don't have a way to run them."

"I'll get them over to Joaquin. He can take care of it and let me know. Are you okay with him coming over, or do you want to go to my place instead?"

"I can't leave Constantine here."

"I didn't think that you would. Wherever you go, your beast comes too."

Constantine stood by me at the door when I peeped through the hole, but the moment he saw it was Enrique, he just wiggled until he got bored. I know he nudged Enrique's thigh, and Enrique patted his head once before Constantine went to his bed. He's thumping his tail right now since we walked past him.

There's nothing beastly about my gentle giant. Just the opposite.

"I don't know, Enrique. I know your property is safer with your guards patrolling, but I have an unreasonable fear of going near your men even though you're with me. It was Andrés and Carlos who spotted the dash cam, but how do we know they weren't the ones taking these photos?"

I shake my head at my own thoughts.

"That makes no sense. They didn't know me when whoever this is took some of them. They had no way or reason to suspect me of anything. I—I'm not even thinking logically right now, Enrique. I don't know what to make of all of this."

"I know, little one, and neither do I, but we'll figure it out together, whatever it is."

"Thank you. I am not usually this easily bothered by things, but it just feels off, and I can't put my finger on it. It's throwing me for a loop. I don't want to see ghosts where there are none."

"No, this is a serious invasion of your privacy, Ellie. I don't blame you for being upset. It was bad enough looking at them the first time, but I'm certain you were looking at it as evidence, not emotionally, as somebody who's had their privacy violated."

"True. It feels different looking at these a second time. All right. I can go with you, and I'd prefer that."

"Of course you're coming with me."

"No, I mean in the same vehicle."

"I didn't think we'd drive separately. Pack a few days' worth of clothes. We'll pack Constantine's food and bowls. We'll take one of his beds, his treats, and his toys. You can stay as long as you want. We can always come back here at any time, either to return your stuff or to get more."

I merely nod. He gives me a kiss and a soft pat on my backside before pointing me toward the stairs. I hear him dialing his phone while I grab my pants from the living room. Then his voice fades as I head up the stairs, but it's still clear.

"Joaquin, I want you at my house with your computer. I have prints for you to run."

Chapter Nineteen

Enrique

I don't want Ellie to know how bothered I am by these photos, but I also won't lie to her about whatever results Joaquin gets once he examines the prints she pulled. I put all the photographs back in the envelope as I speak to him and round up the test kits' results. Once I have those in another envelope I found on the shelves behind her desk, I head to where I've seen her keep Constantine's food.

I grab his bowls and the storage container of food, stacking them by the garage door. I grab his bed as well and toss some of his toys into a reusable grocery bag hanging from the pantry door.

"Thank you for getting all of that together."

I turn as Ellie enters the kitchen. She has a large duffel bag with her, then a smaller looking overnight bag. When my gaze reaches her again, something dawns on me, forcing my attention back to the black duffel bag.

"Yes, Enrique, it's what you think."

She's got her rifle and whatever other weapons she owns in the bag with her.

"Do you object to me taking these to your home?"

"Hardly. I have a full arsenal, as you can imagine, but if you feel more comfortable with weapons you know, then I won't say no."

She nods.

"Funny thing is, I never believed in keeping weapons in a home before I got married. I didn't imagine having them with kids in the house. I wasn't blind to what my dad did, but I was naive enough to think the arsenal he kept was unnecessary. I figured the average person could probably rely on the police coming and are more likely to hurt themselves than not, but this lifestyle required us to have them. We always kept them out of reach of the boys until we were certain they were old enough to understand the danger that went with them. We had drawers installed in the kitchen and bathrooms, bedroom dressers—all over the place—that had special latches that only opened if you knew where to press them. That's where we kept the guns, not in a safe that would take us too long to open. When I moved in here, I thought I would tuck these away and let them get dusty. They had been for a while. Little did I know not only would I need them once, but that I would want them with me just to leave the house."

"I understand, little one. Take whatever will make you feel comfortable while you're at my place."

"I can tell you, panties would make these capris more comfortable, but I don't think I'm allowed to take those."

"Most definitely not. You tempt me to outlaw anything but skirts and dresses."

"You really want free access, don't you?"

"I do. What's yours is mine, and what's mine is my own, and that pussy belongs to me."

She laughs, and it lightens the mood. I'm mostly serious. I say it with a smile, and it calms her.

"Can we go in my car? I'm assuming someone dropped you off because I didn't see headlights pull into the driveway."

"Yes, I had the guys drop me off here rather than at my house. We can go in your car, and my men can surround us."

"All right." She hesitates before she agrees to that.

"Ellie, I understand how nervous you are, but without knowing who sent the photos, there's no way I'm taking you anywhere without additional guards. We can ride in your car, just the two of us, but I want other guards to accompany us."

"I get it, Enrique, and normally that would make me feel better. I'm just on edge now, and I suppose pretty paranoid."

I pull her into my arms, and even though she leans into me, I still feel the tension in her body as much as she tries to relax.

"You're not paranoid. You're responsible and cautious. I'm trying to be the same way. We'll both feel better once we're home and tucked away in our bed."

I don't realize what I'm saying until it hangs in the air surrounding us. I wait for her to tense all over again or jerk away; instead, she sighs. I guess she approves of the idea that we could share a place. I want her to feel at ease in my house and think of it as our home.

I'm not married to the house I live in, but it's more secure than here. If we were ever to buy a new home together, it would have to be in a neighborhood similar to my current one where it's gated, and my property could be too. There aren't too many neighborhoods like that available here. Not even my brother's neighborhood has gated properties.

However, there're still a few houses available in the same neighborhood the Mancinellis, O'Rourkes, and Kutsenkos took over in Queens. It's syndicate Switzerland where nobody violates the sanctity of people's homes, at least not too badly since there could be women and children around.

"Enrique?"

"Yes, just thinking, *chiquita*. Let's get everything loaded into your car, and we can head out."

"All right, would you prefer to drive?"

"It would probably be easier if I did."

She hands me the keys from the hook by the door. It's a key-shaped wood board with hooks. I think it's probably something one of her boys made while they were in middle school if they had woodshop. She grins at me and shakes her head.

"None of my sons made that. I did in seventh grade shop."

It's as though she could hear my thoughts.

"Wait, it's yours? How old is it?"

"Old enough, but it still works. Waste not want not."

"I think it's rather sweet you still have something from your childhood you made."

I kiss her cheek as I hold the garage door open for her. She calls Constantine and snaps his leash on before leading him out to the SUV. I grab the bed and all of his other accoutrements and put everything in the trunk. Neither of us opens the garage door until we're in the car with our seatbelts on. I click the button on the visor, and the door opens.

There are two cars in the driveway right now, which surprises me. There was only one when I arrived. Luckily, she's parked in the third garage, so there's room for me to reverse out of the single and onto the driveway. When I pull even with Matías, I wind down the window.

"Who's that?"

"Andrés."

"He and Carlos aren't on the rotation tonight."

"That's what I told him, but he still insisted on showing up."

"All right. Have him lead, and you follow. I'm taking Elodie to my house. Have the others stay here to keep an eye on the place. I want somebody positioned in the backyard as well. Let the guys know. We'll wait for you on the street."

I wind up the window and sense Ellie's unease about that exchange. I want to assure her, but I don't like unexpected arrivals.

Why did Andrés come?

Why didn't anyone tell me?

I retrieve my phone from my pocket once we're on the street, waiting for Andrés to pull ahead of us and Matías to get behind us. I tap Pablo's contact and put the phone to my ear.

"Ellie, I'm going to speak Spanish only because I don't know where this conversation is going."

"Enrique, I understand. You can speak Spanish anytime you

want. I may have a general understanding of what's going on, but I won't be able to follow all of it. I definitely couldn't repeat any of it in Spanish, and I would never do that in English."

"I know, *chiquita...Hola*, Pablo."

"*Hola, tío. Que pasa?*"

"I'm bringing Ellie over to my house. I need to know if you changed the rotation and sent Andrés over here."

"No, I didn't know he was. Today's his day off."

"I backed out of Ellie's garage, and there was a second car in the driveway. I couldn't see the driver through two tinted windows since the car was on the other side of Matías. He told me it was Andrés. I'm trying to see if it's him right now. The car's passing us to get ahead of me since we're leaving Ellie's neighborhood. I can't be certain. Can you pull up his tracker?"

"Yeah, give me a moment, *tío*."

I wait as Pablo looks up what I need.

"Hey, can you also find Carlos? It should be his day off, too."

"Yeah, I'm looking at both of them. Neither is near Ellie's house. They're both at a casino in Atlantic City."

What the fuck?

"All right. Where are you right now?"

"I'm home. Do you need me to go to your place?"

"Yeah. Where are your cousins?"

"Alejandro's here with me. He's in the living room, and I'm getting changed. *Tres J's* went to *Tía* Luciana's."

Fortunately, my sister doesn't live far from me either, so Jorge and Javier can get to my house even faster than Pablo and Alejandro.

"I want all of you to meet me there. Joaquin should already be on his way."

"Why's he headed there?"

"I'll explain when we're all together, but I need him to run some fingerprints for me."

"Is everything okay?"

"I'm not sure. I don't think so."

"What's going on, *tío*?"

267

"Can Alejandro hear you?"

"No."

"*Tío* Matías lied to me about who was in the other car in Ellie's driveway."

"Is it possible he didn't know?"

"No, they parked beside each other, hood to trunk, so he could speak to whoever. Now they know I'm taking Ellie to my house. I will, but I'll take a detour to get there. I'm in Ellie's SUV. If anybody else shows up at my gate, don't let them in. Call the house and let the men know. It doesn't matter if they recognize them or not. Only you and your cousins are allowed on the property."

"*Tío*, this is serious if you don't want *Tío* Matías there."

"Until I understand what's going on, I don't want anybody other than the five of you."

"Should I tell Papa?"

"Later. Once we have a better understanding of what's going on. I don't want him to think he needs to leave your mama again tonight."

"Okay. What do I tell Alejandro?"

"Nothing yet."

"And if he gets a call?"

I know he means if Alejandro gets a call from his dad, but Pablo doesn't want to say his uncle's name again.

"He can answer honestly. He doesn't know what's going on. Just tell him I need you there now."

"All right, we'll be over there as soon as we can."

It didn't sound like he had me on speaker. I trust Alejandro implicitly, but I don't want my nephew in a position of questioning his father or having to pick between us until I know whether he needs to choose.

I follow the car Andrés is supposedly in as we pass through the neighborhood gate. I go two blocks with Matías behind me. I take an unexpected left, leaving the unknown driver to go ahead of us, and Matías unprepared for my sudden detour. I speed, navigating through the surrounding neighborhood to ensure Matías doesn't catch up with me. I'm certain the mystery driver already noticed we're no longer behind them.

I can see the lights in my neighborhood as I turn the last corner. I glance in the rearview mirror and recognize Matías's car coming up behind us. When I look ahead, I recognize the oncoming car as one from my fleet. They're trying to box us in. I spin the SUV around as I go through an intersection, not bothering with the stop sign. I take the first right, just as Matías becomes visible behind the wheel.

"Watch behind us, Ellie."

"Yes, Daddy."

She's said that playfully and seductively. I love that, but I hate it when I hear her say it out of fear.

"It's all right, *chiquita*. Change of plans. We won't go to my house."

"Where're we going instead?"

"Luis's."

"No, Enrique. Margherita looked tired today. We have to go somewhere else. I don't want this around her, whatever's going on. I don't want her to be a target, too."

"It's not your decision, Ellie, even though I appreciate what you're saying. We have protocols in place for things like this."

She remains quiet as I concentrate on maneuvering. Both cars now follow me, and it won't take long for them to realize the new destination. I just need to keep them behind me rather than either of them getting in front of me again. I'll circle some more blocks, but I'll take the most direct route I can.

A car pulling out of a driveway forces me to slow. When Matías's car gets too close, I swerve around the one that just got in front of me. The driver blows his horn, pissed at what I'm certain he believes is erratic driving. I call it evasive maneuvering. I flick my gaze to the rearview mirror; I only see Matías's vehicle. It makes me wonder if they already guessed where we're headed and if the other car isn't trying to get ahead of us.

"Enrique, up there."

Ellie points to headlights that're barely visible, but they're at a street corner two blocks ahead of us. They aren't moving, and there isn't a stoplight there, only a stop sign.

"I see them, *chiquita*."

I take another unexpected left turn. Ellie reaches back to pat Constantine who whimpers, not liking these unpredictable moves. I pray I don't make him carsick. Dog vomit is the last thing we need to deal with right now, and I'd feel guilty.

As we turn onto a dark street, I turn off the headlights, hoping to be less noticeable if either of our pursuers realizes what road we're on.

Ellie unfastens her seatbelt. I reach for her, but she pushes away my hand. She scrambles into the back seat beside Constantine. She keeps her head low as she urges the dog to sit in front of her as she kneels on the floor. She reaches to the side and folds down half of the back seat. She scrambles to reach her weapons bag.

I peer in the mirror again as I hear the zipper open. It shouldn't surprise me, but it does when she assembles the rifle in the dark. I recognize each sound it makes, and there's no doubting from her speed she's an expert.

She lies on her belly with the rifle propped in front of her on a tripod. She can't shoot with it in that position, but it makes it easier for her when she's ready to get up and fire through the back window. I hate knowing she's in her element, but I don't worry she'll panic. I can just worry the normal amount I would if I were in this situation with my brother or nephews.

"Enrique, there's somebody approaching. They don't have their headlights on either."

"I know, *chiquita*. I saw them."

"How far are we from Luis's?"

"About ten minutes."

"How do you want me to handle this? They won't expect me to be armed. Do I stop them now?"

"No, not yet. We're almost to a vacant lot we can cut across. Once we're there, then we'll make our move. I don't want anyone to see or hear that car crash into something."

"Do you think there's one or two men?"

"I'm really not sure."

But I will fucking find out. To target Ellie is the same as targeting me. There's a short list of people who've attempted it, and no one on it still breathes.

I spot the dip in the curb where I can enter the vacant lot. Thankfully, Ellie drives a sturdy SUV and not some subcompact that couldn't handle the rutted dirt.

"Enrique?"

"Can you get a clean shot?"

I sense her movement because I can't look back right now. There are some deep holes, and I need to avoid them, so she can keep her sights level.

"Yeah. Constantine, down."

The dog shifts and puts his head between the two front seats, his nose nudging my elbow. I reach back to pet him, silently promising him all the treats he can eat for the next month.

"Do you want to talk to them?"

"Can you tell yet if there's a passenger?" I slow down and allow our pursuers to draw a little closer.

"There is."

"Leave him."

"Roll down the window."

There aren't many SUVs with roll down rear windows, but Ellie's is one of them. It makes me wonder...

"Yes, this is why I have the roll down window."

"Psychic?"

"Maybe." Her tone is lighter than I'd expect.

She adjusts her position, coming onto her knees. I take my chances and watch in the mirror as she lifts her rifle while the window lowers enough for her to stick the muzzle out. There's no hesitation. I hear the windshield shatter, then the tire pop. The car careens to the right before coming to a stop.

"Rabbit."

Whoever the passenger is thinks he can outrun a bullet.

"Kneecaps. He's down, Enrique."

Not that the fucker will live, but she blew out his kneecaps. With her caliber rifle, he'll never walk again. I turn the SUV around and head toward the man attempting to commando crawl away from the vehicle. I pull up, so he's on my side. I grab the gun at my lower back as I open the door. Ellie lifts her rifle and draws it back into the SUV. She crawls into the back seat and slips out the door behind me. We point our weapons toward a man I don't know. I kick him in the ribs, noticing his head's bleeding. There's a shard of windshield sticking out of his cheek. He groans but tries to pull himself away. My next kick forces him onto his back.

"Who are you?"

His response is a groan.

"Who are you?"

I place my foot on his chest, pressing against it as I speak. He stares blankly at me as I take a photo with my phone, hoping I'll discover who he is if he refuses to speak.

"*¿Quién eres?*" Who are you?

"*A la chingada.*" Go to hell.

Mexican slang. Interesting.

"*¿Quién te envió?*" Who sent you?

"*¿No te gustaría saberlo?*" Wouldn't you like to know?

Definitely *not* a native speaker. His accent is piss poor when he isn't swearing.

I lean over to Ellie, who has her rifle pointed at his groin, and whisper. "Ask him in Italian if he planned to die today."

"*Avevi intenzione di morire oggi?*"

"*Come ho fatto ieri e come farò domani.*"

She interprets for me. "As much as I did yesterday and as much as I will tomorrow."

Arrogant little fucker.

"*Domani? Hai esaurito il domani quando ti sei svegliato ieri.*"

Ellie doesn't look at me when she shares what she said. Instead, her lips curls in disgust.

"I told him, 'Tomorrow? You ran out of tomorrows when you woke up yesterday.'"

"Can you tell where he's from?"

"My guess is around Venice. He could be *Mala del Brenta*."

Salvatore's linked to them. His niece-in-law twice over is Venetian, and her father is the don.

"Do you know Allegra Carosi?"

"No. Should I?"

"She's Salvatore Mancinelli's sister-in-law. She's married to their don."

"Don Torretta's oldest daughter? I remember the name now. Her daughter's married to Salvatore's nephew Carmine, right?"

"Yes."

"He and Tommaso are allies. Did Salvatore send him?"

Did our plan already get back to Salvatore?

"I don't know."

I back away as I answer, then round the car to see if I recognize the driver. I pull the door open, then shove the slumped body back from the steering wheel. I don't know him. I snap a photo with my phone.

"Do you want me to ask him anything else? Or—"

Gunshots fill the air, and I dive to cover Ellie as the first few pings against our original pursuers' car land far too close to us. Ellie rolls—at least tries to since I'm so much heavier than her—to face where the barrage is coming from.

"Get behind the car."

I give the order as I push up high enough to shield her as she scrambles out from beneath me. She gets to her feet but stays low as she darts to the back of the vehicle. I follow close on her heels. We squat with our backs to each other as we peek around the sides.

"Eleven o'clock."

I have to turn toward Ellie to see what she does. She lifts her rifle and fires. The car racing toward us jerks to the left as she takes out the front driver's side tire.

"That's not the car Matías was in earlier. Do you recognize it?"

"I don't. It doesn't belong to my fleet or any of my men. At least, not that I know of."

"Then where's Matías?"

I shift to sweep my gaze over our surroundings. Nothing moves beyond the car still coming toward us.

"Do you want them to live?"

"No."

My answer is immediate. I don't have to think twice about it. Whoever it is won't give us any more information than the *care mondá*—dickface—cowering in front of me, still exposed to the shooters. Either I'll recognize them or not. A rummage through their wallet or phone will tell me more.

I shift to look over her shoulder as she takes out the front passenger side tire. The silencer on Ellie's rifle makes it nearly soundless, but the glass shattering isn't. With the windshield gone, she lines up the sights on her gun and shoots twice. It's too dark to see the blood spray, but I can imagine what the inside of the car must look like. Her aim is impeccable.

"We need to get back to your car, Ellie."

"What about him?"

She looks back over her shoulder at me and nudges her chin in the surviving man's direction. He's wisely stayed put not wanting to make himself a target. I pivot toward the guy and put a bullet through his forehead. I turn my head toward Ellie as I squeeze the trigger. I want to know what she thinks when I shoot at close range. There's no anonymity to my target. She doesn't flinch.

We both look around, seeing no new threats. We sprint to her SUV, and once more I get in the driver's seat, and she climbs in the back seat. I hear her moving things around in her duffle bag. There's no mistaking the sound of a pump-action shotgun. She loads five rounds before going still. She has plenty of bullets left in her rifle, and now she has the second weapon loaded.

I put the car in gear and press on the gas. I plan to cross the field, get on the highway, and circle around, arriving at my brother's from the other side. Two cars appearing from opposite directions cut those plans short.

Their headlights threaten to blind me since they have their brights on. I'm unprepared to hear Ellie's rifle behind me. My gaze flicks to the rearview mirror, spotting a third car approaching from behind as it swerves before coming to an abrupt stop.

¿Quién carajos son estos hijos de puta? ¿De dónde diablos salen? ¿Dónde está Matáis ahora? Who the fuck are these mother-fuckers? Where the fuck do they keep coming from? Where's Matáis now?

I have plenty more questions, but not a single fucking answer.

Barely taking my eyes off the approaching cars, I give my phone a command. "Call Pablo."

"Calling Pablo." The digital voice sounds ridiculously chipper in this situation.

"*Tío*, I was just about to call. We're all here."

"Ellie and I are at the vacant lot where we're going to put up the grocery store. Get the cleaners here now. We have multiple cars coming at us. Ellie already took out five men, and I finished another. I'm trying to get us out of here, but I have two more cars trying to cut me off."

I need our team to clear the scene of all evidence. It'll never look like anything happened once they're done.

"Who are they?" That's Joaquin, so I hope giving him our only clue might be enough for him to start digging.

"Ellie thinks the guy we questioned was Venetian. He said, '*A la chingada.*'"

"Mexican slang?"

"Yeah, Alejandro. I don't know if he pretended not to understand Spanish, but he didn't respond beyond swearing at me. Ellie questioned him in Italian, but she never got to ask anything significant. The second car arrived, and the men immediately opened fire on us. Ellie neutralized them. I've got cars three and four swerving in front of me, and she took out car five already."

"Enrique, swing around. Get the driver's side closer to them, then stop."

"No, Ellie. We need to go."

"Do it, Enrique. Trust me." She's winding down the back driver's side window as Constantine shifts to the far back of the car.

"*Tío*, you need to get out of there. Go to Papa's."

Pablo's insistent, and my logic says to listen, but my gut tells me to do what Ellie said. I twist the wheel hard to the right, and the tail end swings around. I angled us, so she has a clear shot. As soon as I slow, car doors open, and four men pour out of each car. I watch as Ellie takes out the two on each far side with her rifle. Then she fires her shotgun. She releases the empty shells as the pellets zoom through the air. The greater the distance, the wider they spray. She shoots a second time and fells all four men between the two vehicles.

"Go!"

I don't need her to tell me to drive. We're already on the move.

Chapter Twenty

Ellie

Things you didn't imagine happening tonight for five hundred.

If only this were as simple as a *Jeopardy* category—even a challenging one. But it's not. I felt uneasy while leaving my house, but I'm petrified now. I'm used to working alone. I have Enrique's life to consider, too. I just took a monumental risk. I opened him up to take fire, but I needed to get close enough to shoot them. I knew the buckshot would spray pellets at them, so I had a greater chance of hitting them if they ran toward us.

"*Tío!* What's happening?!" There's fear in Pablo's voice that I'm certain none of them are used to.

"Ellie got rid of that threat."

"Not all of it. Enrique, there's another car behind us. It looks like Matías. What do you want me to do?"

"Papa?"

Fuck. Poor Alejandro. The last thing I want to do is kill the young man's father. But if it's between Enrique and Matías, then Matías's gotta go.

"Nothing yet, *chiquita*. If he gets too close, disable the car."

It's unlike him to let something slip, but I don't think he realizes what he called me before the word left his mouth.

"*Sí, papi.*" I speak barely above a whisper, so I don't think it carried to the call.

"What are you talking about? What's Papa doing?"

Alejandro's understandably upset, and I feel horrible for him. I sense Enrique's hesitation as he speeds up, putting more distance between Matías and us. But the man doesn't relent. His car races after us, and that's made easier once we're back on the street with no ruts to contend with.

"Your father lied about who was in the car at Ellie's and chased us, trying to box us in between him and men we don't recognize."

I know Enrique hates explaining this to Alejandro.

"*Tío*, you have to be mistaken. There has to be a reason. Maybe he's trying to help you."

"Alejandro, my phone works just fine because I'm on it right now. If he was trying to help me, why hasn't he called?"

"Why haven't you called him? *Mierda.* I'm sorry." Shit.

The moment the words leave Enrique's nephew's mouth, he regrets them and wishes he could swallow them back. But I can't blame him. I'd have the same reaction if I were in the young man's position. Enrique lets it go. I know, had it been anybody outside his immediate family, there'd be consequences for that slip.

"Right now, Alejandro, I'm a little busy trying to keep Ellie and me alive. Considering multiple people have shot at us from multiple directions and nearly run us off the road, I haven't had a chance to make too many phone calls."

"Where's Papa now?"

"He's still following me."

I went back to crouching after I shot the men in the last two cars. I lift my head just enough to peer out the back window. Matías is there, but not as close as he was.

I wonder if that's because Matías realizes there's no one else to help him. Or is it because he knows he has people to help, so he doesn't need to stay that close? My mind wars with those two options, knowing either is possible. I disassemble the shotgun and the rifle as Enrique speaks to his family. I put them back in the duffel bag, pulling out my handgun with a loaded magazine and a spare.

I climb back into the front seat as Enrique explains we were headed to Luis and Margherita's, but he's decided we're going to his house after all.

"I'm taking a roundabout way again, so it'll take me a little while. Give me twenty minutes to get there. I'm activating my tracker now. If I'm not there in twenty minutes, you need to find us."

It tempts me to activate mine.

My boys are the ones who'd get the alert. It's in a bracelet they gave me. Not exactly as a divorce present, but as the result of the divorce, because the tracker I wore for nearly three decades linked to Tommaso's system, and I definitely don't want him monitoring my whereabouts. Plus, it wouldn't have done me any good living in New Jersey when all his men are in Boston.

Even though two of my boys are in Boston and one is in Connecticut, if something happens to me, they should know. It surprises me I didn't already think to press the alert. It wasn't that I was too distracted. I've been in more chaotic scenarios than this. It was my implicit trust in Enrique to get us out of this that kept me from thinking about hitting my tracker.

I settle into the front seat, putting my seatbelt on. It's always nerve-wracking being in any type of vehicle chase without a seatbelt on, but there are plenty of times where that's not an option, like tonight. I keep my eyes peeled for anything that appears unusual.

"I'll call you back, Pablo, if anything changes. Remember, twenty minutes."

"All right, *tío*, twenty minutes."

Enrique ends the call, and while we have a moment's reprieve from whatever the fuck is going on, he sticks out his right hand, and I eagerly lace the fingers of my left hand with his.

It's a moment of reassurance for both of us. Part of me wants to ask what he would do if he were in this situation with another woman. Would his ex-wife have been able to handle it? Would she have been anything like me? I know he didn't love her and was glad to be rid of her once they divorced because of her infidelity and betrayal, but I've wondered a few times if I'm anything like her.

I have olive skin and dark hair. Could I look anything like her?

"*Chiquita*, I'm sorry we're going through this, but I'm so damn glad you're so capable. I don't know what I would do if I didn't have you with me right now. I'd probably be dead."

"Don't say that. Never, ever say that. You and I both know the possibilities without you saying them aloud."

"All right, *chiquita*, I'm sorry, but I'm still so damn proud of you. I know how fortunate I am that you have the skills you do. This would be a very different situation if you didn't."

"I'm certain there are other women out there like me you could've fallen for."

"*Chiquita*, there's no one out there like you. That's why I haven't found another woman who makes me feel the way you do. And if you're wondering, no, Daniela never could've done any of this. She would've been more liability than benefit. You two are nothing alike, and that makes me even more grateful for you. You know how much I worry about you, and I'll never stop—especially since this situation reminds us of the danger I bring to you—but I'm so damn lucky you're with me. I don't know that I'd survive this with someone else."

"Daddy, we don't know that this is about you at all. It could be entirely about me, so until we find out otherwise, don't blame yourself for anything unless you want me blaming myself, too.

"Definitely not, *cariño*."

"Then don't take this on yourself. We'll figure this out together."

We fall silent for a moment as we both flicker our gazes to the mirrors. I use the side-view mirror on my door, and Enrique keeps checking the rearview one. We're the only people on this side street, but I recognize where we are, and we'll soon be on the highway. This is definitely a roundabout way to get to his house, but so far I don't see Matías's car, and no other vehicle is too close. I won't let my guard down, though.

We both remain vigilant. I watch the exit ramps and entry ramps as we go past each one, waiting with knots in my stomach and a lump in my throat that this might be the one. That's where somebody catches up to us.

When Enrique pulls off the highway, my gun rests in my lap. I put my free hand on the door, my finger resting over the window button. We think of the same thing at the same time because we let go of each other, and Enrique picks up his handgun while I do the same.

We're both prepared to shoot. I'm left-handed, but I can do most things ambidextrous because it's a challenge to be left-handed in a right-handed world. I can shoot with either, so I'm not worried I won't manage from this side if I need to. Once I get the window down, I can switch hands. I wonder whether Enrique can shoot easily with his left one.

"*Cariño*, I see how comfortably you're holding that gun. I learned to shoot with both hands as well. My father insisted. All of my nephews and my brother know how, too."

I nod. I want to learn more about his childhood, but it saddens me when these brief insights are about how he learned to survive this brutal life. I'm grateful for how normal a childhood my kids had. I'm certain I didn't have the same worries his parents did, and I didn't have to teach my children the same lessons his parents did.

"Don't worry, little one. One of these days, I'll tell you cheerful stories from when I grew up."

I glance over at him, and even though he's still looking straight ahead, he smiles.

"I've already figured out how much we think alike."

"It is rather uncanny, isn't it, Daddy?"

"It is uncanny, and that's how I know you're the only one I'll ever want."

This isn't the right time to make any professions of love and devotion, but I'm certainly tempted. I think my feelings are already there. I've already considered it many times, but I don't want to rush into saying something I can't take back.

When he puts his hand on my thigh, squeezes it, then strokes his thumb along the outside, I think he's thinking the same thing. Neither of us wants to make what could be a deathbed confession when we might survive. This is hardly the most romantic setting, but I also don't want to miss the opportunity in case we don't make it. It could all be over in a blink. I might not have time for a last-minute profession. I'm torn, but I keep my thoughts to myself.

I keep checking my mirror as we approach Enrique's neighborhood. He flashes the headlights four times as we approach a mansion that's enormous for one person. Men pour out of the front door. Enrique's nephews have their guns drawn as the gates slide open. The men patrolling his property have their rifles at the ready, scattered around the circular drive and front yard.

We pull around, so I'm closer to the front door. Alejandro rushes forward to open my door. I have a moment of trepidation he'll drag me out, blaming me for this. I get out, and immediately, the men surround me. But they're shielding me. They're protecting me.

Alejandro's left hand wraps lightly around my upper right arm. He draws me backward as the men move with us, none turning away from the gate. Enrique rushes around to me just as another car swings into the driveway as the gates change direction.

"Papa!" Alejandro's grip loosens for a moment before he realizes what he's doing.

I glance up at the man who looks most like Enrique. I see the anguish because he wants to run to his father, but he remembers his duty is to protect his *jefe* and by extension, now me too.

Men swarm forward, and *Tres J's* bolt to the car. They have guns aimed at Matías, who drops out of view as he leans to his right. No one shoots, but I'm not surprised he tries to stay out of sight. Jorge pulls on the door handle, but nothing happens.

My brow furrows. Something's going on in the car. There's someone in the back seat I didn't notice before. The windows were too tinted, and it was too dark. But I can tell there's a scuffle.

Then there's the sound of a key fob unlocking the vehicle. I look over at Alejandro and realize he has keys to his dad's car.

Armed guards yank open three doors, and Jorge opens the driver's door. Guards pull two men from the back seat. Jorge helps Matías from the car as his brothers rush back to help surround me.

"Papa!"

Alejandro shifts his focus to Enrique, who nods. He lets go of my arm and bolts to his father. Matías has blood dripping from his temple from someone pistol whipping him. He can barely stand, and it wouldn't surprise me if he's seeing stars.

"They have Catalina!"

The sentence hangs in the air before all hell breaks loose.

"Pablo, *Dos J's*, get Ellie in the house. Now. Stay with her. Javier, pull up your mama's location. Make sure she's safe. Pablo, call your dad."

"*Sí, tío.*"

Three voices respond, but I don't budge.

"Enrique, I know that man." I point to the one on the far side of the car who was in Matías's back seat.

"Is he one of Tommaso's?"

I shake my head. "He's a mercenary, too. I've been on jobs at the same place as him. He never knew who I was. If they have Catalina..."

I trail off, not wanting to say what I know is a strong possibility. My gaze meets Enrique's, and I need to say nothing more for him to understand.

"Let me speak to him."

"No, Ellie, this is out of your hands now."

"Do you know him?"

"No, but—"

"Then you don't know the easiest way to get information from him."

"Just tell me, and I'll do whatever it is."

I shake my head again. I still don't want to argue with him in public, but I will if I must. I step around Pablo, my gun aimed at the car, ready to pick off any of the men. I'll shoot any of those men, including Matías, if they look the wrong way at any of us.

"*Ta fille doit avoir six ou sept ans maintenant.*" Your daughter must be six- or seven-years-old by now.

I approach the vehicle and flick my fingers in a come here motion to the two guards surrounding my target. They hesitate and look toward Enrique, who must give them permission because each man grabs an arm and hauls the guy toward me. When he's in front of me, I point to the ground, and the guards press him to his knees. I continue in French.

"How's Marie-Claude, Gérard? Has she started school yet?"

The man's expression is inscrutable.

"I know you got her a puppy three months ago. It would be such a shame if she found it with its throat slit."

The man still looks straight ahead, but I see him clench his jaw. I'm out of the business, but I keep tabs on the people most likely to kill me if they find me.

"What will your wife do without you there when men break in and take your daughter? She won't know what to do since she has no clue who you are. You haven't prepared her for that because you believe no one knows about your real life, but Jacqueline won't be able to protect Marie-Claude or your little boy. Pierre looks so much like you these days, which is surprising since he's not your son."

Gérard Sainte-Croix's gaze flicks up to me. I shrug dismissively.

"He's not. He's Henri Bouvier's. Your wife has a type. She likes blondes. I know you've always suspected it, but it's true. It happened while you were on the Munich job. I'm certain you're wondering how I know. It's because I introduced them. You screwed Don Vizzini over on a job, and Henri owed me a favor. There's no way Pierre's yours since you were in Munich for three and a half weeks. The dates don't line up with when she had him."

I watch him as I mind fuck him.

"You've always suspected he's somebody else's. I have plenty more secrets I can share. How much more pain would you like me to inflict before I get mean?"

"You don't know what the hell you're talking about. You were arm candy for men doing business you know nothing about."

"But I do. Your wife has a birthmark on her left ass cheek. From nursing two kids, her right breast is slightly bigger than her left."

That registers shock on his face, and his body practically vibrates with rage. I step forward since the guards still hold his arms back. I put my handgun to his forehead and turn off the safety.

My bodyguards were often decoys when I wasn't fulfilling my role as an accountant. People suspected they might be mercenaries when they negotiated on Tommaso's behalf. But no one guessed I was the hired gun working behind the scenes. They didn't know I gave the men cues during the meetings where I was seen but not heard.

I've created and kept dossiers on many mercenaries and syndicate men over the years, including information about the people most important to them. It's a type of rainy-day fund. You never know what you might need to make it rain for someone else. It's awfully cloudy today.

I peer down at Gérard and grin as I keep antagonizing him in French.

"Is your daughter's favorite color still yellow? The last I heard, your wife was painting her bedroom to look like it was full of sunshine."

"Stay the hell away from my wife and children."

"Then stay the hell away from my family."

I push the muzzle of the handgun harder against his forehead, not thinking twice about calling Enrique's family mine. It comes naturally to think of them that way.

"If you are who you claim, you aren't family to anybody. You abandoned yours."

"Would you like my sons to prove how protective they are of their mother? I'm sure Enrique has somewhere we can put you until they can get here. In the meantime, I'm certain his nephews have questions for you, too. Where's Catalina?"

"Wouldn't you like to know?"

I look up from Gérard's glowering face to the guard on his right.

"Hold up his hand."

When the guard does, I grab Gérard's middle finger and push backwards while twisting until I feel the pop. I move on to his ring finger, then his thumb. I leave his index finger and pinky how they are.

"You have a choice. You can either answer my question, and all I do is break your last two fingers. Or you can be stubborn, and I'll blow your fucking hand off."

"You aren't doing shit like that with a pistol."

"I wasn't the driver tonight. After what you saw, do you believe all I have is this handgun? Enrique, can you grab my shotgun and my rifle, please?"

I stick with French since I know Enrique understands. It wouldn't surprise me to learn his nephews do, too. I sense Enrique's movement behind me. He hesitates, but then I hear the trunk open. I'm watching Gérard as his gaze darts toward the vehicle, then back up to me.

"You know my reputation—even if you didn't know it was me —and you know how I enjoy hunting. Maybe I should make you run. Can you hide behind a tree faster than I can shoot you? You know what happens to the body when it's hit with buckshot at close range. Is that how you'd like me to begin your torture? Because your fingers were just a hello."

The guy shakes his head, knowing everything I threaten is an understatement. I've hunted for nearly thirty years, and I've yet to miss my target when I make someone my prey.

"So, I'll ask you one more time before I get really convincing. Where is Catalina?"

I grab his pinky and pull it backwards until it nearly touches his wrist.

"She's at a warehouse in Hoboken."

He blurts his answer in English. She's still here in Jersey and not too far away. But I don't know which syndicate has properties there.

"Did you take her there?"

He shakes his head and then tilts it toward the other man who's still standing outside the vehicle. These two fuckers were in the back seat to coerce Matías. I can't blame the man for choosing his wife over Enrique and me. I understand he's supposed to put his *jefe* before everyone else. But I will never fault a person for putting their children ahead of absolutely everything. And I won't fault them for putting their spouse ahead of most things.

Enrique hands me the rifle, and I click the safety back on my handgun. My capris' waistband is snug enough to tuck the handgun against the small of my back. I check the chamber before I aim the rifle at the man who's said nothing yet. I put a bullet through each foot. I recognize the man from photos, but I've never met him before. I use the little German I have with the guy.

"*Ich weiß, wer Sie sind, auch wenn wir uns noch nie gesehen haben. Wie lautet die Adresse?*" I know who you are, even if we haven't seen each other before. What's the address?

The man glares at me and shakes his head while Enrique's guards have to hold him up. I gesture with the rifle to let him sit. When he does, he brings his shins up in front of him. I put a bullet through his left one.

"I can keep going. Can you?"

The man's clearly in agony, despite how he tries not to show it. Blood gushes from his feet and his shin. I comb through my memory for what I know about him. I remember he speaks English, too.

"You have a son at NYU. He lives in an apartment not too far off campus. Does he know you're here in the States, Johann? Is it time for you to have a brief visit? We can bring him here for you."

That gets his attention.

"Stay the fuck away from my son." His English is perfect.

"Then tell me what I want to know. Where is Catalina? What warehouse in Hoboken is she in?"

"Fuck off."

"The faster you give me my answer, the faster I can do just that. I hadn't planned to spend my evening with anybody other than my boyfriend."

I smirk and waggle my eyebrows. This isn't any less of a pissing contest just because I squat, and they stand. I turn my head as though I'm looking toward Enrique, but I don't take my eyes off the guy in front of me.

"Jealous of my plans?" I cock an eyebrow, and the guy jerks back. "Oh, you didn't think I knew about that? You think that's your best kept secret? Hardly. I've known about Gaston for years. I may not have met you before, but you're not a stranger. What would your wife say? What would your other boyfriend, Freddy, say about that?"

"You wouldn't dare. That would put a target on you for life."

"You don't think there's already at least one on me? You were here for all of this tonight. You have far more to lose than I do, Johann. You're here alone with no one to protect you. I'm the one with the guns and men. So, I'm asking you for the last time. Where is Catalina?"

I walk over to him and kick the shin where blood pours from the gunshot wound. He howls and sucks in a breath. He rambles off an address, and I hear Alejandro barking orders at someone. I don't turn to see who Alejandro's speaking to. He might have even called someone. I look over at Gérard instead.

"Is there anything else I should know about Catalina's location?"

Gérard shakes his head.

They're giving in far faster than I imagined. It's a combination of my reputation, Enrique's family's, and the guards. They know their death is inevitable, so they'd prefer to make it painless.

I look between my two prisoners, shifting my rifle between them.

"Eeny, meeny, miny, moe."

I point toward Gérard.

"Who sent you?"

"I don't know. It was anonymous for me. My instructions said to meet Johann, and we'd do the job together. At first, we didn't know why someone wanted us to watch you then kill you. Diaz came around, and we figured he was the reason. We never knew who you really are."

"How much were you paid?"

"Five-hundred-thousand up front, a million when the job is done."

I look over at the German. "What about you?"

"Same deal."

"Is that the price just for me? Or is that price for Enrique? Or is it for both of us?"

"That price is for you. If we take out the *jefe de jefes*, we each get a seven-hundred-and-fifty-thousand-dollar bonus."

I chuckle.

"I've always been expensive, but I had no idea I'd cost more than one of the wealthiest men in the world."

Enrique steps beside me and kisses my temple. "*Cariño*, you are priceless."

With Enrique standing beside me, his handgun pointed toward Gérard, I train my rifle on Johann.

"Who arranged this?"

He hesitates a moment too long, so I put another bullet through his other shin. If I do too much more, he'll pass out sooner and will be of no use to me. Eventually, he'll slide into unconsciousness from the pain and blood loss, so I need information now. I'll take my chances on him passing out in hopes this incentivizes him to spit out the info. Not that he'll survive this, but if he did, he'd never walk again. I've shattered both legs.

"I don't know for sure, but the IP address was from Russia, but that means nothing."

I gesture to a guard. "Can you get his cell phone, please?"

The guy reaches into Johann's pocket and pulls it out. He uses the retinal scan to unlock it.

"Pull up the message."

It requires he have one hand free, so I nod to the guard.

Johann taps on his phone screen, then we watch him scroll until he reaches out with his phone. The guard clamps his hand on Johann's shoulder as I take it from him. He can only keep his arm at the height it's at now. The guard's merciless grip forces his hand down once I take the device. I step back and Enrique takes my spot, his gun now to Johann's forehead.

With my gun pointing toward the ground, I read a post on the dark web with a specific request for my elimination. It describes me as a Mafioso's former wife, not as a Mafia accountant or mercenary. I see Enrique mentioned nowhere. I scan the date and realize this posted shortly after I finalized my divorce. That gives me a moment's pause.

I hadn't considered Tim at all.

I don't know what to make of this.

I never thought he would do something like put a hit out on me. Now I can't help but question all the years we were together. If he hates me enough to kill his own children's mother...

My mind rebels at that notion. While it wouldn't be impossible, it still isn't a theory that resonates with me. I continue to scroll, then tap the back button to see what else I can find in Johann's messages.

There's a more recent one where he explains to the anonymous client that I'm with Enrique. The response includes the bonus for eliminating him. These messages are dated two weeks after we started walking together.

I continue to search the man's phone, finding additional messages with updates for the client. However, nothing gives me any hints about who hired these men.

Alejandro steps beside Enrique, leaving his father leaning against the car. "*Tío*, everything's set."

I know that means they're ready to find Catalina. I look at the guards holding each man.

"Cut off their index fingers and thumbs, so I can get into their phones again once they lock. Take out an eyeball if needed."

"Wait, what?!"

"Gérard, if you've told us all you're willing to say, then I don't need you anymore. I'll get more information out of your phones. All I need you for is ways to unlock it."

I nod to the guards, and they pull the men away. More guards step forward to help restrain the men.

"Wait, wait, *wait*." Johann fights against the men, who try to pull him onto his back.

"If you have something worth saying, you better say it quickly."

"Wait. I know more."

"Get on with it, then."

"There was more than one job post about you."

"Intriguing, but not surprising. Are they recent ones?"

"Yes. There're always posts to eliminate any of us, but recently there've been several placed for you. Even before this one. It's just no one knew the mercenary we were after was a woman. I didn't connect them to you until now. You saw the original one. It described your appearance and age, and that you were once married to a Mafioso. It said nothing about who you worked for or what you did. Once we took the job, the message told us where to find you. It never said why. We figured someone thought you knew too much."

"Was this the highest offer?"

"No." Gérard pipes in but shrinks back when I turn a withering stare at him for interrupting. He had his chance. I return my attention to Johann.

"If this wasn't the best offer, then why take it if you could've earned more with somebody else as your client?"

"Because I don't know who this is, and it described an ex-wife not a gun for hire. I know who some of the other clients are who wanted the unnamed mercenary, and neither of us wants anything to do with them. Neither of us wanted to go after a fellow hitman with your record."

"Do you have the listings on here?"

"Yeah. Keep scrolling until you get to a folder icon. Tap that."

I do as he says, and I see four posts. I open the first one and skim. I look at Enrique and quirk a brow.

"You might want to take this one down."

"What?"

He holds out his hand for the phone and scans the post that describes but doesn't name me. The one overwhelming inaccuracy is it assumes I'm a man. Anybody working as a top echelon international mercenary would know who the mark was, but the job would've entailed searching for me. Until I confessed to Enrique, the only people who'd know it was me were Tommaso, Frank, their *consigliere*—Santino—and me.

Enrique taps on the screen again and turns his hand, so I can read the new post he pulled up. This one's from the Mancinellis. I skim that one too before Enrique moves on to a third one, which I'm certain came from the Kutsenkos, and the final one's from the O'Rourkes.

None of their names are on there. There's no mention of what type of syndicate, but when you've been in this business as long as all of us, little effort's needed to guess which family. They included nothing clearly identifiable, but put in context, the information that's there makes it easy to tell who's who.

Enrique looks between the two men. "No one wanted to tangle with the New York families. This is an outsider."

Johann nods. He's perspiring, the sweat trickling down his cheeks. He's growing paler by the word as he pants. I need this information fast.

"Why risk working with someone you don't know? How can you be sure they won't turn on you or have him turn on you?" I tilt my head toward Gérard.

"As long as I get paid, then I accept the risks that go with this. I always have."

"Who do you suspect hired you?"

"I think it's somebody in the Maldives."

"What makes you think that? You said it was someone in Russia."

"I said that's where the IPN was from, but that I didn't think it was someone there. I didn't mention that when I traced the IPN, that's where it went to."

I grit my teeth as I take the phone back from Enrique and go back to the original message thread. I reread the posting and all the correspondence between the man in front of me and his mystery employer.

"Motherfucker. Enrique, it's my Registered Agent. That's who posted this."

"The one who handles your LLC?"

"Yes, but he has nothing to gain because I tucked all the financials away behind enough walls he can't easily get to them, even as the Registered Agent. He's doing this on somebody else's behalf.

"Do you think they're coercing him into it?"

"Possibly. I don't know why he'd do it voluntarily. I've paid him well for his silence and discretion, but it's possible somebody's paying him even better."

In this world, people will sell their mother's souls to the devil for the right amount of money. I can't help but wonder if that's what happened. Somebody discovered my connection to him, and they're using it against me. I pay him an exorbitant fee for what he does, so he must be making a fortune if they're paying enough to convince him to betray me. Or they have something more powerful to coerce him with.

I go through a rapid process of elimination to consider who else might want me dead. Then I think about who has the resources to figure out who I am. The list isn't that long. I can wager some solid guesses who it is.

"Enrique, I don't think we need them anymore. You need to go."

"Alejandro, Javier, and Jorge will come with me. Joaquin and Pablo will stay with you."

"No, we've been through this before. You're not separating your family because of me. I'm fine on my own. You have men here you trust to protect you when you're alone. If you trust them, then I do too. My skills are obviously enough that I can easily add to my own defense if necessary. The more of you together, the faster it will go and the greater likelihood you'll all come home."

"*Chiquita*—"

I lean over and whisper in Enrique's ear.

"Daddy, you can punish me later. You can command me to do whatever you want. But we already know you won't convince me to back down on this. Save yourself the time and energy rather than arguing with me. Just give in now, and I'll gladly do whatever you want later. I promise."

His skepticism is obvious, but practicality wins when he nods.

"All right, but I wouldn't get used to having your way all the time, *chiquita*, or you will find yourself disappointed."

"I know, Daddy. Hurry and bring your sister home."

We gaze at one another, and now that we'll be apart rather than working together, the temptation to tell him how I feel nearly gets the better of me. His fingers channel through my hair as he pulls me close and gives me a potent kiss that sends me reeling as it intoxicates me.

When we pull apart, we look at each other, and we don't need words. We smile and each dip our chin to acknowledge our feelings. We want to express them now, but we want to say them in private. Enrique and I look back at the men in front of us.

"Little one, I'm not convinced their usefulness is over."

"All right, if you think there's reason to keep them alive, then do so."

"I'll have men take them to our place."

I know what that means, so I don't need an explanation. I've never been to the Vizzinis' place. I don't know for sure where it is, even though I have an idea. I've never wanted to know that about the Vizzinis, and I don't want to know it about Enrique's family either. The less I know, the fewer nightmares I can have.

The men who're holding Catalina—their nightmares haven't begun. But they will when Enrique and his family get there.

"I better show you the panic room if you're going to be here without any of the *niños*."

Chapter Twenty-One

Enrique

"If anything happens while you're upstairs, you come here, Ellie. Hit this button, and the alert will go out to all of us."

I point to the panic button in my panic room.

"Daddy, I know. You explained the button and everything else while you showed me the room downstairs. I grew up in a house with a panic room, and I raised my kids in a house with one. I have one in the house I live in now."

"You do?"

"Of course."

"Where is it?"

"The door is at the back of the hall closet. There are stairs taking you down to the basement and directly through a reinforced door to a soundproof, concrete room. The boys and I built it when I moved in."

"I was going to say that definitely wasn't part of the original blueprints."

"Even a turnkey property needs some personal touches."

"I hate leaving you here, but I prefer you and Constantine be here while I'm gone."

God bless José. He's one of my most senior guards and every animal's favorite person. He slipped over to Ellie's car and got Constantine out while we dealt with our unwanted guests. He took the dog around back and kept him occupied. Though even José wasn't enough to keep Constantine's attention when Ellie walked out to the patio.

The poor dog has glued himself to Ellie ever since he raced over to her. He nearly knocked her over when he reared back onto his hind legs, but he was so gentle when he put his paws on her shoulders and rested his head on one of them. He truly hugged her. He's closer to my height when he stands up like that. He's a few inches taller than Ellie who's about five-six.

Between a panic room off the butler's pantry and the one up here in my bedroom, and her dog, I'm calm enough to leave. I need to get to my sister, but I couldn't leave Ellie without being certain she's safe. I want to tell her to lock herself in one of these rooms until I get back, but I won't keep her a prisoner. I trust my men, but thinking Matías betrayed me is fucking with my head. I'm less trusting than I was.

"Daddy, you're going to keep everyone waiting. I'm certain they're all dressed and geared up now."

"I know."

We step back into my bedroom, and I push the clothes in my closet back into place. I rush to change into a fresh set of black utility pants, black turtleneck, and black boots. I glance over my shoulder and find Ellie staring at my ass.

"What?" She sounds completely unrepentant.

"Come here, little girl."

I wrap my arms around her and kiss her in a way I will never do in public. It threatens to wipe all thoughts of my duty to my family from my mind.

That's a first.

We rest our foreheads together when we come up for air, then I kiss hers before pressing her head to my chest.

"Ellie, I'll be home as soon as I can. I need you to know I will do anything to get to you. I have very few limits to begin with, but there's nothing I won't do to be with you. I need you to understand how deeply I care about you."

She leans back, and our gazes meet.

"Don't make me come looking for you, Enrique. There's nothing I won't do to bring you home."

That's not hyperbole with Ellie. I knew what she could do before seeing her tonight. But that wasn't the same as witnessing it. I hated every moment she was in danger, but I can't help how impressed I am. She's a professional through and through, so I remind myself of that as I lead her back downstairs.

Almost everyone is waiting for us, including Luis. I spotted him as I took Ellie upstairs. It surprises me to see Luciana and Margherita coming out of the kitchen. I glance over at Luis who frowns.

My sisters approach us, and I sense Ellie's wariness.

"Elodie, we wait together when we can, so we have each other. We didn't think you should have to be alone."

Margherita offers her a glass of *guaro*, a favorite Colombian drink made of sugarcane and distilled spirits that looks a bit like brandy. Its official name is *aguardiente*—fiery water—since it's nearly thirty percent alcohol.

Ellie sniffs it, then smiles. She raises her glass to Margherita and Luciana, who join them.

"*Salud.*" Health.

She offers the toast before downing the drink in one swallow. I expect her to cough or shiver or at least curl her nose up at the anise-tasting liquid that's surely burning a hole the length of her throat. I hate the stuff. She hands the glass back to Margherita without batting an eye.

"We'll leave the *niños* home the next time we go out drinking." Luciana gestures at her sons, nephews, Luis, and me.

"Mama." Three exasperated voices grumble from the landing above us, and Ellie giggles.

"Ana don't—"

"Your sisters won't corrupt me. It's far too late for that." Ellie winks at me.

"I'm glad you won't be alone, little one."

"Me, too. Be careful, Enrique. I didn't give in just to lose you the moment I did."

I pull her back into my arms as Luis kisses Margherita. I always feel badly for Luciana when Luis and Matías say goodbye to their wives. I used to stand with her, my arm around her shoulders as we watched what she'd lost. Now she's alone, and it makes me wonder if she'll ever remarry.

But it's only a moment later that *Tres J's* barrel down the stairs from getting changed in the bedrooms they have upstairs and elbow each other to get to their mama while Pablo engulfs Margherita. When the boys are done with their mama, Luis and I hug Luciana, too. Then I do the same with Margherita. I get one last kiss with Ellie, then we head out the door.

"You never lingered over your goodbyes with Daniela."

I shift my gaze to Luis as we step off the stoop together. "I didn't love her."

Luis's expression hardens, and his eyes narrow. He blames Ellie for Catalina's kidnapping. I don't blame Ellie, but I know she's the reason. Blame implies Ellie played an intentional role in this.

"Luis, you didn't see Ellie tonight. You didn't see what she risked to save my life, to get me here to all of you. You didn't see how she handled the interrogation that got us the information we need. She could have saved herself and forsaken me. She could have let me work those men over and possibly gotten nothing. I didn't recognize either of them, and I haven't even heard of them. I could have guessed they had children and tried that approach, but she knew details. She insisted—in front of the men—and I'm *glad* she did. She knows this world. She knew what she risked disagreeing with me, but she risked my rejection to help us. Don't blame her for something she didn't do."

"She caused all of this."

"No, I did. I caused it by wanting her beside me. Place the blame where it belongs. With me."

"Believe me, I do. She's just not free of it."

We arrive at the first SUV, and I look at Javier and Jorge. They're studiously looking anywhere but at their uncles. They're used to Luis and me disagreeing in front of them, but they've never heard us argue about a woman—my woman.

"Take it up with me. Don't hold it against her."

Joaquin, Pablo, Alejandro, and Matías climb into the second SUV. We have two more with men already waiting inside them. I walk around to the far side and climb in as Luis joins me in the second row. We remain quiet as a vehicle pulls in front of us, sandwiching the two SUVs with my immediate family in the middle. When we get on the highway, we'll drive four abreast. This protects us from the sides, allowing Javier and Joaquin to speed or slow as needed if we're chased. It's more dangerous for a car to pull alongside us and try to push us off the road.

Our SUVs are tanks the government should copy. The entire frame and all the windows are bulletproof. The undercarriage is caged with metal plates to protect against Improvised Explosive Devices—IEDs. The tires will roll enough when punctured so we can keep going even after driving over spikes.

All Four Families have vehicles like these for missions. We use the same customizer, and the shop is like the DMZ between North and South Korea—not big enough to stop anyone but an agreed upon neutral area. The only way to tell the families' vehicles—SUVs, town cars, and limos—apart is by the hubcaps. They're personalized, so in a rush, we don't confuse them and wind up with the wrong family if we're running.

"Enrique, you're blinded by charm and a nice pair of—"

"Say it, and I'll beat you for the first time in our lives."

"Eyes. Don't be disgusting. I'm not looking at any woman but my wife."

My brother's getting me riled up enough I'm the one being an ass.

"I'm sorry. I understand your concerns and your distrust of Ellie, but I don't appreciate your distrust in me. I have served our family since I could walk and talk. I've never put myself first, and I'm not doing it now. But my duty doesn't mean I have to grow old alone. I married a woman for the sake of this family, and I bore the humiliation of an unfaithful wife for the sake of an alliance. You will not begrudge me loving a woman who's been more loyal to me in the couple months I've known her than my wife was in the years we were married."

"Loyal? She didn't tell you who she was when you confessed who you were."

"That's not disloyalty. That's self-preservation. I'm not alone, and I'm not a woman. If Margherita were in her position, would you expect her to confess to you her family ties when you have an entire army at your disposal? When you have more wealth than many countries? When you control one of the most powerful empires in the world? I don't blame Ellie for keeping her secrets to protect her family, herself, and even me. I don't blame her for being wary when she purposely left this life behind, and I marched in and dragged her back into it."

"She could have said no."

"And you could say yes."

We stare at each other at an impasse. It's rare we're at odds, but I won't back down on this. If I could forsake my duty to be with Ellie, I would. But I can't, and she would never let me.

We turn away from each other and stare out our windows for the rest of the ride to Hoboken. It's just as well we finished arguing because Alejandro briefs us along the way. All four sets of headlights go off when we're three blocks out. We turned off our phones before leaving my neighborhood. We'll rely on our radios again. There are sixty-five Amerindian languages spoken in Colombia, and my family speaks one of the most obscure. *Macaguán's* spoken by only a handful of people in a remote part of the extreme north near the Venezuelan border. We use it when we're on missions because no one will understand us.

All Four Families revert to their native languages when they

don't want anyone to understand them, but Spanish is too preva-
lent in America. It makes nothing a secret, so our family has
preserved the indigenous language passed down over many
generations from our ancestors before they migrated to Bogotá.
We use it in Colombia too since as few as five hundred people
speak it.

"Ready."

Alejandro's voice fills my ear. As our chief strategist, he's
already planned the mission. It's also his mother we're rescuing.
Matías is with us, but he's injured. He'll stay back with the vehicles with two other guards. I still need to speak to him about what
happened, and until I do, I don't want him in the middle of this.

Javier hands me my rifle, and I fall into formation. Alejandro
takes the lead, but I'm right behind him. I'll never send anyone
ahead of me. The only person ever in front of me is the mission
leader. When we're in the thick of things, I'm just another fighter.
We protect each other equally.

When my nephews were younger and still training, they
believed they had to put me ahead of everyone else because of my
role. I made it clear everyone is equal during missions. No one
sacrifices someone else for me. The best way they can show their
loyalty is to protect each other. That lesson's saved all of us at
some point.

We're wearing our NVGs, so everything is black and green.
We move in formation as the teams fan out when the warehouse is
in front of us. We break off, going to our designated entrances. I'm
with Alejandro and Joaquin. Javier and Jorge work as partners,
and Luis and Pablo are a pair. They're so much alike it's like
watching one man with two bodies. They never need to speak,
just knowing what the other needs or will do. They gravitate to
each other when Luis goes on missions. When he's away and
can't, then Pablo and Alejandro partner.

I watch Joaquin with his lock picking kit as he gets the front
door open. I wait for an alarm or for the door to at least squeak.
Nothing. My nephews and I ease inside and look around. There's
a heavy chemical odor that saturates the air. This isn't some place

to spend much time without a mask. It makes finding Catalina imperative.

Alejandro taps my left shoulder, and I look over at him. He points to a door with a sign saying Office beside it. I nod. His cursory investigation showed no property records for this building, and there wasn't time for Joaquin to dig more. We need to know who owns this place.

Once more, Joaquin jimmies the lock. Immediately, the three of us set to work getting filing cabinets open. Alejandro and I both have our lock kits, too. We comb through documents, and it's only a couple minutes before all three of us look up with a paper in our hands.

"O'Rourkes." Alejandro says it, and Joaquin and I agree.

"What the fuck do they want with your mama? What do they have to do with Ellie?"

I'm going to fucking murder Dillan O'Rourke. I don't give a damn what the rules are about putting hits on your peers. I don't give a fuck about maintaining a balance of power. That *juemadre* —the Colombian slang for son of a bitch—targeted two women in my family. I'll fucking kill the entire O'Rourke clan.

"Trash it."

We work together to pull apart the office. We yank filing cabinets apart, the drawers strewn across the room. Joaquin shoots the fire detector and the sprinklers before we set fire to the papers in the drawers, counting on the metal to contain them long enough for us to get to the others and get Catalina out. We've heard nothing on our radios, so no one's found her yet. I'm the last one out of the office, so I lock the door behind us.

We creep toward the main floor just as voices fill the air. My nephews and I sprint forward, entering the expansive storage area as the first round of gunfire unleashes. I shove Alejandro, who bumps into Joaquin. The three of us dive behind a stack of barrels. We ease around them, flanking men I don't recognize. If this doesn't end fast, a stray bullet's likely to cause something to explode.

My men outnumber them two to one. Our enemy's quickly

picked off, but the clear leader is cornered with three of my guys blocking his escape. I recognize him. As I approach, Pablo's voice fills my ear with one word in *Macaguán*.

"Found."

I look over my shoulder at Alejandro and tilt my head in the direction we came. He takes off to find his mother. Joaquin and I keep our rifles raised as we step around my men.

"Gareth O'Brien, what the fuck are you doing in Hoboken? I thought Seamus made it clear your ass is to never leave Trenton again."

"I don't take orders from Seamus O'Rourke."

"Yeah, you do, but if you're here, does that mean Dillan orchestrated this?"

Gareth O'Brien is young. He's still pretty new to his position as Trenton's mob boss. His father died, and it was a blessing to the world. But Gareth still has a lot to learn, and he's in the shit up to his eyeballs with the O'Rourkes. The O'Briens were already the O'Rourkes vassals. They became mere peons after Seamus practically castrated them for the shit they allowed to happen to the woman Seamus fell in love with. He's just as protective of his wife as any of the other married syndicate men. They must be working their way back into Dillan's good books.

Shame Gareth won't live long enough to do that.

"Fuck off, Enrique."

"He thinks he has balls, *tío*. Should I shoot him and find out?" Javier joins us along with Jorge.

"Not yet."

That doesn't stop me from swinging my rifle around and thrusting the butt into his junk. He doubles over and gags but says nothing. I drive my right fist into his face when he bends forward. The force sends him sailing backward.

"Why did Dillan set this up? Why my sister?"

"Wouldn't you like to know?"

Dumb fuck.

"Yes. That's why I'm asking. You're proving nothing but your stupidity by being evasive. Tell me, and we can come to some resolution that allows you to live. You'll be my bitch now, but you'll survive. Keep testing my patience, and I'll torture you for days before I hack you to pieces and send them to Dillan one at a time."

That doesn't strike fear in him the way it should. That tells me a lot. He doesn't fear failing Dillan. If this was Dillan's operation, and I let Gareth live, then Dillan would go after him. That should make him more than a little nervous.

"It's not Dillan, is it?"

"Didn't take you long."

"Then who is it?"

Gareth's lip curls in disgust, but he says nothing.

Very well.

"Hold out his right arm."

Javier and Jorge step forward to follow my command. I withdraw a knife from my belt. This isn't some pocketknife. It's not a switchblade. It's like a miniature machete.

"You gonna cut off my hand first?"

Gareth's going to wish that's what I planned. It's my turn to remain silent. I need not say anything, since my men know what I'm doing as I step in front of him. I put the blade at a forty-five-degree angle at his wrist while Jorge holds his now bare arm still. When I press, Gareth realizes I don't plan to amputate.

I intend to fillet.

The blade breaks the skin, and I push it toward Gareth. He releases a blood-curdling scream as I work the knife up his forearm. The knife's sharp enough to peel him like a tomato. I see it more like peeling a mango.

"Stop!"

"Tell me who."

My demand's met with silence. I move back to his wrist, ready to begin another cut. I pause, giving him a chance. He remains quiet. Who does he fear more than the pain he's experiencing?

"Who'd you fuck over worse than the O'Rourkes? You're working off a debt to someone else."

"I can't say."

"Why not?"

"You're only going to kill me. They'll kill my family for my failure. They'll torture them if I narc on them to you."

That doesn't narrow it down by much. Any syndicate would do that. But there are only two that would risk fucking with another syndicate's vassal. Both could have reason to target Ellie. Both have reason to target me. It shocks me that either would take my sister.

I pull out my phone and turn it on. My GPS is off, so that helps minimize the risk someone could track me. I wish we had jammers. I tap a number in my contacts.

"What do you want?"

"Always a pleasant greeting, Dillan. Gareth took my sister."

"What?"

I tap the speaker button and hold the phone out to Gareth, who looks like he's barely able to keep from peeing himself. His arm's gushing blood that's pooling at his feet.

"Gareth took Catalina and brought her to your warehouse in Hoboken."

"Feck him up, but that piece of shite is mine, Enrique. We had nothing to do with this. I get to punish him for setting us up."

"If he survives, then I'll drop him someplace you can find."

"Not good enough. Gareth, you better fecking live through whatever hell Enrique puts you through because you do not want what I have planned for you happening to Callum."

Gareth isn't married and has no children. His heir is a second cousin, who's—who was—far more fit to lead. The shit that happened between Seamus and Gareth's family changed the O'Brien family dynamics. Everyone hoped Callum could talk sense into Gareth, but apparently he didn't. The guy's lying dead ten feet from me.

"You're too late for that, Dillan. Callum's dead. Alejandro shot him."

"Then you definitely owe me Gareth. Keep him alive, Enrique. I'm going back to sleep. Call me to arrange the handoff when you're done."

Dillan hangs up before I can argue. Arrogant little shit. But I don't blame him for wanting to sleep next to his wife more than deal with this.

"Save me the time of making two more calls. Save yourself the pain of me hacking off more of you while I do."

I hand my phone to Joaquin. I turn my knife away from Gareth and use both hands to rip his button-down shirt open. I place the blade just above his left nipple and break the skin. His eyes roll back as I slice. Joaquin's hand swipes through the air before it lands against Gareth's cheek, reviving him.

"My uncle didn't say you could pass out. Wake up."

"Call Pasha."

Is it a coincidence they were already giving me a hard time? Was the bratva already watching Ellie before I met her? Did they figure out she took out Ignacio?

"It's the middle of the fucking night, Enrique. What do you want?"

Doesn't anyone say hello anymore?

"Why'd you take my sister, Pasha?"

"Which one?"

"Not funny."

"No. Seriously. Which sister? You must blame me if you're calling, but I don't know what the fuck's going on."

"Yes, you do. You're striking out at me for Ignacio."

"That wasn't you. I heard some hired gun did it."

"You're getting back at me for my connection to that mercenary."

"You hired Ignacio's killer?"

That perks him up.

"No, but I know the person."

"He's one of your friends?"

He.

Is Pasha playing me?

Most likely.

"You could say that. What do you know about the mercenary?"

"He's the only one as good as Robert Simms."

306

The man was a ghost. He kept most of his money under his mattress and wouldn't use anything more advanced than a flip phone. He operated for more than thirty years, but he went too far with the Mancinellis. He paid the price for it with a few bullets through him. I heard about it second-hand, but I'm certain the story was downplayed not exaggerated.

"Better."

"Is that pride I hear?"

"Respect."

"Anton has a theory about who it is."

Here we go. His brother oversees their men's day-to-day assignments. He's as big as Alejandro and nearly as smart. He's a trained computer programmer and isn't a half bad hacker. It's his best friend, Sergei, who's the master hacker in that family. He heads their intelligence gathering.

"What does your big brother have to say?"

"The woman you're dating went out of town at the same time Alejandro went to Brazil. While she's gone, Ignacio and Benicio wind up dead. Alejandro lives. You ordered the hit on my wife's uncle. You used Alejandro as a decoy to make me think you weren't responsible for it."

I remain silent when he pauses for dramatic effect.

"Your girlfriend's flight landed in Rio. On the way home, she stopped in the Caymans. Are you dating her because she threatened to kill you if you didn't put out?"

"Tread lightly, Pasha."

"She's a beautiful woman. You've had a drought for a decade."

I'm merely more discreet than the rest of them.

"I can't blame you for falling for her. Has she been busting your balls?"

"So, you know who she is."

"Yup."

He was fucking with me, saying "he" at first.

"Is that why you were watching her before she and I even met?"

"What're you talking about?"

"The photos."

"What photos? She wasn't on anyone's radar until you couldn't keep away from her and her dog. He reminds me of Sebastian."

"The photos you sent her. The ones from the car parked on her street *before* she and I met."

"Whatever photos you're talking about, no one in my family is responsible for them. We don't fuck around like that. That's *your* family's MO."

"He's been gone a long time."

Luis and Margherita's other son, Juan. My heart aches thinking about him. He broke the cardinal rule that women and children are off limits because his childhood crush—Sebastian's owner—broke his heart by falling in love with and marrying Pasha's cousin. It didn't help that Maksim is the bratva's *pakhan*— my equivalent.

"But your family didn't learn from him fast enough."

"Don't deflect. You know who she is to me. You targeted her."

"No. I didn't."

"She was involved in your in-laws' deaths, and you want me to believe you aren't getting revenge?"

"I've been busy comforting my wife. Your woman did a job, but she wasn't interesting enough to spare a second thought while my wife and her family grieve."

"Then who?"

I know the only other possibility.

"Who the fuck do you think? Call them and let me go back to sleep."

He must have slipped out of his room to discuss this with me because he would never talk about this in front of Sumiko.

Dillan and Pasha are both with their wives, and I'm still chasing down who kidnapped my sister instead of being in bed with the woman I'll make my wife not soon enough.

"Enrique, is your sister all right?"

An ounce of humanity.

"I haven't seen her yet, but no one's told me she's hurt."

"Then take her home and deal with you know who in the morning."

He must be back in his bedroom. A bed creaking confirms it.

"Goodnight, Pasha."

"Night."

There's not a fucking chance in hell I'm waiting until morning to deal with Salvatore Mancinelli.

Chapter Twenty-Two

Ellie

I force myself not to check my phone again. Not even to see the time. It has to be close to four a.m., and I'm exhausted. However, my mind won't settle. I'm in Enrique's bed alone, and this isn't how I thought I'd spend my first night in it. Luciana and Margherita convinced me to come up here. They're in the rooms I discovered they have whenever they spend the night here. Apparently, there are enough bedrooms for each of the five guys to have their own, plus ones for Margherita and her husband, Catalina and her husband, and Luciana.

Instead of looking at my phone, I'm staring out the window. It looks out over the driveway. The view would be prettier if the room were at the back of the house, but it's more practical to see the front. I have the blinds open just enough to see the guards patrolling. I'll see when the SUVs return.

I should try to sleep. It's been a long time since I've been in this position. After the first few years, I got used to Tim being gone for unexpected lengths of time. With young children to run after, I needed my sleep. I don't have that excuse anymore.

I grab my phone off the bedside table and pull up a streaming app. I scroll my choices and pick a show. I adjust the pillows as the opening scene begins. All I needed was something to distract me. Within fifteen minutes, my eyes grow heavy, and my phone just fell forward on me for a third time. I'll let it keep playing, but I reach to put my device back on the table.

As I do, movement outside catches my attention. I prop myself on my elbow as an SUV appears just beyond the gate. My brow furrows as I wait for the gate to open, but it doesn't. Instead, men with their rifles raised rush forward from the side of the house. I recognize the smoke grenade as it sails over the gate. Two more follow it. The circular drive becomes an unrecognizable cloud.

I'm out of bed and through the bedroom door without a second thought. I run to the opposite end of the hallway and pound on Luciana's door then Margherita's. Constantine follows, practically tripping over my heels.

"Get up! Someone's here, and it's not our men. Get up!"

When I hear movement in both rooms, I turn back toward Enrique's. I'm about to go back inside when Luciana calls out to me.

"Could you see the hubcaps?"

I spin around and shake my head. "They weren't through the gate when I went to tell you. Someone tossed smoke bombs." I look toward the window. "Whoever it is breached the gate. You and Margherita need to get in the panic room."

Margherita steps out of the bedroom with a high-power rifle she's carrying with ease. This is a woman who's used to the weapon. Luciana disappears for a moment before coming out with a shotgun.

I suspected these women have killed before, and their bearing now confirms it. Enrique is going to kill us if these strangers don't because I know I won't convince them to hide. The women hurry toward me as I rush back into his bedroom.

"Constantine, bed."

The dog looks at me as though he'd disagree if he could speak, but he follows my command. I pull my rifle from my duffle bag and quickly assemble it. We stay clear of the windows, but Luciana gets close enough to see the SUV.

"I don't recognize it."

"There can't be more men in it than there are patrolling."

"There aren't. It's a suicide mission."

"Or a distraction."

Margherita runs from the room and across the hall into the true guest room. It's unassigned. It also has a view over the backyard.

"There are men coming over the walls."

"Are there enough guards?" I follow Luciana out, so all three of us stand in the hallway, away from the windows.

"There should be."

"I won't convince either of you to go in the panic room, will I?"

"Are you going?" Luciana lifts her chin.

"If that's what it takes to get you in there, then yes."

"There are family heirlooms in this home I won't walk away from. I'm not letting strangers in here to trash my brother's house."

I nod. I understand that. My mind flashes to my house. Could these people have already gone there? Could it already be trashed? Could it be rubble? My security system hasn't gone off, but that doesn't mean someone hasn't figured out a workaround.

"Come with me."

Margherita heads back into the spare room as she speaks. We each take a window, opening it but keeping the blinds mostly shut. I pray no one notices our movements. Enrique's sisters and I watch as men pour out of the summer house at the foot of the garden. It's more like barracks than a guest cottage or staycation escape from the main house.

A couple men scaling the wall fall as they try to get over it. Men who'd already jumped down, stumble forward from bullets fired behind them. I aim my rifle for the drone that just appeared. It's probably the same fucking one that took photos of me. I'm assuming these are the same people who violated my privacy. One shot takes it down. It also gains attention from the men on the ground. An invader pivots toward me, and I see his finger move to the trigger. I don't hesitate. I put a bullet through his eye since his helmet covered his forehead.

Luciana, Margherita, and I open fire. We pick off men who don't belong here, evening the numbers for Enrique's men to finish.

"Enrique!"

I recognize a muffled voice. I leave the window and run back to his bedroom. I open a window as he, Luis, and his nephews shelter Catalina and Matías as they all try to make their way to the front door. I spot another drone, and this one isn't made for aerial photography. I shoot it down, the machine landing close to Javier. He looks up at the same time as Enrique. I ignore the younger man as surprise morphs into rage as Enrique's gaze meets mine. I refuse to cringe. I stare at him defiantly.

I brace myself for when he storms into the room. I look past him to see Luis pulling Margherita into his arms while he chews out Luciana. Enrique kicks the door shut so hard the frame shakes. I lay the rifle on the bed as Enrique points toward his closet while he pets Constantine with the other. Satisfied with a scratch between the ears, my dog senses it's still not time to be in the way.

"Why aren't you in there?"

He stalks toward me, but I stand my ground.

"We decided not to."

"We? You let my sisters convince you?"

"They didn't need to. It was obvious they know what they're doing with their guns, and I saw the proof. We aren't helpless."

"No. You're foolish, which is just as bad."

"No one entered the house. If they had, then the panic room would be the right place to go."

"You conveniently didn't say it's where you *would* go."

He fists my hair with one hand, and his other rests heavily on my throat. I can't move, and I don't want to when he kisses me. I welcome his forcefulness, opening to him as his tongue presses into mine. But when I cross my wrists behind my back, he jerks away.

314

"Touch me, *chiquita*. Hold me."

I wrap my arms around him, grateful he wants a reunion of equals, not a BDSM scene. He wants me to see his dominant side, but he isn't a Dom. I appreciate the nuance. As our kiss continues, our hands skim over each other. I can't get enough. He lifts me, and I wrap my legs around him as he walks to the bed.

"What about outside?"

"My men have it under control."

"Catalina?"

"Safe and unharmed."

I dive in for a kiss. Once Enrique sits, we fumble with our clothes. I'm wearing one of his button-downs that comes to mid-thigh.

"What the fuck are these?"

I pull up the shirt as I rise on my knees. He's already pushed down his boxer briefs, so I push my panties aside. I try to lower myself onto him, but his fingers bite into my ass and keep me from moving.

"Why are you wearing panties, little girl?"

"In case I had to dress in a hurry and because I was in the house with your sisters. It felt wrong not to have anything on under this, but I really needed to wear something of yours. I needed to feel you were around me. I couldn't have everything on display if I moved the wrong way."

He presses me down as he thrusts up. My head falls back as I Kegel around his cock. I work the buttons on the shirt until I can push it apart. He latches on to my right breast and sucks. His arms wrap around my waist, keeping me from doing more than rolling my hips. It's my turn to tunnel my fingers into his hair, holding him to me.

"Daddy, we're both safe. We're home. We're together."

He groans and sucks harder. He devours me, moving to the other side. There's fear radiating from him, and I realize just how much my disregard for his expectations bothers him. He kisses across my chest, over my tits, up my neck, and down to my sternum. He nips and sucks until he marks me where clothes will always cover me. His hands hold me in place, not allowing me any control. He needs that, and I'm fine to relinquish it.

"Daddy, do whatever you want."

He pulls away. "We don't have time for that. I still have things to sort out. But I promise you I will do whatever the hell I can think of when we have our house to ourselves."

Our house.

I love the one I live in now. It's exactly how I want it. It's perfect for me.

But I don't want it to just be me anymore. I want it to be us. To be ours. To be "we" and not just "me." If this is where I can get that, then I hope the next buyer loves my place as much as I do.

"Daddy, fill me with your cum. Know that it's inside me where it belongs. Know that when you allow me to leave this room, it'll drip down the insides of my thighs. I'll be sticky and reminded I belong to you."

"When I allow you to leave the room? Do you think I'll lock you in here?"

"I'd hoped you might tie me to the bed and make me wait for you."

"And when the others ask where you are?"

"Tell them you didn't want me to leave here until you knew it was safe, and I understood you have things to do I can't know about."

"I'm not letting you out of my sight or my reach for months, *chiquita.*"

We observe each other as his hands now lightly hold my hips, guiding me to move slowly.

"I will pump you full of my cum. Then I will spank your pretty little ass. You will dress and come downstairs with me. You will keep from squirming when you sit on your sore cheeks."

"Then I'll suck you off while you sit at your desk and deal with all of this once everyone is gone. You'll hold my head down while I take all of you."

"You'll swallow every drop. Then tomorrow night, I will fuck your ass again. You will have my cum in every part of you. You belong to me, Ellie. You belong beside me."

"And underneath and on top. I belong wherever you are, Enrique."

We haven't taken our eyes off each other.

"I love you."

It's a relief and a joy to say it and hear it.

We come together for another kiss. I rise higher on my knees, and his hand lands across my ass. He does it repeatedly, varying the speed and firmness.

"Count them, little girl. These are for punishment."

"I know, Daddy. One. Two. Three."

I keep counting until I get to forty. He gives me twenty on each side. My ass stings, and I kick my feet as best I can. Each spank pushes me forward, grinding my clit against his pubic bone. I'm getting close.

"You will come this time, Ellie. Normally, I wouldn't reward you during a punishment. But I need to feel you come. I need to pleasure you after fearing I wouldn't see you again, then realizing the risk you put yourself in. They could've shot you through the window. They could've trapped you, leaving you unable to make it to the panic room in time."

"I'm sorry I scared you, Daddy."

"I know you are. I know you can defend yourself, but you don't always have to. Let me protect you. Promise me, please."

I cup his jaw and brush a soft kiss against his lips.

"Can I promise you forever?"

"Do you mean that, Ellie?"

"Yes."

"No his and hers, Ellie."

"Only ours. I want my day to start and end with you beside me. No more wondering if I'll see you that day because we run into each other. No more saying goodbye. Only goodnight and good morning."

"That sounds perfect to me."

He stands and walks into the bathroom, closing the door

quietly. He places me on the bathroom counter. We're away from where anyone can hear us. The hard surface fucking hurts like a motherfucker, but I don't mind once we move together. I hang on for dear life, one hand grasping the edge and the other holding on to his shoulder.

"May I come?"

"Yes. I can't last much longer, Ellie."

"Neither can—I'm coming, Enrique. I'm coming. God!"

"Fuck, *chiquita*."

He pounds into me one more time before we still. I lean back against the mirror, and his hands rest behind my hips as his forehead presses the glass above my shoulder. He kisses my neck. We take a few moments to catch our breath before we straighten. We haven't forgotten about the rest of the world, even if we ignored it for a bit.

"I love you."

We say it together again, and it's perfection.

He helps me down, and I follow him into the bedroom. We both change before heading into the hallway. Luis and Margherita step out of their room together at the same time Catalina and Matías come out of theirs. Catalina looks better than I expected. I see no cuts or bruises. She appears worn out, and she's leaning against Matías.

Enrique wraps his arm around me and whispers in my ear. "I don't know about them yet, *cariño*."

I nod as we all meet at the top of the stairs. I take a tentative step forward. My concern is genuine, but it's also a test. Catalina doesn't recoil or sneer. She offers me a smile.

"Do you need anything? Is there anything I can do?"

She shakes her head and leans against her husband more. "Thank you, though. Matías told me what you did earlier. How you got the information to save me. I saw you in the window too. If two sisters is good, then three is better. We must outnumber my brothers by twice as many. They each talk enough for two of us."

I look at Matías. His face is bruised, and it's not just from where Gérard or Johann hit him with their gun. I couldn't see the damage earlier because it was too dark. But the light in the hallway shows someone beat him before we left my house. There's plenty more to the story. I'll withhold further judgment of the man until I know all the available information.

The six of us head downstairs to the dining room where Luciana sits with the younger men. All five of them devour a heaping plateful of food, and she looks among them indulgently.

When we enter, her smile falters a little, but she soon plasters it back in place. She must have greeted her sister earlier because when Catalina sits next to her, they merely hold hands. Margherita sits on the other side of Catalina and takes her hand too.

As much as they might have made me feel welcome and a part of this family a moment ago, I'm still an observer. There are no more open seats next to the women. Instead, I follow Enrique as he leads me toward the head of the table, but Pablo pushes back his chair and gestures to it.

"Here you go—Elodie."

He hesitates, unsure how he should address me. After all of this, especially since they probably guessed what the couples were doing upstairs, did he think he should call me Ms. McCann?

He looks to Enrique who looks at me and shrugs. I don't know what's going on between them. I shift my gaze to everyone else at the table, and the other men in Pablo's generation are looking at me just as questioningly.

"Pablo?"

"I was just wondering if—should I call you—um—"

"You can call me Elle if you'd like."

That puts him at ease a little more, but I sense there's something else. I look around and settle my gaze on Alejandro. I don't know if it's because of our initial encounter or there's something about him in particular, but I seem to have a soft spot for him. Maybe it's because I know he's always been an only child. Until a few years ago, Pablo had a younger brother.

I wasn't always an only child, but I became one when I was in my early twenties. The car accident that killed my brother was a hit the Volkovs put on him. I suppose I have more in common with Pablo, but I felt like an only child long before my brother died because once he started his training in middle school, he was never around. Maybe because I've felt that way for so long there's a kinship. I innately understand what the others don't because, as far as I know, Margherita isn't an only child. I can't imagine being in her position, though, having lost a son, even if Juan deserved it. Not that I would ever say those words aloud.

"We—um—"

Even Alejandro seems at a loss for words. It's Joaquin—I've already deduced he's the shyest in the group—who finally explains.

"Even at our age, we still call everyone *tía* or *tío*. We wondered if we may call you *tía*."

"Of course you can. Thank you."

That brings a lump to my throat because, even if their parents don't accept me, they do. That's a step in the right direction. Perhaps it'll be enough to bring their parents around if their children can welcome and trust me.

I'll take whatever bones anyone's willing to toss at me right now. After all that's happened tonight, the fact that none of them are chasing me out of the house is a success I'll gladly accept. I take the seat Pablo offered me next to his mother, and Enrique helps ease it under the table for me. He hesitates before walking to the head of the table and taking his place there. It would almost seem cliche if he didn't look like he belonged there so much. It's the same as it was when he sat behind his desk the other day.

The conversation remains fairly light as the men eat. I pick at the food that appeared in front of me. Fortunately, it was a far more reasonable size portion than what any of the men had. Constantine joins us and lays beneath my chair. How he fits places like that is beyond me, but he barely makes a sound only snoring once in a while. He's merely happy to be with me again.

When the men finish eating, I expect them to head back to Enrique's office. Instead, the younger men move to the living room and turn on the TV. It's my generation that heads to Enrique's office. It surprises me that Luciana, Margherita, Catalina, and I are all involved in this conversation.

I remain quiet this time, slipping into one of the two armchairs rather than waiting for Enrique to bring a chair around beside him. However, that doesn't work when he avoids his desk and comes to sit on one of the three love seats in the office.

I vacate the chair I'm in, and Luciana takes it. I move to sit with Enrique, and he takes my hand. His thumb brushes over my knuckles, and I wonder what he's preparing to tell me.

"Do you know who did this?"

"We suspect who's behind it, but until we speak to him, we can't be sure."

"Is it Tommaso?"

"No, though he might be involved."

"Tim?"

"No, I considered it, but I don't think it's him."

"You would have told me right away if it were the bratva or the mob. You're hesitating, so that tells me Mafia. That leaves Salvatore. Is he responsible for this?"

"We believe so, but we're not entirely sure how because it involved the Trenton mob as well."

"So, it involved the O'Rourkes, too?"

"No, Gareth O'Brien worked independently from the O'Rourkes even if he used one of their buildings to hold Catalina."

"Could it have been them working entirely on their own?"

The three men snort in unison.

"Gareth O'Brien is young and inexperienced and mildly stupid, but he's also not brave enough to use another syndicate's building without someone insisting he must and providing some reassurance he could survive the job."

"Does he owe Salvatore something, or is Salvatore using the O'Briens to get back at the O'Rourkes?"

"Either? Both? We're not sure yet."

"All right, so what next?"

"We'll call Salvatore after Catalina and Matías fill everybody in on what happened."

"Ms. McCann, I owe you an apology. As you were putting the privacy glass back up, my phone rang in my pocket. I didn't recognize the number, so I didn't answer it. The person calling sent a text when I didn't pick up. It was a vague warning something would happen to Catalina, so it distracted me. It's why I wasn't attentive enough to walk to the door with you. It's why I didn't sweep the backyard properly enough. Just after Enrique arrived, the other car pulled up. Men climbed into the back seat of mine. They'd already killed Pedro and Diego. The men in the car beside me showed me photos of Catalina bound and gagged as men dragged her from our house. She hadn't even set her purse down before they attacked her."

I look at the woman who sits with her husband's arms wrapped around her. Her eyes are sunken, and she's paler than she was while we sat at the table. Reliving this is obviously unpleasant for her, and I feel badly that she has to, so the rest of us can know what happened.

"What you and Enrique couldn't see was the gun at the base of my neck while Enrique spoke to me. Gérard and Johann insisted I follow you, but I did my best to slow down and lose you a few times in the neighborhood. However, Gérard climbed into the front seat and threw some punches to make me more cooperative. They couldn't kill me because they didn't know their way around here. The bruises—" He gestures to his face. "—weren't as bad as the photos of Catalina they showed me. She was bound and gagged, but I couldn't tell if they had injured her. I couldn't make out what kind of car she was in or where they took her. I didn't think it was a warehouse. I did what I had to keep from antagonizing them. I worried they'd punish Caty instead. I needed to stay alive for her sake and Alejandro's. I wish I could have put you and Enrique first, but she's my wife."

"Matías, I understand this world, and I understand the oath you probably swore was something similar to the *Omertà*, but I will never fault a person for putting their children and their spouse ahead of others. You risked a great deal to protect your wife and to protect Enrique and me."

Catalina opens her eyes and looks over at me.

"I wish I'd been warmer to you when we met. I realized what it must have looked like when you saw Matías and me talking, then looking at you. I have to imagine with everything that happened that was disconcerting. I'm certain we left you with more questions and doubts than either of us intended."

She shifts her gaze to her brother and grins before turning a more subdued expression toward me.

"Matías and I were wagering how long it'll take Enrique to marry you. Before all of this happened, I said the end of the month. Matías said next month. I wish to adjust my bet. I say the end of this week."

Enrique chuckles and playfully clears his throat. We've barely acknowledged our feelings for each other, and they're ready to marry us off. But that's what I alluded to earlier. So much has happened in the past twenty-four hours, never mind the past week or the past few months. I went from being staunchly opposed to being in a committed relationship to now considering remarrying.

I have to give that more thought, but my intuition screams I should seize the opportunity the moment it's available. I tighten my fingers around Enrique's hand, his thumb continuing to stroke the back of mine.

"Catalina, did they hurt you?"

"No. I kept waiting for them to, but they were far gentler than I expected. When I stopped fighting them because I realized they were doing their best not to manhandle me, it got much easier. It was never about me. I was merely a means to an end. Luciana would have been an easier target, but they needed leverage over someone."

I glance at Enrique's other sister, my heart aching for her with another reminder she's a widow. The reminders are constantly there. I don't know how she manages. She's made peace and moved on, or at least, that's what it seems. She may mask a world of hurt she wants no one to see. Or maybe she's hiding it because

I'm here, and she's not ready for somebody outside the family to see her pain. I don't know her well enough to wager more than a guess, but I hope I can get to know her, and she'll come to trust me and see me as a friend. Perhaps I can make it a little easier for her sometimes.

I look to Enrique, waiting for him to step in and question his sister. I don't want to be the one who bombards her, asking her for information. He understands my cue and shifts his attention to Catalina.

"What can you tell us about the men who took you?"

"They barely spoke. When they did, I'm pretty sure it was in Sicilian."

"Did they say anything that hinted whether they're from New York or New Jersey?"

Catalina shakes her head. "No, they could've easily been from either place. They had no American accent when they spoke Sicilian."

I'm dying to ask whether she understood any of it. Enrique's gaze flickers to me before he looks back at Catalina.

"Was there anything you could repeat?"

"No, I didn't understand any of it. It sounded like Italian, but there was too much that made no sense to me for me to follow along."

"Did they say anything to you in English or Spanish?

"No, they didn't say anything to me in either when they first arrived. When I tried to resist them, one snapped 'cállate' at me."

That's not the politest way to tell somebody to be quiet, but it's hardly the worst thing they could say.

"It was strange they didn't blindfold me. They gagged me and restrained my hands and feet, but I saw their faces. I think they wanted me to see how far away they were taking me."

I furrow my brow. Hoboken isn't that terribly far from here. It makes me realize I assume Catalina and Matías live in Jersey. Enrique understands my confusion.

"They live in Queens."

I nod. That makes more sense, but it's still not that far away.

They did it to intimidate her, to make her realize they could go anywhere they wanted, and there was nothing she could do about it. She could watch and wonder, even recognize her surroundings, but they were in control. They didn't fear she'd tell somebody how to get to her or that she could use her surroundings to help her escape.

They were extremely confident, which means they were pros or incompetent.

I refocus on the conversation as Enrique continues to question Catalina.

"Did the men who took you stay at the warehouse?"

"No, I saw them leave, and I don't recall them coming back."

There was a handoff. No one I know outside the Mancinellis and my immediate family speak fluent Sicilian. Tommaso is more than proficient, but he's only fluent in Italian. Stella's family only knows a smattering of Sicilian and barely a working knowledge of Italian.

That's the way it is in a lot of Mafia families these days. They don't even all speak Italian fluently. I did for work, and it was a family tradition to continue speaking Sicilian. My boys speak it and Italian.

It should narrow down who could've kidnapped her. I run through a mental phone book of which mercenaries speak Sicilian. The only ones I can think of are from there. None are Americans. I'll share that piece of information later unless I'm asked for it now. I don't want to interrupt Enrique.

I also don't want to remind anyone why I would know that. It's bad enough this is about me. I'm certain no one's forgotten that. Unfortunately, Luciana wants to know more.

"Elodie, do you know who this could be?"

"I can't think of anyone specific, but I don't know any Americans who aren't Mancinellis who speak Sicilian fluently besides my parents, my boys, and me. If they were more than proficient, my guess is someone hired them from Sicily."

Catalina's brow creases. "Why would they come all the way from Sicily to kidnap me? That seems excessive."

"Either they didn't think they could get to me, or they thought you were better leverage against Enrique and your family."

In other words, I only matter to Enrique. The rest of the family wouldn't try that hard to get me back.

I'm trying to map out all the moving pieces. I have too many questions now to remain quiet.

"Enrique, whose men did you find there? I mean other than Gareth's? Did you recognize any of them?"

"Only O'Briens."

It's been a long time since the Mafia and the mob worked together. They've had a love-hate relationship for decades. The mob's the oldest syndicate in America, but the Mafia eclipsed them. They've had generations-old rivalries.

"Do you think the O'Briens were the ones who contracted Gérard, Johann, and whoever these men were?"

"Gareth could have gotten Gérard and Johann, but I can't imagine he would employ any Sicilians. Why would he want to support them in any way when he has men here to do it?"

I nod at what Enrique said.

"You mentioned Salvatore. What do you think his role is in this? Is he the one who provided them? Could they be Don Torretta's men?"

Luis has been silent so far, but he speaks up now.

"That's my guess. I think Salvatore hired them to do the part of the job he didn't trust the O'Briens to do. He only used them as babysitters. He believed men from Sicily would be harder to connect to him with any solid proof because he didn't think they'd get caught. He also wanted men he knew he could trust to do the job. He won't trust Gareth farther than he can throw him."

"But why would Salvatore go after your sister when I know his family's trying much harder to restore their reputation of no women and children? After what happened with the bratva, they've been much better at keeping women and children out of Mafia business."

Luis's eyes narrow, once more suspicious of me. I feel like sighing and rolling my eyes.

"Stella Vizzini is one of my closest friends. Tori Carosi is my best friend. Between the two of them, I knew Luca tried to prove himself more to his uncle. He thought arranging a marriage with Stella's niece would link New York and Chicago. He tried to expand the Mancinellis' influence practically halfway across the country. I'm certain you know what a disaster that was. Catalina and I don't look alike beyond dark hair and olive skin, but we were both here, and we both left to go home. Matías was with me rather than his wife. Do you think they confused me for Catalina?"

If that's what happened, I feel even guiltier than before. Catalina sits up straighter.

"Two men spoke at once. They told me to be quiet. The one closer to me was louder and almost drowned out the other guy, but now I remember the second one called me a whore when he said it."

My shoulders droop as my gaze meets Enrique. They grabbed the wrong woman. If they're Sicilian, they might not know their way around that well and confused where they were going. Or perhaps they merely followed her not caring where they scooped up the woman they believed was their target. I shift my focus to Catalina.

"I'm entirely the reason they took you. They weren't targeting Enrique's sister. They thought you were me. If they knew anything about me—that I was raised Mafia, was married to a Mafioso, and now I'm involved with a narco—they'd see that as a betrayal and that I've whored myself out to be involved with Enrique. Not only that, but to have an intimate relationship with a man I'm not married to would allow them to feel justified in calling me that regardless of me being middle-aged. I'm so sorry. It seems so weak in the face of this ordeal, but I feel horrible that they caught you in the middle."

Luciana leans forward to look around Margherita. "It could've just as easily been me or Margherita if all of us were here. Catalina and I resemble each other. And from a distance, Margherita's hazel eyes look just as dark. She has the same coloring as the two of us and you."

I know Luciana means to reassure me. However, I'd already thought about how easily she or Margherita could've been the victims instead of Catalina. Knowing there were three women instead of just one they could've kidnapped does nothing to ease my guilty conscience.

I look back at Enrique. I want to ask him how they'll handle this. But that's one question too far. It's none of my business.

I sit back, fighting the temptation to wrap my arms around myself and hunch my shoulders. I lift my gaze and my head to look at Enrique. Most of his expression hasn't changed, but I see the concern in his eyes. I wish it were his arms wrapping around me. All of this is so out of control. I wish I could just hand all of this over to him. Let him deal with all of it.

But I know even though he and his men will, I'm not entirely removed from this situation yet. My past life will always chase me. This could happen again. Not just me being the target, but Enrique's family being collateral damage. I'm selfish to want to have anything to do with Enrique when I bring nothing but danger to his family. The right thing to do would be to walk away.

I hate that idea. And it may be too late for whoever this is not to punish Enrique for his involvement with me. But once this situation is over, then it could just start all over again.

There will always be somebody chasing me, and being more visible now that I'm in a relationship with Enrique will make it easier for people to find me. It'll antagonize more enemies.

This is why I went to such length to hide my identity. I need to go back underground. I need to put distance between Enrique and me. It's the last thing I want. It's the last thing he'll let me do. I need to make the world understand once and for all I'm retired. To do that, I need to remind them how I earned my reputation.

Chapter Twenty-Three

Enrique

It's like Ellie's thoughts are mine. I'm certain what she's thinking. Duty and responsibility war with what she wants. In the end, duty'll triumph over love for her. It's too deeply ingrained in her no matter how much she wants love and how much she deserves it.

There's not a chance on God's green earth I'm letting some shitbags steal my future with her. I know if I can show her a path to us being together, she won't stop until we are. She just needs hope. This is squashing the bit she had.

"Luis, Ellie, and I will call Salvatore. We'll decide what to do once we hear his excuses. Send Pablo in."

I know this announcement pisses Luis off because he refuses to see Ellie the way I do. His role is to balance my power when I risk making a mistake. I know he's also a protective little brother. But he needs to open his mind rather than be so stubborn. This situation is bad enough without my brother making my future wife feel unwelcome.

Catalina, Luciana, and Matías file out of the office, and we wait in silence until Pablo arrives. He immediately senses the silent hostility from his father and Ellie's reserved thoughtfulness. He sits on the loveseat next to Luis. It's a tight fit for both of them, but it allows them to look at us.

I fish my phone out of my pocket and hit Salvatore's speed dial. It rings five times, and I expect it to go to voicemail.

"*Enrique, come stai?*" Enrique, how are you?

"Fuck you."

"I have a wife for that, and I hear you'll have a bride soon, too."

"Your pieces of shit grabbed my sister tonight."

"You don't say."

"Don't be a bigger piece of shit than you already are. Stay away from the women in my family."

"Or what? You'll sic your girlfriend on me?"

Ellie's nails press into the back of my hand. I look down at her, and she juts her chin toward the phone. I nod, and she launches into what must be Sicilian.

"*Stai lu cazzu luntanu dâ me famigghia, Salvatore, o ti fazzu cazzu accussì mali, mi preghi pi aiutàriti a ripigghiàrila. Lorenzo è appena nu cucciolu di casa rutta rispettu a chiḍḍu ca pozzu fari. Ti lassu comu li pezzi di spazzatura pòviri ca la tò famigghia havi statu di quannu partìu dâ Sicilia câ cuda ntra li jammi.*" Stay the fuck away from my family, Salvatore, or I'll fuck your shit up so badly, you'll beg me to help you get it back. Lorenzo's barely a housebroken pup compared to what I can do. I'll leave you like the impoverished pieces of garbage your family's been since they left Sicily with their tails between their legs.

I understand nothing but Salvatore's name and one of his nephew's. Whatever Ellie said, she means it. There's a prolonged pause before Salvatore responds in Sicilian.

"*Ti chiàmunu Ball Buster pi na raggiuni, ma tu non mi fa scantari, signura Vizzini. Ti avìa a pigghiari tanti anni fa. Allura non avìa a lassari quarchi d'unu usari l'òmini ancùora cchî pannolini pi fari nu travàgghiu ca sapìa ca fallìa.*" They call you the Ball Buster for a reason, but you don't frighten me, Mrs. Vizzini. I should have hired you ages ago. Then I wouldn't have had to let someone use men still in diapers to do a job I knew would fail.

I recognize her nickname, and Salvatore used her *old—former*—married name. It's going to be Diaz when this shit ends.

"Enrique, you lucked out this time. You got a woman far too good for you. How you managed that—You must be a *cazzo d'Orro*."

Ellie chokes on a laugh.

"Considering your wife *had* to marry you, and I'm with Enrique because I *want* to be, I'd get off my high horse if I were you, Salvatore. And we both know I'm not the wealthy one in this relationship. I certainly have no complaints, but we all know I'm not with him just because of what he can do in private."

Salvatore arranged his marriage to his wife, but they fell in love almost immediately. It's no secret the man adores her, so he's still close to his in-laws. Her niece married his nephew, so that doubly connects the Mancinellis to the Torrettas. That's why we planned to use them against Tommaso. But that plan came about after someone started watching Ellie.

"Mrs. Vizzini—"

"Ms. McCann, and you know that Salvatore."

She releases my hand and stands as she speaks. She puts out a staying hand and walks to my desk. She grabs a pencil and then looks around. She spots the printer and grabs a piece of paper before scribbling something as she leans over the desk.

"You're barking up the wrong tree. You and that giant dog of yours."

"You should know Constantine's and my bite are worse than our bark. We're both silent but deadly."

She hands the note to me before sitting again.

He told me he had to let someone use men. He didn't say his men, and he didn't say he used them. He gave someone permission to use Sicilians. Who?

I hand the note to Luis, who skims it before handing it back to Ellie. His eyebrows rise, but he offers no other acknowledgement. She reaches for the paper and bends to use the coffee table to write more on it.

Tommaso swore it wasn't him when I called, and I don't think it is. But it's definitely an outsider. I don't believe it's the O'Malleys or the Volkovs. My last job was in Sinaloa. It got messy before I could escape. I think Jesus found me and planned to strike, but then you and I met. Would he do this —take your sister or me—to get back at both of us?

I read her second note and nod.

"How're Luca's in-laws?"

Salvatore's oldest nephew and heir married a woman with connections to the *Culiacán*, the most powerful cartel in Mexico. It wouldn't surprise me if that *cabrón* Jesus Espinoza wasn't behind all of this. He's more than just an asshole, but if Ellie can read my thoughts as well as I think I read hers, I don't want her to know how much I loathe him.

"Fine, last I heard. I don't keep tabs on them, but you should. As we speak, his family's getting to know the O'Rourkes."

I take the pen and paper from Ellie.

Since he didn't hurt Catalina, just scared her, I think it could be him. He wants to fuck with me, but he knows not to push too hard or too far.

I look at Pablo and add a note for him before pointing to the top of the sheet as I hand it to him.

Son.

Pablo looks up from the paper and nods. He fires off a text and will soon know what Santiago Espinoza is up to. The guy lives in NYC because he's in grad school. He'll head back to Chihuahua when he's done. He keeps his distance from us, but we keep an eye on him. We like to know where all our rivals are. Pablo will have an exact address soon enough.

I have another question for my longtime nemesis, sometimes ally. "Sal, did you hire Gérard and Johann?"

"No. I had nothing to do with this, Enrique, beyond staying out of the way."

"And allowing Jesus to use Mafiosos right under your nose. He didn't find them on his own. You found the men for him. Did you pick the shittiest ones, so they'd fuck up? Did you want to prove you're in control? Or did you pick useless ones because you knew the consequences if Ellie or I got our hands on them?"

"This isn't my fight. I brokered a deal, then stayed out of it. I didn't decide who came over."

I won't say anything about Torretta since fucking with Tommaso already involves the Sicilian don. I don't need to play that hand yet. I'm focused on Jesus. We have history, and that *bastardo* has owed me a favor for nearly thirty years. I'm cashing in...after I get some payback.

"Mrs. Vizzini—"

"Stop being a prick, Sal. You know you'll be calling my future sister-in-law Mrs. Diaz soon enough. Until then, use Ms. McCann's name. Being a little bitch about it only makes you look like you have no *huevos*."

Luis sounds bored, but no one misses his endorsement. I glance at Ellie, and she's staring at Luis until she realizes he, Pablo, and I are watching her. She flushes, dips her chin, and smiles.

Whatever she said at the beginning set the tone, and we're getting the info we want without having to beg or even issue that many threats. It's almost too easy, but I won't look a gift horse in the mouth.

"Salvatore, I have never struck your family because Tommaso never ordered it. But I don't work for him anymore, and I'm not married to Enrique yet. I'm a free agent. If you're fucking us over, my earlier threat stands."

"I have no reason to doubt you, Ms. McCann."

Did I hear his voice tremble for a moment? I'd like to think I did. Maybe a healthy dose of fear is why Salvatore's being so cooperative. I doubt it, but I can dream, can't I?

Pablo reaches across the table to show me his phone. I scroll a text before looking up at him. He shrugs, and I nod.

It's not Jesus's son after all.

Pablo's headed out to Jackson Heights in Queens because Jesus is indirectly involved, even if it's not his son. Cormac O'Rourke's there, and he shouldn't be anywhere near our neighborhood. Hopefully, Pablo can kill two birds with one stone and fuck things up for both families.

"This is your last chance to confess to anything else, Sal."

"You're the furthest thing from a priest, Enrique."

"If I find out you're more—"

"Ms. McCann's threat is more convincing than yours."

I look at my brother, and he grins. I suppose seeing and hearing Ellie was what it took. I'm certain he saw her shoot down the drone, and we'll hear about what Ellie, Luciana, and Margherita did in the backyard soon enough. All Luis and I know is that they helped our men from the guestroom. I'm not sure I want to know, but I have to.

"Sal, how's Maria?"

"She thinks she's over the worst of it. The doctor's threatening bedrest if her blood pressure keeps going up. She's never sat still in her life, but she's been the perfect patient. Matteo's the one who's driving the doctor crazy. I've never met a man with more questions. His wife's a damn doctor, and he won't believe her unless her OBGYN says the same thing."

Salvatore's only niece by birth is pregnant with her first child, and it's been high risk since the beginning. She's unlike the men in her family despite being raised with six guys close to her age. She's unjaded. She's a radiologist and has a heart of gold. But she's a

Mafia daughter through and through. God help anyone who looks sideways at her children.

"Give her our best. Remind her she can always call Margherita if she needs anything."

Luis speaks up, since our family sincerely hopes things improve for Maria. My sister-in-law's a midwife. She wound up delivering Alejandro because Catalina got stuck at her house during a blizzard. Margherita braved driving from New Jersey into Queens rather than Catalina trying to get to the hospital.

The syndicate women don't like each other any more than the men do. But they're better at putting aside their pride and offering help when it's needed. They can keep the peace and be civil when it's the right thing to do. But I'd hate to see a fight between any of them. It'd be far worse than scratching and hair pulling. It'd be way worse than punches. As generous as all of them can be, none are nearly as forgiving as the men if they believe someone wronged their family. They'll put a bullet through anyone and walk away with a clear conscience.

"Thank you. I'll remind her. Ms. McCann?"

"Yes, Salvatore?"

"When you realize you're too good for the ape you're sitting next to, and you don't want to help Tommaso, I'll hire you full-time."

Ellie scowls but says nothing. I can't help myself.

"That many people trying to kill you these days that you need a full-time mercenary to protect your sorry ass?"

"You know I'm not one to settle for second best."

Ellie pipes in, her hackles up in my defense. "Neither do I, Salvatore, so I definitely won't settle for anyone in last place."

"You say that now."

"I wouldn't keep insulting my future husband. I'm feeling mighty protective."

Salvatore laughs. "All right, Ms. McCann. We live to fight another day, Enrique, Luis. Goodbye, Ms. McCann."

"It's Elodie. Goodbye, Salvatore."

I hang up since neither Luis nor I care enough to play his game. I look at Ellie and find her already watching me.

"Why'd you invite him to use your first name?"

"He's never used my last name out of deference. It was to put me in my place—at arm's reach. He wanted me to know he'd see me as nothing more than an employee if ever I worked for him. If I'm going to be his wife's equal, then he's going to give me the respect that position comes with."

"Not 'if,' *chiquita*. When."

It's been three weeks since our conversation with Salvatore. My family's watched Jesus's in NYC since both of his children arrived. We haven't struck yet, but we will. I'll let Jesus think he's gotten away with things for a while. He might not have succeeded, but I'm certain he doesn't think he failed. I'll wait for the complacency to set in. That's when I'll strike.

In the meantime, I'm having lunch with all three of Ellie's sons today. She knows I'm in the city for a meeting. She just doesn't know who with. Pablo's with me, and *Tres J's* discreetly spread out throughout the restaurant. I spot Will easily. The brothers resemble each other strongly, and it reminds me of a photo I saw while Ellie and I packed up her house last week.

They rise when Pablo and I approach the table. Will and I shake hands first, the pecking order very real, before the others greet us.

"Thank you for coming down here. I would have been happy to go up to Boston."

Three identical expressions tell me I'm not welcome up there. Not surprising.

We wait to start our conversation until after we order, making small talk until then. I survey them, and they're watching me like I'm a snake they expect to attack at the slightest movement.

"If I'd seen any woman on a ladder looking like she was about to fall off, I would've offered my help. But something about your mother struck me the moment I saw her. When she looked down at me from that ladder, I expected her to refuse and order me off her property. I know she was tempted. Her common sense and pragmatism won out, and I respected that about her from the start. She's easy to talk to, and I enjoyed her company immediately. It didn't take long to realize we had enough in common to chat when we saw each other. Your mother isn't an open book by any stretch. She's a book tucked away in a chained and locked cabinet. But she let me in. I couldn't help but fall in love with her."

"She said you were bossy but sweet." Hunt grins at me, and I know where he got that smile from.

Pablo clears his throat, his water going down the wrong pipe. "Sweet?"

I elbow my nephew. "I can be when I want."

"That's what Mom says, too." Steve's more skeptical than his younger brother.

"I've met no woman like your mother. I don't think there's anyone else like her. I know you know how lucky you are. I can tell just from the way you look right now. I can tell from how suspicious you are of me. I don't know everything about your parents, and I probably never will. It's not my place to know. But I know our relationship will never be like theirs because our situation is far different. I can promise I'll always love, respect, cherish, and protect your mother. She means more to me than anyone else in the world."

"You know she'll never say the same about you." Will doesn't say that to be hurtful, so it doesn't bother me.

"And I shouldn't be. I'm not a parent, so I don't know firsthand the depth of her feelings toward all of you. I have no interest in coming between you and her. I'd like to be in your lives as much as you'll let me, but I won't push my way in."

All three sit back, putting their knives and forks down in unison.

"I'm certain you know why I asked to see you."

Three chins rise in the same mannerism Ellie's given me so

many times. I wonder if it's natural or if it somehow imprinted on them from seeing her do it so much over the course of their lives.

"I'd like to marry your mom. May I?"

There's a protracted silence while they assess me. Pablo's discreetly observing the conversation while he eats. I'm certain he's loving every minute of this. He knows how important this is to me and how anxious this prolonged standoff is making me. It's an emotion I'm unused to.

I watch all three as they speak together.

"Yes."

I didn't see any of them signal it was time to answer. I think it's intuitive. These are men trained, just like my nephews. Ones who can communicate silently because their lives depend upon it. They trust each other as brothers who'll do anything to protect each other. Do anything to protect their family.

I swallow my relieved sigh.

"Thank you. I know this relationship puts you in a tough position, and that's something that weighs heavily on Ellie. She knows I'll never ask you to do anything but protect her. I don't expect your loyalty or anything like that. You're all too old to need a stepdad, but I hope we can be friends."

A wall goes up around all three, and I don't know why.

Pablo gets what I don't. "But if you ever wanted a stepdad, I know my uncle would never say no. He was the fun one when I was a kid. When I was upset with my parents or my younger brother, I would turn to him. He's not a father, but he'd be a great dad."

Oh.

"I have five nephews, so I've never felt like I missed out on having children. But there's something nice about knowing you'll be my stepsons."

It takes a little longer for the wall to crumble around Hunt and Will than it does for Steve. But eventually, they smile again.

"What should we call you?"

"Enrique, if you want."

"Have you already proposed?"

"No. But we've been talking about marriage for the past few weeks."

"When is Mom bringing over the last of her stuff?" Hunt acts casual, taking a bite of his steak when he finishes speaking.

"In the next few days. Do you object to us living together before we're married?"

"Hardly. But we'll be sure to call or text before coming over." Will grimaces, and I don't love recalling what he would've witnessed if he arrived five minutes earlier.

"Does Dad know?" Steve's question has no undertones to it, so I think he's merely curious.

"Not unless someone else told him. We haven't announced it because I wanted to ask you before officially proposing. Should I be worried when he finds out?"

"No. It'll shock him. He knows she's with you, but I don't think he's prepared for her to remarry. Not because he wishes her unwell or because he thinks she shouldn't. She just swore up and down she never would."

"Believe me, I know how resistant she was."

Will looks at his brothers before turning his attention back to me. "Take care of her. She's spent nearly three decades taking care of everyone else. She's had no one do that for her since she lived with our grandparents, and that's not the same. Be someone she can rely on, even when she swears she doesn't need anyone. Even when she tells herself she needs no one."

It's clear her sons know her. I'm glad they want the best for her, that they appreciate her. Steve shifts in his seat. I can tell whatever he's about to say, he wishes he didn't have to.

"Will your father object?"

I look at each young man, and Steve answers.

"No, but he'll have something to say."

"To you or to Ellie? Is his objection because she'll marry into a Cartel family? Or will he object because he doesn't want her to move on?"

"He doesn't want her back. That's not what it's about. She swore she would never be in a relationship again and that her need for independence drove her to leave. She even told him he should remarry because he hadn't run a household before. She took care of everything for everyone. Grocery shopping, clothes shopping, cooking, bill paying, doctors' appointments, all school events. She deserves to be an equal partner, and it's clear she's found that with you. It'll force him to see some of his shortcomings, and that's never pleasant."

"As long as he doesn't upset her, then he's free to think what he wants. But if he contacts her and upsets her like last time, I will suggest she have no more contact with him unless it's about you."

"Suggest?" Hunt's eyes narrow.

"Yes, suggest. I don't dictate to your mother. Your father is her ex-husband, not mine. I won't decide for her who she will or won't speak to, but I will support her if she doesn't want to deal with him anymore."

The brothers stare at me for a moment before they nod. Will holds up his water glass, and the rest of us raise ours.

"Welcome to our family, Enrique. Treat our mom right, and we'll be one big happy family. Make her unhappy, and there will be no remains for anyone to find."

I suppose that's as good a toast as I can expect. I clink glasses with the three young men, and they all grin.

"Seriously, though, we're glad Mom is with you, Enrique." Steve extends his hand, and I shake it across the table before I do the same with Will and Hunt.

The rest of the meal is easy conversation, and their stories about Ellie show their deep devotion to her and an appreciation for what she's sacrificed because she's just as devoted to them. It ends on a positive note, and I'm eager to get home to Ellie.

"Give Mom a hug for all of us." Hunt makes the request, and Will pretends to grimace.

"Call then knock." I grin at the brothers, and they all cringe.

If I'm already mortifying them, maybe I'm already figuring out how to be a stepdad. I won them over, but I may not be so lucky with Tommaso and Tim.

Chapter Twenty-Four

Ellie

"Jorge?"

"Hi, Elodie. I came by to see if you could look at something, please."

I'm in the kitchen grabbing a snack as the young man walks in. He called out to me and nearly scared the crap out of me. I didn't expect anyone to come over. Thankfully, I'm not naked—which I was ten minutes ago while Enrique licked whipped cream off my nipples.

"There's something going on here, and I'm not sure what to make of it."

He sets his laptop up on the kitchen table and pulls up an accounting software I used for years. I slip into the seat next to him, and he turns the computer toward me. My forehead creases, and I feel my "angry elevens"—the deep grooves between my eyebrows—setting in. I got rid of them when I gave up accounting, along with the headaches they caused from squinting.

"These aren't your family's accounts."

"No. They're the Kutsenkos'."

I skim the data in front of me and scroll down before making my way back up. I recognize routing numbers and account numbers because I set up the latter.

"The bratva's paying the Vizzinis."

"And I don't know why, but that's not what's odd, though. I followed the money to where it wound up. I can't figure out whose accounts these are. Do you recognize them?"

My gut screams he's testing you, but my heart's telling me Enrique's nephew trusts me enough to ask my help. I'm far more conflicted than I expected. I don't feel loyal to Tommaso, but my loyalty to my family and the organization I served demands I refuse to help Jorge. My instinct even hints I should sabotage this. But my stronger loyalty tells me to help him, and that's disconcerting as fuck, considering all the things I've done to support the Vizzinis. This is rattling me, and I don't know what to do.

"Jorge, do your uncles know you're asking me? I don't think they want me this involved in your family's business."

"*Tío* Luis will probably bitch about it, but *Tío* Enrique would agree you're the only person I can trust to help me. I usually have no trouble tracing accounts, but this one money trail is odd."

"Do you mind?"

"Go ahead."

I move the computer in front of me, and I click on a few things. I feel more conflicted by the moment. It doesn't feel right helping at the Vizzinis' expense, but what I see makes me want to say fuck 'em.

"Jorge, I really need to speak to Enrique before I go any further."

"What do you need to speak to me about?"

Fucking hell. These men are like fucking panthers. Stealthy as fuck. I didn't hear the garage doors because the kitchen's on the opposite end of the downstairs. I didn't hear either of their footsteps either. I might be losing my edge.

"Jorge asked for my help tracking down some transactions. It involves the Vizzinis."

"Jorge, give Ellie and me a moment, please."

"Do you mind if I take Constantine out back? I'll play fetch with him."

"You'll make a new best friend if you do."

Jorge calls out to my dog who gladly forgets I exist when Jorge picks up one of the tennis balls from the toy basket near the sofa. I watch them head outside before I turn to Enrique.

My toes wiggle in my shoes, and I haven't felt this uncomfortable in a long time.

"*Chiquita*, what's wrong?"

I glance out of the kitchen again and can see Jorge on the patio. The French doors are closed, so he won't hear us.

"Daddy, I don't know what to do. I want to help Jorge because it helps you, but I still have family in the *Cosa Nostra*. Fucking over Tommaso fucks them over too."

"If it doesn't feel right, then Jorge will understand."

"It feels disloyal either way."

"You aren't disloyal to me if honor tells you not to share certain things with us."

"But I've sworn up and down I've sworn off the Vizzinis. That I'm not one of them anymore."

"Do you fear Tommaso will punish Will?"

"That's definitely part of it. But my father still works for Tommaso. My cousins do, too. I'm friends with Tori and Stella, even if I don't get along with Tommaso anymore. If I tell you or Jorge what I already figured out, then it'll be ammunition for you to use against them. It feels like I'm waiting to give myself a self-inflicted wound. But if I don't, then you're the one who might get hurt."

"I'll support whatever you decide."

"I know. That's not the problem. It's the decision that is."

"If you help Jorge, will it be obvious you're the one who did?"

"I don't think so."

"Could Tommaso find out it's you?"

"He might suspect, but unless your family confirmed it, he wouldn't be certain."

"Would revealing this information have far-reaching effects?"

343

"Probably."

"Would it have long-term effects?"

"It could."

"Would it endanger your sons?"

"No. If it would, I'd have said no without a second thought. But it would make life significantly harder if Tommaso found out."

"Would they feel betrayed?"

"They wouldn't like it, but they would probably understand. Daddy, I truly don't know what to do. I knew a situation like this was inevitable, and I knew it wouldn't easy. But this is harder than I expected."

"Is it something you can take time to think about?"

"Probably, but not a lot."

I sigh and wrap my arms around my waist. I wish I could melt away.

"Enrique! Put me down."

I'm unprepared for him to scoop me into his arms and march to his office. He uses the biometric pad, then locks the door behind us. He carries me to a loveseat and puts me down.

"Take your dress off."

"Could Jorge walk in on us?"

"He'd knock and wait to be told he can enter."

Reassured, I slip off my dress. Enrique cups my bare ass and kisses my neck.

"It pleases me to find you without panties, *chiquita*. When I want your pussy, I will have it. You will not put anything between me and what's mine."

He runs his fingers between my pussy lips, and I know he finds me wet. I always am these days.

"Take your bra off."

I follow his orders, and he guides me to put my hands behind my back. He binds my wrists with my bra straps tight enough I can't slip them out. He unfastens his trousers and pulls his boxer briefs down before he sits.

"Come here, baby girl."

I straddle him and ease down his cock.

"*Ay, papí.*"

"That's right, *chiquita*. Why do you call me Daddy?"

"Because you'll always protect me. I can lean on you when I need help or to feel safe. You'll take control when I need a break or when you need the reassurance I'm okay."

"Do I believe you can make your own decisions?"

"Always."

"Do I trust you to make good ones?"

"Yes."

"Then come here."

He opens his arms to me, and I lean against him. The moment my cheek touches his chest, my eyes drift closed. My entire body relaxes, and I feel my shoulders sink away from my ears. He kisses my forehead, and I feel calmer. His right hand cups my ass while his left caresses my back. He says nothing else, just letting me breathe.

I don't think about the situation. Instead, I do my best to quiet my mind. I listen to his heartbeat, which is so strong I can hear the steady rhythm even though my ear isn't over it. It doesn't feel like the weight of the world is squashing me anymore.

"I created an account years ago for money that comes in that isn't from business transactions. It's a place to put money that came from transactions that weren't for goods or services."

"Hush money."

"The account balance will go down if they have to pay for something other than goods or services."

I neither confirm nor deny their regular illegal endeavors because I don't need to. Enrique understands what I mean.

"Only one other person knows how to access this even if other people know it exists. This is usually a final destination, not a conduit to another account."

Hopefully, Enrique picks up on the keyword *usually* because this is where my conflicted feelings stem from.

"I suspect other parties don't know Tommaso is basically robbing Peter to pay Paul. Or in this case, Pyotr and Paolo."

I switch to the Russian and Italian pronunciations, not that I doubt Enrique can follow along. This ensures my meaning isn't lost.

"He's figured out a way to force Pyotr to pay him, so he can pay Paolo. However, neither Pyotr nor Paolo know Pyotr's essentially paying Paolo. Tommaso's just the pass-through. It would seriously displease Pyotr to learn that, and Paolo would *never* let Pyotr forget that."

I'm inching across thin ice right now, and I keep waiting to hear it crack. It'll be an icy plunge if I fall through. Enrique says nothing, just holding me as I piece through how to share without specifics.

"Because Tommaso robbed Pyotr, it'll force Pyotr to recoup his losses. It wouldn't surprise me if Pyotr steals from Paolo, unaware he's basically getting his own money back because he won't know Paolo's even involved. That Tommaso paid Paolo with the money he got from Pyotr."

I squeeze my eyes shut tighter. I'd shake my head if it weren't against Enrique's chest. But I continue working out the situation aloud.

"It won't end there. Instead, it'll just escalate. Paolo has plenty of people who owe him favors right now, so he'll call in one or two from someone specific—Chucho—to get what Pyotr took in what Paolo will claim is an unprovoked attack. Without Pyotr or Paolo knowing the role they play in this tragedy, it will be an unprovoked attack."

I'll stick with the metaphor as though I'm telling a fictitious story rather than telling Enrique what I suspect's happening.

Tommaso probably extorted the Kutsenkos for fucking up the deal with Ignacio. If that's why Tommaso received the money, the bratva must not know for sure that the Boston *Cosa Nostra* ordered the hit. Tommaso's probably sending the money to Salvatore for something or other. Who knows what right now? He breathed in the same hemisphere as Salvatore for all I know.

Salvatore's going to call in favors from Jesus Espinoza—Chucho's a nickname for Jesus—to go after the bratva once he realizes it's the bratva who stole what was originally theirs. I doubt Jesus told Salvatore he figured out who I am, and that a woman was his target when he asked for men to do the job.

It wouldn't surprise me if Salvatore isn't punishing Jesus for sucking him into *Culiacán*, Cartel, and Boston *Cosa Nostra* business. He'll probably tell Jesus his restitution is dealing with the bratva about what Salvatore will consider stolen money. Salvatore will probably use Jesus to settle some old score with Enrique.

The Kutsenkos will invariably discover what Tommaso did with the money, and it'll piss them off that even a penny went to the New York Mafia. Salvatore won't let them live that down: Tommaso duped the bratva.

"When Chucho does those favors to hurt Pyotr, Chucho'll think he and Paolo are even. But one favor will lead to another. The second favor will be to settle an older score of some sort with an enemy from south of the border. However, Chucho's doomed to fail from the start. This enemy south of the border is also Chucho's nemesis. This enemy's learning about this as I speak. This enemy—Kiko—is likely to deal with Chucho because Kiko's involvement is even more personal than anything Chucho did to Pyotr or Paolo."

I'm certain Enrique knows I mean him. I couldn't be clearer since Kiko is a nickname for Enrique.

"When Chucho disappears, Paolo honestly can say it wasn't him. The tricky part is Chucho has connections to a fourth player who has ties to one of Chucho's kids. Patrick'll get sucked into this because Patrick and his family'll be honor-bound to defend Chucho who just went poof and disappeared."

All Four Families will wind up involved. When Jesus disappears because Enrique finally gets fed up with him and all the shit he's caused, along with Jesus's decades-old debt, it'll draw in the O'Rourkes because of their ties to Jesus. If only Cormac O'Rourke weren't tied up with the Espinozas, but love makes strange bedfellows.

Salvatore will cry foul since the Mancinellis have familial ties to Jesus, too. Pushing Jesus into Enrique's hands allows Salvatore to be rid of a pain in his ass without betraying his nephew Luca who brought Jesus into the mix a few years ago.

"If all goes to Paolo's plan, Paolo will have three enraged syndicates blaming each other for Chucho's involvement. It'll deflect everything from Paolo. He's counting on Kiko being too busy to punish Paolo for his role in what happened to two women Kiko loves."

Tommaso is so far in over his head he'll look like the toddler trying to play with the big kids. He'd be smart to just fade into the background.

It's all so fucking complicated though, and I have to run through all the players to be sure I've forgotten no one.

The Kutsenkos—Maksim, aka Pyotr—hate the Mancinellis—Salvatore, aka Paolo.

The Kutsenkos pissed off Enrique by causing problems with his deal with Ignacio. Tommaso's pissed at the Kutsenkos because he got fucked over, too. Maksim's now paying Tommaso, so he won't tell anyone—Enrique primarily—that they fucked things up. But Enrique already knows the Kutsenkos are involved. My guess is primarily Pasha who's married to Ignacio's niece.

The Kutsenkos will go after the Mancinellis because they need that hush money back somehow, and Salvatore's as good a target as anyone.

Salvatore will want revenge against Maksim for that, and since Jesus complicated things by going after me and not telling Salvatore the truth, Salvatore'll send Jesus after Maksim.

Except Enrique has the oldest grudge against Jesus. He'll want first dibs because of the past and what Jesus just did to Catalina and me. If Enrique goes after Jesus, Salvatore will have to protect Jesus because Jesus is now related by marriage to Salvatore's nephew Luca.

The O'Rourkes will come to Jesus's defense because of Cormac's connections to one of Jesus's kids.

Salvatore will try to fade into the background and let the Diazes, Kutsenkos, and O'Rourkes war with each other.

"You deduced all of that from looking at a couple bank accounts?"

"And nearly five decades of life among syndicates. If I were in Paolo's place, that's what I would do."

"And if you were in Kiko's?"

"I'd make sure Chucho understands he needs to pay off his old debt to Kiko before he worries about anything else. If he does that, then they're even. Chucho might live if he's still useful to Kiko. Kiko might also remind Pyotr that if he hadn't tried to fuck with Kiko first by going through Tommaso, he wouldn't have to deal with Paolo or Chucho at all. If Chucho does this—makes restitution to Kiko and stays out of things with Pyotr and Paolo—then Patrick never gets involved because Chucho's no longer in danger of dying."

If Enrique gets Jesus to man up finally on their old bargain, then Jesus can slink back to Chihuahua and be out of everyone's way. Enrique can remind the Kutsenkos they're the real reason all of this happened, and Ignacio would still be alive if they hadn't tried to fuck Enrique over.

If the Kutsenkos leave Tommaso alone, then they have one less thing to deal with Salvatore over. Salvatore gets iced out since Jesus won't be his bitch. The O'Rourkes have no reason to interfere, and Enrique's settled things with no one blaming him.

"Little one, I think you're brilliant. I think Kiko would be wise to follow that advice. Thank you."

"You're welcome, *papi*. Thank you for listening to my convoluted story rather than pressing me to pick."

"I'll never ask you to, Ellie. I understand how stuck in the middle you are. I'll shield you as much as I can. I'll make sure my guys ask me before approaching you about anything like this. I'm certain Jorge meant no harm by it."

"I never thought he did. And I'm happy he wanted my help and doesn't think I'll try to usurp his position. I won't stand in your way, but I also can't always make it easier."

"I get that."

"I know you do. That's why I'm so comfortable right now. I'm

349

not scared. I'm not even nervous or anxious. I don't feel guilty either."

"I think I should say thank you a little more thoroughly."

I grin and nod. He pulls my bra off my wrists and flips me on my back. The submissive position with my hands behind me let me feel like Enrique had control of everything as I divulged complicated information that put me in a position where I had no control. I hate feeling out of control unless Enrique is there to reassure me he can handle it.

I reach my arms over my head, holding onto the end of the loveseat. He thrusts into me as I push my feet into the cushions, rolling my hips to match his movement. It's short, hot, and fucking intense.

"Daddy, I'm ready to come. May I?"

"Yes, *chiquita*. I'm there too."

"I want to feel your cum in me."

I strain, my body tensing and squeezing around his cock as it pulses inside me. I gasp as I come back down off my burst of sexual euphoria. I'm pulled back to reality when Enrique withdraws. I want to wrap myself around him and keep us joined, but I know he has things he must do now.

"If you're going to need to make calls or meet with your family, I can take Constantine for a walk."

Enrique hesitates, and I realize that was a thoughtless suggestion. Being outside the gates will spike his blood pressure.

"Actually, you know what. I have some writing I should get done before I fall behind on a deadline. I've had a lot of time away from my computer, and I need to get back on schedule. I'm going up to our room."

I grab my clothes and hurry to put them back on while he straightens his pants and dictates a text to have everyone meet at his house.

"Ellie, if it comes down to eliminating Jesus, do you want to know?"

"To satisfy curiosity or because you want me to do something?"

He stares at me in disbelief. "I am *not* asking you to do a job for me. I meant do you want to know what's going on? Or would you rather wash your hands of all of this?"

"Whatever you think's best."

He wraps his arms around me and gives me a kiss that leaves me wanting rounds two through a hundred of what we just did on the loveseat. A bigger part of me than I want to admit wishes I could be involved in this conversation, but it's none of my business. I don't want to get sucked back in any further. I'll let Enrique handle it.

Chapter Twenty-Five

Enrique

"Jesús, no me importa una mierda." Jesus, I don't fucking care.

I continue the conversation in Spanish, too pissed off to think in English even though I've been speaking it for more than fifty years.

"We square up on your debt once and for all. You owe me for helping you secure your position. If you want to remain the boss, then you'll fucking pay up. I want the Texas port and the border crossing in New Mexico for as long as I want. Your men not only won't get in my way, they'll also make sure my men can cross back and forth any time they want. Make sure Border Patrol doesn't fuck it up."

This *cabrón* thinks he has a leg to stand on to negotiate with me. He's fucking out of his mind. I've listened to him give two excuses, and I'm unwilling to listen to a third.

"Shut up. I don't care where your family is or who they're involved with here. That's your problem. You should have thought about that before you crossed the border. You can go back to Chihuahua and watch your plants grow. If you don't, I'll set fire to all of it."

He knows I really mean all of it. Hundreds upon hundreds of square miles of crops that make his tequila, pot, and cocaine. I'll leave nothing, and his enemies can pick him apart like he's roadkill.

"Fine."

"And?"

"And what, Enrique? You're getting even greedier with age."

"The 'and what' is that you apologize to my woman. You stay the fuck away from her and her family because they're my family now, too."

"You want me to apologize to the person who started all this?"

"She did a job just like any other mercenary any of us have hired. Don't hate the player, hate the game."

"Fine. Should I send you a basket of pears or something?"

"You can apologize right now."

Ellie came back down from our room after I strategized with my nephews. Luis had to fly down to Colombia this morning to sort out some shit with one of our mules. Fucker got himself locked up. Since I've been speaking Spanish throughout this call, Ellie's just sat quietly. I don't know how much she's understood, but I don't think it was much since I was speaking faster than usual.

"Speak."

The call's already on speakerphone, so Ellie can hear Jesus.

"*Señora*, I apologize for drawing you into all of this. You wanted to get out, and you weren't working for the Vizzinis anymore. I should have dealt with Tommaso since you just did your job. I'm sorry."

He practically chokes on the first and last sentences.

"Let's put this behind us."

Ellie doesn't accept his apology, and he knows it. But he also won't push the issue. He's lucky she isn't assembling her rifle right now.

She was ready to go after her Registered Agent who hired Johann and Gérard for Jesus, but he took his own life when he discovered how badly he failed because even the obscene amount of money Jesus paid him wasn't worth it. He didn't want to give her a chance to find him.

She doesn't need to know everything else I'm planning for Jesus. I'm certain she knows it's not over, but her role is. She stands, and I press a quick kiss to her lips before she slips out of my office.

"Do we have a deal, Jesus?" I'm calm enough now that I lapse back into English.

"Yes. But we're even after this."

"Until you fuck up again."

"Fine."

"I'll be in touch."

"I'll await your call, *el patrón.*"

"*A la chingada.*"

I hang up. Patronizing fuck calling me *el patrón*. That title's far beneath me, but he knows he can only push so far.

"Where do we stand on everything else?"

Alejandro crosses his arms and smirks. "The ships are well on their way to the Port of Nagoya, and there's not shit Maks can do about it."

Jorge's already smirking as he drums his fingers on the armrest of his chair. "The IRS is breathing down Pasha's neck, and he's running in circles to keep them from digging in too many places. It's great."

Pablo looks up from the text he was reading. "Salvatore just got a pissed off call from Don Torretta about Tommaso doing business with the Razzanos. Salvatore was on his way to a meeting on Staten Island and turned around. From what I got from our guy in Palermo, Tommaso's fucked every which way from Sunday."

"Make sure he deduces this is his punishment for involving Ellie while leaving no proof we caused it."

"Already taken care of."

"Shocking the O'Rourkes actually had nothing to do with this. I was certain they were up to their asses in it when we found the O'Briens."

Javier says what we've all thought since we rescued Catalina from their warehouse. One of our informants already told us Seamus lost his ever-loving mind and went on a rampage. The O'Briens are short another dozen men. Their newest pot shipment from Jamaica now belongs to the O'Rourkes. Gareth's in the hospital and will be for at least another month from what Seamus's ham-hock fists and size fourteen boots did.

"When Jesus is out several million over the border deal, they'll have something to say, especially Cormac."

I've been watching the last man standing in that family. Cormac's getting way too close to Jesus's family for my comfort, so I'm waiting for the perfect opportunity to shake shit up. There's going to be a reckoning between the Mancinellis and the O'Rourkes one of these days, and I pray I'm there to see all of it. Maybe Ellie and my wedding reception since they'll be on their best behavior, and I'll consider it a gift from both families.

I need to propose before I make plans for the wedding and reception, but that'll happen soon enough. For now, I'm content the pieces have all fallen into place to deal with the other families.

"That fucker can go to hell."

Javier shrugs at my scowl and proclamation. I'm going to kill Salvatore. This might be the year I really do it. That *hijo de puta* just can't leave well enough alone. He came to Tommaso's defense and is trying to smooth things over for him with the Torrettas. Now I have the Vizzinis *and* the Torrettas planning to fuck me over because I'm pissed the Vizzinis fucked Ellie over.

"*Tío*, we'll deal with them another way. When God closes a door, somewhere He opens a window."

"Or you could just leave it alone."

I turn toward Ellie as she walks into the dining room. She comes to stand beside me, and I greet her with a peck on her lips. We've only been apart ten minutes, but I love how I can do that whenever I want. We finished moving her in two weeks ago, and it's been bliss being together whenever we want. We're good at reading each other and knowing when we each want space but gravitating toward each other when we want to be together. We've fallen into easy routines of dividing the household tasks, and it's as though we've always lived together.

"Enrique, let it go, please. He'll fuck up some other way soon enough. Deal with him over that, but move on from this. It'll freak him out more if you drop it. It'll leave him worrying and wondering what's coming next. It'll distract him, and he'll open himself up to something else. Strike then. No one will think you lost. They'll think you're plotting. Keep them guessing, but in the meantime, don't let him occupy your mind."

I want to believe Ellie, and she's right to an extent. Much of syndicate life is machismo. No leader wants someone to one up them. None want to appear weak. None want someone else to get the last word. It's better to change the subject.

But Salvatore is the one I'm super pissed at. He could've let me deal with the Vizzinis and stayed out of it. He could've even helped repair the rift after it happened. But the nosey fucker just had to butt in. And that fucking complicates shit.

"Javier, check on the sparrows and get back to me."

"*Sí, tío.*"

My nephew offers us a smile before heading out, leaving us alone. The Italian sparrow is the national bird, so when we can't use the Mancinelli name, that's how we refer to them. The sparrow is a sturdy bird that can survive much, but they're small and can be crushed or scooped up and torn apart by a larger bird of prey.

The nickname's fitting because I intend to crush the Mancinellis' Bronx new housing project. They're about to have a walk out. None of those construction workers will show up. Fuck their union. I'll make sure they're paid—not to go to work. Salvatore's budget will skyrocket once he has to find people willing to work for him—which he won't—not to mention the hit he'll take on wasted equipment and supplies. His client will shit a brick, and it'll look horrible in front of the city, who he's pandering to for a large, low-income, bond-funded project.

"Daddy, I'm serious. I know things are always in the works, but I don't want the constant reminders of the life I tried to leave behind. I don't want it to be the focus of our new life together."

Then I'll have to do a better job of not discussing it around Ellie.

"Daddy, don't you think I'll know you're still dealing with them? There's no way I won't know that my boyfriend is engaged in a feud with my old boss."

"I don't want you caught in the middle, Ellie. But I won't let this go. It's not about Tommaso right now. It's tangential."

She stares at me for a moment before nodding, and I can tell she's retreating. I don't want this to be our first fight, and I don't want this to put distance between us. I wrap my arm around her waist and pull her close, but she doesn't relax against me like she usually does. I rest my free hand heavily at the base of her throat, causing her head to tip back. I feel a sliver of tension ease from her. I increase the pressure, and her shoulders relax. I squeeze a little more, and her body presses into mine.

She's giving me control. She may not agree with how I'm handling this, but she needs to feel someone has control without it having to be her. Or maybe she feels like the situation is still out of control, but she's glad I'm controlling something. She's called me Daddy twice. That should have been my clue.

"*Chiquita*, I'll sort it all out. I'll keep you and my sisters safe."

"I know you will. I just wish you could move onto the next disaster. One that doesn't involve me or the family I once belonged to and worked for."

"Do you still feel guilty about this?"

"How can I not?"

"Because what's going on now isn't because of you."

"Don't treat me like I'm simple. Whatever you planned to do to Tommaso made its way to Salvatore. You've probably already dealt with Tommaso for his role in things getting fucked up with Ignacio, or maybe you were going to hold him harmless for that. But whatever you tried to do, you did it because you're pissed about how he treated me. Now you're pissed Salvatore protected him somehow. I may not have been privy to all the Vizzinis' inner workings, but I knew enough to accomplish my missions. I know how syndicates operate. I know what slights can be overlooked and which can't. I could ask you what happened, and I could ask what you plan to do. But I won't. I know you won't tell me, and I won't make you lie to me. How this plays out isn't me guessing. You might keep the specifics secret, but don't think you can keep how things work from me."

"And if I don't want you thinking about this? If I want you to let me worry about it?"

"The only way you can control my thoughts is to make sure there's nothing to think about."

I squeeze her throat tighter and pull her fully against me.

"Or I give you something else to think about."

I dive in for a kiss, and she surrenders immediately. Rather than return my embrace or run her hands over me, she crosses her wrists behind her. I adjust my arm around her arms and waist. I keep increasing my grip on her throat until she has to pull away. She tilts her head back, and I nip at her right earlobe.

"You'll let me worry about that for now. All you need to think about is how I'm going to fuck you until you scream. Until you beg me to stop because it's too much. Then you'll beg me for more. I'll watch your beautiful ass turn bright pink. I'll play with your sensitive nipples while I suck on them. And I'll make your cunt ache for me while I play with your clit."

"When, *papi?*"

"Right now, *chiquita.*"

I shift us until she's leaning over the dining room table. I pull her yoga pants down and enjoy the view. I love looking at her ass and thighs. I love thinking about her legs wrapped around my waist. I love sliding my hands over her ass, always having something to cup and hold.

She angles herself, so her top half presses into the wood. She's kept her hands at her lower back the entire time. Her left cheek rests on the table, and her eyes are closed. She trusts me and whatever I do. She shifts onto her toes to get more comfortable, and it pushes her hips back. I can't resist the temptation. I grip her hips and grind my dick against her ass. When I take a step back, her fingers uncurl, and she snags hold of my shirt. I move out of her reach and bring my hand down across her ass.

"OW!"

It wasn't a light tap. It wasn't a medium one to warm her up. It was a sharp crack she wasn't expecting. I land another and another, her ass blossoming into a rosy pink immediately.

"Do you know why I'm spanking you this hard?"

"Because you can?"

"Yes. Because you love it. You love knowing that when you give me control, I take it. I'm not a man to be toyed with. When something's given to me or I take it, it becomes mine. I take care of what's mine and treasure it. I hold on to it. You belong to me, Ellie. You have since the moment I saw you, and you will until my last breath. I will find you in the next life and the one after that until eternity. When I want to fuck you, I will. When I want to make love to you, I will. You can always tell me no, but if you don't, I will take what I want when I want."

"Yes, Daddy."

We both know there are elements of truth to what I'm saying, but much of it is role play. She loves it as much as I do. I've never been so possessive of anyone or anything in my life. I have three siblings, and as the oldest, I've always felt responsible for them. It's meant sharing even when I didn't want to. Most of the time, I enjoy sharing with them now. It's the same with my nephews. But I want Ellie all to myself.

I don't want to lock her away from the world. I don't want to take her out of some gilded cage just to parade her around town at events. I want to know I can make her happy and protect her. That she doesn't need to turn to someone else because I can't do those things. I want her to know she has all of me. That she possesses me heart, body, and soul.

An all-consuming need to be inside her sweeps over me. Every thought I had a moment ago on how to tease her evaporates. I unfasten my pants, pushing them and my boxers down. I grab her hips and thrust into her.

"AH!"

Her mind's unprepared for my force, but her pussy is slick. It's easy for me to enter her. She wants this already.

I fight not to thrust repeatedly until I come. Not yet. I reach around her, my fingers seeking her clit. When I find it, I roll it between my thumb and index finger. I pinch and pull her pussy lips until I come back to her clit. I rub slow circles that soon have her shifting with impatience.

"You come when I say you can. Your orgasms belong to me. I can give them, and I can take them away. You need me as much as I need you."

"Yes, Daddy."

"You crave this as much as I do."

"More."

"Impossible. No one can want another person more than I want you. I'll do anything to make you happy, Ellie. Anything."

"Marry me."

The words fly from her mouth, and we both take a moment to realize what hangs in the air. When it sinks in, I pull almost all the way out. I see the immediate hurt on her face. She's unprepared for how I hammer her cunt, thrusting over and over. My hand tangles in her hair as I lean over her body.

"If that's a proposal, I accept."

She looks over her shoulder as best she can.

"Do you mean that?"

"We've always been on the path to marriage. I will love you for the rest of my life, Ellie. You have all of me, and I want you to keep it. I want to grow old with you beside me. I want to fall asleep and wake to you. I want to love and cherish you, hold you in good times and bad, care for you in sickness and in health, until death parts us only to do it again in the afterlife."

Her hands grip the edge of the table as she moves her hips with mine, pushing them back to allow me to bottom out when I'm in her the deepest. Her clit rubs against the hard surface, and I know she's straining to get off. I don't stop her because I want her to come.

Just not yet.

"May I come?"

I pull her away from the table and pull out far enough to spank her.

"No."

I push her back over the table, my hand in the middle of her back.

"Will you marry me, Enrique?"

"Yes."

This isn't how I thought a proposal would go. I'm not such a prince that I'll turn it down because it isn't the fairy tale I envisioned.

I retreat, keeping her from the pressure she needs on her clit, before I spank her again.

"I love you, Daddy."

"I love you too, *chiquita.*"

It's like every spank—every dominant action on my part—frees something in her while she submits. Her feelings aren't a surprise or a secret she's suddenly revealing. But it's the dynamic, the openness. It's what we need because when this is over, we'll go back to me keeping secrets. We'll go back to her not having control over what happens outside our door.

This is who we are, and this works for us. I wouldn't have it any other way.

"Daddy, please. I need to come."

I trap her between the table and me. I plunge into her over and over, forcing her clit to grind against the table. She holds onto the edge, and the weight of our bodies makes it creak while the power of our bodies moving together inches it across the floor.

"Come, baby girl."

She rubs her clit faster until she screams.

"*Ay, papi!*"

Fuck. I love hearing that. I don't hold back. I explode inside her, feeling rung dry by the time my cock's done. I draw her arms out in front of her and stretch over her, entwining our fingers. I kiss the back of her shoulder, along the top to the crook of her neck, then her cheek. We stay joined until my body refuses.

"Don't move, Ellie."

I see the flash of sadness as I pull up my boxers and pants. I know she wants me to stay with her, to hold her. I will in a moment. I rush to my office then hurry back. I help her off the table and turn her toward me.

"Keep all my cum inside your sweet little cunt. Catch any that drips on your thighs. Know that body belongs to me."

I drop to one knee and fish out the ring box I just put in my pocket. I snap it open.

"My body belongs to you just as much, Ellie. You have my heart and what's left of my dark soul. The only light I have comes from you shining on me. I love you, and I want you to know that'll never change. That when I pledged to take care of you—when I started the moment I met you—it's because I've always intended to do it for eternity. Will you marry me, *chiquita?*"

"*Sí, papi. Sí* a million times."

I slide the ring on her finger, but she's watching my face not my hands. When I stand, she launches herself into my arms. I sweep her into them and carry her to our bedroom. It's only as I climb the stairs that she looks at her ring.

"Oh my God, Enrique. This is exquisite!"

"I hoped you'd like it."

"I love it. It's stunning."

My sisters helped me pick it last week.

"Did I ruin things by asking in the middle of sex?"

I grin and steal a kiss.

"I knew you didn't ask because you were carried away. It's one of the most intimate things we share with just each other. I think that was a perfect time to ask."

"Are you bothered I asked you rather than the other way around?"

"I just asked you, and you said yes."

"You know what I mean."

"No. It might be traditional for the man to ask, and as old-fashioned as things are for our family, I see no reason a woman shouldn't ask if that's what she wants."

I lower her to the bed and lift off her shirt before unfastening her bra. I pull down the covers for her, and she slips beneath them. I strip off my clothes as she watches, her eyes feasting on me. My dick twitches back to life. When I get in beside her, she wraps her hand around my length and slowly strokes.

"When do you want to get married, Ellie?"

"Soon. Will it be the way it is in Boston? The ceremony is private, but the reception is for everyone and their mother?"

"Pretty much. The ceremony will be our family and my most senior men. Then the reception will be the who's who, including the other families. My brother will be my best man. Can you come up with eight bridesmaids?

"Eight?! I don't have eight female friends."

"My five nephews and your three sons."

"My boys? You'd ask them to stand up with you?"

"Of course. Why wouldn't I?"

She swallows and smiles.

"Ellie, I'm never going to parent them or try to replace their father. I hope the four of us can be friends. But they're my family now and have been since the first time I kissed you. Just like everything else has been a foregone conclusion, so is them being part of my immediate family."

"Thank you, *mio caro*." My darling.

"You must have eight female friends or even four."

She averts her gaze, her hand no longer stroking me.

"Ellie?"

"The only two women I'm close to are Tori and Stella."

Shit.

Me persecuting Tommaso puts Ellie in an even shittier position than I considered. The don's wife and sister won't even come to the wedding, let alone stand next to Ellie, if I keep going after them. Even if it's through Salvatore, it'll put a rift between them they may never overcome.

I have only seconds to work through this as she speaks. I can put the past where it belongs for Ellie's sake since my grudge against Tommaso really is about how he treated her. He knows I don't like him, so that should be enough to keep him on his toes. Salvatore's been a pain in my ass for decades, and the old goat will remain that way since he and I are both in great health. We've survived into our late fifties for a reason—to piss each other off to no end.

"What about Kathleen?"

Ellie's chin draws back as her brow creases and lips turn down.

"I don't know. The O'Rourkes didn't disown her, but she's no longer one of them. It doesn't mean it'll thrill them to see her sitting with Frank and the others at the reception. I assume if I invite Kathleen, then Frank will come. If I invite Tori, then Santino will be there. And if I invite Stella, that means Tommaso too. There's not a chance in hell those three men would send their wives down here and not be there to guard them the entire time. It means the Boston don, *consigliere,* and former underboss who was the *capo dei capi* before that would be at our wedding. That'll piss off everyone in your organization."

"Not if I tell them it won't."

"You know that's not how it works. They'll resent me and question you."

"Ellie, I've been *el jefe* for thirty-four years. I've lasted longer than nearly anyone else anywhere in this hemisphere. I've been questioned, doubted, and resented the entire time. I've also put the Cartel ahead of me in everything. Every decision I make is with everyone else's wellbeing in mind. I considered them before I pursued you. I've thought about the organization and my family throughout this. I'm not pussy whipped. You don't lead me around by my balls. My love isn't blind. I know I'm a better man and a better leader with you by my side."

I'm hard again. No surprise with Ellie on my mind and her body next to mine. I draw her over me, and she takes me into her slick cunt. I cup her ass as she rests her head on my chest. This is how we've always been meant to be.

One.

No end.

No beginning.

"I love you, Ellie. Whatever comes up, we'll figure it out together. But the future—ours personally and the organization's—is us united as one."

"I love you, Enrique. I'll stand beside you when I can. But I'll also stand behind you to support you whenever you need me."

"Plan your wedding, little one. I'm marrying you in a month."

"Yes, Daddy."

It's only mid-morning, but we doze off. Syndicate life is back to homeostasis, but Ellie and I are just beginning our life together. There's no direction but forward. I've been a king on his throne alone. Now I have the perfect queen to rule alongside me.

Epilogue

Ellie

There have been seven momentous days in my life. The day I married Tim. The day I killed someone for the first time. The three days I gave birth. The day my divorce went through. And today—the day I married Enrique.

Three I could've lived without. Four are days I will treasure above all else.

Today is the only day without fear or trepidation. Today is the only day with absolute certainty and peace of mind.

The past month has been a haze of activity. I had a manuscript to finish, which I fell behind on. It released last week, and I'm still riding the high from that. Wedding planning was—interesting.

We're in NYC. Every company I contacted from the reception venue to the florist to the baker—everyone—practically laughed in my face when I said my wedding was in four weeks. Until...

The name Enrique Diaz means even more than I realized in this city. He's somewhere between a man and a myth. Whether he's known for his legitimate wealth or the rumors about his ties to the underworld, everyone I spoke to became far more helpful once I shared my fiancé's name. Amazing how that worked.

"Have I told you how happy I am, *cariño*?" It's what he calls me in public now.

"I think you did, but I can't remember."

He kisses behind my ear as we take our place in the receiving line.

"Blissful, little one. Happier than I knew was possible."

"I feel the same, *mio caro*." It's what I can call him in public.

We greet our guests. I'm friendly with most people, but I understand this is as much about business as is everything in our lives. Enrique and I are the producers, directors, and stars of this Off-Broadway show. I have a role to play now as *la patrona*. It's the same as Stella and Sylvia Mancinelli play as *la madrina* of their *Cosa Nostra* branches. They're the Godmother, and I'm the Lady Boss. Whatever our title, it means the same thing.

I stand beside Enrique, an ice queen to outsiders when I must be, and the arms of compassion and mercy when it's needed within our community. Right now, I'm somewhere in between.

I greet our guests, and when the Kutsenkos and O'Rourkes arrive, I pray none of them recognize me. It surprises me when I recognize Jesus's daughter accompanying the last O'Rourke through the line. Enrique keeps them chatting as Salvatore and Sylvia enter the ballroom. Salvatore and I have met a couple times, but we mostly know each other by reputation. After my conversation with him last month, I'm uncertain how he'll react to seeing me again, even if he knew he would.

I watch the other Mancinellis enter, and my gaze lingers over a woman with the Mancinellis' underboss. I shift my attention from her to Jesus's daughter. I hide my confusion, knowing I'll ask Enrique later. The conversation soon answers some of my questions, but I'm only left more bewildered.

The women are ready to draw blood when they confront each other. I don't need a fight at our reception. Certainly not one between two women. The men may all have at least a knife, but they aren't carrying their guns. If they get in a fight, they'll throw some fists, and someone's bound to be stabbed. But they'll stop when they remember where they are.

Two women?

I guarantee they have knives. I also guarantee if they fight, it won't end until one of them is dead. It doesn't matter where they are, who's here, or what they're wearing. The men might fight till first blood. These women will fight till last blood.

I listen to the conversation as it nears a standoff. I'm confused about how they don't know each other. I glance up at Enrique, and I know in an instant he orchestrated this. Somehow, he ensured the O'Rourkes went through the receiving line directly ahead of the Mancinellis. He made sure Jesus's daughter and her O'Rourke date were at the end of the family pack. He knew they'd run into the Mancinelli underboss and his wife. This unpleasant confrontation will get back to Jesus, and it'll complicate his life tremendously. Enrique banked on that.

Enrique's arm tightens around me as we watch the women negotiate moving their conversation somewhere more private, and the men in their lives exchange anxious glances before agreeing to step out of the reception. I won't say anything to Enrique until later, but I don't appreciate him using *our* reception for *his* machinations.

"*Chiquita*, it was inevitable they'd meet. No, I didn't orchestrate them coming through the receiving line so close together. No, I didn't expect them to challenge each other practically to a duel right here. But I knew it might cause a scene, and I know Jesus is up to his eyeballs in shit right now."

"You risked all that to inconvenience Jesus on our wedding day. The man isn't even here."

"But his son and daughter were along with his niece. He may never repair the damage that just happened to his relationship with his children. He should've thought about that before keeping those secrets. While he's distracted with that, he won't pay attention to you."

"Enrique—"

"Ellie, I didn't plot this. I didn't use our reception as a guise to lure those women into an argument. That's how life unfolded. I made the best of it."

"You could have warned me, so I didn't stand there, looking lost in front of strangers."

"Your composure was impeccable."

I stare at him for a moment. I get a lot of this life is about *carpe diem*. If you don't seize the day, you not only miss opportunities, sometimes you wind up dead. I don't begrudge him that.

"Just keep me informed, please."

His hand trails down my hip from my waist, over my ass to my hand. He's discreet as he cops a feel then laces his fingers with mine. He brings the back of my hand to his lips.

"I'll do better. I'll need reminders."

"Thank you."

I turn toward him, and people tap their knives against their glasses. I'm happy to kiss the man of my dreams.

Enrique encircles me in his arms, and the moment our lips meet, the rest of the world melts away. We're not indecent, but we don't care who watches. Our foreheads press as we break the kiss. The evening passes with food, toasts, and dancing. We cut the cake, and neither of us considers smashing it in the other's face.

That just isn't us.

But we might have licked frosting from each other's fingers when we fed each other. I toss my bouquet, and a young woman I don't know catches the flowers. From the corner of my eye, I notice Javier observing her. She's connected to the bratva, but I don't know how. It's not by blood. I can't tell if they have a past, but something tells me fate made her catch the bouquet.

Enrique wishes our guests goodnight, encouraging them to enjoy without us. I'm certain the three other families will since it's an open bar. They'll drink just to run up Enrique's bill. All the men are as massive as the Diazes, so they can easily manage three drinks to every other person's one. The Russian women have been drinking vodka since they were five, and I've heard the O'Rourke women used to get a tipple of whiskey in their sippy cups.

It was a relief to see the O'Rourkes welcome Kathleen, even if they weren't warm to Frank. She's still one of them at heart. Her cousin, Donovan, once led the family, but we're all better off for him being dead. She blends in with Donovan's sisters like she's the fourth one. She sounded more like the younger generation's aunt than an alienated cousin-once-removed.

"Are you ready, little one?"

Enrique helps me onto the super yacht moored at North Cove here in Manhattan. We're taking our time sailing down to the Caribbean where we'll spend three weeks on a private island he just gifted me. I wasn't sure what he handed me when I looked at a land deed, then aerial photos.

"So ready, *papi*."

He opens the door to our cabin, and I realize he meant for more than just our honeymoon. To the left is a Saint Andrew's Cross, and to the right is a spanking bench. At the foot of the bed is a swing I point to.

"That. I want to try that first, Daddy."

He's already sliding the zipper down my modestly cut but ornately embroidered ivory gown. He pushes it down to find I'm only wearing a garter belt and thigh highs.

"You're leaving those on. You're sexy as fuck, little one."

I help him out of his tux. He's gorgeous as sin, and every single woman—and several of the married ones plus a few guys—noticed.

Mine, bitches.

He's soon situated on it, and I slip my feet into the stirrups, straddling him. Our foreplay was undressing each other.

"Fuck, Ellie. The feel of slipping into you."

"It's divine."

He pushes off, our bodies guiding the swing's momentum. It's the most erotic position I've ever had sex.

"I fantasized about a man like you when I was younger. I convinced myself they only existed for other women. As much as I feel like I'm in a dream, I know this is real. You make me happier than I ever thought I deserved to be, Enrique. I love you."

"And I love you. I never once want you to doubt those words are the truth and that I'll mean them for the rest of time. I didn't need a wife, and I didn't want one until the moment I met you. Then I knew. Life tried to tell me to be patient, but once upon a time I thought I knew more. Now I understand fate always planned for me to find you."

We move together, kissing while our hands explore. Every movement, every motion brings us closer to ecstasy. When we're finally there, we burst into it together. We've fought to be together. We've fought beside each other. It may be a fight to stay together. But what we've brought together, no man can put asunder.

Javier never imagined a ghost from his past would be on the other side of the hotel door he just burst through. Discover what happens when the first of the *Tres J's* falls...for wrong woman—the bratva *pakhan's* sister-in-law in *Cartel Viper*.

Would you like to join Enrique and Elodie for an extra scene with these sex toys once they're home? Subscribe and get your free download here.

Bonus Epilogue

Enrique

"Javier?"

"Sí, tío?"

I look over at Ellie who shrugs, but I suspect she knows what's going on with our nephew.

"You're awfully distracted. What's going on?"

"Nothing. Just thinking about Carmine and Gabriele. I don't know what they're up to, but I know they're trying to fuck me over somehow."

That puts my hackles up. I get protective fast when it comes to my family. It doesn't matter that Javier's in his early thirties. I changed his diapers and burped him—he spit up *all the fucking time*. If someone's giving him crap, then I'll come to his defense in a heartbeat.

Ellie squeezes my hand under the table.

"Javier, are they messing with you because they think you have something they want?"

"Definitely not. They wouldn't want anything to do with what's going on. I think they just want to watch me squirm."

Ellie looks at me as Javier stares at his computer screen. Ellie mouths her thought.

"A woman."

That makes my eyebrows shoot up. She mouths to me again.

"Later."

What did my wife figure out that I haven't?

"You've been off since our reception. Do you need anything?"

I press a little more, but Javier's always been the most reclusive. He isn't the shyest, but he's the most introverted. He'll withdraw if I don't get an answer now but keep grilling him.

"Nothing I can't figure out once I do a little digging. I think they're trying to get in the way of a deal I want to do. But I won't let them mess this up. Anyway, I need to go. I have a meeting."

Ellie licks her lips before she speaks, and I want to pounce. We've been married for two months and been back from our honeymoon for one. I can't get enough of her. I doubt I ever will. Even after a month away—we extended an extra week—I want her near me every waking and sleeping moment. That's unrealistic and obsessive, so I give her space. She has things to do and so do I, so it's not like I'm up her ass around the clock. Only every few days while I make her come.

"Javier, I'd go slowly. I don't know anything specific, but something tells me she's fragile. Something happened, and she needs time to heal."

My nephew's head snaps up, and he stares at Ellie. His dark gaze spears her, and a lesser person would shrivel under his probing stare.

"What do you mean?"

"I don't know anything specific, but I think Madeline is even warier than I was. From what I can tell, she moved back to Jersey unexpectedly. I don't think she planned to move back in with her parents after living on her own for years in Albany."

"How do you know?" Javier grimaces when he realizes he barked at Ellie.

"*Tia* Margherita told me a little about her. After all, *Tia* Margherita's lived next to the Doyles since before Madeline was born. She and Luis used to be best friends with Susan and Killian."

She shifts her gaze down to the table. She knows what happened between Juan and Laura Kutsenko née Doyle. I had to fill her in on more of the family history, and that included Pablo and Juan growing up next door to the *pakhan's* wife and how my family's actions ruined Luis and Margherita's relationship with their neighbors. They used to share Sunday dinner every week. Madeline's Laura's younger sister.

I glance down at the tattoo on my inner forearm. I still have a large cross on it with four initials. P on the top, J on the bottom, L on the left, and M on the right. Pablo, Juan, Laura, and Madeline. The sisters grew up calling me *tío*. Laura's threatened to dig out the L and M with a rusty butter knife if my family goes near hers again. If Javier's got his eye on Madeline, I better sharpen the knife before I hand it to Laura. Maybe it'll be less messy and painful if I do.

"I'll keep that in mind, *Tía* Elle. Thank you. *Tío*, I'm going to take off. I want to get in line tonight for the new collection's release tomorrow."

My nephew collects something he'd kill me if I ever divulged, but he's been doing the camp out overnight to be at the front of the line deal since he moved to America just before he turned twelve. He could order the stuff online, but it's tradition because Jorge and Joaquin go with him. It's pretty much the only innocent thing the brothers do together these days.

"Have fun. I'll talk to you tomorrow."

"Bye, *tía, tío*."

Ellie and I watch him head out of the living room, and we hear the front door close. I look over at Ellie, waiting for her to explain.

"Margherita said Madeline told no one when she first arrived. She went to a hotel or something for a few days. I think she didn't want her parents, Laura, or her in-laws to see whatever condition she was in."

"She looked fine at the reception. She even caught your bouquet."

"On the outside. Who knows how she feels?"

"True. Speaking of feelings…"

Ellie practically winces. She knows what's coming. I stand from the sofa, still holding her hand. She rises with me and glances toward the stairs. She follows me to our bedroom, and I push aside my clothes and press the button that opens the door to the panic room. We did some redecorating in here. It now has the Saint Andrew's cross, swing, and spanking bench that were in our yacht cabin during our honeymoon.

"Strip, *chiquita*."

"*Sí, papi.*"

She hurries to obey, slipping off her blouse and jeans. She's wearing a bralette since it's easier to get off than unclasping a bra. She's not wearing any panties because she owns none. She tried while I was away unexpectedly last week. She thought she'd have time to ditch them, but I caught her in them. I followed through on my threat from before we moved in together. I burned the entire pile.

"Do you know why we're in here?"

"Because we both love when you tie me up?"

"There is that. Try again."

She sighs as her lips purse and twist to the side.

"Rather than tell you that I didn't want to talk about it when I had to deal with Tim, I told you nothing happened."

"And did something happen?"

"Yes."

"What happened?"

"I'd rather not talk about it."

"Was that so hard?"

"No, Daddy."

"You know I won't force you to tell me your thoughts. But you also know I worry when something's bothering you."

"I didn't want to worry you, and that's exactly what I did."

"I know I can't fix everything all the time, Ellie. But please don't shut me out. You know I'm a man who craves control. Without it, someone always gets hurt or something always goes wrong. I'm not such a control freak I don't understand there are things beyond my reach. But if it's something like making you feel better or at least sharing the burden, then please let me."

"I do, and I will in the future. But you can't fault me for not wanting to add to your list of crap going wrong. I want to shield you as much as you do me. You know I'm as protective of you as you are of me."

"And I love how you love me, *chiquita*. I've never felt so cared about in my life. But it doesn't feel great knowing you're avoiding telling me something. I get that's the height of hypocrisy, too. And it's not like I don't think you can do things for yourself, but I swore I would always take care of you."

"And you do. But you're right. I avoided telling you what was bothering me, even though I knew you could tell. The things you keep from me aren't as frivolous as Tim complaining about me refusing to do his taxes. It's just things have been quiet with all the Vizzinis since the wedding. I didn't want to stir up trouble."

"I get that. But this is about you and me and how we handle things that come up."

"I'm ready for my spanking."

We're not truly into domestic discipline. I'm not a Daddy Dom, and despite calling her little girl, she's not a Little. We talked about this earlier, and I know she feels guilty. I know it wasn't dealing with Tim that bothers her as much as regretting shutting me out. I teased her that a spanking would clear the air. I didn't think she'd agree to it, but I think she wants to restore the balance we've had since we got together.

I walk her over to the spanking bench and help her to step onto it. She leans over, grasping the upturned handles. She's shifts until she's comfortable. I love the view from the side, hints of her tits peeking out. I love the view from behind, her ass on display. I barely notice her scar, but I know she still feels self-conscious at times.

I move to the rack that holds the floggers, crops, paddles, and various other implements I bought the evening I sat outside her spare bedroom door along with what we ordered while on our honeymoon. I select a long-handled crop and a short-handled paddle. I step beside her and run my hand down the length of her back then over both perfect globes. I knead the flesh before bringing my hand down across both cheeks.

She sucks in a noisy breath but does nothing else.

I switch to the crop, flicking my wrist. I swat her all over her ass, no pattern or rhythm to predict. When her skin's a light pink, I switch to the paddle.

"This'll hurt, Ellie. What's your safe word?"

"Mushrooms."

"This is a punishment, but it's not meant to harm you. If it's too much, you tell me. Don't convince yourself you can take more. You safe word immediately."

"Enrique, I know. I won't put you in a position where you regret sharing this with me or make you feel guilty because I didn't speak up. I don't want to ruin this or your trust in me. You don't have to remind me every time. I'd never do that to you."

"Thank you, *cariño.*"

"You're welcome, *mio caro.*"

I eye her ass, deciding where to land the paddle. I bring it down with a sharp slap, and she shrieks. I give her no reprieve, spanking her again and again. She stomps her feet and cries out.

"Daddy! Ow!"

"It's supposed to hurt, little one."

"Is it really supposed to hurt this much? You didn't even punish me this much after the home invasion."

She realizes her mistake bringing that up when my next spank will likely leave a bruise. I dial back the force since bruising her isn't my intention. That comment just struck a nerve. I never want to be as terrified as I was pulling into my driveway to see my house under attack, knowing my woman and my sisters were inside. I never want to be as furious as I was seeing Ellie peek out through the window, knowing she'd exposed herself long enough to fire the shot that took down the weaponized drone. It could have shot her.

"Ow! Please, Daddy. Fuck! It hurts."

I ignore her as she cries out again and again. I watch her body for any signs she's truly in distress, but I see none. I would know. I've spent decades torturing people. I know what they can withstand and what they can't. I know the tells people have, and I see none in Ellie.

"No! No! I don't like this anymore. Stop, Enrique."

"Safe word."

She snaps her mouth shut. She doesn't want it to end. Not really. I give her a stinging blow to her horizontal cracks before walking around to stand by her head. She looks up at me, and I nod. She reaches out and pulls my jogging pants and boxer briefs down. I draw the head of my cock over her lips three times. She opens for me, and I risk her biting me as I slide in and bring the crop down on her ass at the same time. She sucks instead of biting.

Each time the leather crop lands across her ass, she draws me in deeper. It's sweet torture. She's excellent at what she does, so it's not long before I'm fighting not to come.

"Little one, three more. Then you're going to suck me off, and I'm going to come down your throat."

She nods her head, and I do as I say. I finish her spanking, loving how her ass is a deep pink. I thrust, holding her head in place but careful not to choke her. She works me until I can't stop and spill down her throat. When I'm done, she licks me then her lips. I help her off the bench and carry her to a sofa. I stretch out, and she lies over me.

"You know you didn't mention asking Luciana about putting my house on the market, Enrique."

"You said you wanted to sell."

"I did, but I didn't tell you I was ready to put it on the market. There are things I want to change like making the panic room look like a cellar and changing the entrance from the back of the hall closet to a door in the pantry. You just swooped in."

"I thought I was taking something off your plate since you have another deadline with your editor."

"I know, but the path to hell is paved with good intentions. I think you might need a reminder that you don't make all the decisions now."

"What did you have in mind, little one?"

"I think you deserve getting edged tonight."

"Is that so?"

"And I think you're going to do that thing with your tongue and my clit."

"Oh?"

"And a few other things I'll come up with between now and bedtime."

"You think you're going to punish me, *chiquita?*"

"Mhmm."

"And if I refuse?"

"You won't, Daddy. I'm certain of that."

"And why's that?"

"Because if you don't let me, I'll tell Luis you took the last *three* servings of your sister's *postre de natas.*"

The milk pudding is Luis's favorite and one of the best desserts Catalina makes. I love it but not as much as he does. That didn't stop me from going back for two more servings. I might have suggested there wasn't any more after the *niños* got their servings rather than admit I ate the last of it.

"You wouldn't dare."

She cocks an eyebrow. I kiss along her neck as I tickle her. I love listening to her giggle.

"Enrique! Stop. I've had three large babies. You can't tickle me like this. I'm over forty!"

I tug at her earlobe with my teeth as I stop.

"I love you, *chiquita*. But we'll see who comes out the winner when you edge me tonight. You might dole it out, but will you be able to take it when you don't come either?"

"Oh, I intend to come. And you'll love watching every minute of it. And I love you too."

We cuddle together, and I've never been happier than I am since meeting Ellie. I may be the king of this castle, but she's the queen of my heart.

Don't miss the next installment

Preorder Javier and Maddy's story now.

Javier—I may have walk in her door, but I barge into her life. Two reversed numbers lead me to the wrong address. One word and one look are all it takes for me to be hooked. I may lust for her, but I can never love her. She doesn't need my dark past, deadly present, or likely short future anywhere near her. Now enemies she never imagined are harbingers of death. Will it be hers? Only I make her feel safe. Only I can protect her. You *might* fear my uncle. But you *need* to fear me.

Maddy—He doesn't recognize me, but I know who he is. He's the one man my family will never approve of. I came back to start over again, and he's my new beginning. The pleasure he gives me when I'm in his arms surpasses all my fantasies–even the ones he's in. There's one major problem. My sister's married to his enemy. People underestimate me since I'm the nice sister, but I'm silent and deadly. I slide next to you, strike when you're not looking, and sink my fangs in.

We're a match made in Heaven because there's nothing we won't do for each other.

Sabine Barclay

Meet Javier and Maddy in *Cartel Viper*, coming June 2025.

Thank you for reading
Cartel King

Sabine Barclay, a nom de plume also writing Historical Romance as Celeste Barclay, lives near the Southern California coast with her husband and sons. She loves her days at the beach soaking up way too much sun, a good Netflix binge, and a strong hot chai. Her heroines are independent women who can defend themselves but love their Alpha heroes who want nothing more than to protect their soulmates in her Mafia Romances. She's Gen Y/Oregon Trail and loves creating engrossing contemporary romances that will make your toes curl and your granny blush.

Subscribe to Sabine's bimonthly newsletter to receive exclusive insider perks.
www.sabinebarclay.com

Join the fun and get exclusive insider giveaways, sneak peeks, and new release announcements in
Sabine Barclay's Facebook Dubious Dames Group

Do you also enjoy steamy Historical Romance? Discover Sabine's books written as Celeste Barclay.

The Ivankov Brotherhood

Bratva Darling
BOOK ONE SNEAK PEEK

LAURA

As I sit across from the four Kutsenko brothers, I press my lips together to keep from drooling. No four men should be so strikingly handsome. Not all from the same family, anyway. I fight a valiant battle against letting my gaze drift toward the eldest, Maksim, whose ice-blue eyes bore into me. After years of negotiating billion-dollar investment contracts while facing countless ruthless businessmen, I've learned to keep my expression studiously blank. But it's a true struggle today. Instead, I focus my attention on the squirrelly lawyer sitting across the conference table. While he's disingenuous with each comment, he's a good negotiator. But I'm better. How cliché am I?

While I feel Maksim watching me, I focus on Dmitry Yakovitch as he continues to argue the merits of the venture capitalist company I represent, RK Capital Group, merging with Kutsenko Partners. What he means is the merits of Kutsenko Partners acquiring RK Capital Group, then stripping it and making it another money-laundering shell corporation. While most people in New York have little awareness of the Russian mafia, I do. The Kutsenko brothers' names appear on no titles or deeds anywhere in New York City, but it wasn't difficult to determine which shell companies likely belong to them. Their assumption that I'm unfamiliar with them is proving beneficial to me as they continue to whisper amongst themselves in Russian. I think they may even believe they're convincing me that they don't speak much English.

The senior partners of RK Capital Group know who I'm negotiating with, though they may not know I'm aware of these Russians' more nefarious operations. They've given me the go-ahead to agree to a merger with an eventual acquisition, but only for the right price. A price to the tune of twenty billion dollars. Considering an investment firm like Goldman Sachs is worth nearly one-hundred-and-twenty billion dollars, my clients' asking price appears reasonable.

"Mr. Yakovitch, I shall stop you now." I raise my left hand, pen caught between my index and middle fingers. When I have his attention, I lean back in my chair and casually twirl the pen over my index finger and thumb. "Fifty billion is my clients' asking price. You know that. Your clients know that. RK doesn't oppose the merger. What they oppose is the insulting offer you've made. It's nearly noon, and I'm hungry, Mr. Yakovitch. I have a delicious ham sandwich waiting for me. I even have three chocolate chip cookies waiting for me. If we aren't going to make any progress, I shall let you go, so I can move onto my eagerly anticipated lunch." I cant my head just enough for me to appear as though my gaze rests solely on the opposing attorney's face, but I can see each Kutsenko brothers' reaction. My face battles yet again against showing my emotions as I fight not to smirk. Their muted but surprised expressions confirm what I already know.

"Please tell your clients to make a reasonable counteroffer, or I will conclude this meeting and enjoy my ham sandwich and cookies."

Dmitry glares at me before turning to Maksim and his three brothers. In rapid Russian, he doesn't interpret my suggestion. Oh no. There's no need for that. I can't catch every word because his voice is too low. But I catch something along the lines of "The bitch refuses to budge. What now? A fucking ham sandwich. More like a stick up her ass."

Maksim swivels his chair to look at his brothers. In Russian, he says, "Fifty billion is ridiculous. She's not so stupid or naïve not to know that. My guess is they'll settle for twenty billion. We offer fifteen."

"That's barely better than what we already offered," Aleksei, the second-oldest brother, argues. "She'll be eating the fucking sandwich and dipping her cookies in milk before we walk out the door. We need the buildings."

"We offer twenty, Maks," Bogdan, the youngest, insists.

As I watch the brothers discuss, their voices barely lowered, I pull my lunch sack from the black leather satchel by my feet and set it beside my laptop. It's a ridiculously pink floral bag with an embroidered monogram, the L and D overlapping. It's an empty prop, but they don't know that. I watch as five sets of eyes narrow. I offer a smile that would appear innocent in any setting other than this meeting. It's patronizing, and I know it.

Bratva Sweetheart
Bratva Treasure
Bratva Beauty
Bratva Angel
Bratva Jewel

Do you also enjoy steamy Historical Romance? Discover Sabine's books written as Celeste Barclay.

The Mancinelli Brotherhood

Mafia Heir
BOOK ONE SNEAK PEEK

LUCA

Every head turns toward the liquor store's back door as it opens. A gorgeous blonde steps out, and I wish I had the time to appreciate her beauty, but she's about to die. Carlos and his men draw their guns and pivot toward her. My men pull their weapons too, but we keep them pointed at the Mexicans. The woman stands like a deer in the headlights for a second before ducking behind the industrial garbage dumpster like a frightened rabbit. Three shots hit the metal almost at the same moment. That's all it takes for my men and me. The two bodyguards standing with me aim for a guard each, and I set my sights on Carlos. We squeeze our triggers, and the men fall.

Screeching tires tell me Carlos's driver takes off. I hear more gunshots as at least one soldier in my cars tries to shoot the escaping vehicle. Glass shatters, but the sedan keeps going. I hear more tires squeal as one of my SUVs takes off and chases the guy. I holster my gun and wave my men to do the same.

I inch forward toward the trash can, but I see the shadow shift.

The woman bolts from the other side. She's still the frightened rabbit, but I'm the fox pursuing her. She's fast, I'll give her that. But she has to be at least a foot shorter than me. My legs are a lot longer and cover a lot more ground with each stride.

She weaves among the cars, most likely believing it's harder to hit a moving object. She isn't wrong, but I have no intention of shooting her. I push myself harder and pounce as she darts out and tries to cross the last stretch of parking lot to reach a better lit area near a bus stop. I lunge.

"Stop running, *piccolina*. I won't hurt you."

I wrap my arms around her and pull her back against my chest, but I'm quick to spin her around and put space between us as I grasp her arms. Of course, she fights me.

"If I wanted you dead, I would have shot at you, too."

"It doesn't mean you won't kill me after."

She's breathless as she continues to struggle. I almost let go to take a step back, insulted at what she implied. But I can't blame her. If I were a woman, I'd be terrified of the same thing.

"I'm not going to rape you. I'm going to talk to you."

"Talk? You are not a man who talks if you just killed a guy."

"To keep him and his men from killing you. I told you, if I wanted you dead, I would have shot at you too. And I wouldn't have missed."

She stops struggling against me, but her eyes continue to dart from one place to another, trying to find somewhere to flee. I know I can keep her in place with only one hand, so I release her left arm. I still have a firm hold on her right one, but I haven't held it nearly as tightly as I could.

"I'm Luca. I know you figured out you interrupted something you shouldn't have. Did that man know who you are?"

"Yes."

"What about his driver? Would he know you?"

"Yes."

"Do you have a name?"

"Yes."

"*Piccolina*, we won't get very far if yes is all you can say. Are you willing to answer me with more than one word?"
"No."
I knew that was coming, and I grin. I can't help it. I wasn't wrong about her being gorgeous, but I doubt she wants to know that's what I think. At least, not if I want her to know I won't assault her.
"Fine. I have more than twenty questions I can ask that you can answer with one word. Do you work at the store?"
"Sometimes."
Ah, an improvement.

Mafia Sinner
Mafia Beauty
Mafia Angel
Mafia Redeemer
Mafia Star

Do you also enjoy steamy Historical Romance? Discover Sabine's books written as Celeste Barclay.

The O'Rourke Brotherhood

Mob Boss
BOOK ONE SNEAK PEEK

DILLAN

I hate meetings like this. I don't need to wear pants from some shitty off-the-rack suit that are too tight to *try* to make my dick look bigger. I'm secure in my cock size, and I don't need to show how big my balls are for people to know I run this part of the city. I loathe strip clubs too. I'm past the point where naked women make my jimmy do jumping jacks. I can appreciate a hot bod and gymnast level strength, but it does nothing for me. These douchebags? They're practically ready to come in those cheap arse pants. Why am I here? I keep asking myself that.

Seamus and Shane are doing just fine with these negotiations. I'm just here to look good. I'm the muscle today. Or rather my name and my position. Who the fuck thought— way, way back in the day —that giving the mob hierarchy nautical names was a good idea? Fucking Skipper. This isn't motherfucking Gilligan's Island. None of these numb nuts are the Professor, even if they think they're fucking Mr. Howell.

But who is that? If this is *Gilligan's Island*, then she's Mary Ann.

I glance at Seamus, but he's focused on the Albanian he's trying not to lose his shite at. Shane smirks at me when I dart my gaze to him. I cock an eyebrow as the waitress walks over. She's definitely not a dancer. She has too many clothes on. But you can barely call the pieces of thread she's wearing clothes. She's got on a bikini top that's barely more than pasties, and the skirt she's wearing would make my Catholic grandmother do somersaults in her grave.

It's the standard uniform for this place, but somehow it doesn't look right on her. Not because she doesn't have a banging body because she does. Not because she's a butter face— but-her-face — as in great bod, not so great face. She's beautiful in a super under-stated way. That's part of what makes her look out of place. She has next to no makeup on. I think those are even her real eyelashes. The natural beauty is drawing way too much attention.

"'Scuse me."

She tries to step around Zef Hoxha, the *kyre* of the Albanian mafia here in New York. When he reaches out to grab her wrist, I'm out of my seat with my hand around his. He never gets a chance to touch her because my hold is so tight he can't bend his fingers. I keep squeezing until it must feel like I'll snap the bones.

"No touching."

Zef drops his arm as much as my hold allows. I let go and stare at him before I tilt my head toward the waitress. I narrow my eyes, and he knows what I expect.

"I apologize, miss."

"That's all right, sir. Here's your drink."

She's polite as she hands him his glass. Unfortunately, to put down the rest, she has to bend forward, giving everyone a view of her glorious cleavage. Tits and arse are what sell here, and she has them in spades. I'm certain it's why my cousin hired her. If I sit down, everyone will know I'm just as guilty as these fuck nuts because she's made my dick do something that hasn't happened in a strip club since I was like twenty-three. I'm now thirty-three.

Mob Star
Mob Princess

Cartel King

Mob Saint
Mob Bride
Mob Knight

Do you also enjoy steamy Historical Romance? Discover Sabine's books written as Celeste Barclay.

www.ingramcontent.com/pod-product-compliance
Lightning Source LLC
Chambersburg PA
CBHW020526110726
47899CB00004B/1259

9 781648 398315